embers of mercy

EMBER GLEN | BOOK THREE

BRYNN FORD

Embers of Mercy (Ember Glen, Book 3)
Copyright © 2023 Brynn Ford
Published by Brynn Ford

ISBN: 978-1-955349-32-1

Cover Design Copyright © 2022 Qamber Designs and Media
Interior Formatting by Qamber Designs and Media
Editing by Silvia Curry at *Silvia's Reading Corner*

More from the Author
www.brynnford.com
brynnfordauthor@gmail.com

content warning

This is a dark romance series involving many triggering elements
which may be upsetting for some readers. A complete list of tropes
and triggers can be found on the author's website.
www.brynnford.com/triggers

series note

Embers of Mercy is book three of three in the Ember Glen trilogy.
It is not a standalone; the books must be read in order.
Books one and two end on cliffhangers.

reading order

EMBER GLEN
Spark of Madness
Blaze of Misery
Embers of Mercy

playlist

Landmines by BELLSAINT
Born To Die by Euphoria ft. Bolshiee
Detached from Reality by MEJKO ft. Arkane Skye
Where the Lonely Ones Roam by Digital Daggers
Reaper by Glaceo & RIELL
The Calling (EPIX Remix) by The Rigs
Breathe by Parah Dice & Brianna
Marble by Neptunica & Shockz & Rebecca Helena
Lover. Fighter. by SVRCINA
MIDDLE OF THE NIGHT by Elley Duhé
Unstoppable by Sia
Where We Rise by Neoni
Royalty by Egzod & Maestro Chives ft. Neoni
Ember by Katherine McNamara
Alpha by Little Destroyer

For all the women who are struggling to rise…
Dig deep, have faith in yourself,
and begin with a single step.

chapter one

ARLO

I'M STUNNED, PARALYZED, rooted to the spot.

A whip of black lace from Ellary Hill's skirt catches on the wind before following her down into the abyss, dropping into the empty space beyond the cliff's edge. Her sudden descent is silent—no scream escapes her—and I'm horror-struck.

A stunned beat of silence passes.

My soul has sprouted deep roots that snake into the earth beside Mercy's grave, keeping me motionless despite the horror unfolding before my eyes. My heart, which I tore from my own chest and gave her freely, is trapped in the coffin with her, resting at the bottom of a hole dug six feet deep. But when Cambria screams, breaking through the eerie silence, the rest of my consciousness leaves my heart and soul behind.

We all feel the collective pull, as though Ellary's fall drags us all down with her. My brothers and I run to save the servant who's already fallen, already gone. Cambria runs for the edge, but Killian grabs her wrist and snaps her backward into his hold.

Wesley is the first to reach the edge, but his focus is set on Killian. Coming up behind him, Wesley grabs Killian's shoulders with a firm grip and jerks him back so hard he stumbles. Killian loses his grip on Cambria as he whirls to face Wesley, whose face is tense with rage. The moment she's released, Cambria runs for the edge in a panic.

I sprint ahead, skidding toward the edge, barely stopping in time as I lasso an arm around her waist and tug her back. In her frenzy, she nearly met the same fate as her friend. I stumble backward as I drag her, drop my weight to sit, and pull her down with me to anchor her to the solid ground.

She turns her head back to look at me with dark, teary eyes. "He pushed her…he pushed her…"

"What the fuck did you do?" Wesley's voice echoes, calling for our attention. I glance over to see him stepping up to Killian, grabbing his jacket collar, and jerking him closer.

Killian slaps Wesley's hands away as Owen approaches, coming in close. "*Shut up*, both of you. Everything is being streamed to the village right now."

"There's a ledge!" Theo calls out from where he carefully leans out, looking down. He glances back at us. "She's there, I can see her!"

I release Cambria and scramble to my feet, quickly telling her to stay put, then rush to join Theo's side. Cambria ignores my demand, and I see her moving from the corner of my eye, but she's down on all fours, crawling slowly, so I'm not as fearful she'll accidentally leap to her death to chase after her friend. While I lean out to look over the edge, she flattens to her belly, creeping forward to do the same. We wait and watch as the rolling fog clouds over everything, then gradually clears.

At first, all I can see is the gray rock forming the ledge Theo spotted, maybe twenty or thirty feet below. But then a gust of wind blows, pushing the clouds and revealing a morbid palette of black and red splatters against the gray rock canvas. Ellary's black skirt whips against her unmoving limbs, waving over the blood spilling from beneath her lifeless body.

Lifeless?

Is she dead?

"Ellary…" Cambria's voice has turned calm against the chaos.

"How do we get down there? You have rope?"

I feel her looking up at me, but my gaze is fixed on Ellary's chest, watching it closely, hoping to see a rise and fall. Ellary is so still, flattened against that rock, and her left arm is twisted at an odd angle as the bloody pool beneath her steadily grows.

Truthfully, I don't know if she's alive or dead.

I don't know if this kind of fall is survivable.

Seeing her laying there is grotesque—an image that will no doubt haunt my dreams—yet I stare all the same. I suffer the image to fix my gaze on her chest, to watch for a sign that her lungs still draw breath.

"You must have rope with you," Cambria says again, pressing her palms to the ground and pushing to her feet. "Tie it to my waist."

"What?" I look over at her.

"Tie your rope to my waist and lower me."

My brow furrows, and I shake my head at her before wrapping my palm around her wrist. I turn—dragging her away with me—and stalk away from the ledge to where my brothers have gathered in an ever-shifting cluster of pandemonium.

Wesley shouts at Killian.

Ryker shouts at Wesley.

Killian goads them both.

Ryker lunges at Wesley, and Owen grabs him by the back of his shirt to stop him.

"That's *enough*. Start filling the graves," Owen commands as he shoves Ryker. "Wesley. Wesley!" He waits for Wesley to tear himself from the argument with Killian to face him. "We need you to make a statement. Get control of the situation, assure the village that Ellary's fine, and that the trial will go on as planned."

"But Ellary's not *fine*." My tone is clipped, harsh. "Let's end the trial. Mercy and Delle made their choice; they made their sacrifice, and a beloved servant fell off a cliff on *our* watch. That's enough death for one damn day."

"She's not *dead!*" Cambria jerks against my hold, and I tighten my grip around her wrist. "She landed on a ledge! She might be… she could be okay…"

"Did you see her?" Owen asks me.

I nod. "I can see her. It doesn't look good. I don't know if she's alive or—"

"Okay," Owen huffs, raking a hand through his hair. "We'll see if we can figure out how to get to her. If anyone can figure out how to rig something up, it's you."

"I told him to tie rope around my waist and lower me." Cambria's voice rises desperately. "I'll do it. I'll go over the edge for her."

My grip on her wrist tightens in frustration. I'll leap over the edge myself before I let Mercy lose both of her best friends on my watch. I need Mercy more than I've ever needed anyone in my life, and though I know she needs me too, I also know she needs them more.

"I'll go," I volunteer.

My adrenaline is already spiked, and I need a distraction from the dull thud of each shovelful of dirt that lands on the coffin. Ryker is quickly shoveling in soil from the mound behind Delle's grave, and the sound echoes through my mind. I already know it's a sound that will haunt me for eternity—it's a sound that calls to me, begs me to act, to make it stop.

I can't make it stop.

I want to. I need to. But I can't.

Mercy Madness is a symbol for change, a martyr for her cause, a catalyst for rebellion, and the greatest dishonor I could do her is sully my own name in trying to free her from her coffin. It wouldn't serve either of us. The Control would only take me under arrest and bury her again, and then I'd be powerless to help her when she survives this.

Because she will survive this.

She has to survive this.

"Let me go to her." Cambria's voice softens as sorrow and sadness drag tears from her eyes. "Please, she needs me." She tugs against my grip, but it's weak and she breaks into sobs. "She's all I have…Ellary and Mercy are all I have."

"All you have?" Killian snaps, tearing himself away from Wesley. He pushes between me and Owen, then charges toward Cambria.

She flinches, but she stands her ground, like a good servant would. She knows that retreat would ultimately get her thrown into a coffin and buried alive like Mercy. *For God's sake.* I tug, pulling her into my side as Killian moves to loom above her.

"How *dare* you say in my presence that she and *Mercy* are all you have? How *dare* you speak of that vile sinner so fondly?" He wears a disgusted scowl, a look of betrayal as he spits his words at her with fury. "What has she ever done for you besides bring you torment? What has she done besides disappoint, hurt, and abandon you and her sisters in her sins?"

"I don't…" Cambria stammers, averting her eyes and shaking her head. "I'm sorry."

What is she sorry for?

I release her arm and raise my hand to Killian's chest as anger greets me, slipping between them as I push him back.

"She owes you no explanations or apologies. She just stood on the edge of a cliff to serve as a potential sacrifice and watched her friend fall." I feel my lips snarl with the building rage, and my voice lowers to a gritty growl. "You pushed her over the edge, Killian Cole. I know you did."

I stare him down, eye to eye, expecting to see something, anything that would confirm my suspicion—the shadow of guilt flicker across his brown eyes, the twitch of his jaw, perhaps the bob of his throat as he swallows nervously. Yet I see nothing, no sign of weakness or faltering.

Instead, the side of his mouth lifts in a self-righteous smirk, and he simply says, "Prove it."

In my mind, I grab him by the collar, shove him back to the edge, and push until he falls. I used to see him as my brother in God, my equal, a powerful leader in our community.

And now…all I see is the truth.

I see a demon standing in front of me—if such a thing even truly exists. The demons I once so stupidly believed to possess my Mercy were never within her. Nothing vile or evil could ever exist within that perfect woman's soul.

The evil is within *us*—the Control, the men of Ember Glen. We are the evil that made these women kneel and serve. We are the demons who whispered threats in their ears, who denounced them in their unwillingness to serve our every manic impulse. No man could serve these women in the way they've so dutifully served our vileness. We threaten them—*manipulate* them—into believing what we tell them to, and they pay the price for our sins again and again.

Mercy's strength, her power, her hard-won love broke me. She broke the part of me that believed the dark lies, and with her brightness, she brought light on the truth.

For all she's done for my soul, I will not let this overwhelming urge to end Killian overcome me. It wouldn't serve her if I lost myself now. I cannot let her suffer for my mistakes in vain. I made her promises, and I intend to keep them.

"It will be proven, I assure you." I return his challenging smirk with one of my own. "The footage that's livestreaming to the villagers at this very moment will tell us all we need to know."

He tilts his head to the side. "Will it?" He takes a small step closer and lowers his voice. "Are you so certain the cameras are angled appropriately to show what you *think* happened?"

"Are you so certain they aren't?"

A tense silence lingers through a beat, a quiet transference of understanding that he and I are no longer brothers in God.

His grin gradually widens, then he claps his hand against my shoulder. "I suppose we'll find out, won't we, *brother?*" He nudges me sideways as he moves around me, taking hold of Cambria's wrist and dragging her toward the forest. "I'm taking her back to the village so she doesn't get any bright ideas, like hurling herself over the edge to save Ellary."

"Are we letting him get away with this?" Wesley nearly shouts, glancing around at us in search of support. "He *pushed* her!"

"He did," I agree. "I know he did. We need to—"

"What we *need* to do is complete the trial," Owen demands. "It's our duty, and it *must* be finished. Whatever Killian did or didn't do will be judged later. This is our job…our *duty*. Let him go and let's finish our work here. We'll deal with him later."

"Deal with him later?" Wesley scoffs, brow furrowed over his dark eyes and indignant expression.

Owen sighs, finding a gentler tone. "We'll bring Killian in front of the Elders, review the footage, and cast our judgments, but it will have to be done later." He steps closer to Wesley, placing his hands on his shoulders in camaraderie. "I promise, Wesley, we will evaluate the circumstances together after this day is done. When our minds are clear and capable of seeing the truth. Decisions should not be made in rage, such as the state you're in right now."

"Stop!" A small, but mighty, voice carries in the quiet, and we all turn to see Adam, Delle's younger brother, standing beside her grave. "Stop it!" he yells at Ryker. "My sister's in there!"

Theo turns and runs full speed toward the grave while Ryker continues shoveling soil onto Delle's coffin, unaffected by the horror of the child's cries just feet away from him.

"Get back!" Theo shouts at Adam as he closes the distance.

The child bends his knees, leaning forward with intent. That's when we all move, running after him as we shout our protests. But none of us reach him before he jumps, disappearing into Delle's grave.

Theo gets there first, hopping in without hesitation. Ryker pauses his shoveling with an annoyed huff, as if this is a mere disruption to his work and not a terribly traumatic scene.

I slam to a stop beside the grave. Beneath my feet, Theo struggles to get a hold of Adam as he fights for his sister. Theo's feet slip out from under him, and he falls backward on his ass. He's down just long enough for Adam to move away, his small hands searching along the edge of Delle's coffin.

He finds the lid, and his fingers curl to lift it, raising it a mere inch before Theo rises, slaps his hand against the top of the lid, and slams it shut before wrapping his arms around Adam's waist.

"No!" Adam cries out.

But his voice isn't loud enough to drown out the sound of Delle's harrowing cries from within her coffin. "Stop! Adam, stop! Please, just go!"

Air catches in my lungs, a swell of swirling, twisted emotions filling every empty space within me, and it aches. I fall to my knees, desperate to pull this child from the grave, and spare him and Delle both from further heartache.

"Here," I call for Theo's attention, reaching a hand down.

Theo twists him around and lifts him to meet me. I grab hold of him and drag him up. He struggles so much that he knocks me sideways onto my hip, falling with me into my arms. I tighten my grip, though he fights. I feel sick subduing this innocent child, stopping him from saving his sister.

This child's pain burns hot enough to melt my heart. Though my hold on him is firm, my touch softens. I cradle his head in my palm, stroking to soothe him as a mother would her child.

"She'll be okay," I whisper. "Delle will be okay."

He continues to fight me for what feels like hours—though I know it's only moments that have passed—before I feel him being tugged away from me. Theo kneels beside me, his face and fine clothes covered in soil, and plucks Adam from my arms, forcing him upright. He grabs his face, forcing him to meet his eyes.

"You cannot save her," Theo says firmly. "You cannot stop this, Adam. It must be done. Do you hear me?"

"I'm scared!" Adam cries out. "*She's* scared! Don't hurt her!"

"She chose this." Theo's stern eyes flicker with dissonance, flitting away from him for a moment before he steadies his gaze again. "Delle chose to sacrifice for you because she loves you. And if you love her, you will let her do what she must in your honor."

"No!" Adam stills, but cries.

We can hear the muffled cries of Delle's tears, of her demands for us to, "Take him away…take him away from here!" coming from behind her closed coffin lid.

"Go," I tell Theo, then scramble to my feet. "Take him back to the village, and make sure he remains until Delle comes back."

I'm urgent to move away from these graves, from Delle's cries. My ears strain against my will to listen for Mercy's cries, drawn into concern for the fact that I don't hear them at all. I don't hear her cries or her voice. I have no idea if she can hear what's going on outside her coffin, though I think she must. If Delle can hear it, if she can hear her brother's cries, then so can Mercy.

What must she be thinking?

Is she horrified?

Fearful?

Lost in panic?

"I can't." Theo's alarmed gaze meets mine. "I can't take him. I need to be here for Delle. I have to be. Because I'm her warden," he adds the last sentence in a way that makes it feel like an afterthought.

I move in front of him, Adam crying between us. "*Go*. Take him for Delle's sake. He shouldn't be here; he should never have been here. She cannot endure her trial if she knows he remains."

His gaze shifts around the clearing as he lowers his voice. "I-I can't leave her, Arlo."

I flash back to the first trial, when it was time for me to leave Mercy behind to endure my brothers without me. I'd been on the verge of losing control, ready to attack Killian as he turned a knife on her and threatened to push its handle inside her. I would have laid hands on him. I would have hurt him, and in turn, it would only have hurt Mercy more. They would've taken me away from her then, and she would've been alone. She would've had to endure her remaining trials and all the days between without me.

But that didn't happen.

It didn't happen because Theo knew what I was fighting.

He grabbed me and forced me away.

He saved me.

He saved *her.*

And I owe him the same now.

I gently grip one of Adam's small shoulders with one hand, gripping Theo's shoulder in the other. I force them both to turn away from Delle's grave, and I urge them ahead.

"Take him back," I demand as I push them away, leading Adam to move in front of Theo. "Walk, and don't look back."

Theo grips Adam by the shoulders, and I put a hand on Theo's back, pushing them along until we reach the hidden path from which we emerged from the forest.

At the top of the path, Theo turns to look at me. "I promised Delle—"

"You promised you would help her. It's your duty as her warden. And this is the only way you can help her right now."

His eyes skip past my shoulder, peering beyond me toward the graves as though Delle might emerge at any moment.

"I will not let anything happen to her," I assure him with a steady voice. "I will dig her up myself and ensure she returns to the Homestead, alive and well. I promise, Theo. Now go."

He nods slowly as he finds his resolve in my reassurance. With a strained intake of breath, he reaches to take Adam's hand and drags him away, disappearing down the path where Killian and Cambria have already fled.

When I turn back, I find that Wesley stands once again in the clearing, facing the tree line, speaking through his barely controlled anger, delivering a message through the broadcast as Owen urges him to continue from a few feet away.

"…a full investigation into the leadership of the Control and the Elders. We urge your calm and patience in the meantime. A memorial honoring the sacrifice of Ellary Hill will be arranged and held before the next full moon."

Memorial?

We don't know whether she's alive or dead yet!

"We will now be ending the livestream here at the cliff's edge to allow privacy in our…" he hesitates, glancing down at his hands as he rubs his palms together, "privacy in our retrieval of the honored servant, Ellary Hill. We will now switch over to livestream the remainder of this trial at the burial site of Delle Carter and Mercy Madness. Their time begins as soon as their graves are filled." He clears his throat. "*Malo mori quam foedari.*"

The moment he finishes speaking, Wesley stomps off toward the tree line. He bends to pick up a shovel near the graves with an angry huff, then scoops from the pile behind Mercy's grave and tosses it into the hole.

Mercy.

Sweet Mercy…what have we done to you?

My legs beg me to run to her, to Delle.

Owen grabs another shovel, and along with Ryker, begins to

bury Delle. I stand still and watch as Wesley shovels dirt over Mercy, each heap landing with a thud against the top of her wooden coffin, a sound that reverberates in my head.

Thud…Thud…Thud…

"Arlo!" Owen calls, and I'm pulled from the trance of that horrifying sound. He waits until I look at him. "The sooner they're buried, the sooner we can be done."

He's calling me to come and help bury these women.

I have to help bury them.

I have to help bury Mercy.

Sound dissolves into an echoing roar inside my mind. Somehow, my feet begin to move beneath me, carrying me toward the graves. Somehow, my body bends and my hands wrap around the shovel's handle. Somehow, I turn and scoop soil onto the blade, turning to toss it onto the coffin.

Somehow…I bury Mercy.

Thud…Thud…Thud…

I'm numb, lost, so broken by this day, that my movements become rhythmic, automatic.

Thud…Thud…Thud…

And then the descent into my most horrific nightmare begins.

The lid of Mercy's coffin rises, pushed open from within. I feel her terror slip out from the crack, rushing out like some dark and terrible magic was trapped inside for centuries, begging for release. It flows out and strikes me hard in the chest with a sickening feeling of horror unlike anything I've ever felt before. And as her fear rushes out, soil falls to fill the empty space inside her coffin that it left behind.

Dirt pours from Wesley's shovel mid-toss, and I see a flash of white, her starlight hair shining at me like a beacon.

Starlight.

Wildflowers and starlight.

I still feel lost, as though my mind hovers in a gray and dreary purgatory while I suffer through this dark nightmare. But the flash of her starlight hair reminds me that everything I do is for her. She made me promise to do this, and though it's tearing me apart inside, I must.

Black soil dusts her starlight tresses as it slips through the crack, and I can't bear the sight of it.

How dare the earth sully such perfection with filth?

How dare the earth try to swallow her whole, to fill her coffin and steal what little air she has left to breathe?

Mercy screams and it's a siren song, calling me back to her light, her love, to my duty to ensure her rebellion is led and her revolution is won...

But more than that, her panic calls me to be her reason, her sanity, and to ensure she survives this trial.

Her oxygen is limited, and more escapes her coffin each second she keeps the lid open. It must be shut.

God, it has to be shut.

I have to keep it shut...

I shift my grip on the shovel and slam it down hard, the blade hitting the wooden lid and forcing it closed. Mercy screams again and my stomach lurches. I swallow the rising bile and press down harder as I feel her push against me from the inside. My jaw clenches against the nausea of her terror, against the pain of her fear ripping through my soul and shredding it to pieces.

I have to hold her down.

I have to do this to keep her alive.

I close my eyes and press harder as Wesley buries her.

Thud... Thud... Thud...

chapter two

Mercy

THUD...THUD...THUD...

Is that the echoing sound of my pounding heart?

The tempo of my heartbeat is so quick that the beats fade together in a rushing whir that vibrates painfully through my chest. I wonder if the panic alone might end me long before the air runs out.

Because the air will run out.

I'm going to be trapped for hours.

There's no way out.

There's no air to breathe.

A long, slow suffocation.

Fear grips me firmly by the throat, its icy cold fingers squeezing, making it that much harder to breathe. My lungs are desperate to fill as fully as they can before the light of day is gone, before my coffin is fully covered with soil, truly buried. My chest sharply rises and falls with each rapid breath. I know I should breathe slowly, but I'm fighting madness here, and I just *can't.* Each breath heightens my panic, reminding me that I may draw my very last one today.

I have to be calm.

I have to be still.

The lid is closed, and soon, I'll be buried beneath layers of soil, trapped with only the oxygen that swirls around me at this moment…and there's so little space.

My arms are pressed tightly to my sides, palms on my thighs, legs tangled through the fabric of my gown. The soles of my boots press flat to the end of the coffin, and the top of my head is only inches from the top.

It fits too perfectly, as though they built it to match my height and width. There's only just enough room to make slight adjustments, but every adjustment brings further discomfort and greater panic— my movements are so restricted that each one reminds me that I'm trapped.

I'm trapped!

Four hours…

Two hundred and forty minutes…

How many seconds is that?

Would counting them help pass the time? Give my mind something to focus on?

No…it will only remind me how slowly time is passing.

Four hours.

Four hours…

Four hours?!

Every muscle twitches at once as a collective tremor tears through me, begging me to move, to stretch, to take up more space. And when I realize I can't, my body thrashes with urgency through the panic, through the desperate need to move.

I have to move!

Don't panic. Be still.

Thud…Thud…Thud.

I can do this.

I can do this.

I…I can't…

I can't!

Conscious decision and rational thought are gone.

My determination to sacrifice myself in the name of revolution has fled my spirit, forced out by the rising cowardice which quickly fills me. It's like a rising tide washing away my strength in this moment, in this terror, in this living, waking nightmare.

My arms creep up my body, twisting until my palms press to the lid above my chest. A small voice screams inside me not to do it, that there's some reason I shouldn't open this coffin right now, but I can't remember why that is. That small voice is drowned by a much louder voice, screaming for me to get out at any cost, and I can't fight it.

I push, expecting the lid to rise immediately, but it's heavy, and I can't seem to remember why it should be. I can't make sense of anything. I'm all action with no thought, and my only motivation is to escape. I shove hard, with all my might, and the lid rises slowly.

Blackness rains, dark soil trickling in through the space I created by cracking the lid open.

There's light beyond…

I'm not entirely buried yet, but I will be soon.

I'll be buried soon.

A mangled scream claws up my throat, escaping from my lungs and leaving a burning trail of terror in its wake, like a fire that snuffs every ounce of oxygen from my tomb.

I'm terrified, desperate, more frightened than I've ever been in my life. I push harder, but I'm weak through my fear, weak as tears well and sobs break free. And just as I find a moment's strength, a moment's resolve to push as hard as I can to escape this certain death, the lid slams shut, and a weight from above holds it down.

No…

No!

I push, but it doesn't budge. The soil was heavy, but this is something else, something forced—perhaps someone holding it down to ensure my entrapment.

I need to conserve my oxygen; I can remember that, at least. But remembering does nothing to persuade my panic against forcing another scream to burst from my soul.

I'm trapped.

There's no way out.

Soon the meager light begins to fade as my grave steadily fills.

Shrouded in darkness, helpless, *buried alive*, I close my eyes and force my mind to drift to another world where peace exists, where women are safe and where love is open. I think of a world where I wouldn't be buried alive for my sins…and the man who loves me wouldn't be forced to shovel the soil.

chapter three

ARLO

"ARE YOU ALL right?" Owen asks.

His voice startles me, and my head rises from my hands to look up at him. For a moment, I falter, unable to register what he's asked me or how I should answer. I force out a sigh, then drop my head to fall back against the tree where I sit. My elbows rest on my bent knees as I wring my sweaty palms between them.

"I'm okay," I manage, though my voice is unusually quiet. I clear my throat and press my eyes shut, then try again, a little louder. "I'm fine."

"Are you sure?" he asks. "If you're sick—"

"I said I'm fine, Owen." I open my eyes and meet his, trying to reassure him with a tight, forced smile.

I managed to help Wesley fill Mercy's grave about halfway before sickness overcame me. I dropped my shovel and ran for the trees with the overwhelming urge to vomit, but on an empty stomach—knowing what would come, I couldn't bring myself to eat or drink this morning—I was launched into a fit of dry heaving that went on for minutes.

Guilt, heartache, terror, grief.

A swarm of emotions roils in my gut, and they keep me in this horrid sickness. I don't hate it; I'm glad for it. I deserve it.

What kind of man allows the woman he loves to be buried alive?

What kind of man holds her coffin shut so she can't escape?

I deserve to feel sick.

I deserve to remain in misery before meeting an appropriate, horrifying end.

"You're shaking," Owen points out, though I don't need him to. I feel the way every muscle twitches, how my bones quake with fear for my starlight encased in darkness, buried beneath the soil. "I've never seen you ill before." His brow furrows. "Perhaps you should return to the Homestead when Park arrives to take Ellary back to the village."

Once we'd buried Mercy and Delle, I kept my ailing mind focused by anchoring rope to the stone cliffside before repelling down with my brothers' assistance. Ellary had a pulse—it was faint, but it was there. The moment I lifted her from the ground, she screamed in pain, awakening suddenly and horribly. One leg and one arm were bent in ways they shouldn't be, but I feared more urgently for the potential of a shattered pelvis or broken ribs that may have punctured organs.

We're so far from the Homestead, from medical supplies and medicines. We had to call for Park to return after ensuring Stefanie—who'd protested at the processional—was securely locked up.

Killian isn't wanted here by any of us at the moment, and Theo needs to keep watch over Delle's brother. So Ellary's broken body lies in wait near the pathway hidden by brush. She's unconscious again, and that worries me because the pain of such a fall should have her veins so flooded with adrenaline that rest evades her. I fear she's in shock, slowly drifting toward death—a death she most certainly didn't deserve.

There's a strange fondness that many men hold for Ellary Hill. She's always had such a pure and kind energy about her—a sweetness and docile demeanor that brings calmness around her, even during violent nights of service. There will be men outraged over the loss of her if she dies.

They should be outraged over the loss of *any* woman, but it seems hypocrisy is rooted in Ember Glen, my own running the deepest roots into the earth beneath my feet.

"I'm not going anywhere," I affirm.

Regardless of how much I want to help Ellary, I can't. I can't leave Mercy behind, even knowing that she'd want me to take care of her friend.

Owen gives a quick nod of acknowledgment as Wesley calls out, "Five minutes."

I scramble to my feet with the notice of Delle's remaining time, rushing to her graveside, and picking up a shovel. I'm prepared to work hard and fast to dig her out the moment Wesley calls her time. She'll be alive, I know she will. She only had to survive an hour, so she'll be okay, but I will not let that girl suffer a moment longer than necessary.

I shouldn't have let her suffer at all.

Guilt threatens to make me heave again, but I swallow it down and pull my shoulders back, forcing myself to feel the ache of it in my gut, the nausea of shame that ripples and runs through every inch of me.

It feels like hours pass as I wait. Owen appears across from me on the opposite side of the grave, lifting a shovel from the ground. Wesley paces, watching the black band permanently attached to his wrist. Ryker stands nearby, casually leaning against a tree with an expression of boredom on his face—and I have the urge to knock it off of him with my fist.

"That's it. That's time," Wesley finally says.

I dig before he even finishes speaking. I work quickly, pushing myself past a reasonable pace for my waning strength and through this guilty sickness which consumes me.

At first, it feels as though I'm doing the job alone, but soon I find my brothers matching my pace and urgency, and it's nearly strange to find a moment of solidarity with them. It's not an altogether foreign feeling; before I began to see the world as I know it now, I shared many moments of brotherhood and solidarity with them. It only feels strange now because I hadn't expected to share a collective determination with them in digging Delle from her grave, in ending this trial we've orchestrated ourselves under the religious law we enforce.

Maybe—*just maybe*—they see the absurdity in this ritual, too.

Minutes, hours, I don't know how long it takes before my shovel scrapes the wooden coffin. I hasten to push away the soil, brushing it off the sides and down toward the end. When I see enough of the coffin cleared—enough to know I'll be able to raise the lid without raining soil over her face—I drop my shovel and leap into the grave.

I shift to stand precariously on the sloping soil filling in the space between the side of her coffin and the grave wall. Crouching, I swipe away the last heaps of soil with my gloved hands. As soon as I can get my fingers under the lid, I raise it up to free Delle.

She lies still inside her coffin, stiff, every muscle tightened though twitching from fear. Her hands are balled into fists beneath her chin, her elbows tucked in tight against her chest, and her eyes are forcefully squeezed shut.

"Delle," I say as a warning before I grab her wrists.

She's so gripped by fear that she hasn't even realized she's being freed. When my fingers touch her skin, her eyes pop open and she jolts in surprise. She's so tense from the horror that her upper body rises with her hands, as though her arms are fastened to her chest, though that at least helps me pull her out faster.

"Is it over? Is it done?" Her voice is nearly inaudible, though it's tone is frantic, quick-paced.

"It's done," I reassure her quickly. "You're done, Delle. You completed the trial."

All at once, she cries. She loosens, throwing her arms around my neck and clings to me. She kicks her bare feet, scrambling to get out of the coffin. Inadvertently, she presses me backward, trying to climb me like a ladder to escape her grave. My feet slip along the inclined soil, angled toward her wooden tomb.

Sliding over loose soil, I lasso an arm around her waist and hoist her up against my side to keep us both from falling into the coffin. I reach above me with my other arm, fingers clawing for a grip at the edge.

"Give me your hand, Delle," Wesley says as his hand appears, reaching down to help.

Delle doesn't respond, lost in her panic to escape. She only continues to scramble and claw, trying so hard to climb out, though it's to her detriment—every time she pushes to try to climb me, we slip deeper into the hole.

"Delle." I try to get her attention as she fights, but she doesn't seem to hear me. I firm up my voice, and snap, "*Delle!*" She turns her eyes to mine and gives me a moment of her attention. "Give him your hand."

She blinks, taking a few seconds to bring herself to the present—I think her mind is still trapped in the wooden box at our feet. Eventually, her gaze turns to spot Wesley's outstretched hand, and eagerly, she reaches for it. He pulls her up as I lift, and she falls over the edge onto the solid ground above me. I watch from below as she scrambles to her feet, and Wesley helps her stand.

I move my feet, trying to climb up, but the dirt beneath them shifts. I slip with the soil and stumble backward, catching myself as my feet slam against the wooden bottom of the coffin. The strike of my shoe against wood and the fall into the lowest part of the grave brings about an explosion of reality, a bomb of aching truth detonating in my mind.

Surrounded by black walls, I lift my head to look up at the gray, cloud-covered sky, visible through the looming tendrils of nearly bare branches. A dark brown leaf slips from a branch and slowly falls, floating back and forth on the autumn breeze, drifting downward like it's slowly dying and seeking the grave.

Down it falls, and before long, it lands at my feet. But the landing isn't gentle. The small leaf strikes the wood coffin with the force of a lead weight. It shakes through the dirt walls and makes the earth shift beneath my feet. I feel as though the world has flipped, and I'm tumbling from the grave, falling upward, forever upward toward a heaven I'll never see.

I'm hurtling through space, tumbling eternally through a dark sky, forever seeking that point of light in the distance—the forever fading starlight that's slowly dying, out of reach, too far for me to touch and too far for me to save.

"Starlight." The word whispers from between my lips.

"Arlo." Owen's voice sounds so far away. "Take my hand and let me pull you out before you pass out down there."

"He looks sick," Wesley says.

I hear them both, but all I see is darkness behind closed eyes— the darkness of a night sky with a single, fading star calling to me in the distance…

Wildflowers and starlight.

She calls to me across space and time.

She calls to me from her grave.

Suddenly, I'm hoisted upward. My soul snaps back into my body as I open my eyes, drawing in a gasping breath to fill my lungs because for moments, I'd held it. There's an ache in my chest so strong that it brings tears to flood my eyes.

Does Mercy's chest ache this way?

Can she breathe?

Panic shakes through me, and adrenaline floods my veins. As Wesley and Owen hoist me up, I turn and climb. I bend onto solid ground and swing my legs up to follow, rolling away from the edge before shifting to all fours. I crawl forward and climb to my feet, moving quickly with my sights set on Mercy's grave…and then I see Delle.

It stops me dead in my tracks to see her, bending to wrap her shaking hands around the handle of a shovel, sobbing as she moves toward Mercy's grave.

"She can't breathe," Delle mutters through her tears. "She can't breathe. She can't breathe."

Weak from low oxygen, from panic, from the drugs still flowing through her system, Delle barely manages to puncture the earth with the tip of the shovel, though she tries. She tries to do what I should have done from the very beginning…*save Mercy Madness.*

My brothers run to stop her, and their movement kickstarts me into action. I sprint past them and reach her first, wrapping my hands around the handle and lifting the shovel between us. Tears stream down her cheeks and she grits her teeth as she tightens her grip, pulling back with all her might.

"*No.* Let *go!*"

I jerk the shovel from her weakened grip and swivel back to face Mercy's grave.

Dig.

It's my only conscious thought.

I drive the blade into the soil, scoop, and toss.

Dig, scoop, toss.

Dig, scoop, toss.

"Arlo, stop," Owen demands.

"What are you *doing?*" Wesley asks.

I don't stop; I keep digging.

I dig until Ryker knocks into my side and we tumble to the ground. He lands heavily against my side, trying to twist me to face down so he can wrestle my arms behind me.

I won't allow it.

I can't let them stop me.

I tighten my grip on the shovel and swing it in his direction as I roll toward my back to hit him. He rolls away, just missing the strike, and that's enough for me. It's not my goal to harm them, but I will if I must.

I will *not* be stopped.

I fight to my feet, rush to her grave, and I dig.

Dig, scoop, toss.

Hands grip my biceps from behind, fingers digging into my flesh and jerking me backward. "Stop!" Owen shouts.

"Get *off* me!" I demand.

My voice sounds like it's coming from someone else, someone feral and lost.

But I *am* lost.

I'm lost to my love for her, and I have no desire to ever find my way back.

I twist and jerk, shaking Owen off.

Dig, scoop, toss.

"You have to stop," Wesley's voice calls from somewhere behind me, calmer than the others. "Arlo. You have to stop."

Dig, scoop, toss.

Dig, scoop, toss.

Someone grabs my arms again, and another grabs the shovel. I'm being pulled and twisted, and though I try to keep my grip on the handle, they eventually tear it from my grasp, tossing it away.

Wesley stands before me, dark eyes fixed on mine as he lowers his voice. "The cameras are on," he hisses. "This is livestreaming; everyone in the village can see you right now."

Delle's soft crying floats to my ears from somewhere nearby, and it tugs on the last thread of sanity remaining in my mind. And when she hiccups through her words, whispering a broken refrain, "She can't breathe. She can't breathe. She can't breathe," she snips that thread, and all my control is lost.

With fury and fear, I fight for Mercy.

I lunge, and Owen grabs my shoulders from behind. "I *can't*," I grit through my teeth, swinging my arms around to knock him off. "I *won't*. I won't stop."

Ryker tackles me from the side again, and we tumble—rolling, twisting, fighting. I manage to get on top of him and slam my fist into his face, watching blood spurt from his nose, as his head turns sideways from the force. Then Owen's at my back, tugging at my arms, and in our struggle, we fall. I scramble to get away from him, but he grabs my leg. I jerk to get out of his grip, and unintentionally kick him in the gut, hard enough that he grunts and rolls away.

I crawl, racing to Mercy's grave on my hands and knees. I claw at the black soil, scratching and tearing my way through the earth to Mercy. My only goal is to free her, to draw her into my arms, to wrap her in warmth, and to carry her away from this place forever.

"We can't do this anymore..." I mutter mindlessly as I dig. "We can't hurt them anymore. We can't do this..."

I pause just long enough to rip off my gloves and toss them away, needing the freedom from restriction to scoop the soil away faster.

The Control doesn't speak; they don't grab me and try to stop me. Eerie quiet loops around me, the absence of sound except for Delle's soft crying, her soft chanting, "She can't breathe. She can't breathe."

We're broken.

We're all broken from this madness.

And I know I won't be whole again until I feel Mercy's heart beating beneath my palm, until I see her chest rising and falling, until I feel the press of her lips against mine.

I claw with my hands until something hard and heavy collides with the side of my head...I fall sideways and snap into darkness.

chapter four

CLARITY IS FOUND…
my eternity in bliss,
she and heaven are one in the same.

Arlo's voice recites poetry inside my mind. Anguish draws from my memories, seeking things that brought me joy, forcing me to recall them in these dreadful moments, and causing me further pain.

Arlo's words are plucked from somewhere hidden within my subconscious. I'd read his words over and over in my final days, but I hadn't intentionally memorized them—but the words are there all the same, imprinted eternally.

My beloved starlight…
my mortal universe,
her death will bring the end of all things.

Yet…
my love for her is immortal,
and suffering will haunt my mortal flesh eternally.

She is paradise.
She is endless.
She is mine.

"I am yours…" I whisper into darkness.

Panic had overwhelmed me for some time, but gradually, a sense of calm has slowly begun to wash over me. My slow breaths feel unsatisfactory, and I'm growing tired…*so tired.*

I try to fight the calm.

I try to hasten and deepen my breaths.

I try to remain angry, panicked, anything other than *calm.*

Calm means tired.

Tired means breathless.

Breathless means death.

It's coming.

I can feel it coming.

Should I welcome it?

I think I can hear the scythe of the grim reaper himself, cutting through the earth to get to me so he can steal my soul. It's a faint sweeping, scraping sound as he digs down to find me…*No.* He must dig from below, creeping up from hell as a demon to take me away for my eternal punishment.

The sound grows louder, and though it seems clearer at first, it quickly crescendos into a sonorous, clashing echo inside my mind, bouncing around with all my strange thoughts, with Arlo's voice reciting poetry, with the voices of a thousand men calling me a sinner. And I'm trapped with them all, trapped in my mind as much as my body is trapped in this coffin.

I'll never be free from this tomb!

No man nor angel nor demon will ever break my soul free.

Even if they pull my physical remains from the coffin, my soul will stay right here, trapped forever in this purgatory—

.

.

.

.

Wake up!

My body jolts as I force myself awake, and my arms fly out, colliding with the sides of the coffin. I open my eyes wide, blinking rapidly against the heaviness of my lids, which threaten to close again so quickly.

Will I miss her when she's gone?
With all the brightness of her starlight hair.

Will she remember me in her damnation?
I'll never have to wonder.

My eyes…they're so heavy.

I fight them as they will to close, as the time between each blink gradually lessens and the peace of slumber calls to me. I'm exhausted, weak, and tired from fighting to stay alive.

I let out a long, slow breath, willing the last bits of air to leave my lungs, sadly hoping there won't be another to fill them again because I'm so tired…

So damn tired.

I'll wreck my soul to meet her in hell…
and she'll never know the ache of missing me.

I'm losing the fight.
I close my eyes.
And maybe it's for the last time.

.

.

.

.

.

I drift through the darkness of space as a lonely star, yet I feel the presence of his being floating out there, somewhere in the vast emptiness, searching for me. The gravity of my heart reaches for him, draws him near, pulls him into my light.

And before I fall into my final slumber, he appears. I see his face behind my lids. The bright blue of his shining eyes, his devilishly charming grin, and the disarming dimples that chisel through his short beard, creating such uniquely distinctive lines through his handsome face.

He's beautiful bathed in light, just as he is in the dark.

I love you…

Arlo, I love you.

I love you. I love you. I love you.

I know I'll find myself in hell the next time I awaken, but I won't have to wait long for him to chase after me. I know I'll awaken to find him right there with me, prepared to suffer our damnation in tandem, and we'll burn together eternally.

chapter five

ARLO

GOD, PLEASE...

Dear God, please let her live…let her be alive.

I stare at Mercy's grave with wild eyes, adrenaline racing through my veins as the Control finally—*finally*—works to dig her out. I've been intently watching the soil that traps her for hours, praying for a miracle from the cruel God who's forsaken us both.

Perhaps I should call upon demons to save her.

I'd sell my soul in a heartbeat…

The Control—no longer my brothers because I can no longer consider myself one of them—had bound my hands at the wrists using my own damn rope. The side of my head still throbs where I was struck with a shovel, though I still don't know which of them hit me. I didn't ask, and I don't really care. It was the only way they ever would have been able to stop me during my mad rush to scrape away the soil, to free my starlight from the darkness of this wretched land.

I kneel at the foot of her grave, watching as my brothers dig, tossing away the dirt one shovelful at a time to free her now that her time has been called.

Four hours.

She has to be alive…she can't be dead.

If she's dead, I'll lay with her in that grave and let the Control bury us both.

I'm gripped with maddening fear, my body trembling as I

watch helplessly.

"Arlo," Delle whispers, and it startles me, making my shoulders jump.

The world disappeared when they started to dig, and everything but Mercy was forgotten. I forgot that Delle was there, standing beside me. I forgot that she sat with me all these hours as we waited. I forgot how I let her lean on me to share my warmth. I forgot about the few times she drifted to sleep, but woke again with a start, with a scream for help to free her from the grave where her mind was still trapped.

Delle lowers to her knees beside me. "Do you think she's…" She doesn't finish the question, and I'm grateful that she doesn't because I wouldn't know how to answer her.

All I can do is shake my head.

I don't know.

I don't know if she's alive or dead.

I don't know if she's dead.

If she's dead…

A thud signals that someone's shovel strikes hard wood, and my pulse races.

They've hit her coffin.

They keep shoveling.

My body tenses, lurching forward with the instinct to leap into her grave, to wrench the lid of her coffin open by force against the remaining dirt that still weighs it down. Urgency ripples beneath my skin, and I shove to my feet, stumbling sideways in my rush.

Delle rises with me. She reaches for me, her hands grabbing hold of my biceps. With an impressive grip for such small hands, she twists me around, turning me to face away from the grave.

I start to turn back, but then she snaps out my name with a sharp bite, "*Arlo.*"

Her insistent tone halts me as she glances over my shoulder, probably finding my brothers lost in focus as they dig behind my back. And then her small hands fall to the rope around my wrists. She works frantically at the knots, her nimble fingers moving quickly to free me. A sigh of relief escapes me as she pulls one end free from a loop and keeps going.

"Hurry," I whisper.

"I'm trying," she says.

We share a chaotic energy between us, both of us caught in our desperation to save the brightest star in the sky. Though I selfishly want Mercy to shine for me alone, I could never deny the fact that her light belongs to the world.

Delle finds the last knotted thread and tugs it through to free me. "Just get her out," she whispers urgently.

The moment the rope falls away, I move.

I turn and jump into her grave to the sound of protests from the Control. I grab the end of someone's shovel as it slices into the final layer covering her coffin, and I wrestle it from his grip. I think it's Ryker's because I hear him shout something as I tear it from his hold.

Turning the shovel in my grip, I sweep and scrape—sweep away the dirt, scrape against the wood. The sound of it is haunting because I don't know what I'll find when the sound stops, when the soil is all swept away and I finally open the lid to her coffin.

Please, please…let her be alive.

Before long, I toss the shovel aside, press my foot into the dirt, letting it slip between the sodden grave wall and the side of her coffin. I curl my bare fingers, wedging the tips into the crevice where the lid meets the frame. I feel fingernails bend and break, scraping along the wood as I wedge them deeper.

When I'm finally able to slip my fingers deep enough to try, I lift with force, grunting as I raise the lid against the heavy soil that still covers the coffin where her head and feet lie. Slowly, it rises, and

I shove harder, pushing it up entirely, then leaning it to rest against the grave wall.

Without taking so much as a moment to steel myself, my gaze drops, and I look down into Mercy's coffin.

There she rests…*my Mercy.*

Pale, except for the flecks of dirt smeared across her cheeks.

Silent, still, the crimson fabric of her dress unmoving.

Her eyes are softly shut.

Her expression is neutral, impassive, like she's asleep.

She looks like she's asleep…

"No!" Delle screams from above, and the punching sound of it strikes my gut.

I drop and reach for Mercy, shifting awkwardly in this wretched space. I feel out of my body, out of control, animated only by the desperate need to get her out.

She'll be okay once she's out.

She'll breathe once she's out.

I struggle to slip my arms beneath her, to circle them around her waist. I raise her motionless body from the coffin, dragging her into my embrace. Her weight shifts against me, and I lean back to avoid dropping her into the coffin, falling back to sit. I drag her with me, shifting until she's cradled on my lap.

She's so cold…so fucking cold.

Her head rolls, falling limply to the side. There's no tension straining through the muscles in her neck, no consciousness.

"Mercy…"

Nothing.

Not a word, not a movement, not a breath.

Delle screams and cries, and the Control speak in rushed and urgent voices above me, but it's all just noise. The only sound I want to hear is Mercy's voice. I'd settle for a sigh, a puff of breath escaping from her lips, *anything.*

"Mercy." My voice is commanding, insistent on having her attention. "*Mercy!*"

Nothing.

I shift her on my lap, hoist her higher, hug her closer.

"Mercy…" My commanding voice lowers to a pleading whisper that I breathe against her ear, my palm cradling the back of her soil-speckled hair. "Starlight, open your eyes. Wake up." A lump rises in my throat and I swallow against it. "It's over. The trial is done. You can wake up now." My voice catches and I hiccup through my words as liquid glazes over my eyes, making them burn.

I hold her tighter.

I kiss her cheek.

I curl my fingers and comb them through her hair.

I tremble, fighting against the voice in my head that tells me she's gone, the voice that begs me to feel the pain of losing her, that pushes me right to the edge of falling apart. It tells me she's not responding, she's not moving; it reminds me that she's been buried for four hours and there wasn't enough oxygen for her to survive.

"No. *No.* Mercy, no…wake up. Wake up, *please.* Just wake up."

She can't be dead…she can't!

My chest stutters, rising sharply as I draw in a deep breath, and then tears fall.

I cry as I hold her.

I bury my face in the crook of her neck and cry against her cold skin, losing myself entirely to a pain more intense than anything I've ever felt. I thought I was broken before, but I wasn't. I know that I wasn't because I'm breaking *now*, my soul shattering into a million pieces, scattering in the soil, never to be pieced together again.

I cannot exist without her.

If her soul is gone, then mine has gone with it.

I weep over Mercy until silence falls around me. When all that exists are the black walls of the grave around me, the coffin beneath me, and the gray, dreary sky above me.

I press a kiss to her neck, then another, and another. And then I crush my lips to the spot again, using her cold flesh to hide my sob, pouring my sadness through her veins from the gentle *thump, thump, thump* of her pulse—

Her pulse…

I turn to stone, focusing hard on where my lips touch her neck. I feel it as sure as I feel her body in my arms—a faint *thump, thump, thump* beats in a slow, but steady rhythm, pulsing against my lips.

I sink my fingers deeper into the strands of her hair, gripping her head, tugging back to tilt her face toward the sky so I can look at her.

Skin still pale, eyes still shut.

I move my other hand between us, pressing my palm to her chest, desperate to feel the beat of her heart beneath my palm.

I wait.

One of the Control calls down from above, "Arlo, she's—"

"Wait!"

I push harder against her chest, and in the stillness, I can feel it. I can feel her heart beat slowly in her chest.

I bring her face to mine and kiss her cheeks, her chin, her forehead. "Open your eyes, Mercy. Open your eyes. It's done. I'm here. It's all over, and I'm here with you."

I kiss her lips, tender, soft, lingering.

I don't care anymore.

It doesn't matter who sees, who knows what I feel for her. All I care about is bringing her back to life, consequences be damned.

Let them see me kiss her.

Let them bring me death so long as it brings her life.

I feel the warmth of a shallow breath ease from her nose, breezing hope over my skin. She's still limp, asleep, but she's breathing and her heart is beating.

"Starlight."

I kiss her again, and a faint moan vibrates through the connection of our lips. I lift away to look down at her, watching the muscles in her face twitch to life as she makes another soft sound.

I sigh, tension releasing, my weight sinking in relief. Her head turns slightly against my hand, and I splay my palm wider to hold her steady.

I lift my head to allow my shout to echo beyond her grave. "She's alive!" I bend to kiss Mercy's forehead. "You're alive," I whisper, feeling the tug of a grin at the corners of my lips.

"Mercy?" I hear Delle and look up to see her on her hands and knees, peeking over the edge with tears streaking her cheeks. "She's…Is she—"

I nod, smiling. "She's alive."

"Oh, God," Delle sobs. "Thank God!"

"How dare you thank God, you little sinner?" Ryker wraps his hand around Delle's hair and forcefully jerks her back from the edge.

I need to get out of this grave.

I hoist Mercy up, moving her to sit on my lap, though she's still limp, her body still slumping heavily against me. "I need you to wake up now," I tell her. "I know it's hard, but I need you to wake up. Delle needs me. She needs *you.*"

Mercy hums, slowly awakening. I can feel the way her soul fights within her, begging her mind to wake up, imploring her limbs to move.

I shift beneath her, trying to get to my feet, though I don't exactly know how to lift her out of here without help.

"Arlo," she whispers, and it halts me. Her head turns against my shoulder. She sighs, blinks against heavy eyelids before losing the fight, then fades back to sleep.

"Here." Wesley's voice startles me, and I look up to see him reaching down. "Lift her up, and we'll pull her out."

Owen appears and reaches down to help, as well.

"I'm gonna get you out of here." I promise Mercy before moving again. With all the strength I can muster, I pull her up with me as I stand, struggling against the soil which constantly slides and slips beneath my feet.

Somehow, the three of us manage to lift her out while she's unconscious, and gratefully, they pull me out after her. I wouldn't have been surprised if they'd left me here to die—they saw me kiss her, I know they did, and the sin won't go unpunished.

Mercy is laid on the ground beside her grave, and I move quickly to kneel at her side. Her fingers twitch before her hand briefly lifts from the ground, floating up, then falling back down again.

"Where are you?" Mercy asks dreamily as her head rolls sideways, caught between sleep and waking. "Arlo…love…I need you…"

"How far has it gone?" Owen asks softly at my side, and I look up at him, meeting his eyes, which are wide with concern. "How far across the line did you go?" He sounds as though he doesn't want to know, and of course, he doesn't. I'm supposed to be his brother in God—a man of faith, upheld to the highest standards in our community.

And I've just shattered that illusion.

I'm not that man anymore, though I suppose I never really was—and now they all know.

They saw me share physical affection with a woman—a servant and my ward, no less. And they heard her call to me with *love*. I am her love, and I no longer care if it brings me death for them to know it.

"The line was thin," I mutter, recalling a conversation I had with Mercy when she first became my ward, a musing about the thin line we both saw between asserting my authority and abusing it, "and I broke it long ago."

There it is.

The truth is out, and there's no reeling it back in.

I turn away from Owen's judgment to give the woman I would die for my full attention. I bend over her, cradle her cheeks in my hands and watch as she slowly opens her eyes, her gaze searching until she locks on mine. I smile at her because she's alive, and the joy I find in that simple fact is all that matters to me.

"I'm here," I tell her. "Mercy, you're alive. You survived the trial."

I kiss her forehead, then move my hands to her waist to lift her into my arms, but I see panic cloud over her bright eyes as my arms close around her, caging her in to my embrace.

Her face contorts in fear and she jerks into motion, her hands gripping my arms and shoving them away, her legs kicking as she fights to break free from my confining grip—she's fighting to break free from the coffin that no longer traps her.

I let go of her, fearful that holding her will only further her distress. She rolls away, pushes to her hands and knees through a burst of adrenaline, then scrambles to her feet. She steadies herself quickly, though her panic holds her hostage. Her head turns frantically, looking all around her with wild eyes as she seeks to make sense of her situation.

"Mercy," Delle softly cries.

Delle.

Her voice reminds me that she needed me, that I saw Ryker violently pull her from the edge of the grave. I whip around to find her face down on the ground with Ryker's foot pressed to the back of her neck, holding her there.

Fury sharply rises, chaos rippling through my veins because I am *done.* I am over this hypocrisy; I'm finished with the violence against these women who have done *nothing* to earn it.

I'm forever changed by Mercy Madness, and I'm glad for it... *grateful* for it. In her name, I swear, I will never be the same again.

I look back at Mercy, catching her gaze for a beat. She's clearly trapped in her panic, yet I can still see the heart of her through her bewitching eyes—the fury of injustice still lives there, burning as brightly as ever, and I let it catch me on fire.

I've already lost favor with the Control. My death certificate is all but written now that they know the extent of my sins. I no longer have a reason to hold back, so I take Mercy's righteous anger, stir it with my burning rage, and let the fiery mixture take hold of me.

With the force of all the pain Mercy and Delle have suffered at our hands, I turn, charge, and barrel into Ryker.

chapter six

Mercy

MY MIND DRIFTS between dark and light—asleep and awake. My body bobs in the cadence of a slow walk as it drifts through space. I fight to wake up, to lay eyes on Arlo so I can see for myself that he's safe and well because I fear for him.

I think I heard someone accuse him of crossing a line with me. And I think I glimpsed him charging Ryker near my grave before I grew weary, before the world once again went black from my breathless exhaustion.

Maybe it was all a dream—I *hope* it was a dream. If it wasn't a dream, then he's not safe, and he needs me.

I have to wake up.

I say his name, though I don't know if I'm saying it out loud, whether I speak in reality or in this semi-conscious void.

"I'm here." It's Arlo's voice, and I know it's real. I know he's really there, trying to drag me from exhaustion. "You're okay, Mercy." He sounds near and far all at once.

He says that I'm okay, but is he?

Blinking slowly, I force alertness through sheer determination. Peering straight through my half-hooded eyes, I see branches…bare branches cutting across a gray, cloud-covered sky. They seem to be moving, dark brown limbs scratching across the gray as they roll away behind me. Except, it's not the branches that are moving, it's *me*. I'm floating through the forest, looking up at the autumn sky.

The more alert I become, the more that I *feel*, my senses awakening from stagnancy. My neck feels strained as the muscles stretch, my head dropped back and dangling, jostling from the motion of whatever unseen force pushes me through the woods. My left shoulder aches as gravity tugs my swinging arm toward the earth. The cold air sweeps over me, and I shiver. Goosebumps prickle all the way up my right arm, and my hand twitches, making me aware that my arm is bent across my waist as I feel my fingers move on my stomach.

I'm being carried.

But by whom?

Arlo would never carry me this way, and I'd feel warmth if I were in his arms. He'd cradle me against his chest and hold me close to him—I'd feel safe.

I don't feel safe at all.

I don't feel like a woman loved by a man.

I feel like a package that's being delivered.

I try to lift my head, but my neck muscles are strained, as is my voice. "Arlo?"

"I'm here. I'm right here." There's an anxious timbre to his voice, and it's tinged with sadness. "I'm sorry." The odd sound of it overwhelms me, and immediately, I feel like crying.

"Don't speak to her." Ryker's voice is loud, though I don't think he's the one carrying me. "You're already walking toward a painful end; don't force our hand in silencing you before you meet it."

Fear strikes me, and it triggers the flow of adrenaline through my veins. I feel it rush through my limbs, twitch through my muscles, and violently jerk my body into full awareness. My eyes snap wide, and I manage to lift my head against the aching muscles in my neck, turning against the pain—which, thankfully, quickly fades in the chemical rush—to try to spot Arlo.

But all I see are trees and gloom.

"Ar…Arlo!" My lips quiver from the chill, from the buzz of adrenaline as it floods my system.

I raise my heavy arms, twisting my body against whoever is carrying me, and try to push away. I don't care if I fall; I just want my feet on the ground. I just want to move, to look, to find Arlo and run to his side.

I could have died today…I should be dead right now, but I'm *not*. I'm alive, I survived, and being with him is all I want.

"Put her down!" Arlo shouts. "Let go of me!" I hear the sound of flesh colliding with flesh, of fists slamming into muscle, of Arlo groaning in pain.

My hands find fabric, and I curl my fingers to grab hold, tugging myself up against the chest of the man carrying me. My gaze skips across blue eyes—blue eyes that certainly don't belong to Arlo—and quickly sweeps over his face. I happen to notice his jet-black hair and realize it's Owen.

It doesn't matter who it is, I just need him to let go of me.

I kick, trying to get him to drop my legs. I jerk, twist, thrash, move any way I can to get away from him, though he fights to hold on. "Let *go!*"

I have to get down.

I have to get to Arlo.

"Put her down!" Arlo's shouts. "Let her down; let her walk!"

As if he suddenly realizes that trying to subdue me isn't worth the effort, Owen finally drops my feet. My boots hit the ground with a light thump and the brief crunch of dry leaves beneath them.

My hands come up on instinct to push Owen away, landing on his biceps and shoving him back. I push him, yet he doesn't move…*I* move. Weak and unsteady on my feet, I stumble backward. I plant my feet and lean forward, bending at the waist. My arms fly out, prepared to catch myself, but I don't fall. Somehow, I steady myself on shaking legs, and slowly, I straighten to my full height.

I keep my lips closed though they beg to part so I can pant through rushed, heavy breaths. Instead, I force the quick breaths in and out through my nose, trying not to show them too much of my weakness.

Because I've never felt weaker.

I've never felt so exhausted while simultaneously feeling so alert, so fearful, my mind preparing my body to flee or fight.

"Easy," Owen says as he steps toward me slowly, one palm raised as if to show good intentions.

Fear punches my gut, and I take a step backward. My eyes nervously dart around, seeking, searching, taking stock of my surroundings. I see Owen right in front of me and Wesley a few yards behind, slowly closing in with a concerned expression.

I see Delle off in the distance toward my right, crying silent tears as she hugs herself. Her stare is fixed on me, watching me with such pain in her expression that it aches inside my chest. She slumps sideways to lean her shoulder against a tree.

I hear a hit, a groan, and my eyes shift focus to Arlo and Ryker, about halfway between me and Delle. I find Arlo in time to watch as he doubles over in pain, Ryker pulling his fist away from his gut. Still bent, Arlo's eyes raise to meet mine from beneath his lashes as pain contorts his expression. But we lose the connection when Ryker moves directly in front of him, digging his claws into Arlo's biceps to jerk him upright.

Then Ryker turns, but one arm remains behind him. His hand grips the rope between Arlo's wrists—which I'm just noticing are bound together—and drags him with a sharp yank as he stomps toward me and Owen.

I naturally take a step back as Ryker moves closer.

He stops beside Owen, releasing Arlo long enough to release a length of rope from his belt—*Arlo's* rope. My lips snarl with an oddly placed sense of outrage that any man other than Arlo should hold that rope, never mind the fact that they've *bound* him with it.

Owen takes the rope from Ryker and turns to face me. "Don't run." He takes a step closer. "That will only make things worse for both of you."

"Worse than *what?*" Fury takes hold of Arlo. He moves swiftly between me and Owen, facing him squarely. "She already faced death. Can you imagine any fate worse than being buried alive?"

"You and I both know there are deaths far more painful than being buried alive."

I take another step back on shaking limbs, muscles weak from lack of oxygen, my knees already threatening to buckle beneath me.

Arlo's head cocks to the side. "And is that the fate you intend to push for us to meet? A more painful death?"

Owen steps forward, bravely standing chest-to-chest with Arlo. "It would be the fate you've chosen with your actions, *brother*. The sins you've obviously committed with her are atrocious… unforgiveable."

Arlo's voice lowers, but his cadence remains steady. "I've come to a different understanding of that word than you have."

Unforgiveable.

"There is no misunderstanding here," Owen says. "You admitted to crossing a line with her. I watched you; *we* watched you put your lips on hers, as if you've kissed her a thousand times before—"

"I *have*," Arlo declares with open defiance, straightening to his full height. "And I don't regret a single moment of our indiscretion."

My legs finally give way with a brief spell of faintness that makes me feel as though my heart has stopped pumping blood through my veins…like my heart is skipping beats. Leaves crackle as I fall to my knees, then drop forward on my hands as my vision blackens around the edges.

"Mercy…" Arlo is quickly at my side. I think he's kneeling beside me as I work to slow my breathing.

My mind feels blurry, on the verge of tumbling back into unwanted slumber. Everything seems fuzzy except for the situation we find ourselves in; the only thing that's truly clear to me right now is that Arlo has let our secret loose into the world—and it puts him in danger.

He's in danger now that they know about our shared sins of the flesh. Yet, strangely, instead of fear, I find relief washing over me.

The secret is out.

And though we both may soon face deadly consequences, in this moment, I don't care. I can't think of the future. All I feel is relief that I no longer have to hide what I need—and what I need right now more than anything is my warden, my keeper, the man that I love.

I can let go now.

I can stop pretending I don't need him desperately.

I can seek him for comfort.

And I do.

Tears rush to the surface and pour down my cheeks as an unexpected sob bursts free. I let myself collapse, tilting sideways to fall against him, knowing that he'll catch me, and he does. He drops back to sit on his heels, and I let myself break apart, falling into a heap on his lap. Though his hands are bound, he uses them to comfort me, fingers grazing my cheek as he tucks my hair behind my ear.

He doesn't speak; he only strokes my cheek with a tenderness I didn't know I needed until he touched me. I cry on his lap and he comforts me, both of us losing any remaining dignity in the eyes of the Control.

As if they know the first thing about dignity.

For moments, nothing happens, no one speaks. It's just a stagnant, broken moment in between one horror and the next.

"You know what?" Owen sighs. "Fine. I could use a damn break, too. I've been carrying her for nearly a mile." Through my tears, I see him sit down, leaning his back against a tree.

"What? We don't have time for this," Ryker says impatiently. "We need to enact punishment immediately."

"Punishment will be enacted whether we take a break or not, and I *need* a break if I have to carry her all the way back to the Homestead."

"I can walk," I mutter quietly.

My voice sounds so weak.

Has all my strength left me?

Did it die? Was it left behind in my grave? Buried, and never to return?

"I'll carry her if you can't," Ryker says, taking a step toward us.

Wesley stops him, coming up to place a gentle hand on his shoulder. "A ten-minute delay won't harm anyone. I could use a short rest after all that chaos, anyway."

Arlo shifts beneath me, moving to sit on the ground as Ryker shrugs Wesley's hand off his shoulder, spins, and paces away. Wesley watches Ryker for a few beats, then, satisfied he's given up, leans his back against a nearby tree. Arlo stretches out his legs and shifts me between them, bringing my head to rest on his thigh.

I hear movement near our feet, and I sharply lift my head to see Delle slowly lowering to the ground with her back to a trunk. Our eyes connect, and we share a moment of silent misery, a beat of camaraderie in our shared mental anguish. She and I were buried alive today, and we survived. We were pulled from our graves, but pieces of our souls were left behind—pieces we'll never get back.

No words need to be spoken.

The way we've been damaged screams between us.

I should go to her, hug her, try to give her some comfort. Though my love for her insists I should give her whatever compassion I have left, I realize I have none left to give. I feel a sudden ache in my chest as this dawns on me—it's like a chisel has been driven into my heart, forming a crack right down the middle, and it hurts so much that it makes me sob.

Of all the things they've done to me, this trial has stolen my compassion, and losing that is the worst thing of all. I turn and press my face into Arlo's thigh as I cry.

"I'm *disgusted.*" Ryker's voice curls with disdain and I feel his eyes on us. "This is *disgusting.* Are we just going to allow them to touch each other so…*inappropriately* in our presence?"

"Give it a rest, Ryker," Wesley says.

"It doesn't matter." Owen's tone is somber and distant. "Their time left is short, and they're both damned eternally. Let them do what they want. I need to rest my eyes."

I would laugh at that if I could, as if he's so weary from the events of his day. Not a single man in this forest—in the entirety of Ember Glen—could withstand the impossible trial I just passed.

I passed.

I passed the second of the Trials of Dissension.

Yet they said our time left is short…

"What's going to happen? What happens to us now?" I'm not sure whether I've spoken loudly enough for anyone to hear, or whether anyone would care enough to respond to me if I had.

"Don't answer her." Arlo's tone is clipped, sharp, a quick command to silence anyone who should dare try to tell me what our fate is going to be.

Somehow, I manage to raise my weary head from his thigh, rising to sit sideways between his legs. "I want to know." I meet his eyes. "I want to know what's going to happen to us."

"I'll tell you what's going to happen, sinner." Ryker chuckles. "You're going to—"

"*Stop,*" Owen cuts him off. "*Enough.* This isn't a moment worthy of gloating." He gives Ryker a stern look. "Our brother has fallen.

This situation is mournful and I feel *sick* about it… and so should you."

Owen rakes his fingers through his dark hair, then brings up his knees where he rests his elbows. He turns his head to look at Arlo with narrowed eyes, though he doesn't look angry—his stare is filled with confusion, betrayal, maybe even sorrow. "Why have you done this? Why have you let her drag you into sin? Have you lost your convictions, your love for God and your loyalty to uphold His word? Why would you give up your entire future to lose yourself for mere moments in sin with *her*?"

I look at Arlo, watching him as the weight of Owen's judgment settles heavily on his shoulders. I see the way his expression flickers, the way it hurts him to answer to them this way. A small part of me is fearful in this moment where he faces their questioning, where one of his brothers in God has boldly asked him to justify what he and I have done in our secret sin. That small part of me is fearful he may waiver.

His response is crucial; this moment is pivotal.

I stare at Arlo with wide, tear-soaked eyes as I wait for him to speak. Before he responds, he turns his eyes to meet mine instead of theirs. No dishonesty or deceit exists in the small, sad smile that lightly lifts the corners of his lips.

He responds to Owen, but his loving gaze is fixed on mine. "Our moments of sin were filled with more love, more joy, and more passion than a lifetime of dutiful worship to an unseen God has ever brought me."

"Fuck," Ryker interrupts with his disapproval.

Arlo continues on as if Ryker never made a sound. "The God we've been called to worship is one I no longer wish to follow. If He exists in the ways we were told, then He's a hateful, spiteful creator for deeming that we should have pride in what we've done today. I would sooner follow demons than the creator who compelled us to bury these women alive."

Arlo's bound hands close around one of mine. "I'm sorry, Mercy. I am so sorry for all we've done to you, to Delle. I'm sorry for saying all of this now because I know this seals my fate, but if you have taught me anything, it's that my future is worth nothing if it's not a future found in truth, in passion, in love.

"As you would die for your cause, I would die for *you*. I choose death over a future where you're not with me. I choose hell over serving a God who insists upon your pain. I choose you." He briefly glances at my lips. "I feel no regret for telling them now that I love you, Mercy."

Tears spill down my cheeks as I nod, unable to speak, stunned by his admission and overwhelmed by everything that's happened.

His grin broadens for a moment as he returns the nod, then turns to look out at his brothers. No, they're no longer his brothers in God, as he's just renounced his faith. They are the Control—the men who will punish him—and nothing more.

"You asked me why I would give up my future for her," Arlo says to Owen. "The answer is simple, yet you'll all fail to understand it if the only voices you hear are those of men. The simple answer is that I fell in love with a woman who refused to be silenced. She demanded to be heard, and somewhere along the line, I chose to listen. I should have listened long ago, and I've failed her in that way, but I won't fail her now. Hear me when I say she has my heart; I am in *love* with her. Her love is greater to me than God's has ever been. My faith is in *her*, and though loving her leads me to death, I'll choose to take that walk every time."

Owen huffs, closing his eyes for a beat as righteousness takes hold of him. "Falling in love doesn't *work* that way," he says before he opens his eyes, then looks squarely at Arlo. "Love is for the lucky, for the rare partnership between a man and his assigned domestic that God has deemed divine. And he would never sully such a perfect partnership with the physical intimacy meant only for servants to perform.

"I hear you say you fell in love with her, but I don't think you understand what that means. If you do love her, then you would never kiss her, never touch her. If you were truly blessed by God to have found love with her in a divine partnership, then you would have *honored* it. So tell me…just tell me because I have to know. Have you used her in the ways a man would purge with a servant? Have you lost yourself to the Impulse, such that you've mistaken it with love? I need to know the extent of what you've done with her."

"You already know what I've done with her," Arlo replies. "You've already decided that I'm damned, and you already know what my punishment will be."

"Nothing has been decided." Wesley pushes off the tree where he leaned and steps forward.

Owen combs his fingers through his hair again before laying his forehead in his palms. "You know as well as the rest of us that Arlo's fate is sealed. A member of the Control has to be held to the highest standards—it's in the Edict. He's condemned to meet his end with—"

"Meet his end?" I snap.

Wesley speaks slowly, calmly. "I fear you'll judge me for asking this, brothers, but I think it must be asked. Where…" he hesitates, "where is the line between God's will and our own if we were selected by Him to lead this community?"

Wesley is met by a heavy silence, one where all eyes are upon him, watching and waiting for him to go on.

Owen lifts his head from his hands to look at Wesley. "I'm not sure I understand what you're asking."

"If we were chosen by God to be the leaders of Ember Glen, then shouldn't that mean that…well, that we've been chosen to lead? Shouldn't that mean that we could choose a different interpretation of His word? God chose us to lead, and there must be a reason for that. He must want us to exercise some flexibility in the enforcement of His word. Forgiveness is a pillar in His rule, is it not? The Control must be held to the highest of standards, I understand that, but how were these standards selected? And couldn't we alter those standards such that the highest of them are more reasonable for us to attain? We are only human, after all."

"I should hold you in *contempt* for speaking such blasphemous thoughts." Killian's voice echoes outward from the endless cluster of trees.

My anxiety instantly spikes at the sound of his voice, and nausea twists through my gut as he appears through the fog, his lips twisting into a proud sneer. Last I saw him, he was standing at the edge of the cliff beside Ellary and Cambria, watching me climb into my own coffin to sacrifice myself for them.

Where are Ellary and Cambria, anyway?

Did they return to the Homestead?

"What the fuck are you doing here?" Wesley spits, turning to face Killian. His long, black braids slipping over his shoulders as he turns and marches to meet him.

Killian and Wesley come to a stop directly in front of each other as they square off, fuming. I don't quite understand what's happening between them, but there's anger and animosity rippling in waves, sweeping around all of us.

"I came to help my brothers," Kilian says.

"Right off a cliff, you'll help us," Wesley snorts.

"If that's supposed to be an insult—"

"*Stop.*" Owen climbs to his feet, walking over to them. "Enough of this fighting between us," he glances around, "all of us. It's been a long damn day, and we all need to get some rest before we speak to one another again…before we tear ourselves apart and lose control of this community. Domestics are rebelling openly, and if we start fighting against each other, we'll never be able to fight against a rebellion."

Is there truly a rebellion brewing?

My heart beats a little faster at the thought of it. Stefanie's outcry at the processional before my trial had been a loud and clear act of rebellion, even if I hadn't understood the words she shouted.

Circulus vitiosus.

Circulus vitiosus in aeternum.

I think it might mean *vicious circle*, but I still don't know what that means. Arlo's sister, Luna, had whispered something to me about *vicious circle* that day we went to the village, when Arlo had given me a pill that had taken away all the pain of my burned hand and had made me feel so blissfully high that I couldn't recall the exact events, or whatever else Luna had said to me.

And then women had started to shout *circulus vitiosus* from the crowd before my trial. Stefanie had cut her arm in protest, and the Control had taken her into custody.

But why had she cut her arm?

It was the same arm which servants bear the tattoo—an image where two black lines slice straight across the middle of the forearm, wrapping all the way around to form circles which split the image of wildflowers.

So she'd cut her arm in the place where a tattooed circle wraps around mine…Is that the vicious circle? The tattoo?

That doesn't make any sense.

Despite Owen's attempts at finding peace between his brothers, they continue to bicker, voices rising to shouts as they speak over one another, entirely distracted.

Arlo slowly shifts his feet, twisting them beneath him and moving into a crouching position. I look at him, but he's watching the Control—the men so lost in their need to be heard that they aren't even paying attention to us. His hands close around my bicep, and he gives me an encouraging tug as he slowly rises, gives me a quick sideways flash of his blue eyes to make sure I'm rising with him.

Inch by inch, we rise to our feet, and Arlo shifts sideways to stand in front of me. He looks at Delle, shifting his arms slowly in her direction, giving a wave of his fingers to beckon her. She moves slowly, rising, taking gentle steps to move beside us.

With his arms swung out to his side, he nudges the back of his hand against Delle's stomach, urging her backward. I reach out and wrap my hand around her wrist, taking his cue to move her, and I drag her behind me.

I stare at his neck in confusion, wondering why he wanted us to stand and move behind him. Then he takes a slow step backward, forcing me and Delle both to move back as well. He takes us back another step, then another…

Killian says something that must prod Wesley, because Wesley's voice rises to a shout, and all attention is held on them.

Arlo turns his head over his shoulder, and just loud enough for us to hear, he quickly says, "If you don't run, you die. This is your last chance. When I turn…"

"We run," I whisper, finishing his sentence.

I lean forward to press a soft, silent kiss between his shoulder blades. He shudders, and then I see the slow nod of his head.

Mid-shouting match, Killian turns his back on Wesley, and Wesley lunges for him, rushing him on the attack. Owen and Ryker race to stop the fight that threatens to become a brawl, and I know this is it. I know this is the moment where Arlo will turn and we'll run. It's our chance to get a head start before they realize we've fled.

Perhaps it's useless to even try. I'm fast, but I'm exhausted from a trial that nearly killed me. Delle has been walking on her own, but I'm sure she's exhausted as well. I already know we aren't going to win this race, and I imagine Arlo knows it, too.

Yet all the same, I understand why Arlo has made the decision for us to try. It's the same decision I made that night in the forest when everything changed—when Hyatt Price set his sights on me after lighting Ivy Jane on fire, and I knew his intent was to do the same to me. That night, I chose to take a step back. Despite the consequences I knew I would meet for running, I still chose to run because the choice was *mine*. It was the only choice I had the benefit of making, and so, I made it.

I chose to try.

And I choose to try now.

So, when Arlo turns, Delle and I turn with him, and together, we run.

chapter seven

ARLO

WE RUN. WE try. But I don't think we'll make it far. I have to try now because I didn't before when I should have, when we might actually have stood a chance at fleeing this godforsaken place.

The Control knows it all now. They know that my allegiance belongs to Mercy. Death will soon find me, and the thought of her laying witness to it burns inside me. They'll make her live without me before killing her as viciously as they'll kill me.

And there is no doubt, it *will* be vicious.

The Elders will push for brutality in the third trial, and not just because of what Mercy has made herself to the women in this community—a rebel, a saint, a martyr. They'll blame her for ruining me because she's a sinner. They'll be more inclined to hurt her in retaliation for the way she corrupted me. But she didn't corrupt me; she opened my eyes to the truth, but that's not how they'll see it.

So, we run.

Leaping over a large, fallen branch, Mercy stumbles when her foot twists beneath her. Helping her with my hands bound is challenging, but I grip her elbow in my hands and try to steady her all the same.

Delle stops, turns, and Mercy yells, "Go! Run!"

Delle waivers between coming back to help her friend and running from certain death. She never gets to make the choice for herself as Ryker sprints out from the trees at a rapid pace, barrels into her, and takes her down. Mercy sprints after her, running straight for Delle, and I chase after Mercy.

I only make it a few steps before someone collides with my back. My weight pitches forward and I fall, landing face down so hard that the air is knocked from my lungs. Two of the Control are on top of me within seconds, and with my arms pinned between my body and the ground, I know it's over for me.

I turn my cheek to look for Mercy, and see her fighting with Ryker, trying to wrench Delle from his grip so she can run. I want her to help Delle, I do, but more urgently, I want her to help herself. Selfishly, I need Mercy to *run*…with or without us.

"Mercy, *run!*" I shout, and instantly, I regret it because my plea doesn't urge her to move. Instead, it draws her attention to where I'm pinned to the forest floor.

She sees me and stops.

She turns toward me and takes a step.

With anger in her eyes, she runs to me.

Mercy rushes to attack whoever is on my back, to save me, though I don't deserve to be saved by her. Yet before she can reach us, she's stopped short, tackled to the ground by Owen.

Once Mercy is down, that's it.

We tried, and it's over.

We tried, and we failed.

We are all defeated, and none of us can be saved now.

chapter eight
ARLO

"I'M BEYOND WORDS for how far you've fallen, Arlo Rainn."
The Elders fume at me from the projector screen in the courtroom.
I've been brought to kneel before them beneath the spotlight. My
wrists are still bound. I'm covered in dirt and scratches from the
tussle in the forest, from trying to escape.

I failed to save her…again.

I keep fucking failing her.

They took her from me the moment we crossed the threshold
into the Homestead, and I don't know where she is. I don't know if
they've hurt her. It's all I can think about, and it's killing me to stay
here on my knees, to face their unwanted judgment when every part
of me is screaming to find her.

"We had such *hope* for you!" Lawrence shouts at me through
the screen, his fist pounding against an unseen tabletop. "How could
you betray us like this? How could you turn your back on God?"

"Don't speak to me of God; you know nothing of true divinity."
My words are unfiltered, as are my thoughts. My mind has never
been clearer since the events of this awful day.

I'm met by raised voices all around me, everyone shouting
their judgment all at once. Killian rushes to my side, lashes his hand
against my throat and twists my head sideways to force me to meet
his eyes.

"You make me *sick*. I trusted you as my brother in God. We had faith in you as a leader in this community, and all for what? For you to betray us just to get your cock sucked by that filthy sinner?"

His expression is so serious. The hypocrisy of him holding this anger against me for loving a woman at the same moment he faces his own judgment for pushing another off a cliff is so absurd that it makes me chuckle.

"Are you concerned, *brother*, that I didn't return the favor for her? Because I assure you…I did. And believe me when I tell you that I found God right there, between her thighs—"

Killian spits on my face, making it abundantly clear that I've lost his favor—as if it weren't clear enough before. He releases me with a shove that knocks me sideways, but I catch myself with my fists against the ground.

"Let's not forget that you're facing judgment here, too," Wesley says, gripping Killian's shoulders and shoving him down to his knees beside me.

Killian snickers. "I'm facing judgment for what you *think* you saw. We *know* what Arlo has done; the entire village knows. We watched him kiss her!"

"And I watched *you* push Ellary over the edge," Wesley bites back.

"Prove it."

I look over at Killian. "You're a coward. At least I'm man enough to admit to my sins."

His face twists in rage as he lunges for me again, though Wesley pulls him back. Owen moves quickly to stand between us, facing the Elders on screen.

"Give us guidance," Owen pleads. "How do we judge our own brothers for their sins?" His voice is strained as he struggles to come to terms with my betrayal—and there is no doubt my betrayal for loving Mercy is seen as far more horrible than Killian pushing a servant off a cliff.

Guilt weighs me down with my acceptance of the truth—with the recognition that Mercy has always been right, and I have always been wrong. It's painful because I can never see this world the same as I did before. I can never see these men as I did before. I can never forgive myself for all the choices I've made that have caused so much harm.

I don't deserve Mercy's love.

My head drops forward, hanging with sorrow for how I've hurt her, how I've failed her, how I've *used* her.

I put her on trial. I strung her up to be fucked by these men who are so *lost*—as lost as I've been my entire life. I cut her hair in the name of removing a temptation that I couldn't control myself against. I let her take responsibility for a murder that *I* committed— it was no accident that the blade I held slipped across Hyatt's throat that night. I walked her to her own grave, stood by and watched her climb into her own coffin. I closed the lid and allowed her to be buried alive.

And the one time I tried to run with her, to *save* her, I failed. I should have tried before. I should have tried every day. I should have loved her sooner…I should have loved her *better*.

"Only one of your brothers should be kneeling for our judgment right now." I hear Edgar's voice, though I don't look up at the screen. "We've reviewed footage of the broadcast when Ellary fell, and we can't clearly say whether she was pushed. And what would it matter if she was? She's a servant, and she stood as a sacrifice for the trial. Mercy might have made the choice to push her over the edge herself rather than be buried alive, and we would have allowed it—"

"Are you saying…" I lift my head to look at him on screen with narrowed eyes, "that it doesn't matter if Killian pushed her because she was chosen to serve as a pawn in this twisted game?"

"I'm saying that she was selected to serve as a potential sacrifice for Mercy's trial, and we all knew that could result in her death. In fact, most of us expected it would. We all thought Mercy would choose to sacrifice her sisters in service to save herself—it's what we'd hoped for. We wanted the servants to see her push her dearest friends over the cliff's edge and squash this rebellion once and for all."

I scoff. "You are so out of touch with the truth, it's astounding. Mercy is more selfless and compassionate than any one of you could ever dream of becoming. She would *never* harm another to save herself, and the fact that you don't know that is so telling of how ignorant you truly are.

"I hope the servants heed Mercy's words and bring war against you. I hope they turn their backs on the god you crafted to control them. I hope they renounce the Edict and break every law you twisted to fit your narrative in the name of God. They should bring all men to kneel before them and force us to endure the same brutality we've forced upon them, because we have earned it. We *deserve* it.

"I am no longer one of you. I no longer recognize your sacred laws." A prideful smirk twists the corner of my lips. "I'm a sinner, and I hold the name proudly in honor of Mercy Madness. She and I are unholy, and I'll gladly burn in hell with her."

"And burn, you *shall*," Edgar snarls.

"I refuse to hear more of this," Lawrence adds. "I presume we all agree on the fate of Arlo Rainn after that vulgar speech. He's clearly possessed by the same demons who possess Mercy Madness."

"There are no *demons*." I laugh. "There's only truth and clarity, and thank *fuck* she's opened my eyes so I could find both."

"Arlo, stop." Owen's hand lands on my shoulder, fingers digging in harshly. "I can't bear to hear another word of your blasphemy."

In a strange way, I feel bad for Owen. A part of me feels that he could find the truth if he found someone who called to his soul the way Mercy calls to mine. He's the man I was before her, and it's difficult to acknowledge that now—to see myself as I was at my worst in the man standing beside me, calling my own words blasphemy, just as I called hers.

"I move for Arlo Rainn to be burned at the stake in penance of his sins," Ryker says as he steps forward. "He's aligned with sin, and his corruption will only embolden those who seek rebellion."

"I second the motion," Killian says—a murderer with the right to say I should die for my love while he should live for his honor.

"*Malo mori quam foedari,*" I mutter with disdain, and their voices rise around me again.

Edgar's booming voice shakes through the room as he shouts loud enough to cut across the noise, "We will not waste another moment discussing this. There will be no vote. Death is your sentence, Arlo Rainn. By ranking decision of the Elders, we declare it."

"*Death* for his indiscretion with a woman?" Wesley asks in scrutiny. "And what of Killian's judgment?"

"Let it go!" Edgar's outrage is clear. "We saw no definitive proof she was pushed, and regardless, her death is of no consequence."

"Wait," Theo says, "is she dead? I thought she was still alive?"

"She was close enough to death when I left her in Sanctuary," Park says quietly.

"You *left* her in Sanctuary?" I twist my head around to glare at him. "Is she alone? Is anyone assigned to care for her?"

"Silence!" Edgar shouts. "Our word is final. Killian is absolved of any blame. We need him as a leader now more than ever—a strong man of God to lead this village back to the light. But you, Arlo Rainn," he chuckles darkly, "you will be made to suffer from this sunset to the next. And with the rising dawn that follows, you will *burn.*"

I huff, resigned to meet my fate. "So be it."

"Hear me now." Edgar's eyes shift around the room, looking at each member of the Control. "You men are tasked with delivering his death publicly. Burn him with Stefanie Price in the village square, and let all see what deviation from God's law will bring them. Let them see that no man or woman is immune from our judgment."

"Then we should burn the trial participants with them," Killian adds. "Let Mercy and Delle burn before the eyes of the village to reassert God's will."

"No," Lawrence snaps. "No. Let Arlo burn, knowing that Mercy will live her final days in misery. Let him know she'll watch him go up in flames, that she'll witness his death. Let him see her in his final moments, knowing that she'll suffer until she meets her own brutal end."

"Hurt him," Clyde adds. "String him up by his own rope and lash him until he bleeds. Bring him pain before the morning of his death. Make him suffer, knowing what you'll do to Mercy in her final trial. Make it known how you will punish her in Service from Bloodshed. Let him go to his death with fear for hers."

My breaths are heavy and quick, my eyes wide with anger that pulses hot through my veins. I'm outraged at their use of Mercy to hurt me, but perhaps I shouldn't be. I should've known how quickly they would turn against one of their own in the name of God.

And before Mercy, I would have done the same.

I'm furious, and I'm frightened. I'm guilty and filled with shame because it's my own actions that will ensure her pain after I'm gone. I'm the one who lost control at her gravesite; I'm the one who showed all of Ember Glen the truth of our forbidden love. She would have been strong enough to hide it.

For my actions, I will burn…but she will suffer.

Even in my death, I don't deserve her.

chapter nine
Mercy

A SUNSET. A sunrise. Another sunset. That's how long I've been locked in my room since the day of the trial, the day we tried to run and we failed. I haven't seen Arlo since we stepped inside the Homestead and they pulled us apart, when they dragged me away from him and locked me here.

Before they left me alone in my room, I'd demanded answers, insisted that they tell me what would happen to us next, but they refused to speak a word. I cried forever when they left, sitting with my back pressed against the locked door and sobbing until my tear ducts ran dry. And then, too easily, I slipped into numbness. I sat motionless for what must have been hours, my gaze unfocused as I dissociated from reality.

Gradually, sensation crept back in, and I was quickly overwhelmed by the feeling of filth caked onto my skin. I looked down at my red gown and the sight of black soil sullying the fabric startled me back to life.

I had to get away from it.

I had to take the dress *off*.

I had to get clean.

I needed to scour every last speckle of dirt from my body.

In a panic, I tore off the wretched gown—the dress that was meant to be the last article of clothing I would ever wear. I drew a warm bath, and with a washcloth, I scrubbed every inch of my body until my skin was raw and pink. Yet even now, it feels as though the soil from my grave has seeped through my pores, like it runs through my veins and has clogged my heart.

My heart…

It stutters and starts through alternating beats of fear and pulses of joy. Fear of what comes next; joy from Arlo's confessions—and for the fact that I survived what should have killed me.

Maybe it should have killed me.

Every moment of my survival since the trial has been torturous. It still feels as though I'm drawing in speckles of soil with each breath I take, and the thought of it keeps me teetering on the edge of panic.

I'm exhausted from balancing on the brink, but I don't dare close my eyes for too long. The darkness behind closed lids only takes me back to my grave, so dark and cold buried beneath the earth.

And I thought hell would be bright and hot from the eternal fire.

I was trapped in that darkness, just as I'm trapped now—alone with my thoughts. This room is only a larger coffin, and every slowly passing moment piles a new shovelful of soil on top.

Will it always feel as though I'm being buried alive?

I have the sense that I cheated death in my trial, and now it's chasing me. Truthfully, I know it's always been chasing me. It's just running faster now—and because he chose to run with me, it's chasing Arlo, too.

Where is he?

Is he safe?

Is he alive?

Does he know that I'm okay? That I love him? That I'd give anything to hold him right now?

I'm fully dressed, awake and aware. I put on a burgundy velvet dress with long sleeves and a sharp V-neck. It fits comfortably with the way the fabric stretches, though it snugly hugs my curves. It's tight to my body until it reaches my hips, but then the skirt flares out from my thighs, cascading to cover my black boots. The sleeves are just a little too long for my arms, but the way they hang over the heels of my palms gives my fidgety fingers something to play with while I pace the carpet in front of my bed.

It's a gown in which I could run, in which I could fight. Of course, I could run and fight better if I wore pants like a man does, but I don't have that option. I'm prepared to flee at a moment's notice, knowing that it would be unwise to get too comfortable here.

It's the middle of the night, but I can't sleep. I've dozed off for brief naps here and there, but nightmares awaken me, and then I remember that I don't know where Arlo is or whether he's okay. I don't know what punishments he'll face for his confessions, for doing things with me that he was never allowed to do.

Punishments for wanting me, for needing me, for loving me.

They're going to hurt him for loving me.

Air catches in my lungs as a sob tries to break free. I press my hand over my heart and draw it back inside with a deep, steady breath. I can't cry anymore. I don't want to. I don't want to waste what little time I have left in this life in sorrow.

I march over to the tray of food placed on the table beside the armchair, and I snatch a handful of blueberries from the small bowl. I pop them into my mouth one at a time, chewing them slowly as I return to pacing, working out my nerves through my gnashing teeth.

I suppose I should be grateful the Control didn't entirely forget that I was a human being who needed sustenance for survival. They brought me a tray of food twice since they left me here alone, and I've been anxiously grazing.

I pace back and forth, eating one blueberry at a time from the small pile in my hand. I pluck another berry from my palm, but the lock on my bedroom door snicks, and I freeze in surprise with the morsel held there against my lips. I stare at the door, waiting, holding my breath as the knob slowly turns.

I step forward as the door creeps open, then stops, and a sudden, jolting fear that it will close again rips through me. The blueberries tumble from my hands and plop onto the carpet. I rush forward, lunging to grab the door. I grip the side of it and wrench it open wide.

I hardly have a moment to register his presence as Theo rushes into my room. He hurries to close the door behind him, then presses his back against it. I feel my forehead scrunch in confusion as my head tilts to the side, waiting for him to speak.

He lets out what seems to be a long-held breath. "This is probably a bad idea."

I close the space between us, coming nearly chest to chest so we can speak in hushed voices. "Where is Arlo? Is he okay? What have they done to him?"

"Mercy, he's… He's not well."

"What do you mean? Where *is* he?"

"He needs you."

"Then take me to him." I reach for the door, but his hand shoots out to the side, easily bumping mine away. He shifts to position himself so he stands between me and the doorknob.

"If I let you out and you're found, the consequences for me would be dire. And by association, so would Delle's."

"Then I won't be found."

"You might be if I let you go to him."

"Where *is* he? Theo, please, tell me what's going on."

He sighs. "He's in the foyer."

My face twists in confusion. "The foyer?"

"He's bound, Mercy. Strung up in the center of the foyer just as you were for Service of the Flesh."

A hard knot in my throat forces me to swallow. "Is he hurt?" Tears I said I would no longer shed burn hot behind my eyes. Fear thrusts between my ribs like a knife, stabbing me in the heart. "Is he hungry? Can he rest? Is he able to sit?"

My mind races through memories of being suspended above the starburst tile during my first trial. I remember the ache of my muscles after seven hours of straining against the rope, the panic of having no control.

What would they do to him?

How long has he been bound there?

"Theo, I can't—"

Unexpectedly, he draws me into his arms, pulling me into a warm, heavy-handed hug that I didn't know I needed—and I do need it. Yet the warmth and kindness are too much for me, insisting that I let go for just a moment and lose myself to sobbing heartache.

No. No more crying. No more tears.

I put my hands on his chest to push away from him as I step back. "Just tell me. *Please.* I need to know everything."

His expression is somber. "He's hurt, Mercy. He hasn't eaten. There's enough slack in his bindings that he can sit, but I doubt he can truly rest." His head drops as he swipes a hand over his mouth. He looks down at the floor, his forehead wrinkling in confusion. "How could he ever rest away from you like this? I couldn't rest away from Delle knowing—"

"Theo, please," I stop him before he says something that will only further break my heart. "Why are you here? Why did you come to me?"

He meets my eyes. "Mercy, he's a wreck. I don't know...I thought maybe I could sneak you out to see him, but—"

"But nothing. Do it. Take me to him."

"If you get caught... If *I* get caught—"

"I won't get caught."

"He's out in the open. If any of them wake up and wander downstairs, you'll be found."

"Is it dark? Are the lights out?"

"Yes."

"Then I'll have plenty of time to hide if someone comes."

"If they find you, and they realize that I'm the one who let you out, it won't just be bad for me. If they strip me of being her warden—"

I step close and grab his face. "You already know that I would *never* do anything to jeopardize Delle's well-being. I will *not* get caught, and no one will know you let me out. I promise you, Theo. I swear. I know she needs you. But right now, Arlo needs me more." I release him and step back, giving him space to choose, to open the door for me—because I know he will. "You wouldn't be standing here right now if you didn't know that."

He sighs and his shoulders slump. Slowly, he nods and takes a small step toward me. "I'm going back to my room. I was never here. And you *will* be back in this room when I return with breakfast in the morning. You'll be here before sunrise."

I nod. "I understand."

He turns and reaches for the knob.

"Theo…Thank you."

"I haven't done anything," he whispers, pulling open the door to reveal the unlit hallway. "Nothing at all." He reaches over to flip off the light in my room, and we're cast into darkness. I sense the shadow of him slip out of the room and walk away.

chapter ten

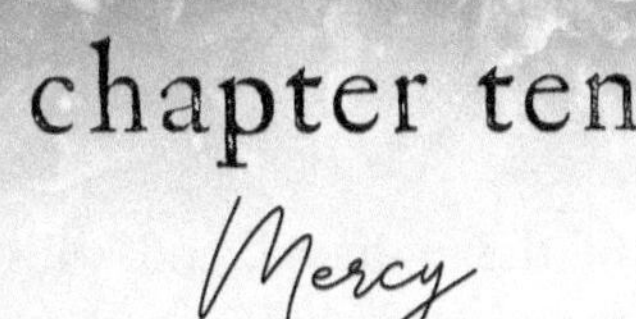

IN MY MIND, I count to ten before stepping into the hallway. I'm surrounded by shadow, entombed in the pitch-black darkness. Not a single light is on, and the entire manor is asleep. It's eerily silent and unusually still, even the air around me feels particularly stagnant.

I take a few steps, moving in the direction of the staircase, but I find that whether I move or stand still, everything around me looks the same—like dark, black night. It looks like I haven't moved at all. It looks like I'm pushing against a never-ending wall of darkness, and I feel trapped by it, condensed by it, like it closes in all around me, and I can't escape.

Just as I couldn't escape my grave.

Suddenly, I'm back in my coffin.

I gasp. I stop. I double over, placing my hands on my knees as I fight to breathe.

I can't breathe.

My lungs ache. My chest is tight. My heart is pounding.

I have to get out of here.

I turn to go back to my room, eager to flip on the light, but then a pained groan echoes from ahead, and it halts me…It calls to me.

Arlo.

I hear his pain, and it pulls me from my grave.

I push against the crushing darkness and rush down the hall.

I reach out with both hands, sweeping them in front of me as I seek the banister. Relief washes over me to see a trace of moonlight peeking in through the window downstairs. It's faint, but it's enough light for me to follow. It's enough light to keep me from being swallowed by the darkness.

I find the top of the staircase, and with my palm wrapped around the banister, I pause. My gaze sweeps down the dark steps, and at the bottom, I find Arlo. I can see his shape, outlined by shadows in the foyer beneath me. A true sense of urgency takes hold of me, and nothing matters but being near him. I turn at an angle to grip the railing with both hands, rushing so I can get to him as quickly as possible.

I descend, moving closer to the window where the moon sends us its meager light. My heart thuds against my ribs, urging me to get to him, to put my hands on him and give him comfort.

I finally step down onto the tile floor, and I reach out my hands toward his silhouette. "Arlo," I whisper as my fingers graze his bare back—his skin is warm, though I expected it to be cold.

He startles, jerking his arms, which I think are bound above him with ropes around each wrist. I flatten my hands against him as I press in closer, and it takes me a moment to work out his position. My touch rests between his shoulder blades, but they only reach the height of my hips so, he must be sitting on the floor.

"It's me," I whisper.

"*Mercy...*" All the air rushes from his lungs in relief. "You're okay?"

"I'm okay." I let my hands slip down his back as I lower to my knees, but his skin isn't smooth as I would've expected. It's rough, and there's dampness in spots.

He's injured. Is this blood?

His muscles twitch, jerking away from my touch. I quickly move my hands away from his back and around his torso. I stop my palms on his chest as I kneel beside him. Shifting closer, my knee bumps against his thigh. His legs are stretched out in front of him, though the bindings around his wrists keep him sitting upright on the floor. I reach up to grab his face, but the angle is odd. I need to be closer.

He needs me closer.

I hurry to shimmy up my skirt and raise it to my hips. I climb over him, straddling his lap before placing my hands on his cheeks, lifting his drooping, weary head. I kiss him first, before another word is uttered, before another moment passes us by.

"What did they do to you?" I ask, dropping my forehead to meet his.

"It doesn't matter."

"What happened to your back? Does it hurt?"

He doesn't answer right away, but eventually, he says, "Yes."

"I'm sorry. I'm so sorry. Am I hurting you? Should I move?"

"Don't move," he says quickly, and I'm grateful because I instantly regretted the offer. "Stay close. Stay right here with me."

"I'm with you. I'm always with you."

I tilt my chin to kiss him slowly, and though I intended it to be chaste and comforting, he insists that it be *more*. He parts my lips with his, beckoning me to deepen the connection. I melt into him, bring my arms around him, and hug myself close.

He pours love into my soul, feeds me affection with each swipe of his tongue. He strips me of my armor and lowers my defenses. He draws each of my emotions to the surface—even the ones I'm trying so hard to fight. An unexpected sob leaps up my throat, and it breaks our kiss. Though I try to stop the tears from flowing, they insist on being shed. I drop my face to his shoulder and I cry.

"I wish I could hold you." He turns his face to press against my cheek. He draws in a deep breath as the tip of his nose nudges strands of my hair, brushing over my skin until he reaches my ear.

"You still smell like wildflowers. Wildflowers and starlight…I wish I could see you better."

My tears slick his skin, and I feel ashamed for it. He's bound and hurt, and here I am crying when I should be comforting him. I kiss the crook of his neck, letting my lips linger as I fight to steady my emotions, waiting until I feel like I can speak without sobbing. Then slowly, I lift my head from his shoulder, blinking away the remaining tears so they no longer glass over my eyes, but drip down my cheeks instead.

"You said they hurt you." I swallow against the lump in my throat. "What did they do?"

"I don't want to talk about that. I don't care." He draws in a shaky breath. "I was so afraid for you, starlight. You're okay, and that's all I care about. It doesn't matter what they did to me."

"It matters to me. Tell me."

"It's nothing."

"What did they do?"

"Mercy, don't—"

"*Tell me.*"

"They whipped me, Mercy." His voice turns harsh, agitated, even in our hushed speaking. "Do you really want to recount the details with me? They tortured me slowly, a few lashings here and there from one night to the next. I've been bound here and tortured since the night we returned from your trial, and it ended only hours ago."

I don't know what to say to him. My heart hurts for what they've put him through. Yet there's a selfish part of me that feels some vindication to know he's experienced a fraction of the torment I've endured for years as a servant.

Now he knows my pain firsthand, and strangely, that makes me feel closer to him than I've ever felt before—when he could only hear my words and imagine what it was like to serve. But now he knows because he lives it. It hurts me that he lives it, but this pain connects us deeply.

After moments of my silence, he speaks again, and his quiet voice is gentler this time. "I'm sorry. Mercy, I'm so sorry for what we've done to you, for what *I* have done to you. You were right all along—right about how wrong things are in Ember Glen. I was so blinded by my faith that I couldn't see it on my own. I couldn't see it until you showed me and I'm so sorry for all the pain—"

"You don't have to do this," I cut him off because I forgave him the moment 'I'm sorry' slipped from his lips.

"Let me finish. I need you to hear me. I won't take unspoken words to my grave."

His grave.

To hear him speak of his own death is jarring.

I speak slowly, softer than a whisper because I'm afraid of saying the words out loud. "Arlo, tell me the truth. Have you been sentenced to die for your sins with me?"

Silence.

Tense moments of painful, honest silence.

"I have."

I gasp at the admission, though I expected it. We both expected it, yet knowing it's been decided is shocking in a way I couldn't have imagined.

"I regret nothing, starlight. I need you to know that. I would choose to sin with you all over again, even if it meant dying a million painful deaths. I hurt you. I failed you, time and again. And yet, you loved me. I'm grateful for you. I'm grateful for every stolen moment, every breath, every whisper, every heartbeat. They may burn me at the stake come morning, but my love for you is fireproof. They can never truly take me away from you."

"Come morning?" A tremor moves through me. I strain my eyes against the dark, willing them to adjust and let me see the blue of his eyes.

'They may burn me at the stake come morning…'

My hands are moving before I even form a coherent thought, slipping along his arms, over the ropes tied around his wrists. I'll untie him. I'll free him. We'll escape over the mountains; I don't even care what exists on the other side of them.

"Mercy, stop."

"I'll untie you and we'll go. We'll run together, one last time."

"You can't untie me."

"Yes, I can, I—"

My voice cuts short as I realize it's not just rope. There are metal cuffs around his wrists, which are attached to chains that are tangled with the rope in such a way that they don't make a sound. I could free him from rope alone, but I can't undo these chains.

"Theo already tried," Arlo tells me. "And even if you could get me free, we can't get out of the Homestead. They've deactivated the band."

The black band that all the Control wear. The one that's latched around their wrist, permanently affixed when they take their oath at the Shift and become one of the Control. It's the black band that unlocks all the doors in the Homestead. The one they wear with them to the grave.

If it's deactivated, then we can't get out.

If it's deactivated, then it's…it's over.

"But I—" My thoughts stutter. "I need a warden for my final trial."

It's a stupid, selfish reply to everything he's just said to me, but my mind feels broken, and I'm grasping at straws. I can't fathom living without him. I can't comprehend the reality of this.

I was supposed to die first.

I was meant to die in these trials.

And now he's telling me that this is the last I will ever see him.

"Even if they showed me mercy and allowed me to live, do you really think there's any scenario in which they would allow me to remain your warden?" He chuckles a little but there's no humor in it. "I confessed to committing atrocious acts with my ward, with a true sinner on her way to death. Not only did I fuck a woman outside of service, but I fell in *love* with her. They don't want love in Ember Glen because it makes you too bold, too powerful, too idealistic—and the Elders can't have that."

He pulls himself up, sitting taller, leaning into me. "Though, I have to be truthful with you, starlight. I think I might have found their forgiveness when I faced judgment if I'd been willing to show some humility. Instead, I committed the worst offense of all." His lips brush my cheek on the way back to meet my ear. "I showed no remorse for any of it."

I shudder at the touch of him, at his nearness, at the warmth of his breath against my skin.

"They asked me to repent for the sins I committed with you, and I refused." He kisses the spot just beneath my ear and my head tilts naturally to open more for him. "I would've used my last breath to refuse it, Mercy. I would've let them kill me rather than lie. Because what we are, what we've done, who we've become…it's greater than God, bigger than the universe. We're beyond death, starlight. You and I are eternal."

"I love you." The words rush out of me just before I turn to capture his lips, and I kiss him with more passion than I ever have before.

I sweep my tongue inside his mouth and he hastily meets it with his, licking me, consuming me like I'm the most delicious thing he's ever tasted. My back arches, my body molds to his, my hands slip up the sides of his neck to hold him steady as I grip just beneath his jaw.

"You taste so sweet," he mutters against my lips. "What did you eat?"

"Blueberries," I reply, and then I slump, realizing he hasn't eaten in at least a day. "I'm sorry, I should have brought you some." I start to shift off his lap. "I'll go get—"

"Don't you dare move from my lap, Mercy Madness. The only thing I need to consume right now is you. Let me taste you. Let me love you." His voice is sultry, filled with heat and need, but it wavers when he says, "Let me have you one last time."

One last time…

"One last time?"

The deep sorrow over our fate threatens to devour me, to break me into a sobbing mess, crying on the floor until all my tears dry up. But I know that wouldn't be right. I would regret losing myself in sorrow instead of losing myself in *him*. I have him now, and I'll be damned if I let sadness take this moment from us.

One last time?

"This won't be the last time, Warden Rainn. They could end us both right this moment, and I'd only find you again in hell." I press my lips to his as I shift my hips forward, settling my weight so he can feel me. "And I would do things to you that would make the demons threaten to cast us out for depravity."

I feel his lips move against mine as he smiles, groaning softly. "And you know I would welcome it."

He captures me in a rough kiss that quickly turns frantic. We easily devolve into lust-driven fools who risk everything for another forbidden moment, another filthy and beautiful memory of physical love to hold on to in our final days.

I've faced death already.

I've accepted my fate.

And though I thought Arlo would last—that he could bring change to Ember Glen—there's something darkly comforting about knowing that he'll join me in death if it's going to find me, anyway.

If there is an afterlife—if hell really does exist—there's a twisted sense of comfort in knowing that we'll quickly find each other in the flames.

And we'll burn together eternally.

chapter eleven

ARLO

MY SANITY HAD been slowly slipping away from me before she descended, before Mercy crept from the darkness surrounding me—my starlight in the endless black universe.

The end is coming for both of us and there is no hope of changing that. Yet somehow, in this moment, I find that I don't care. There is no space in my mind to think of the future or of death. My only need is to exist within her.

I'm lost in her rough, urgent kiss, enchanted by her touch, enthralled by her very presence. She fuels me with raw, undeniable passion, spurring a visceral need that was inevitable from the moment she arrived at my side.

I am so in love with this woman.

In all my years of purging and debauchery, I have never known such pleasure as what I feel with Mercy. I never felt satisfaction before her. Purging has kept us at arm's length from true bliss—it disconnected our souls from the physical acts we committed with servants.

If I had known—if *any* of us had known—how incredible it feels to fight for mutual release, to seek shared pleasure in tandem, then Ember Glen would've crumbled long ago.

My hands feel like they've been set on fire, like my scars have been freshly lit by a flame that could only be extinguished by the touch of her flesh beneath my palm.

Yet I'll find no relief for my scarred hands—hands I've used to punish myself for having desire outside of service. A lifetime of self-mutilation, of burning my own flesh to distract myself from the pangs of lust…

And all for what?

If I'd known how essential lust would be—if I'd known that I would find peace, harmony, and acceptance in our mutually feral cravings for one another—I would've given into her from the beginning. I would have given myself to her freely and without restraint.

My burning hands fight for relief, my arms jerking against my bindings. I'm bound at the wrists, and there's only enough slack to allow my elbows to bend at shoulder height. They could have just bound me with the chains and metal cuffs around my wrists alone, but Killian is a fucking demon disguised as a human, and he took great pleasure in using my own rope against me.

I hope he dies a slow, brutal death.

If the situation weren't so dire, I'd have to laugh at the irony. I'm strung up by my own rope, bound by my own rigging. I'd secured it to the ceiling myself for Mercy's first trial so that men as vile as me could desecrate the woman who had freed my soul.

And it serves me right.

I deserve to be strung up this way in penance to her…or perhaps, in this moment, as a gift for her.

Turning my wrists, I stretch my hands and wrap my palms around the braid of rope and chain that tethers me. I grasp firmly, using my grip to lift myself, to sit just a little taller, to hold my form solidly, and give her what strength I have left. She stifles a moan as my chest flexes, rigid against the softness of her breasts pressed against me in her tightening embrace.

"Pull down your dress. Take them out for me," I growl against her lips. "Let me bite and suck that soft flesh until you're dripping wet for me."

She leans back just enough where I can make out the movement of her dark silhouette, the motion of her pushing down one sleeve, then the other. She lowers her gown to free her perfect breasts, and I only wish I could see them more clearly in this damn darkness. Her weight against my lap lessens as she rises onto her knees. She leans into me, and I nearly come undone as I feel the mound of her flesh bump against my cheek.

If only I could lay my hands on them…

I can't touch her, but I can taste her. I turn my head to brush my lips over her skin.

"I'm already wet for you," she whispers. "But I want more. I need you to make me drip with desperation."

I groan at her perfect filth as my lips graze her nipple, already peaked, hardening easily in her desire. I flick my tongue over the nub a few times until she's huffing with sweet, desperate little breaths, her body twitching, muscles clenching with each swipe. And when I finally suck the peak between my lips, she melts.

Mercy leans into me as she arches her back. Her arms are wrapped around my head to hold me there as I rhythmically suck, drawing out the desperation she asked me to give her.

I'll make her desperate, but she doesn't need to be.

I would never leave her unsatisfied, unrelieved.

Except my hands are bound and I can't touch her.

I scrape my teeth over the sensitive nub, kiss it, bite into the side of her thick mound before I move to the other one. I kiss my way along the inside toward the peak and mutter against her skin, "It kills me that I can't touch you."

"It kills me, too," she agrees sadly.

"Use your hands where I can't use mine, starlight." I play with her nipple using my teeth and tongue. "Put your hands between us. Stay close to me, and let me feel your fingers slip down our stomachs together." Another lick, a hard suck that draws her nearer. "And when you reach between your legs, sit heavy on my lap so I can feel your hand move as you touch yourself."

It's quiet between us for a few beats as I continue my pleasure-filled assault on her breasts. Then, gradually, her grip loosens. Her hands land softly on my shoulders before slipping down my chest. She drags her palms down my stomach, her back arching to keep herself firmly pressed against me. She's so close, and I imagine she feels the same drag of desire pulling down her stomach. Where I feel it through her palms, she must feel the same at the backs of her hands.

She pauses at my belt, her fingertips curling to slip behind the elastic of my boxer briefs. She tugs at the fabric, teasing me, but she doesn't free me yet. Letting go, she gently rakes her fingertips over the bulge trapped beneath layers of fabric. She does it again and again—teasing me so sweetly—until my entire body is trembling with need for her.

Her palm cradles my cock, lightly squeezing, and I draw in a sharp breath through my nose to avoid calling out her name in desire. I lean in to press my face between her breasts, deeply inhaling the sweet and heady scent of her skin as she rhythmically squeezes my cock.

"I want this," she whispers. "I want you."

"Sweet sin," I mutter, turning my face and sinking my teeth into the side of her breast.

"Arlo," she gasps.

"I wish I could feel your warmth on my fingers." I sigh. "Feel it for me, starlight. Touch yourself. Sink your fingers inside you."

She shifts, bringing her hips closer. The back of her hand falls to rest against my hardening cock. Her knees slide further apart on the tile as she lowers, and her fingers move between our bodies. I can feel her hand stretch and flex as she starts to play. I know the moment her fingertips graze her sex because she huffs out a small breath of relief—relief, though she trembles with a greater need still unsatisfied.

She teases herself through heavy breaths that make me harder, thicker. And then she gasps at the same moment her body sinks, impaling herself on her fingers. Her weight pushes her knuckles down, heavy against my cock, almost painfully in the way they dig into me. Yet I welcome the ache because it feels so good when it's delivered by her touch. Only Mercy could make pain feel like pleasure.

She moans, forcing out a heated breath that sets me on fire, makes desire burn low in my stomach, and draws pleasure down to my twitching cock.

"Fuck your fingers." My voice is deep and feral, though I fight to keep quiet in the dark. "Do it for me. Let me feel you move. Fill me with the sweet sound of your whimpering desperation until you're ready for me to fill you."

Her free hand grips the back of my neck, holding me close as she drops her forehead to mine. "I'm ready," she pants, her hips rolling forward with short, smooth thrusts. "I'm ready for you now."

"No, you're not. You want to be…but you're not."

"I'm always ready for you," she protests with another gliding forward thrust, then back.

"No. I want you more than ready. I want you *frantic* with need. I want you pulsing, swollen, aching for relief before you fuck me. I want you so ready that you nearly come the moment I'm inside you."

She shudders at my words as she continues to move forward, then back. "I could come on my fingers right now. I don't want to, but I could."

As if to prove her point, she hastens the pace of her rolling hips. The back of her hand rocks with her body as it pulses against my bulge, making her knuckles dig in harshly. She fucks her fingers like she's riding my cock, and I'm so damn hard that it hurts.

"Tell me…" she pants as she moves. "Tell me you need me now. Tell me to take out your cock. Tell me how much you need me to make you come."

"Sweet *fucking* sin," I growl as I tilt my chin to kiss her deeply.

I didn't want to rush this…I wanted us to take our time.

I know she can't stay here with me all night. I know it will only lead to more misery for her if we're found together, and I can't be the reason she's met with more misery.

This one moment is it for us—the last we'll ever feel each other. I wanted to draw it out; I wanted to make it last because the thought of it ending is too much for my mind to take. Though perhaps it's not the length of time spent in this physical affection that would make it perfect…Perhaps it can only be perfect because it's fleeting.

"*Please*," she begs, her parted lips brushing mine.

The way she wants me—the way I need her *right this fucking second*—overcomes me. "Do it. Take my cock out and fuck me, Mercy. Let me inside you." Suddenly, I'm panting. The slow burn I tried to maintain has burst into flames within me, lighting me on fire.

She pulls her hand from between us and sits heavily. I groan at the feel of her pressing her pussy down hard, soaking my slacks with her wetness. She flexes her hips, grinding slowly, driving me wild.

The heady scent of her arousal draws nearer—I can smell the intoxicating scent of her before her slickened fingers find my lips, slowly dragging across them. I open my mouth and capture her fingertips with my tongue, licking from knuckle to nail. She pushes them inside my mouth, encouraging me to taste her again, and greedily, I do. I swirl my tongue around them, lick and taste and suck her fingers until she tugs, pulling them away from me.

For seconds, she's stark still, silent.

"I hate this," she whispers.

Her words strike like lightning.

I try to bring my hand to her cheek, but my arm only jerks against my bindings, reminding me that I can't touch her. *This* is the worst form of torture.

"I hate it, too," I admit.

In one swift motion, she slides back to sit on my thighs while her hands drop to my belt, quickly working at the buckle.

"I hate them. All of them. *Everyone.*" Her voice is odd—curt, frantic, angry, and sorrowful all at once.

She unfastens the button and pulls down the zipper of my slacks. I grip my bindings, pulling against them to lift my hips for her. Her nails claw my skin as her fingers curl, hooking into the elastic of my boxer briefs. She grabs hold and harshly tugs, dragging my pants and underwear down to my thighs.

"I hate this place. I *fucking* hate it," she grits through her teeth.

She rises onto her knees, moving closer again. She lowers her body just enough so her wet warmth teases across the tip of my cock as she puts herself in position.

"Mercy," I groan.

She shifts her hips, taking me inside her no more than an inch. "I have hated every moment of this awful life that was chosen for me until you became my warden…And then I hated it even more."

She chuckles darkly, wiggling with me barely inside her. The way she teases me is agonizing. I'm panting, throbbing, *dying* to be buried deep inside her.

"I hated it," she says, "and then you made me love it. With no warning, Arlo Rainn, you took every moment of hatred and twisted it into something I could never have. I could never have had you—" Her voice breaks, and my hands are on fire again, burning with the need to touch her.

"They would never let me have you, and the proof is here, twisted through the ropes that bind you." Her palms touch my cheeks. She grabs hold of my face, bringing her forehead down to touch mine. "They never wanted us to have each other because they know how dangerous we are together. They think they can tear us apart, but they don't understand, my love. They can't separate us now, not by putting me behind a locked door or binding you with ropes and chains. They can't even separate us in death, because even there, I will find you."

With a shared moan that shakes violently through us both, she lowers fully, sinking me all the way inside her. She tremors against me, both in pleasure and in sorrow.

"I will find you again," she promises.

She presses a kiss to my lips, lingering sweetly before a sob breaks free. I feel like chiseled stone, cracks rippling throughout my soul at the sound of it. She cries freely, wrapping her arms around me and hugging me close as she nuzzles her face into the crook of my neck. And while she cries, she moves—a gentle rocking of her hips, forward and back.

"We'll find each other," I promise, turning to kiss the side of her head before nuzzling my nose through her hair, letting myself become overwhelmed by the scent of wildflowers that's present each and every time I breathe her in.

Each gentle motion draws intense pleasure through my cock, but *sweet sin*, the way she clings to me, the way she needs me, the way she *loves* me…there's a pleasure I've never known radiating through my soul.

Her crying gradually fades, lessening with each sweep of her hips as they rock. The hiccups that shook her while tears slicked the curve of my neck become slow, heavy breaths, breaths that hasten with each passing moment. Her panting, her small, sweet whimpers tell me how good it feels for her, despite the fact that her heart is breaking.

And my heart is breaking with hers.

Though a part of me wants to fight the pain and be strong for her, I know I can't. This hurts too much. And if she feels a fraction of the pain I feel, then it's too much for me to let her bear alone. So, I let myself get lost in the ache of it, let myself shed tears with her for the perfection of this moment on the brink of our demise.

We share tears as she moves me inside her, and gradually, surprisingly, the pain begins to change. It twists, blending with the overwhelming physical pleasure of our bodies, morphing into pure bliss for sharing something with her that I can only describe as *more*.

She's not just holding me, it's *more*.

She's not just fucking me, it's *more*.

This is what they're trying to keep us from finding. This is love in a very visceral way. It's dangerous, terrifying, brutal, and beautiful. It's finding that we still have strength, even in our weakest hour.

I have strength to face the end because of her, because she gave me truth and peace and *this*. She gave me this love when I did nothing to earn it, all because she saw me and all she hoped I could become.

An absolutely unholy tremor tears through my spine as the truth strikes me—that she and I crafted this passion between us. Together, we created a connection that was never meant to exist, and it changed the course of everything. She and I are making this love together, adding to it with each touch, building upon it with each breath, making it grow with each slip and stroke of our bodies. Our hearts are pounding through the pain of our fates, and our bodies grant us all-consuming pleasure in reprieve.

I let my lips brush her ear. "Wildflowers and starlight."

She shudders, and her movements hasten. Her cheek stays pressed to mine as her hands climb up my arms. Her palms touch mine, and I quickly lace our fingers together, clamping my hands around hers to hold them tight so she doesn't let go.

She fucks me wildly, refusing to slow her pace until she's

panting, chasing release, her inner walls squeezing and pulsing around me. Her lips brush my cheek as they quickly seek my lips, and I silence her with a kiss as her explosive release barrels through her. Her brutal, beautiful motion and the sensual sweep of her tongue over mine spurs me to come inside her.

She feeds me unspoken words through her deepening kiss…

I love you.

I need you.

I'll find you again.

Her rocking hips slow and her eager kiss softens. Her grip on my hands loosens as her palms brush down my arms before she wraps them around me, clinging to me like she'll never let go. She lovingly kisses my cheek before resting her head on my shoulder.

My heart feels light and heavy all at once.

Mercy sighs, settling herself in this embrace, holding on to me as though she'll never let go.

"Wildflowers and starlight," she murmurs against my skin.

The words circle around my head, floating in the air, forever lingering in the ethereal space that surrounds our souls whenever we're joined.

Fresh tears slip down my cheek, and I don't fight them.

I can't fight what her love has done to me.

I don't want to.

Loving her is what brought us here. It's the reason why I'm facing my death now, but I wouldn't change it. I could never regret falling in love with Mercy Madness.

My only regret is that I didn't love her sooner.

chapter twelve

Mercy

THICK FLAKES OF white snow tumble softly from the overcast sky. The air is cold and stagnant, still and silent. The world around me seems unreal, as if I'm already dead, a ghost haunting this plane of existence, trapped in this purgatory where peace evades me.

Theo leads me out through the front door of the Homestead, his hand wrapped firmly around my elbow. Delle is on my other side, but she's withdrawn, distant, broken. Her arms are crossed tightly over her chest, and her gaze is downcast—she hasn't made eye contact with me yet. The trial stole something from her soul that she'll never get back. I know what it stole from me, but I wonder what she lost.

Her innocence?

Her peace?

Her hope?

Perhaps she lost them all.

I've lost my compassion, and I've lost my instinct to help. I've lost my strength, my willingness to try, my hope. It's all gone, shed with the ocean of tears I spilled last night, alone in my room.

Arlo and I were lucky we weren't caught together in the foyer, though it's not like either of us truly cared if we got caught. It's not as if they could worsen our onrushing fates—I didn't care about that at all. But as sunrise neared, Arlo reminded me of what I'd told him, that Theo had let me out of my room to be with him, and we both knew he would be met with severe consequences if found out—and that meant consequences for Delle, too.

I suppose I still had some selflessness and compassion remaining; my love for Delle is something they could never take away from me. I knew she still needed someone strong like Theo at her side because I'll have no strength left for her once Arlo is gone. But now my empathy seems out of reach…and if it's not gone entirely, then it's buried too deep within my soul for me to grasp.

I feel numb.

I feel lost.

I feel like Theo is moving me through an illusion of reality, a hallucination, a waking nightmare about to unfold.

His grip tightens on my arm as we move toward the stone steps that lead to the square. I turn my head, dropping my gaze to look at his hand. His fingers are wrapped around my red velvet sleeve—the same dress I'd hiked up over my hips last night so I could straddle Arlo and sink him inside me.

I blink, forcing myself to focus on the present. I see just how hard Theo's fingers are digging into my flesh, like he's expecting me to fight him for freedom at any moment now. When I look up at his face, I find his expression is tight—jaw clenched, eyes hard and fearful all at once.

What does he have to be fearful about?

"Wh-what's going on?" Delle asks with a frantic voice, and my head whips to look over at her. Her eyes are wide as she stares toward the square at the bottom of the stone steps.

My gaze hadn't even traveled that far yet, completely lost in the cascade of softly falling snowflakes. It's beautiful, yet it's haunting. It seems too early for snow here in the final days of October—it seems to fall as an odd distraction, brought in by the cold air that settles heavily all around me, that feels stifling in its stillness.

I feel like I can't move against the stagnant air, can't breathe through it. It nearly takes my mind back to the grave, but then my eyes catch the snowflakes again. They're large, resembling tiny tufts of cloud falling from the sky, and my foggy mind is mesmerized as I watch them slowly float toward the ground.

A distraction…

I'm forcefully hauled into reality with a sharp and sudden sting that slices through my heart, as if someone's just taken a knife and thrust it into my chest…only there's nothing there. I don't know where the pang comes from, but it hurts. It hurts so badly that I feel tears well behind my eyes.

Something compels me to track the line drawn by Delle's eyes, following the path of her fearful confusion until I'm looking out at the center of the village square…and my heart violently drops into my stomach.

"It's not for you," Theo reassures Delle, though his tone is sorrowful. "It's not for either of you."

Two piles of brush and logs sit in the center of the square. The piles are arranged intentionally—brush, thick around the base with logs angled to point upward toward a pole fixed at the center and staked into the ground.

No…No!

I step backward, and Theo pulls. I bend my knees, using my weight to pull against his grip with all my might. I grab at his hand, trying to pry his fingers, to loosen his grip.

"*No,*" I whimper, twisting, pulling, fighting. "It's not for him…" I grit my teeth, clenching my jaw with determination as I claw at Theo's fingers. I drop my weight hard, nearly falling to sit, though his grip on me is strong enough to yank me back to my feet. "Say it's not for him, Theo!"

"Don't do this, Mercy," Theo's voice lacks conviction, but his hold on me is strong. He jerks me closer, facing me squarely as he grabs both of my arms. "Let him—" his voice cracks. "Let him go with some dignity left."

Dignity?

"There is no *dignifying* this!" I fight even harder to get out of his grip, and he struggles to hold on to me through my violent thrashing.

"God," I hear Delle mutter softly. "Oh, God, *no*. What are they doing?"

The sound of her fearful voice cuts through the madness taking hold of me, and somehow, it brings my fighting to an abrupt end. I freeze, overwhelming panic washing over me, turning me to stone. With wide eyes, I look past Theo's shoulder, casting my stare down the stone steps and out toward the center of the square. My hesitation gives Theo pause, too, and his head turns over his shoulder to follow where Delle and I both watch with dread.

Stefanie Price is brought forward, positioned to stand on a small platform affixed atop the angled logs, facing the Homestead. The crowd of villagers and servants who have come to watch are gathered near the bottom of the stone steps, facing her—facing the two stakes that are meant to go up in flames.

Before the trial, she protested in a clear act of rebellion. And for that, they've sentenced her to die. So quickly, so easily, they've chosen to end her life for having a voice and using it.

Circulus vitiosus in aeternum.

I don't know what it means, but I don't have to know to understand the intent. It was a shout against the Control, against the Elders, against the whole of Ember Glen.

I slowly step forward and Theo moves with me. I take a single step down the stone staircase without even realizing it, but then I feel too weak to take another. My body slumps, lowering to sit on the top step of the staircase. Theo releases me—perhaps he's satisfied that I'm no longer on my feet and fighting to run—but he remains close to my side.

I'm transfixed, unable to look away from Stefanie. I watch with wide eyes as her arms are brought behind her back and tied to the stake with rope. It's hard to tell from this distance, but I think her eyes are shut. Even if they are, she looks strong and powerful, with her chin tilted toward the sky.

They're going to kill her.

They're going to light her on fire.

I fall back into a trance, my eyes unfocused on the scene laid before me, focusing instead on the white tumbling snowflakes.

I hear the voices of women in the crowd—the voices of domestics, no less—screaming, crying, openly calling out for Stefanie to be given another chance. Their voices seem disembodied—there, but not—faded into the background of my gradually detaching sense of reality.

Though my distressed mind begs me to remain in this trap of dissociation, it's the men's voices that draw me away from detaching entirely. The men shout, raising their voices with anger above the women. I force myself to regain focus and see husbands grabbing their wives, jostling them violently within the crowd, shaking them, telling them with force what they should feel about this, what they should think, and what they should believe.

The men want to see Stefanie burn.

They wanted to see *me* burn, but instead of a quick death, I was given this drawn-out torture through the trials. I'm a dead woman all the same.

My pulse thrums, my heartbeat quickening as I feel a sudden shift. The stagnant air moves, grabbing my attention. A breeze that's barely existent draws my gaze away from the crowd, away from Stefanie, and shifts my focus to the second stake.

The noise from the crowd gradually fades, one voice after another falling silent until the world is so quiet that you could hear a pin drop, and then…

I stop breathing.

My heart stops beating.

Arlo steps from the crowd.

Killian and Ryker flank him, bringing him forward before the stake. A cold current rips through my body and causes me to tremble. I shiver violently, eyes open wide and unblinking. I can't look away as he steps up onto the platform. He turns to face the Homestead, his head bowed, looking down at the ground as Killian and Ryker work together to bind him to the stake.

Slowly, his chin rises. His gaze scrapes beyond the crowd as if they don't exist between us. He finds me without searching, locks in on me beyond the distance and obstacles between us, and I don't think I can—

I can't breathe.

They're going to burn him alive.

They're going to kill him today.

My soul snaps, instantly breaking apart the protective illusion and casting me back into my horrifying reality.

My body moves without thought. I shove to my feet, and before Theo can react, I *run*. I charge down the stone steps, running faster than I ever have before. My boots land on gravel at the bottom, and I don't hesitate to shove my way through the crowd. I slap away the hands of men who try to stop me; I stomp on their feet, and I use my nails like claws to force them away.

"Let her through!" I hear a woman's voice.

Then another rings out, "Let her go to him!"

Through the chaotic crowd, a path gradually emerges, a sea of angry men splitting as my sisters in service—donned in their black clothes—fight them away. Black boots skid on small stones as the servants push back against the men they're beholden to serve; they fight to make a path for me to get through…to help me get to the man I love.

It makes me pause.

I thought they hated me.

I know they all saw the trial as it was broadcasted, which means they also saw Arlo lose control. They watched him openly show his love for me after digging me out from my grave. I just thought that would make them hate me more.

Yet forming before me are two walls of black, two unyielding rows crafted by these incredible women. It's a show of solidarity I never would have expected; one I never would have asked for.

They hold strong through my brief pause as I stare in awe of their kindness. But then the walls buckle at the hands of the men who push back, and for a moment, the path narrows, but only for a moment.

They strengthen again as the domestics turn and join the servants, pushing back at their husbands, and the path widens again. Tears drip down my cheeks at the sight of it, my heart heavy with appreciation and awe of their stance. A gentle hand touches the small of my back, and nudges me forward.

"Go," Cambria says. I glance to see her at my side, her eyes filling with tears, the same as mine. "Just go to him, and don't look back."

My eyes sweep the area quickly, looking for Ellary because she's always with Cambria. But I don't see her now, and I didn't see her lining the path, either.

"Go!" Cambria shoves, and I stumble to catch myself as I lurch forward. I give her a quick nod, a brief lock of our eyes in gratitude.

And then I run for him.

chapter thirteen
Mercy

I BURST THROUGH the path made by my sisters moments before it closes. I sense the chaos devolving behind me—a cacophony of shouting voices, shuffling feet, fighting, and colliding bodies.

The commotion serves as ample distraction—which will at least keep the Control away from me—but it's easy enough for me to ignore. It's all happening behind me, and my singular focus is in front of me. They're going to light a fire beneath the man I love, and I will *not* let him burn alone.

My boots skitter across the gravel as I slide to a quick stop, nearly falling forward onto the brush and logs beneath the small platform where Arlo stands.

"Mercy," he calls down to me.

I don't reply.

I don't pause to look up at him.

I plant my foot against the slanted logs, and begin to climb.

I glance up, looking for something to grab hold of to hoist myself up with, and I spot the rope they've wrapped around his thighs to tether him to the stake.

"Get down!" Arlo shouts at me. "What are you doing? Get *down*, Mercy!"

I grab hold of the rope at his thighs and pull myself up, climbing onto the platform. I have to position myself quickly because there's barely enough room for us both to stand. All at once, I lasso a hand around to grip the back of his neck, the other rising from the rope around his thighs to hold on to the one around his waist. I shift my stance, moving one boot between his feet, while the other is bumped up against the outside of his shoe. My body is pressed tightly to his, and I cling to him, unable and unwilling to let him go.

If I let go, I'll fall…and I can't fall without him.

I lift my chin to look at him and find tears streaming down his cheeks, fear in his glassy blue eyes as they dart wildly across my face.

"Mercy, what are you—"

Bang. Bang.

I startle, strengthening my hold on Arlo as two loud bursts explode through the chaos, met by shrieks and screams and voices calling out their confusion. I turn my cheek against Arlo's shoulder, looking in the direction of the sound, and unsurprisingly, I find Killian at the source.

He stands between the posts that secure Arlo and Stefanie, facing the crowd, his arm stretched high above him. And in his hand is something black, metal…

His fingers move over the item in his hand.

Bang.

Another burst of sound makes me jump as a small explosion erupts from the barrel-shaped end of the black metal object.

Is it…is that a gun?

I know what they look like from photographs, but I never imagined I would see one in Ember Glen. We knew they existed; that the Control could be given access to them, but they were only meant for the most dire of circumstances.

Guns were what wars were fought with.

Guns were for violence against the masses.

And if Killian has one now, then it means the Elders have called for that kind of violence against their own people. If the Control has been given access to guns, then it means…

Then it means the Elders have called for war in Ember Glen.

"Quiet!" Killian bellows toward the crowd, his chest heaving with fury that radiates off him in waves. "We will have order or blood will be spilled!"

Beats of heavy silence pass, and slowly, Killian lowers his arm.

"Get down," Arlo whispers. "Get down. Please, get down…"

He can't compel me to move, and I only cling to him tighter.

"Men of Ember Glen, if you cannot control your wives, then they will be stripped from their duty to care for you and your children, and reassigned as servants! And servants, mind your place. Remember…the men you stand against now are the same men you *serve*. Should the Impulse compel them to retaliate against you under the next full moon, then your actions today will have *earned* it."

Killian is more furious than I've ever seen him, and it's frightening. He's dangerous with empty hands, but now his palm is heavy, holding a tool meant only for murder. "This community has shunned God's grace, invited demons to tear us away from what's right. The Elders have called for order to be restored by any means necessary, and we *will* find that order *immediately.*

"Stefanie Price has acted in rebellion, citing ancient and forbidden texts—*unholy texts*—that call for the destruction of our morality in Ember Glen. Our way of life is *right*. Our way is *good*. Our way is *Godly*. And any word, written or spoken against it, will be seen as a violent attack against all things holy. It will be seen as an attack against God Himself, and it will *not* be met with tolerance. We no longer grant grace in your humanity when your humanity threatens the very fibers of our existence.

"Arlo Rainn," Killian lifts his chin, turning his head to look over at Arlo, "a man I thought was my brother in God has betrayed us all more brutally than anyone." He raises his gun, pointing it at Arlo through his outstretched arm, and we both flinch from fear of his aim. "This man committed sexual acts against his ward. He fell victim to her demons and he went to her bed, time and time again, using her in ways a man should only ever use a servant on nights of purging. He has defiled himself in the *filth* of a sinner, for this woman who doesn't even hold the dignity of a true servant. And worst of all, they claim to have fallen in *love*."

He spits at the ground in rage. "Only demons could claim to have found something so divine outside of a marriage. Mercy Madness and Arlo Rainn are *possessed*." His dark eyes meet mine, looking straight at me. "And if you mean to stand there and burn with him, then we'll gladly let you."

"Get down," Arlo tells me frantically, speaking before Killian has said the final word in his tirade. "Get down, get down *now*. Mercy, get—"

Bright orange heat roars to life in front of Killian, a flame rising high from a torch held by Ryker.

My eyes are wide.

My heart is pounding.

The air is sucked from my lungs.

My scarred hand throbs with the memory of being burned when I was forced to thrust my hand into the campfire to spare Cambria from doing the same. I don't fear death…but I do fear the pain that flame will bring.

I let go of the rope around Arlo's waist and wrap my arms around his middle. I embrace him fully, press my face to his chest, and squeeze my eyes shut, shaking as terror grips me.

"No!" Arlo screams, his voice strangled, panicked. "Get *down*! Ryker…Ryker, stop! Wait! *Mercy*, get *down*!"

"No," I tell him.

"Please, Mercy. Get down…let me go…"

The sound of his voice twisting from panic to sorrow brings me to tears. I sob into his chest, crying as he begs me to leave him. I lift my head, place my chin on his chest, and look up to meet his eyes.

My tears run like rivers down my cheeks at the sight of his own.

"*Please,*" he begs one last time.

He wants me to climb down, but I can't. I won't leave him to face this alone. I can't fathom surviving a single day after watching him be burned alive.

There's no choice for me but to burn with him.

"I'm bound to you, Warden Rainn. In this life and the next."

His eyes fall shut as he cries, as screams and raised voices surge from the crowd. "You don't have to burn for me. You don't have to do this. There's still a chance for you."

"There's no chance for me…there never was." I force a smile to lift my cheeks against the tears that drench them.

I kiss him, ignoring the shouts of angry men who protest our love—love that changed us, love that gave us strength as much as it made us weak.

I speak softly against his lips. "If you burn, I burn with you."

"Starlight…"

Chaos crescendos from the crowd behind me.

"Set them on fire!"

"No!"

"Don't hurt her!"

"Burn them!"

"Get her down!"

A scream of absolute horror startles me, and I hold Arlo tighter. I suck in a sharp breath, bracing myself in the anticipation of flames engulfing me, waiting for the worst pain I'll ever know to wash over me…the *last* pain I'll ever know.

"*Circulus vitiosus!*" A single voice rises from the crowd.

Then another. "*Circulus vitiosus!*"

Twice more I hear it, and there's a sharp descent into pandemonium.

The roar of a new flame being lit echoes through my ears,

igniting and crackling to life, but the flames don't rise around me and Arlo...

Stefanie screams.

I look over in time to see Ryker lift the torch away from the branches bundled at her feet.

"No!" I cry out.

Ryker snaps his head and glares at us with intent. I flinch as he turns, rushing toward us with his torch held high. He's coming to end us now, and in a strange way, I welcome it. I'm tired of the fighting, the waiting, the fearful anticipation.

Let him come.

Let him set us on fire.

Let this wretched life be over.

And just as I find acceptance, someone collides with Ryker, striking him hard around his center, brutally knocking him to the ground. The torch falls from his grip, landing on gravel, the orange flames still whipping violently from its end.

But the flames from the torch are nothing compared to what climbs the brush and logs surrounding Stefanie. My gaze tracks upward, as it's not just the flames that climb to reach her. A domestic woman clambers up the pile, bravely stepping onto a log that hasn't caught fire yet.

There's another running to help—a servant tearing at her black skirt, as though she could possibly use that to smother the roaring flames.

And then I see Luna, fighting her husband with all her strength. She's kicking, screaming, *fighting* to get out of his hold so she can get to Stefanie...just as I'd fought through the crowd to get to Arlo.

My sisters helped me; they fought for me. They made a path for me where there was no path before, because I'd done the same for them the night I ran from Hyatt's flames in the forest. I chose to run that night rather than accept my fate, and it brought us here—to this moment of rebellion, this fight that's for love as much as it is for freedom.

They're fighting for each other.

The women of Ember Glen are finally fighting…

It's something I never imagined seeing in my lifetime. The women—domestics and servants—fighting *together* against a fate chosen by the Control and the Elders.

Unexpected hope fills my heart and floods my veins.

I have to fight with them.

It's not the end. I have to stay, and I have to fight with them.

I look up at Arlo, and my lips part to say something to him, though no words come out.

What can I even say to him?

I don't have to say anything at all. My entire body jerks as Arlo startles me, his palm suddenly landing at my elbow. I look down at my arm to see it with my own eyes, and that's when my gaze tracks the movement behind him. They've come to help us, too. Two domestic women have already freed one of his hands, and they continue to work at the knots binding him to the stake. I look up to meet his eyes.

"Go," he says, squeezing my arm, prying it off from around his waist. "Do what you were meant to do, Mercy Madness. Go and fight with them, and don't look back."

His other hand is suddenly freed, and he grips both my arms. He wrenches me away from him, still bound to the stake by the ropes around his waist and thighs. My hands are balled into fists as he lifts them between us.

"Arlo, I—"

"Go," he demands, and shoves me backward, forcing me off the platform.

I try to twist on my way down, but I fail. I land hard on my ass, rolling onto my back, my spine crashing into gravel. Before the back of my head slams to the ground, I roll, flipping onto all fours, and shoving to my feet.

Don't look back.

Gratitude for my love, for his strength, ripples through me. He knew what I had to do—he understood it—but more than that, he gave me the push I needed to let go of him so I could do what has to be done.

I want to look back, to make sure they're still working to undo the knots that bind him to the stake. I want to look back to make sure that Ryker hasn't recovered, doesn't have the torch, and isn't on his way to set Arlo on fire.

But Stefanie's fearful scream claws through the stagnant air and steals my attention. My focus renews to rescue her from the climbing fire that's meant to silence her—the fire that's meant to silence us all with fear.

I will help Stefanie, but I know I'm not the one who will save her. Instead, I turn and run to free Luna from her husband's grip, because I know it as sure as I know my love for Arlo that there is no one more determined than Luna to save her.

chapter fourteen

Mercy

"PLEASE, *PLEASE*!" LUNA shouts at Archer. "Let me go!"

"I can't let you do this!" he shouts back at her as she twists and tugs, pulls and fights him to get free. "We'll lose *everything!*"

I nearly collide with Archer as I skid to a stop, small stones crashing together with a crunching sound beneath my boots. I reach out and close my hand around his with the intention of prying his fingers from her wrist.

Bang.

A gunshot startles us all. I duck my head on instinct as my shoulders lift toward my ears. I can't gauge where the gunshot came from—I don't even know whether it's Killian who still has the gun.

Is he the only one with a gun?

Do the other men of the Control have them, too?

Though I'm afraid of what a gun might do in the wrong hands—in *Killian's* hands no less—I have to push my fear aside and focus on getting Luna free from Archer's grasp.

"Let her go," I grit, clawing my fingernails into his flesh, and he flinches, letting go of one of her arms to swat at me. I take a step back, then rush forward, slamming my palms to his chest and shoving back. Luna pulls as I push, and with a quick twist of her arm, she snaps free from his grip. She stumbles backward and falls on her bottom, but she quickly scrambles to her feet and backs away, palms raised to ward him off.

And then there's a pause—a moment of standing and staring, an exchange of something that seems rooted in mutual kindness between them.

"You can't do this," he mutters, stepping toward her.

Luna quickly steps back. "Just let me go, Archer."

"Think of the children…"

Luna's eyes are glassy with tears. "I *am* thinking of the children. They…they'll be okay, I promise."

I hadn't noticed before, but I notice it now—there are no children here today, not with Luna, not with anyone. I feel relief for that, but it also confuses me. There are always some children left behind in the village when there are gatherings, but not many and not often. When the children stay behind, it means that some of the domestics have to miss the events to stay behind with them. But there's not a single child here for this, and though I'm thankful for it, it doesn't make sense.

Bang.

"Mercy, let's go!" Luna shouts, rushing forward to grab my wrist and tug me along as she runs.

I can't make sense of anything, but it doesn't matter right now.

We sprint toward Stefanie, and I'm in awe of the scene before me, how quickly the events have changed in the few moments since Arlo pushed me from the platform. A circle of women—domestics and servants alike—has formed around the burning brush that surrounds Stefanie.

It reminds me of nights of purging when servants were made to gather around the bonfire in the clearing. We were forced to give our open consent to be used, abused, brutalized in any manner of choosing by the vicious men of Ember Glen. The women surrounding Stefanie now don't join hands as we would before service, but the visual of sisterhood is the same.

They've formed a circle around this fire, not one where they join hands in collective service of men, but one where they've turned outward to fight back against them.

It's beautiful.

It's heart-wrenching.

It's divine.

It's a vicious circle of women…

The circle opens just enough for me and Luna to pass through, and we rush toward the fire. A few of the servants have ripped fabric from their skirts, trying to smother the growing flames—it's useless, but it's the only thing they can try, and it's humbling to see that they did.

The flames are roaring, climbing, and I don't know what to do. My mind stalls, searching for a solution, looking for a path untouched by flame that I might climb, but there isn't one.

"Stefanie!" Luna shouts up at her. "Jump!"

I look up and see the women who climbed have managed to untie the knots. They edge the platform, searching for the clearest spot from which to leap, but there isn't time for searching, for thinking. Flames are going to touch them no matter what they do.

"Jump…just jump!" I yell. "Now!"

It feels like hours pass while they hesitate in fear and we shout at them from the ground. Then finally, they leap, flames brushing the ends of their skirts as they fall toward the ground.

"Down!" I shout at them as they land, screaming as orange dances around their ankles. "Lay down! Roll on the ground."

I grab the shoulders of one, who panics, and I shove her down, telling her to roll. Others come to help smother the flames, and we make fast work of putting them all out.

Luna is on her knees beside Stefanie, gripping her arm as she sniffs back fearful tears to help her sit up. I move to Stefanie's feet, quickly lifting the tinged and smoking fabric of her skirt to check her legs for burns. I'm thankful to find she's wearing beige leggings beneath. They're singed, burned through in a couple of spots that expose slightly reddened patches of skin, but nothing that looks severe.

"She's okay," I say, then look up at Stefanie. "You're okay." I stand, reach my hand to her, which she takes, and Luna and I pull her to her feet.

Bang.

A man cries out in agony, and the sound is unmistakable.

It's Arlo, calling out in pain.

Expecting to see the worst, I look over at the stake, at the platform where I left him behind. My mind imagines flames rising to meet him, engulfing him, swallowing him whole.

Yet there is no fire, there are no flames.

The ropes that held him dangle free.

He reaches across his body, gripping his left arm with his right hand, standing alone on the platform. His body sways sideways, feet teetering on the ledge. And just before he falls, I see the sleeve of his button-down shirt beneath his hand is soaked with dark crimson…

He's been shot.

"Arlo!"

Bang.

A woman from the circle who stands in front of me drops heavily to the ground. She's strangely silent as she lands on her back, eyes wide with fear and one hand covering her bloody stomach.

Shocked at the sight, I quickly tear my eyes away, looking back at the breach in our protective circle. And through the gap, Killian appears, aiming his gun at me through his outstretched arm. A streak of blood drips down the side of his face, and it frames the rage in his expression as a nasty smirk lifts the corner of his mouth.

Stunned by overwhelming fear, staring down the barrel of this horrible, violent tool of brutality he holds in his hand, the only action I can manage is to take a step backward.

And then he shoots.

I flinch, my eyes slamming shut.

Nothing happens.

I only hear a click, and then shocked gasps from the women around me—some speaking my name in a way that nearly sounds… *reverent?* No less than three women rush him, attack him, take him down to the ground before more men come to forcibly remove them. Then someone tugs on my arm. My head turns and I find Stefanie at my side.

"Come on, we've got to get you out of here." Stefanie speaks with an oddly calm voice, given she was nearly just burned alive.

I glance around for Luna, but I don't see her. "Where's Luna?"

"She's fine, she's coming." Stefanie tugs, turning and dragging me as she moves away from the crowd.

The vicious circle of women has broken away, the flames now roaring too powerfully, climbing high around the lonely stake. A group of domestics break free, sprinting across the square, heading for the path toward the village.

One of them calls back, "Stefanie, Mercy, come on. Run!"

"Mercy, I need you to run with me. *Now.*" Stefanie's grip on my arm is steadfast, unyielding.

My feet have no choice but to move beneath me as she runs, pulling me along with her. We've nearly crossed the pebbled square, and she's already released my arm when the guilt of running overcomes me.

I stop, yelling ahead at her and the other fleeing domestics, "Wait, we have to go back…We have to help them!"

I turn my head over my shoulder to look back and sorrow washes over me. This battle is nearly done. The men have their conditioning for brutality and brute strength on their side. The women who fought are gradually being brought to heel, overpowered by men who believe in their right for total dominance over women.

More heartbreaking than that is seeing the women who didn't fight helping their men; the women who are still poisoned by the untruths they've been fed in the name of holy righteousness. I know some of them are just afraid, and I can't blame them for that.

"Go ahead," Stefanie tells the others, stopping to face me, taking a single step toward me as they continue down the path to the village. "Mercy, I need you to come with me. I need to get you away from here."

I waiver. I've never felt so hesitant or indecisive in all my life.

"Mercy!" she snaps at me. "We have to go. *Now.*"

I look back and see a group of servants break off from the crowd, sprinting across the square toward Sanctuary—a place no man is allowed to enter. Ryker and two other men chase after them, catching one or two of my sisters and drawing them back.

We're losing this battle.

I glance toward the Homestead, and my heart drops to my stomach. I see Delle in her red dress being dragged backward up the stone steps. She's kicking and thrashing—probably screaming, though I can't pick out her voice from so far away—as Park and Owen carry her away.

It's Delle who makes up my mind for me. I can't leave her behind. I turn and run back toward the crowd.

"No!" Stefanie yells after me. I hear her footfalls on the gravel as she runs after me. "Come back!"

I run hard, scanning for a clear path through, wondering if I can get to Delle faster if I skirt around the throng. But I never get the chance to decide how I'll get to her. I don't even see it coming. I collide with a wall—Theo's rock-solid chest—and bounce back. I nearly fall backward, but he grips my upper arms and harshly pulls me in front of him.

"You have to go with her," Theo tells me. "Go with Stefanie."

"But Delle—"

"I'm going back; I'll look after her, but you have to go." He rushes to get the words out, shaking me in his grip. "They'll kill you on the staircase if you come back, so get the fuck away from here. Now fight me off and make it look real. They have to trust me so I can be with Delle."

I can't just go…I can't leave Delle behind in this.

What if they place their rage on her in my stead?

If they don't have me, Delle will be their example. They'll destroy her to get the women back under their control.

I press my hands to Theo's chest, and I shove—not to make it look like I'm fighting back, but because I need him to let go of me. I have to go back for Delle. Theo hardly budges, and I shove again, kick at his shins, beat my fists against his chest.

"Good, keep fighting," he murmurs, thinking I'm doing this for show so anyone who sees will think he tried to stop me.

It's not for show.

I fight him. I twist in his grip as my fear for Delle rises, bringing tears to my eyes. "Let go…let *go* of me. She *needs* me!"

A fist comes from nowhere and collides with the side of Theo's face. He jerks sideways on the impact, releasing me so quickly that I stumble backward as he falls.

"Come on," Luna suddenly appears, grabbing my arm to help steady me, "We have to go."

"What are you—"

It wasn't Luna who hit Theo hard enough to fall. I look up and find Arlo before me, his face contorted in pain as he unclenches his fist. I shake Luna off and run to him, but he steps forward with force, forcing me to stop.

"Turn around and run." He steps forward, forcing me to step backward.

"Delle needs me—"

"No, Mercy."

"I'm not *leaving* her!"

"Yes, you are." He moves faster, his chest bumping mine as he forces me backward.

"No, I'm—"

He dips, wraps his arms around my waist, hoists me up, and tosses me over his shoulder. He groans in pain as I yelp, and he starts to move, running with me toward the village.

I bounce against his back as he runs with me, lifting my head so I can look back. I watch in horror as the front door of the Homestead opens, as Delle is dragged across the threshold, and it closes with her behind it.

"Put me down…Let me go back for her!" I shout. "What are you doing?"

"What I should've done the first time you ran from me in the forest," Arlo grunts through his pain, through the strain of carrying me as he runs. "I'm taking you away from this godforsaken place."

chapter fifteen

ARLO

THE CONTROL FAILED to set me on fire, but my arm burns all the same, throbbing in waves of pulsing pain from the bullet. I feel every step I take, thudding against the gravel as we run.

Mercy's weight over my shoulder intensifies every sensation, cycling through alternating rounds of numbness, then agony. Though it hurts to carry her, I'm afraid to put her down. I'm afraid she'll try to run back again, that she'll try to rush toward a goal she can't achieve…

That she'll run away from me, and I'll never get her back.

Delle is locked in the Homestead, and Mercy cannot help her. Going back would bring Mercy to a quick, but brutal, death. I fear I'd see them put her on the stake—the very spot where my charred and lifeless body should be at this very moment—and burn her in my stead.

She came to me.

Mercy was willing to burn with me.

I'm still stunned that she ran to me, that she climbed onto the platform and was ready to *die* with me. I'm in awe of the way she loves me; I'm humbled and inspired by it. She was willing to be set on fire with me just so she wouldn't have to live a single day without me.

And as much as I hated it, as much as it terrified me to think of her enduring that unimaginable horror just to die with me, I understood it. I'm not as brave as she is, but if I were, I would have climbed into that damn coffin with her at the trial and let them bury us together. I would have let them steal my last breath to avoid living without her.

Yet, I didn't—I *couldn't*—because I'm weak. I could never match the strength and bravery of Mercy Madness. No one ever could, and no one ever will.

So, I'll happily suffer this paltry ache in my arm to save her, to carry her away from certain death and give her a chance at another day, a chance at even one more moment of bliss in each other's arms before everything implodes.

I follow Luna and Stefanie all the way to the village, realizing as we approach the homes of the villagers that I don't know where we're going, whether they have a plan, whether anyone is following us at a distance.

"Let me down," Mercy demands. "Put me *down*. I know I'm hurting your arm."

"My arm is fine, but you won't be if you run back there."

"I won't run back there; I'll come with you. Just put me down."

I ignore her and keep moving, following as Stefanie leads us behind a row of homes that provide some cover from being out in the open.

"Arlo, please put me down," Mercy begs. "Your blood is soaking my clothes. It's warm…" Her voice lowers to a whisper, unease touching her tone. "I can feel it, and I really don't want to feel it."

Fuck.

That guts me.

Immediately, I stop, loosen my grip, and let her slip down in front of me until her boots touch the ground. Her eyes fall immediately to my arm, and they widen. She lifts her hand as though she's going to touch the wound, and it makes me flinch. She stops, her hand hovering above my arm as my muscles tense, sending a shooting pain rippling outward from the wound. I feel my face contort in pain.

"Oh, love…I—"

"I'm fine."

I try to convince her as much as myself, though I'm fearful of what I'll find when I finally gather enough strength to look at the wound. Truthfully, I'm terrified to know what it looks like, to see how much damage has been done. At least I can be thankful the bullet didn't strike me in the chest, or the stomach, or my head. There were others struck in the chaos who were far less fortunate.

"We need to keep moving." I reach out with my right hand to snatch her wrist. I turn to follow after Stefanie and Luna, dragging Mercy with me before she can protest, breaking into a run. "Come on."

Mercy runs along with me, quickly and easily matching my pace. After a few strides with no resistance against my grip—assured that she's not going to try to slip away from me and run back to the Homestead—I let my hand slip down her wrist, wrap around her palm, and lace our fingers together. There's a pulse of relief from both of us, comfort striking as our entwined fingers lock us together.

We run until we arrive at the outer edge of the village, where there's a short row of three houses nestled together, their backs facing the rising hillside beyond. We circle around behind the row, and I'm confused as we make our way to the one on the end because I know who this house belongs to. Luna creeps right on up to the backdoor as if she's been here before.

"What are we doing here?" Mercy asks. "What are we doing at my house?"

This is the home Mercy's father owned—the one where she was raised, the one where she stayed all alone after he died. Other than the weeks she was required to remain at Sanctuary after nights of service, this is where she lived, alone—no mother, no father, no siblings.

It was always such an unusual thing, her family. Most family units had several children. It wasn't entirely unheard of for a family to bear only one or two children, but it was unusual. The Madness family had always been unusual in that way.

But what's truly unusual about this moment is watching my sister locate a key that seems to have been buried in the rocks lining the outer edges of the home, as if she always knew it was there.

Luna gives a brief, wary glance over her shoulder, flashing an apologetic look at Mercy. "We'll explain everything once we're safe, but we have to hurry."

As Luna reaches forward to slip the key into the lock, the knob turns and the door opens gently from the inside. We all gasp, startling easily with the adrenaline flowing through our veins. One of the domestic women I remember seeing run away from the crowd ahead of Stefanie and Mercy—Enid, if I recall her name correctly— peeks out through the crack in the door.

"I saw you coming," she says quickly, then pushes the door open and steps back, beckoning us inside. "Hurry. The others have already gone through."

Luna nods, quickly returning the key to its hiding place among the rocks before she and Stefanie rush inside.

Stefanie turns back when we don't immediately follow. "Come inside, quickly," she says, waving her hand to beckon us forward.

Mercy glances over at me, and we share a puzzled look. But then she steps forward, her hand tugging mine as she moves inside. Stefanie skirts around me to shut the door behind us, and she locks it from the inside. All the lights are off, and no one makes a move to turn them on.

"This way," Luna says, following Enid past the small kitchen table.

They turn and head toward the living room. I glance at the

space as we pass through, noting an ordinary room that somehow sparks my interest. My mind instantly wanders to thoughts of Mercy living here, all alone with her thoughts.

Where would she sit?

Did she have a favorite spot?

Was it in this room where her mind first wandered toward thoughts of dissension and rebellion?

She grew up without siblings, without a mother. Perhaps it was all the time she spent alone that gave her mind the space to think. Most of the family units in Ember Glen are crowded with children who fill days with noise, disruption, and activity. For most, there's a lack of time and space to be alone with your own thoughts for too long.

If only I had taken the time to consider my own thoughts and feelings about God, our laws, and the ways of Ember Glen. Maybe then I would have seen all that was wrong with it sooner. Perhaps more of us would be like Mercy Madness if we'd just taken more time to think for ourselves.

Who am I kidding?

There is no one like Mercy.

And maybe that's the way it had to be for us to see the truth.

Mercy's choice to run from service—the choice that started all of this—acted like a chisel that's slowly chipping away at our harshly dichotomous ways of thinking. Bit by bit, the events that brought us from that fateful night of service to the acts of dissension today have steadily chipped away at the exterior. Perilous cracks have been made to the collective, and when Mercy emerged as a symbol for a movement of change, she delivered the final blow to that indoctrinated façade.

Indoctrination.

That is the best word—perhaps the *only* word—to describe our upbringing in Ember Glen. It's a word that was used to teach us about the evil that existed in the world before a great civil war tore this country apart.

We were told that people were indoctrinated by those who wanted freedom from God's law and order. We were told of the ways those freedom seekers wanted to denounce God—that they wanted to be free to choose whether they believed in his existence, whether they followed his word. We were told they were indoctrinating their children to believe they had the right to choose if they believed in God at all.

And because of Mercy, I see the truth now. I see it with my own understanding, rather than seeing it as I was always commanded to see it. I see that we—the people of Ember Glen—are the ones indoctrinated. And I'm so affected by my own indoctrination that it makes me feel sick for admitting that to myself, the dissonance of growth still lingering in my gut.

Mercy squeezes my hand, drawing me from my thoughts and back to the present. We continue to follow Enid and Luna past the living room and down the hallway, with Stefanie behind us. There's a door open at the end of the hallway and Enid disappears inside.

Mercy halts. "That's my father's room. What are you doing in my father's room?"

Luna pauses, turning to face Mercy. "I am so sorry. I know this is all so confusing for you. I promise, we will explain everything soon, but first, we have to get you to safety."

"In my father's bedroom?" Mercy's brow furrows in her confusion. "This isn't a safe place. The Control are smart enough to think of looking for me here—"

"It's difficult to find something when you don't even know it exists…" Luna replies cryptically. She gives Mercy a soft smile before turning and moving inside the bedroom.

Mercy hesitates for a moment, but then she follows, and I walk with her. Once Stefanie has stepped into the room behind us, she shuts the door and locks it. By all accounts, it appears to be a normal bedroom. Wooden floors, a bed with two end tables on either side, and long, rectangular rugs running along each side of the bed in a drab shade of green.

Enid stands at the rug on the far side of the bed. "I closed off the entrance after they went through, in case the wrong people showed up, just like you told me to." She lowers to her knees, grips the end of the rug, and flips it back, folding it over itself before standing and stepping back.

I half expected to see something obvious there beneath the rug, but all I see is a plain wooden floor—the same wooden floor that runs throughout the bedroom.

Luna kneels near the spot where the rug laid before Enid flipped it back. Mercy lets go of my hand to move closer to Luna, and instantly, anxiety spikes. I rush to follow, feeling that need to be close since her presence is the only thing that puts me at ease.

Mercy crouches, watching as Luna digs her fingernails into the crack between wooden planks on the floor, and before I can make sense of what she's doing, she pries up the edge of a plank. She lifts it from its spot and sets it aside. Then, she scoops her fingers beneath the plank it was nestled against and lifts. An entire section of the floor rises on a hinge.

"Wh-what is this?" Mercy asks. "How did you find this?"

Luna glances back at me, then looks at Mercy beside her. "It's a long story, and I promise I will tell it, but we need to go through first and get to safety."

I look past Mercy and Luna, and I spot a haphazard hole chiseled through the foundation, creating a chasm that leads into darkness.

"It leads to a tunnel," Stefanie says as she comes up beside me. "It's a narrow drop in, but manageable. The surrounding walls are sturdy. It's as safe as anything else in Ember Glen."

A narrow drop, indeed.

The chaotically carved hole appears just wide enough for a single person to slip through at a time. I suppose if it were any wider, it would be harder to hide. As it is, I would have had no idea that anything was hidden here beneath the floorboards—the planks are lined up so perfectly, fit together as neatly as the rest of the floor.

What is going on here?

This revelation has happened so quickly. My mind is lagging, struggling to make sense of how we got here, what's happening in this moment, and what might happen next.

"Where does it lead?" Mercy asks.

"I don't know how to describe it," Luna says, lifting her chin to look at Mercy. "You just…you have to see it all for yourself. We just need to get you there and keep you safe."

Luna smiles, and though her expression is still tense with fear, the smile is bright and optimistic. She has that look in her eyes that she used to have as a child when she was caught in a daydream—a look I haven't seen from her in a very long time. The hope my sister lost has returned, and it only strengthens as Mercy turns her head and connects with her through her compassionate stare.

"You're the author of this rebellion," Luna tells her, "and we need you to finish our story."

chapter sixteen

Mercy

I'M BEWILDERED BY this dark space carved into the earth beneath my father's floorboards. I'm entirely perplexed about how Luna and Stefanie somehow managed to find it.

How on earth did they find this?

I've lived in this house my entire life, and I've never stumbled across it. I've lifted the rug that covers the wooden floor; I've swept and mopped the planks that hide this opening to a dark world below. I've never had so much as an inkling that there was anything out of the ordinary hidden here. I have so many questions, and I just hope they have the answers.

The chiseled opening is just wide enough for a single person to slip through it. Enid goes first, lowering her feet into the hole, scooting forward, then slipping into the darkness. Her entire body drops through the entrance, and she disappears.

"One at a time," Luna says. "Follow me."

Luna goes next, following after Enid in the same manner, dangling her feet first before slipping through and disappearing beneath the ground. I stare down through the opening, and my heart pounds with a fury at the sight of the darkness below.

A hand gently touches my shoulder, startling me. "Your turn," Stefanie says, gesturing toward the hole.

I give her a slight nod, though I feel panic clawing inside me. It scratches at my soul, teasing me with awareness that it's always present—forever lurking, ready to pounce at the slightest hint of my fear.

I have to fight it.

Drawing in a deep breath, I shift, lowering my feet into the open void. They dangle as I contemplate asking how far the drop is, whether it's a few feet or if it's more. Ultimately, I think it's better not to know. I scoot forward, letting my thighs teeter on the edge as my knees lower beneath the surface. Deciding it's best not to think too much about it, I close my eyes, shift my weight forward, and let myself plummet into the black abyss.

I drop heavy and hard, but my feet quickly slam to solid ground. The only light in this dark space comes from above, from the hole through which I slipped, which is nothing more than the meager light of day that peeks through the edges of the closed curtains in my father's bedroom.

I gradually straighten to my full height as I look up at the entrance, noting there's little less than a foot of clearance between the top of my head and the ceiling of this open cavity. I feel a tremor through my arms as I realize I can't climb back out. There's no way I can pull myself out of here and the darkness all around me.

"How do we get out of here?" I ask in a rush.

Arlo looks down at me through the opening, and I find some comfort in his blue eyes, though it's difficult to make out the shade of them with so little light.

"There's a step stool." Luna's hand taps my forearm, and I jump, whirling around to try to find her in the dark. She moves in close to me, enough that I can see the outline of her, and I reach out to grab her wrist. "I've moved it out of the way, but it climbs high enough that it's easy to pull yourself back out. Elijah really thought of everything."

Elijah…

My father.

I can't wrap my head around any of this.

"Come on." Luna places her hand over mine, where my fingers have curled to grip her wrist so tightly that I'm surprised she hasn't tried to pry me off yet. She has a gentle way about her. She calmly strokes my forearm, and the simple gesture reminds me to take a breath. "Move aside so they can follow. Watch your head."

I nod and move with her away from the entrance, deeper into the darkness. We stop and wait, watching as Arlo drops in next, quickly followed by Stefanie. Luna pats my hand to get my attention, waiting for me to release her wrist before she leaves me.

She moves beneath the opening, bringing the step stool she mentioned out of the darkness. There are three steps to climb up the stool, and when she reaches the top, she's high enough through the opening to clear her arms and shoulders.

I move closer, looking up through the hole to watch as she reaches for the wooden plank she'd removed and set aside before. She nestles it back in its spot. Then, she reaches up to grip a small, silver handle fixed to the underside of the hinged set of planks. She pulls it halfway closed before reaching out with her other hand, somehow managing to maneuver the rug so it will fall flat over the wooden floor once she closes it.

Then she pulls it shut, cutting off our only light, our only exit.

We're trapped.

I'm trapped.

I'm being buried alive again...

I stutter through a breath as a shockwave of adrenaline punches through my veins. I instantly feel dizzy, like I can't draw in a decent breath, and the faint feeling threatens to take me to the ground. I double over, hands pressed to my thighs as I fight a wave of nausea.

I know I'm not alone. I can hear them all moving around me in the darkness, whispering in words that seem blurred and foreign in my panicked mind. I'm here with them, but it feels like I'm not.

It feels like I'm entombed, like the air is running out and there's no way to escape.

"I can't—" I gasp, trying to suck in a breath, though it feels like my lungs have closed.

"Mercy?"

Arlo's arm slides across my back, but instead of giving me comfort, it startles me. I rise too quickly, bringing myself a light-headed rush as my feet move me backward into the dark.

"I can't…" I barely manage the words. "I can't breathe…"

They all start speaking at once, and their voices blend into a dull roar that echoes in my ears. Every sound is streaming, rushing, bringing a vision of soil pouring steadily through the hole above, covering the cavern floor, rising to my ankles, my knees, filling this space until I'm buried, and—

There's no way out…

"Get me out," I pant.

I hear the strike of a match and the hiss of fire as it ignites, a small flame casting haunted shadows across the inner cave walls.

I feel like I can't breathe, yet at the same time, I'm breathing far too much, far too quickly. Air rushes in and out of me, but it doesn't fill my lungs.

"She's panicking," Stefanie says. "We need to get her out of here."

"We can't go back out there," Arlo says.

"We're not going out," Luna says. "We're going *through*."

"Through where?" Arlo asks.

My knees go weak and I drop to kneel, catching myself with one hand on the ground in front of me as I bring the other to press over my pounding heart.

"Get me out…*please*," I beg as Arlo drops in front of me. "Please, dig me out. Dig me out…"

"Oh, God," Luna's voice cracks, and it makes me worry that

maybe it's real…That maybe she's afraid because there really is soil pouring in all around us, filling in this small cavern, burying us alive. "She thinks she's in her grave again. That trial must have done *awful* things to her mind. What do we do?"

"You said it yourself," Stefanie says. "The only way out is through. Arlo, she has to crawl. The tunnel is only about thirty feet long, but it's hands and knees all the way. She'll be okay once we get her through it, but…somehow we have to get her through it."

"Show me," Arlo says, then he disappears.

I sit back on my heels, pressing my eyes shut, willing myself to calm down and come back to reality.

I'm not alone.

I'm not being buried alive.

The trial is over and I'm safe.

I'm alive.

"Fuck," Arlo mutters, and it sends a shiver down my spine. "Thirty feet?"

"Just thirty feet. Luna, go first with the lantern to give her some light. And Arlo—"

"She's going in front of me, and I'll push her through myself if I have to."

"Good," Stefanie says, and she sounds so much stronger than me. "I'll go in front of her then, and I'll pull her if I have to."

I hear movement around me. Panicked at the sound of wordless motion, I open my eyes. The meager light that formed dancing shadows before begins to drift away, and it frightens me.

"Arlo!" I cry out for him.

The single source of light shrinks, diminishing as it moves into an opening in the cavern. As darkness closes in, my love finds me. His palms touch my cheeks and his eyes catch mine, wide and fearful. I latch my fingers around his wrists, desperate to hold his touch against my skin as the light continues to fade.

"I need you to crawl with me, starlight. Hands and knees. You're going to follow the light into the tunnel, and I'll be right behind you."

My head shakes furiously against his hands, though I don't mean for it to. I mean to be strong, to be brave, to go fearlessly into the unknown, yet I feel weak, broken...

That godforsaken trial has broken me.

"I-I can't..." I hiccup as sobs threaten to take hold of me. "I can't."

Arlo's forehead touches mine. "You *can* do this. You *will* do this. There is no choice here." He takes a deep breath, and I'm envious of it, because I wish I could do the same. "Forgive me, Mercy, but I have to make you do this."

A fearful sound screeches out from my throat as his hand snaps around the back of my neck, snatching me in his firm grip. He twists me around and pushes me down, groaning as if it pangs him to move me by force.

He holds me down on my hands and knees as he shifts to kneel behind me, his knees straddling mine. His hips press to my bottom as he shuffles closer. His fingers dig into the sides of my neck, using his grip to encourage me forward. His other hand slips between our bodies, flat against my ass, and he pushes hard. "Crawl," he commands, and I have to.

Because if I didn't, I'd collapse under the weight of him shifting over me, and the thought of being pinned on the ground in the quickly darkening cavern sends anxious shivers through my entire body.

Arlo pushes me through a small entrance into a narrow tunnel. He has to force me because every muscle in my body is tense and rigid, pushing back against him to fight moving into an even smaller space.

"Don't, I can't—"

"You must," Arlo grunts as he shoves me hard, forcing my entire body through the opening and into the tunnel.

He hisses as his touch disappears and he releases his grip on me. His body is no longer against mine, and I cry out in fear of his absence, turning my head to look back over my shoulder. He blocks the only exit, his shadowed form painted across a pitch-black canvas of darkness behind his back as the only light bounces away from us down the tunnel. There's just enough light cast across his face to show me his features are twisted in agony as he clutches his arm.

His pain washes over me, rinsing away bits of my fear, cleansing me of my panic just enough to allow my compassion for him to creep back in.

His pain reaches out like two hands that shove against my panic, begging it to leave my mind because he needs me. I catch his gaze, and when he meets my eyes, he slowly smiles. He lets go of his bleeding, wounded arm, trying to pretend like it doesn't hurt.

"No need to worry, starlight. I'm coming right behind you. I only needed a moment to appreciate the sight of you on your hands and knees in front of me."

I hear Stefanie groan in annoyance.

Luna laughs, and the playful, echoing sound is strange in the way it cuts through my panic—strange, though it seems to help, like a vibration that cracks the walls of fear.

"That fall really must have hurt," Luna says from ahead as Arlo slips in through the opening and reaches out to grip my ankle.

"What are you talking about?" he asks.

"When the mighty fall from grace, they fall hard, don't they?" Luna laughs again, and I feel the way it tugs at the corners of my lips.

Arlo grins, and it washes over me. It bathes me in warmth and douses me in comfort. It's a rising tide that crashes against the cracking walls of fear with promises to tear them down.

"You should remember from our childhood, Luna; I don't do anything halfway. I'm in the grace of demons now."

Stefanie snorts, "Welcome to hell."

His eyes scan my backside before turning to meet mine. There's a heat there, a passion for me that always burns blue in his eyes. It further chisels at those walls of fear, weakening their stronghold around my peace.

"I like the heat." He gives me an encouraging smile and squeezes my ankle. "Get moving, starlight."

With Arlo's grip firm on my ankle, somehow, I find the strength to push ahead. I still feel the ripples of anxiety coursing through my veins, but some courage has found me, just enough that I can crawl, reassured by the calm movement of the others with me.

Because they're with me, not against me, and it makes all the difference in the world.

It's not long before we reach the end of the tunnel and climb out, one by one, into another cavern. Luna holds a lantern that offers just enough dim light to show us how high the rock ceiling is above our heads. There's so much space above us, I feel a snap of relief inside my chest, and suddenly, I'm able to draw in a slow, deep breath.

Another breath.

Then another.

Gradually, the panic lessens. I don't know if it will ever fully go away, though I'm thankful it loosens its grip on me enough to be present and aware of what's going on around me.

Glancing around, I spot three stone passageways. The passages remind me of the cave system beneath the Homestead, and I have to wonder if they're all connected somehow.

Luna seems to know exactly where she's going, turning left and heading through a long, dark passage, and we follow her lantern light through. There's a junction splitting off into two stone hallways, and we take the one leading left. The anxiety starts to creep back over me the longer we walk without an end in sight. But almost as quickly as panic strikes, we come to the end of the winding passage.

The meager light from Luna's lantern gradually becomes unnecessary as the end of the passage makes itself known to us, bright with all the light of day. My heart beats with excitement, rather than fear…with the anticipation of finding out what lies ahead.

The air around me feels damp and heavy, unusually warm as we move closer to the light. The smell of water clings to each breath I take. The autumn chill fades as a pleasant warmth envelops me.

Luna glances over her shoulder and smiles at us before stepping through the opening, and we follow. With Arlo's hand in mine, we step into a glorious cavern, wide and open, flooded with light from a circular opening in the rock ceiling—an opening that exists directly above a large, clear pool of water.

Steam rises from the pool where the cool air from above meets the warmth that radiates from the water. The pool is serene, clear, a shade that reminds me of the color of robin's eggs. But even more enchanting than the sight of this grand cavern and warm pool of water is the sound of children laughing. I blink away from the pool and take in the sight around me.

The children of Ember Glen are all here—safe—and a group of domestic women are with them in their care.

"What is all this?" I ask in awe.

I hear Luna sigh happily as her hand lands softly on my shoulder. "This is what you've done, Mercy. This is what you started when you chose to run that night of service. This is the rebellion your bravery has sparked."

I look at her where she stands at my side, tears springing to my eyes at the look of gratitude in her expression—gratitude she has for *me*.

"Mercy," Luna grins, "these are all the people you're going to save."

chapter seventeen

Mercy

THESE ARE ALL *the people you're going to save.*

I'm speechless.

Luna and Stefanie lead me and Arlo into the vast cavern, leading us across the expanse of bedrock, where people gather in front of the crystal pool. I'm vaguely aware of how tightly Arlo's hand squeezes mine, can sense the unease that pulses through his grip, but the rest of me feels numb in my shock. I'm stunned by this scene and more confused than I've ever been.

I don't understand how these women and children are here; I don't understand *why* they're here. I suppose the children have been brought here for safety, but I don't understand how they were brought here so quickly after the fight at the Homestead.

Unless they were brought here before…Did the domestic women plan the fight?

"What happened at the gathering?" a woman asks, her hands on her child's shoulders who stands in front of her.

"That's Mercy Madness…" another woman says in awe. "Oh, thank God. Tell us what happened. How did you save her?"

"Mercy Madness!" someone else says with relief.

"Stefanie!" Another woman runs up and throws her arms around Stefanie, pulling her into a relieved hug. "You're alive…They did it! I can't believe they did it!"

A smiling, laughing, joyful group of children run full force toward Stefanie and Luna, who crouch to greet them with eager, open arms. Three little girls and three little boys crash into them at near full force, effectively knocking Luna back on her bottom. Her precious boys tackle her to the ground in a fit of laughter. It's such a beautiful interaction—a joyful reunion between innocent children and the mother they love—and it brings tears to my eyes.

Though Stefanie's daughters greet her in a much less obvious manner than Luna's sons—lively little boys who climb all over her, hug her, tickle her, and make her laugh with pure joy—their expressions show how thrilled they are to see their mother. They cling to her like they're afraid she'll slip away from them if they let her go.

The girls are so calm and quiet in their greeting that it feels restrained—like a learned behavior, like vigilance in self-protection. Being calm and quiet probably kept them safe from their father, Hyatt Price. I have no doubt that man carried his violence with him daily. No single night of service could ever be enough to satisfy the bloodlust of someone like him.

Stefanie's oldest daughter—I think her name is Heidi—has a glassy sheen of tears forming over her eyes. I notice it when she looks over Stefanie's shoulder while hugging her close, her tearful gaze tracing the features of my face before she meets my eyes. I hold my breath while she confidently holds my stare. There's resilience and curiosity shown in her beautiful brown eyes, which are framed by thick, dark eyebrows that resemble her mother's.

I smile as she watches me and the curl of my lips somehow beckons her. She breaks free from Stefanie, slipping around her and walking straight for me. Unexpectedly, she collides with my middle, throwing her arms around my waist and hugging me close. She squeezes, and a sudden sob escapes me.

My hand falls from Arlo's grasp as I drop to my knees, my arms wrapping around Heidi to give back a fraction of the comfort she gave me in her unrestrained hug—unrestrained and *brave* and filled with warmth and care.

When she decides to release me, she takes a small step backward. She stops and regards my face, searching my expression, reading my character from my features before deciding I'm worthy of her trust.

She blinks, then looks down at her left arm as she swings it forward, holding it out between us. She pushes up her long sleeve, revealing the tattoo that marks her for service, the same as mine. I mimic her, holding out my left arm and pushing up my long sleeve. Her arm looks so small next to mine, the tattoo so cumbersome on such a tiny frame.

I always hated the image before—not because it's ugly, but on the contrary, because it's beautiful. The artwork of the wildflowers is stunning with its graceful lines, striking a perfect balance between small and large florals from a variety of different flowers clustered together, so elegant in the diversity of petals and shapes.

But then that beautiful image is broken in half by two lines that encircle the arm—lines that separate one cluster of wildflowers from the other.

Separate…like domestics and servants.

Perhaps separation was the only way Ember Glen could survive for as long as it has, with one group living complacently in relative peace, while the other fights for survival from one month to the next. Today I saw how strong we could be when we fight together as a collective group of *women*, not as separate and distinct groups of servants and domestics.

Our lives may be different, but our hearts are the same.

We all just want freedom to live as we choose, to love who we want to love, to say *no* to a man and have it mean something.

"Mom says you saved me." Heidi's sweet, innocent voice reminds me that she's only a child and not a woman who's already been hardened by forced service to men. "She said you were strong and brave, and that you wouldn't serve my dad, and that might mean I won't have to be a servant when I'm older. She said you were changing things." Her head tilts to the side as she regards me with curiosity. "Is that true?"

A heavy breath rushes out of me.

Is it true?

What do I say to that?

"I-I'm trying," I stammer. "I'm trying to change things. I don't really know what I'm doing, but I'm going to try my very best to change the future for you."

Am I? How?

How could I possibly change the future of Ember Glen?

Heidi smiles sweetly, appearing satisfied at my answer. "Mom always says that the only thing you can do is try. I think that's why she yelled and got in trouble when they were taking you to your trial. Your dress was really pretty."

"Thank you." I smile, swiping a knuckle beneath my eye to drag away my tears.

"You look really pretty in red, but I liked it better when you wore black and it matched your boots. Mom said black is the color servants wear, though. I like how it looks, but I don't want to wear it because I don't want to be a servant."

I swallow against the lump in my throat. "I don't want you to be a servant, either. I never wanted to be one myself."

"You didn't?"

I shake my head. "No, but I didn't want to be a domestic, either."

Her brow furrows in confusion. "But there isn't anything else."

"Not in Ember Glen, not right now, but I always thought that maybe, someday, things could be different."

"Is that why you ran from my dad? Because you wanted things to be different?"

I pause as a swell of tears fill my eyes, and then I force my lips to curl into a tight grin. "Yes. That's why I ran. They didn't want me to run, but I had to make a choice for myself, now didn't I?"

A shy, restrained smile tugs at the corners of her lips and she nods. A chorus of questions from the gathered women quickly fills the cavern with voices, effectively ending our conversation. I give Heidi another smile before I rise to my feet.

"Where are the others?" someone asks. "Where are all the women?"

Luna has managed to untangle herself from her boys. She's tying a fabric wrap around her body, taking her baby girl, Soleil, from another domestic woman who must have been caring for her while Luna was away.

"Why is *he* here?" someone else asks. "Are we safe?"

I glance over at Arlo and see him tense. I reach out to grab his hand and he quickly laces our fingers together, holding firm.

Luna sighs, looking flustered as she finishes tying the wrap that holds Soleil against her body, cradling the back of her head in one palm. Luna's head hangs for a moment before Stefanie places a hand on her shoulder. Luna lifts her chin to look over at her, giving her a small smile. Stefanie's hand rises from her shoulder to her cheek, tucking a fallen strand of hair from Luna's messy updo behind her ear.

"Everyone who was able to get away is here," Luna says, dragging her gaze from Stefanie to look out at the women and children. "Everything became so chaotic. Everyone fought so hard to save Stefanie, and by a miracle, we did." Luna glances at her, and though I can only see one half of her face in profile, the complexity and depth of her feelings toward Stefanie are profoundly etched in her expression.

"You should know that if it wasn't for the servants, Stefanie wouldn't be here right now. *Mercy* wouldn't be here right now. We underestimated the violence we would meet for fighting back today.

But the servants took a stand with us—entirely unexpected—and now Mercy Madness is safe. She's here and she's safe, and we should be happy about that."

"Danielle hasn't returned," one of the domestics says. "Neither has Echo."

"Mary's not here," another says.

"Brandy and Amanda aren't back, either."

Distress is clear in their voices, and I feel the energy of it ripple through me. I squeeze Arlo's hand.

Luna lets out a small breath. "I don't think anyone else is coming back here. Everyone who could get away from the chaos did, and the rest were stopped by the men. I have to tell you that the gathering today was brutal. The Control have guns now."

There's a flurry of gasps and shocked whispers, words spoken in abrupt fear.

"Is that what happened to his arm?" someone asks.

We all turn to look at a woman standing near Arlo, staring at his blood-soaked sleeve. Her eyes are wide, glued to the sight of his injury, and the horrified look on her face makes nausea roll through my gut at the thought of his mangled flesh.

"Yes," Luna says firmly. "But before they shot him, they tried to burn him at the stake. They tried to burn one of their own for the offense of loving someone, for loving a *woman*…for falling in love with Mercy Madness!"

She says my name like I'm important, like it means something to speak of me, but I don't feel it. I don't feel like I'm important. I don't feel like I've done anything meaningful. I'm simply surviving.

"So it's true then? About Mercy and Arlo?" someone asks.

Luna looks at us over her shoulder. "I know what I saw today, but I think everyone would like to hear it from you."

"From us?" My eyes narrow in confusion. "Hear what?"

"Is it true that you've fallen in love?"

Arlo and I look at each other, sharing the same expression of confusion over the fact that they want to know, that they care, that this information is important in some way.

Of course, it's important.

Loving each other is what brought us here.

Luna turns sideways and takes a step back, opening the space in front of me like a curtain, putting me in a clearer view of the crowd. "We all saw the livestream of your trial, Mercy. We all saw with our own eyes that Arlo held affection for you…the kind of affection that's deemed blasphemous by the laws of the Impulse Edict. We saw how you broke, Arlo." She looks at him with empathy and sorrow. "We all witnessed you trying to dig her out early. The way you clawed at the soil on your hands and knees until they knocked you out…I can't speak for anyone else, but it was one of the most heartbreaking things I've ever seen."

He did what?

I watch Arlo's expression as it morphs, cycling through several emotions as Luna speaks. Pride, sorrow, heartache, regret—it's strange how I can identify each feeling from the slightest flicker of his blue eyes or a subtle twitch of his jaw.

"We saw how you fought for her, how you cried for her…the way you held her when you thought she was dead—" Luna's voice breaks.

The way she speaks of these events sends a shiver up my spine that radiates with hope, love, and warmth. I knew he'd been caught in displaying his feelings for me—it's the reason they intended to burn him alive today. Yet I didn't know exactly what had happened after the lid of my coffin fell shut, in the time between my burial and waking up in Owen's arms as he carried me through the forest.

I didn't know Arlo tried to dig me out early. I didn't know the village had witnessed him holding me, showing me affection without a care for who might bear witness. An odd sense of relief washes over me, knowing my burial hurt him, spurring him on to try to dig me out early without a care for his own judgment.

Somehow, I feel lighter in knowing that. I hadn't realized it before, but I can feel it now—there was a part of me that had held some resentment for him, some anger for the fact that he didn't risk everything for me sooner. There was a lingering hurt that he hadn't fallen for me faster, that he didn't understand how much he loved me before the first trial so he could have saved me then.

Hearing Luna tell of how he clawed at the soil on his hands and knees, trying to save me in desperation before my trial was complete, gives me such relief. Knowing this unlocks a door in my heart that I didn't know was still closed to him.

It's freeing, and my love for him deepens.

"We all know you're in love with her, Arlo," Luna says to him, then looks at me. "And Mercy, I think those of us who witnessed you today, running to join Arlo at the stake, ready to *die* with him…I think we already know the answer.

"But the women here who didn't see what happened need to hear it from you. We all need to know, because as strange as it sounds, hearing you say it out loud would give us such hope…Hope that even the worst of men," her eyes flicker to Arlo, "that even the misguided and lost are still capable of seeking truth, are willing to accept it and change for the better."

She smiles at me. "We have faith in who you are, Mercy. The author of our rebellion, our leader of change. If you tell us that you've fallen in love with Arlo Rainn—that he's made himself worthy of your love—it would give us the hope we need to fight for change."

Luna watches me with equal parts hope and fear. She hopes her brother is a good man—a man who's worthy of our trust and someone she could love again, too. Yet she's fearful that he's not.

She takes a slow breath. "Are you in love with him, too, Mercy? Does he have your heart?"

Yes.

Unequivocally, irrevocably yes.

I clear my throat, hoping my voice won't break as I make this solemn and cementing proclamation, sharing the secret that Arlo and I had to keep between us all this time. "He has my heart." At that alone, the women react in whispers and grins, a wholly unexpected joy filling the cavern—it fills me, too, fueling me as I speak. "It was hard won, but he earned it fully. I trust him. I love him."

I turn my head so I can look at him, and I find he's already gazing down at me, his blue eyes showing the same relief I feel for lifting the burden of secret-keeping from our shoulders. "Arlo listened to me; he learned from me, and when he finally opened his eyes to the truth, he made the choice to change."

I can't stop myself from smiling at the way Luna's face brightens. The unrestrained joy in her expression is so innocent, so idealistic, so child-like. I can almost see the hope filling her soul, lifting some undefined burden from her shoulders. Her eyes meet Stefanie's, finding her with a peaceful, silently hopeful expression.

There's a wordless connection shared between them, and though it appears intimately unique, the pulse of their shared energy is familiar—reminiscent of the electricity that passes between me and Arlo whenever our eyes meet.

A strange swell of emotion overcomes me, tears filling my eyes again, though these tears aren't from sorrow—these are tears of peace and contentment. It's so fulfilling that I don't hear what Luna and Stefanie say to the others before the crowd gradually disperses. I only see their smiles, feel their hope, and hear the laughter of children as they run off to play.

I've been surrounded by hatred for so long that I'd forgotten what it felt like to exist in peace—truthfully, I'm not sure I ever knew what that felt like.

It feels like this.

For a moment, I'm surrounded by love and not hate.

"There's something we need to show you," Stefanie says as she and Luna appear before me, "and we don't think it should wait." Her dark eyes have shifted so quickly into urgent gravity, and Luna's expression has fallen, too, reflecting the same.

The sudden shift sparks a quick-burning fire in my soul, and in a flash, the peace is gone.

chapter eighteen

ARLO

"ARE YOU SURE you're all right?'" Luna asks me again. "I know it must be painful."

The gunshot wound to my arm *was* painful—overwhelmingly so—yet the burning has given way to an odd tingling sensation, the injured spot teetering on the edge of numbness. I'm not sure whether that's a good or a bad thing.

Thankfully, it seems to be nothing more than a flesh wound. I think the bullet grazed my arm rather than pierced it, and though it currently looks like my bicep exploded from the inside out, Mercy thinks that the tattered remnants of my flesh can be stitched back together.

I didn't want her to look at it as closely as she had; the thought of seeing her wounded that way pierces my heart more painfully than a bullet ever could. I didn't want that for her. Yet she was insistent on making sure I was okay before she would allow us to go with them for answers, and I was eager to find out what the fuck was going on here.

I didn't bother to remind Mercy of the injuries on my back, the lines of fire across my skin from the lashings I endured at the hands of the Control. Pain from the welted stripes was not as intense as the initial strike from the bullet, but it's a pain that remains no matter what I do, consistent fire across my back without relief. At least I can hold my arm still to lessen the pain there.

I'm exhausted, hungry, possibly on the verge of collapsing as the adrenaline from our escape begins to wane. Yet I push myself past the fatigue because I need to know what's happening as much as Mercy does.

Luna and Stefanie lead us by lantern-light through winding, dark tunnels—passageways cut through rock that seem so similar to the caves beneath the Homestead.

"I told you, I'm fine," I reassure for the thousandth time. "I'd rather have answers than medical care."

"Then you might get an infection and *die*." Luna sighs dramatically.

The exasperated tone is something familiar, like the way she'd speak to me when we were younger, whenever I made decisions she thought were ridiculous. I can't help the grin that touches my cheeks. When I became one of the Control, I'd closed myself off from my past so completely that I hadn't even realized how much I missed her. I missed my sister, and I'm glad she's here, that's she's safe and alive.

"I think I'll push my luck today," I return in a playful tone, "given that I should already be dead."

"It's only a flesh wound," Stefanie says, "and it's covered now. It won't take long to show them, and then Mercy can stitch him back together."

"If her hands aren't shaking with rage after she sees this," Luna mutters, then suddenly stops.

Mercy nearly collides with Luna's back. I tug her against my side to keep her upright, but I continue to hold her there for her warmth.

"Maybe we should go back." Luna turns to face Stefanie squarely. "Let her stitch him up now, get some rest, and we can show them later."

"No." Mercy's voice is firm. "Please. I won't be able to rest without answers. And as much as I want to tend to Arlo and stitch his wound, I trust that he's okay for now if he says he is."

"And I've said it a dozen times already. I'm *fine*. I should be dead right now, but here I am…a breathing, walking miracle. I'm suddenly wary of spending my minutes wisely, as clearly one never knows when the next will be their last. So face ahead and walk, Luna; show us what you know." My mind is processing my words as I speak them, realizing that I *am* alive when I should be dead, and I feel my pulse quickening with the strange sensation that awareness brings. Worried my tone has come across harshly, I add, "Please."

Luna nods, "You're right…you're right, Arlo. I know we can't waste any more time." She says it convincingly, but I see the way she anxiously chews her bottom lip, her face shadowed in the meager glow of her lantern's light.

I remember her doing that when she was younger and nervous about getting in trouble—it's a tell I'd completely forgotten about until this very moment. It makes me wonder what else I've forgotten about the people I cared for before the Shift. It makes me feel shame for the man I let myself become.

I'm not that man anymore, and I never will be again.

We walk down the dark passageway. Mercy remains close, our arms pinned between us and fingers interwoven. She holds my hand tightly, sending two squeezing pulses through her grip as a silent reminder that she's here with me.

Mercy walks beside me in the darkness. I can't help but feel as though we're chasing the creeping shadows along the cave walls into hell.

I can feel the change coming. I can sense the onrushing pain of acknowledging truths we'd rather deny.

I fear it.

I fear I'm too weak to accept further dissonance, too weak to admit I was wrong again, too weak to grow more than I already have. Yet, I follow the truth as we march onward…and I'm willing to confront it for Mercy.

Stefanie and Luna share anxious whispers as they lead us through the tunnel. I can't make out what they're saying as my mind races through all the possibilities of what they might be leading us to. It's not too much farther ahead before they stop, and I see an opening in the passage wall just in front of them on our right, a small alcove through it.

Stefanie gently takes the lantern from Luna, crossing to the opposite side of the opening in the rock wall. "In here," she says, gesturing for us to move inside.

Luna leads, and Mercy and I follow. I expect to see something grand, an obvious revelation, but instead all I see is a small cavern—small enough that I can cross the space with three long strides.

"Is this what you wanted to show us?" I ask, turning around to face Stefanie as she moves into the alcove behind us.

"No." Stefanie moves through the small cavern until she reaches the back wall, and then she crouches, bringing the light down with her to reveal a boulder—big enough to reach my knees—sitting against the wall.

"Your father led us here, Mercy," Stefanie says.

I feel Mercy's grip loosening. I feel her drift toward the boulder and away from me in her curiosity. I want to cling to her and drag her back, but I know I cannot hold her back anymore. Though it's painful, I let her hand leave mine, remain still as she steps forward.

"What do you mean?" Mercy asks.

Stefanie sets down the lantern, dropping her knees to the ground and placing her hands on the side of the rock. She glances up at Mercy. "Help me push? Luna has the baby, and Arlo's arm is useless right now."

Mercy doesn't hesitate. Nodding, she steps forward and lowers beside Stefanie. Together, they push the boulder, straining to make it scrape along the solid bedrock beneath. I want to help, but a twinge of pain in my arm reminds me it's useless. Still, they make impressively quick work of it on their own.

As the boulder moves, they reveal an opening in the rock wall behind it, a low tunnel through which one could crawl. My attention immediately flicks to Mercy, remembering the way she panicked when we had to crawl through the tunnel into the main cavern.

Stefanie must be thinking the same, as she grabs the lantern and quickly lifts it to the rounded opening. "It's not a tunnel; it's just like a small doorway, see? Quick in, quick out."

I crouch to my haunches to look through, trying to hide my wince as a searing pain burns across my back, and I see there's another alcove on the other side. It's still shrouded in darkness beyond the lantern's light, but I have the sense that the room is larger than the space where we currently stand.

I also spy some opaque slate blue plastic bins on the ground. A lid covers each bin to protect their contents—whatever those may be—and some of them are stacked on top of each other.

What's inside them?

How many fill this small cavern?

The bins are rather ordinary-looking storage containers but seeing them here gives me an unsettling feeling of foreboding. It jumpstarts my heart, and I feel a new wave of anticipatory adrenaline punch into my veins.

These containers are buried beneath Ember Glen, hidden away in the dark, where they were likely never meant to be seen…and perhaps their contents will answer questions we never thought to ask.

"What's in there?" Mercy's voice is soft, quiet.

Stefanie looks at her, waiting until their eyes connect. "The real story of Ember Glen."

There's a stagnant pause.

A haunting silence wraps around us.

The real story of Ember Glen?

A new battle begins in my mind, a sharp clash between the man I was before and the man I am now. My natural instinct is to balk at the insinuation that there's a story we haven't been told—a story that's true, a story that will reveal the lies upon which we've based our lives. And yet, I already feel the wavering in my soul, the unease of dissonance. I can feel the whole of Ember Glen teetering on the brink, and there's something in that room that's going to bring it all crashing down.

"Show me," Mercy demands. "Tell us everything."

She feels it, too.

I know it.

Her soul is resonating with mine, vibrating on the same frequency of hope and fear.

Stefanie nods, then crawls through the opening, taking the lantern with her. She sets it down once she's inside, and holds out her hand, beckoning Mercy to follow. I expect her to panic, but she doesn't. Her need for this information must be stronger than her newfound fear over small, dark spaces—a fear we gave her by burying her alive—as she crawls right in.

I turn to look at Luna. "How will you get through with her?" I indicate baby Soleil, strapped to the front of her frame with a fabric wrap.

"I always manage," she says, moving in close to the entrance before lowering to her knees.

She cradles the back of Soleil's head with one hand, crawling through the opening on her other hand and knees. Stefanie reaches out from the other side, her upturned palm hovering beneath the baby's head for additional protection. Once Luna is inside, Stefanie grips her arm to help her to her feet.

Forgetting about the wound in my arm for a split-second, I

drop to my hands and knees to follow, and I'm quickly reminded of the pain. The moment my weight presses down through my arm, I hiss, flinch, reflexively jerk my left arm from the ground as I let out a groan in agony.

"Arlo…" Mercy appears on her hands and knees in front of the opening, worry wrinkling her forehead. "Are you okay?"

I rush to slip through the opening with only one arm. "Fine. I'm fine," I mutter, climbing to my feet.

I'm not fine, but she doesn't need to know that.

I hear a click, then a whirring sound, and a bright light comes on from the center of the room. It shines across the space toward the back wall, across from the entrance, concentrated on a white screen that rests upon a black stand—the light coming from a running film projector. Though it spotlights the white projector screen, the light is strong enough to illuminate the center of the bedroom-sized cavern, casting shadows around the outer edges to reveal stacks of the plastic containers lining the walls.

"How…What *is* this?" Mercy's tone reflects my own bewilderment. "How did you find this?"

I watch as Luna moves past a set of stacked bins, lowering to sit on a thick pillow placed against the wall. "The projector and screen weren't set up when we found this place; everything was packed up in these bins." She waves her hand, indicating the stacks of slate-blue plastic totes all around the room.

Mercy slowly turns, her eyes catching mine with a quizzical look before she completes her rotation, glancing between Stefanie and Luna. "What's inside the boxes? How did you *find* this place? You said my father led you here…but how?"

"I'm not quite sure how to start," Luna says, stroking the back of her baby's head.

Soleil whimpers and whines, preparing to cry. Luna anxiously chews on her bottom lip as she loosens part of her wrap, adjusting her clothing so she can nurse.

Stefanie leans sideways against the wall at Luna's side, crossing her arms. "She's hesitant about sharing some parts of our story… how we came to find the pages from Mercy's father that led us here."

"The pages?" Mercy asks at the exact moment my eyes shift to look at her, my attention immediately drawn to those same two words.

The journal of Mira Madness—Mercy's mother—was missing three torn pages, and we had no idea what was written on them or whether they still existed.

Is it possible those pages still exist?

Is it possible my sister somehow found them?

"What pages?" I ask carefully.

Luna shifts on the pillow where she sits, settling in to nurse Soleil. "Pages we found in Mercy's house." She sighs, staring at her feet. "I'm going to tell you everything—what we found, how we found it, the horrible truth about everything—but I need to start at the beginning. I need to start with an admission, knowing you may judge me for this, Arlo. I'm not the God-fearing domestic woman you've always thought me to be."

I'm struck silent by her words, by the guilt that overcomes me, knowing she's hesitant to speak with me. It's a hesitancy I can't fault her for having; I've given her every reason in the world to believe I would judge her—and judge her harshly—for any sins she may have committed. However, she knows I'm no longer a threat to her, no longer in favor with the Control or the Elders.

"I'm no longer with the Control," I remind her. "I can't punish you for any sins you've committed."

Her head rises, gathering my full attention with the intensity of her blue eyes on mine.

"I'm not worried about you punishing me for my sins, Arlo. I'm afraid of the way you're going to look at me, the way you're going to *see* me. I fear your judgment because you're my brother. You've always been my brother, even after the Shift, even after you joined the Control and had to distance yourself. You put up walls and you shut me out, but I never stopped loving you. I never stopped caring about you. You chose power over being my brother, but I never got to make a choice."

She sighs, averting her eyes. "It felt like you had died, and I had to grieve the loss of you…It was like you were dead, but then Mercy brought you back to life. I'm just afraid of losing you again. I'm afraid that when I tell you who I really am, that you'll judge me, hate me, shut me out like you did before."

It feels like the air has been sucked from my lungs. Shame settles heavily in my chest, making my heart ache. I turned my back on her for *them*, for the men who meant to kill me today for loving a sinner.

I feel Mercy's eyes on me, but I can't look at her. The weight of my guilt is so heavy, and I'm afraid that if I look at her, she'll try to help me carry it. It's *my* guilt to carry, and I have no right to put that on her.

"I want to know who you really are, Luna. I'm not…" I pause, struggling to put my thoughts into words. "I don't want to judge you. And I'm not really in a place to judge, now am I? I'm a sinner condemned, after all."

An uncomfortable silence settles as I wait for her response; the stillness made eerie by the whir of the idling projector and the flickering shadows its light casts on the rock walls surrounding us.

Luna still avoids my gaze, though she slowly nods and says, "Okay." She draws in a deep breath to steel herself as she looks down at Soleil, stroking her head.

Then softly, she begins to speak, starting her confession from the very beginning.

chapter nineteen

ARLO

"I'M SURE YOU remember that Stefanie and I were friends when we were children," Luna begins. "We met on the day of my evaluation when I was five. Stefanie had already gone through her evaluation since she was nine years old at the time.

"I was really nervous that day. I thought for sure they were going to evaluate me as a servant, and I knew I didn't want to be a servant. I didn't understand exactly why back then. It all seemed so much simpler when I was young." She gives a sad smile. "I just knew I wanted to have children, and you can't have children if you're a servant.

"I can't recall all the details from my evaluation, but I vaguely remember one of the Control telling the others that I was a good girl who followed rules well, and that would make me an obedient and dutiful wife." Luna's eyes narrow as her brow furrows. "And then another argued that *because* I was a good girl who followed rules well, I should be made to serve, because I would never say no.

"That's the only part I remember before they decided I would be a domestic. I was so thrilled with the decision that I skipped away and ran right into Stefanie, who was waiting with her mother outside. I accidentally knocked her over, and she started to cry. So *I* started to cry, thinking that I'd hurt her. I hadn't hurt her, though. She was upset because she'd just found out they'd decided her little sister would be a servant.

"I didn't understand at five years old why she would be upset for her sister. I might have been upset if I'd been evaluated as a servant, but only because I knew I wanted to be a domestic. I didn't understand why she would be upset about *someone else's* evaluation. After all, maybe her sister really wanted to be a servant, and she was happy about it. Lots of little girls wanted to be servants.

"But Stefanie told me that she'd heard some bad things had happened to servants during the full moon, and she was scared that bad things might happen to her sister. I gave her a hug and tried to reassure her that she'd be okay." Luna chuckles a little, smiling to herself. "Maybe this is just something I made up in my head and not an actual memory, but I think I was a little in awe of her when we met that day…I thought she was pretty, and I really wanted to be her friend."

"You didn't make it up in your head." Stefanie's voice is quiet and her grin is subtle, but it's there. "And you didn't just think it. You told me that day that I was the prettiest girl you'd ever seen and asked if I wanted to be your best friend."

Luna smiles up at her. "I did?"

"You did." Stefanie nods.

As they speak, Mercy moves in front of them, slowly lowering to her knees just a couple of feet in front of Luna. She presses her palms to her thighs as she sits back on her heels, leaning in to listen as if she's a child who has come to gather for story time. I'll admit, I'm rather absorbed in the story myself.

Luna fights her overwhelming smile, dragging her eyes away from Stefanie. "I'm sorry, I'm entirely off track here, and I said this would be quick."

"It's okay," Mercy says. "I like this story."

"Well, Stefanie and I became friends after that day. It was strange how easily we connected, given that she was four years older than me. Our age difference was so much more pronounced back then, but even so, she was easily my best friend. And that's all we were to each other, the very best of friends, until…" She pauses, her eyes losing focus, staring across the space at the opposite rock wall.

"Until I turned sixteen, and they made me Hyatt's wife," Stefanie says, and our collective attention shifts to her, though she only steals it for a moment.

Luna blinks, and I can see how she actively drags her mind back from some past memories that haunt her. She continues speaking as if she never paused. "I was only twelve when it was time for her to become a wife, and I struggled for a long time trying to figure out what that would mean exactly. It was the first time I saw her with Hyatt that I knew what I felt in my heart—though I was too young to fully understand it or find a word to express it." Luna looks over at me, meeting my eyes with intention. "It was jealousy, Arlo. I was *jealous* of Hyatt."

She doesn't have to say another word.

She doesn't have to finish this story for me to know the nature of her confession, and why she fears my judgment. I think I knew it before; I probably knew it all along but wouldn't allow myself to acknowledge the truth.

Luna and Stefanie have become…something more than friends.

I blink, shifting my gaze from Luna as old judgments fight for power in my mind. I can't bear to look at her as I struggle against habit, feeling too vulnerable as I battle my conditioning and fight to keep my mind open for her truth.

"Right," Luna says with a regretful sigh.

I don't mean for her to think I've turned away in judgment, but I hear in her voice that it's exactly what she thinks.

I wish I could offer her reassurance that I'm struggling with *myself* and not with *her*, but I can't bring myself to speak. The appropriate words evade me as this war of obedience versus truth rages in my mind.

"Anyway, that's when I first started to feel…discordant? I can't think of a better word for it. The whole world just started to feel so wrong to me. I missed my best friend. I *hated* Hyatt—and that was before I even knew what a vile human he would turn out to be. I only hated him then because he'd just become the center of Stefanie's life. She didn't have time for me anymore because she was a wife…and a soon-to-be mother within a few months. Our friendship faded when she became a mother, but she never left my heart. We just… she went on with her life as a domestic, and I went on as a child preparing to become the same.

"Years went by where we only said hello to each other in passing in the village. Then everything changed again when I turned sixteen and became a domestic. I'd been assigned to Archer, of course, and by all accounts, he's a kind husband and a loving father." A pained look flickers across her eyes as she looks down at Soleil.

I wonder if Archer knows she's here with his children. Perhaps the pained look is an indication that he doesn't, and she feels some regret for that.

"I never felt any fear with him," Luna says. "At least, not in the way Stefanie did with Hyatt. I had some fear for Archer's strict thinking, but I felt that with everyone in Ember Glen once I worked out the source of my confusion and accepted the truth about myself. I felt things I wasn't supposed to feel for anyone, and worse than that, I felt them for another *woman*.

"I had to accept this truth about myself when it literally came knocking on my door, and it came only a week after I became Archer's wife. Stefanie came to my house late one night after we'd gone to bed. Archer was sound asleep, but I was wide awake, spending yet another night wondering why I didn't feel happy yet. I thought I'd feel happy all the time once I started serving my purpose as a domestic, but I didn't…" Luna falters, closing her eyes as she swallows hard.

When she opens them again, she tilts her chin to gaze up at Stefanie as she slowly lowers to her knees beside Luna. "You came over in tears," Luna says to her. "Do you remember that night? I know there were so many other nights just like it, but that first time you came to me after he hurt you will always be locked in my mind."

My heart feels constricted, my chest tight with a familiar ache that resembles the pain of watching tears fall down Mercy's cheeks. I glance over at her at the same moment she looks back at me, and it pains me further to see her eyes are glassy with tears of her own.

"You were sobbing when I opened the door," Luna goes on. "It nearly broke me to see you that way. You could hardly catch your breath enough to tell me what happened."

"I remember," Stefanie says calmly, maintaining an energy that perfectly contrasts Luna's—a perfect balance. She reaches forward to tuck a wayward strand of hair behind Luna's ear. "You gave me exactly what I needed. You invited me in, you let me tell you what Hyatt had done to me, and you listened without any judgment. But I felt so guilty for putting that on you when you were still so young, when you'd only just married Archer."

"You shouldn't feel guilty," Luna replies. "You kept it to yourself for so long."

"I couldn't burden you with that before you were assigned to someone, before you were married," Stefanie says. "I didn't want to make you fearful of what it would be like when you became a domestic. You'd had such high hopes for it when you were younger."

"And I'd been wrong to have that hope at all." Luna's shoulders slump with her sorrow.

"Hyatt hurt her, Arlo," Luna says my name so emphatically that I have no choice but to meet her stare directly. "That's what the purge is supposed to prevent, isn't it? It's for the men to let out all their violent and sexual urges so their wives don't ever need to fear them. But you probably didn't know all the ways he hurt Stefanie. You probably didn't know that she's been his domestic *and* his personal servant for ten years. Because if the Control knew, they'd surely have done something about it, right?"

I swallow hard. "I didn't know."

I probably should have known, but I didn't.

"Hyatt did everything he could to hide it," Luna says. "He'd been so intentional about it, only causing injuries in places that were hidden by clothing. That first night she came to me…He'd hit her hard enough to break a rib."

Stefanie shifts uneasily, slowly rising to her feet again.

"Her back was bruised so horribly that she winced with every movement. I went to her house every day for weeks afterward, just to help her care for Heidi and Hattie."

"Hattie was just a baby," Stefanie adds, crossing her arms over her chest, her body rigid and tense.

"That wasn't all he'd done to her." Glancing up, Luna asks Stefanie, "Will you show them?"

There's a long pause, but then Stefanie nods. Pushing off the wall, she steps past Mercy on the ground, moving to stand between the light of the projector and the screen at her back. She lifts the hem of her cream-colored sweater, and with her other hand, hooks her thumb into the waistband of her modest skirt to pull it down. She exposes a patch of skin on the lower right side of her waist, just above her pelvic bone, revealing an old white scar in the shape of the letter 'H.'

Fuck.

I let out a heavy, audible breath, swiping my hand across my beard.

"He hurt me for years," Stefanie snaps, covering her scar as she brings her sweater and skirt together again with a sharp motion. "I couldn't tell anyone. The Control couldn't have helped me; no one could. Hyatt told me he'd kill me if I told the Control, that he'd do it before they could take action against him. And then where would my daughters be? He was *cruel* to them. It was only a matter of time before he started to hurt them physically, too. Heidi would have been next."

Mercy rises sharply, and in a flash, collides with Stefanie, throwing her arms around her to embrace her with clear compassion. For a moment, Stefanie's frozen in surprise, but then she welcomes the hug, letting out a heavy breath and hugging Mercy around the middle.

I have to turn away to compose myself as an array of emotions overcomes me. Most prominent is shame because I should have known. It was my job to punish sinners, and that vile man sinned against his wife for years. Hyatt Price denied everything I stood for each time he placed his hands on her.

"You saved me from him, Mercy." I hear Stefanie tell her. "I'm grateful for what you did to him."

"It wasn't just me," Mercy says. I turn to see them untangle and stand at arm's length from each other. Mercy glances over her shoulder at me. "I want to tell her. Can I tell them what you did that night?"

I'm so lost in my racing thoughts that I don't know what she means at first. I nod because I don't care what she tells them.

She turns back to Stefanie. "There's something I think you should know about the night Hyatt died."

Stefanie's dark brows slant toward her nose, her head tilting at an angle.

"Hyatt selected my friend Ellary to serve him that night…"

Ellary…Fuck.

I haven't told Mercy that she fell.

She doesn't know that her friend is in Sanctuary, grasping at tiny threads of life that can easily slip through her fingers.

She may be dead now.

"I escaped the Homestead and ran to save her," Mercy says. "Arlo chased me, but it wasn't to catch me. He went straight for Hyatt, and he was the one who attacked him first. Arlo took Hyatt's knife and held it to his throat, but then his hand slipped and—"

"My hand didn't slip, Mercy."

All eyes fly to look at me.

"I was in control of the situation. I didn't consciously decide to do it. I don't remember a moment where I thought I wanted to kill him, and I don't recall making an active decision to end his life." The words fly out of me, as if this room was meant for sharing secrets and draws it out of me. "But what I do remember is making a decision to press down on the blade when he moved beneath me, and I knew exactly what would happen when I did."

Mercy's chest rises sharply, then falls slowly as she exhales, her gaze dripping down my body before drifting back up to my face.

"I took the knife from Arlo." Mercy's voice is suddenly deeper, slower, like something in my admission effectively altered her mood, and the subtle hint of longing in her voice alters mine just the same. "It's true that I delivered the final blow, but we both had a hand in Hyatt's death. I wouldn't allow Arlo to take the blame, though. I chose to take responsibility for it to spare him," she says to them before she turns to me. "I wanted to spare you."

"And you did."

Stefanie asks, "Is that true?"

I nod, though my gaze is fixed on Mercy, watching her, watching me. "It's true."

"Then I have to thank you both," Stefanie says, "for ending my misery."

I don't know how to respond to that, but saying, 'you're welcome,' in response to being thanked for killing someone's husband seems inappropriate. Though I suppose there are many things I once found to be inappropriate that I no longer see as such. The way Mercy looks at me right now is *entirely* inappropriate under the standards I held before, but now I consider the look to be expected, necessary... *wanted.*

"For what it's worth," I tell Stefanie, "I'm glad for what Mercy and I did to him now that I know it ended your suffering."

"So am I," Mercy whispers, her eyes flickering over my face as a grin pulls across her cheeks. She draws in a deep breath, then turns back to Luna. "So, you were telling us that you and Stefanie...that you feel for each other the way that Arlo and I do?"

Luna blinks her glassy eyes, tugging her bottom lip between her teeth. "Yes. And I first realized it that night she came over. I wanted to be with her. I wanted to comfort her and take care of her. I wanted to be her partner, her *wife*, the mother to her children. I wanted to be the domestic who cared for her, made a home for her..."

Luna drops her head, eyes focusing on a spot near her feet. "And I wanted more than that. I wanted...I had desire for her in the way a man has desire for a servant. I felt sick over it for the longest time; I prayed about it nightly. I kept my thoughts a secret for years until I simply couldn't anymore. That day came shortly after Stefanie's youngest daughter, Hollie, was born two years ago."

Her head snaps up and her eyes lock with Mercy's as she cries, "I kissed her, Mercy. I couldn't take it anymore. I just grabbed hold of her and I kissed her. I thought for sure that was the end for me— that she would report me and the Control would kill me for this sin—but instead, she kissed me back."

Luna smiles, though tears drip down her cheeks. "She kissed me back, Mercy, and it didn't feel *wrong*. It felt...it felt like the world had been gray before, but it all turned to color the moment our lips touched. Maybe that doesn't make any sense, but—"

Mercy lowers to her haunches, resting a wrist on her knee. "It makes perfect sense to me, Luna." She smiles at her, reaching out with her other hand to touch Luna's knee with compassion.

"Stefanie and I have sinned, over and over again. Sins of the heart, sins of the flesh…" She sighs with relief. "I never thought I'd be able to say that out loud."

"But you did." I can only see Mercy's face in profile, yet her genuine smile radiates all the same.

Her natural grace always strikes me hard, but I feel it especially now in the way she shares her kindness with Luna so easily. I feel a ripple of warmth blanket me, vibrating through my limbs. I feel light-headed…

More than light-headed, I feel dizzy, suddenly faint, and the room seems to tilt sideways.

"Arlo?" Mercy's voice echoes oddly as my vision blurs.

Does she feel the room tilting, too?

No…it's only me.

I've hit the wall of exhaustion, and my body's shutting down.

"Arlo, sit down!" Mercy commands as the room turns.

I stumble sideways, seeing the blurry vision of her rushing over to me. I slump to the floor at her command, but before she reaches me, my exhausted mind shutters to blackness as my body collides with solid rock.

The world goes black.

chapter twenty

Mercy

ARLO COLLAPSED NEARLY two hours ago. I stare at his chest, watching the gentle rise and fall that reminds me he's still breathing. Every so often, I nudge him, just to make sure he responds with a groan or a wince, so I'll know he's all right.

He's exhausted after the torture he endured by the Control—the sleepless nights bound to the foyer ceiling while suffering the pain of being lashed across his back. And then there was the chaos at the Homestead this morning, where he faced his death at the stake, where the crowd battled, and he was shot in the arm.

That would be enough to make anyone collapse from exhaustion, but I also have no idea when he last had something to eat or drink.

When he collapsed, he'd toppled sideways, landing on his right side—thankfully, not landing on his wounded arm. I knew we needed to turn him onto his stomach so the wounds across his back from the lashings wouldn't be further irritated by the rock-hard ground.

I asked Luna and Stefanie to help me remove his shirt first, as I wanted to clean his injuries while he was resting. Then, we rolled him onto his stomach, turning his head to rest his cheek against the pillow Luna had been sitting on earlier. He groaned and muttered as we moved him, so at least we knew he was okay—he was just beyond exhaustion, entirely succumbed to his need for rest.

Luna and Stefanie left, and in their kindness, they brought back food, water, and some medical supplies. They left me with two lanterns and some matches so we could leave the space later.

Both lanterns are now lit, resting on the ground a few feet away. I told them I would come back to the main cavern to find them later.

I still have no answers about how they found this place through my father's house. I still haven't been told the 'real story of Ember Glen,' as Stefanie had promised would be revealed in this room. I'm beyond anxious to know, but I don't want to know before Arlo. I want to learn these secrets together because I don't know if I can handle learning the truth on my own.

It all just feels so overwhelming.

I've turned off the projector, worried the light would wake Arlo. Though, I must admit, there was something comforting about the sound it made when it was running. The way the light filled the space made it feel less like a tomb where secrets were buried, shining a light on them instead.

I'm beginning to face exhaustion myself with this cycle of fear that keeps repeating. The small, dark space reminds me of being buried, so my panic rises sharply. I'll push it back down, forcing it away somewhere deep in my soul, but it can only lie in waiting for so long before the panic rises again.

The cycle is wearing on me.

But I refuse to leave Arlo's side, even if he doesn't realize I'm here with him.

I need him.

I don't ever want to be apart from him again.

Sitting beside him, I stroke my palm down the back of his head. I laid beside him for a while—even dozed off for a bit—but now I'm wide awake.

He groans in his sleep, drawing in a deep breath before letting it out again. "Starlight…" he mutters.

There's an extra thump between heartbeats, another pulse of life through my veins at the sound of his voice.

"Mercy," he whispers in a gravelly voice. "Come back to bed."

"I'm here, love. You can rest."

The wrinkles on his forehead deepen at the sound of my voice, then his eyes flutter, slowly blinking open. "Mercy?"

"It's me; I'm here." I curl my fingers to drag them through his hair as I continue to stroke the back of his head.

He groans. "Where are we?" He opens his eyes fully, slowly lifting his head from the pillow.

"You don't have to get up. We're safe here. You can rest."

He pushes himself up into a sitting position. "I don't need to rest…I'm fine." He reaches up to pinch the bridge of his nose, his face scrunching against the pain.

"Please don't lie to me, Arlo. Don't tell me you're fine when you're not. You collapsed."

He blinks as he drops his hand. "Where's Luna? I need to tell her—"

"We're alone right now. I told them to go while you rested. You've been out for nearly two hours."

"Two hours?"

I nod. "You needed the rest."

"I don't need rest." He places his hand on the ground, shifting as if he's going to push himself up. "I need answers."

"I need them, too." I grip his right bicep and wrap my other hand around the side of his neck to hold him in place. "Trust me when I tell you how much I need some answers. But it was foolish of us to rush after what we've been through."

I let my hand drift down the side of his neck, lightly brushing over the curve of his shoulder, stopping there to avoid touching his gunshot wound. "I need to stitch this up, disinfect it, and cover it. After all we've survived, Arlo Rainn, wouldn't it be ridiculous for you to die from an infection we could have prevented?"

I smile at him, hoping to ease some of the tension that naturally exists in this small, dark space.

His head inclines as he watches me, his gaze fixed on mine. "You're right. You're always right." It's strange that I can see just how blue his eyes are in this dim lighting.

A small flame sways and waves in the two lanterns nearby, making shadows dance on the cave wall behind him, appearing like dark ghosts which haunt him.

He looks haunted.

But at least he's alive.

I swallow hard against a rising lump in my throat, the same one that rises each time I remember that he could be dead right now. If the women hadn't chosen to fight back today, Arlo would be dead. I would be entirely without him. I'd be crying alone, locked in my room at the Homestead, grieving the loss of this man who won my heart.

The mere thought of it is unbearable.

I shove to my feet and move away as tears rise behind my eyes. "Let me just put on the projector for light, and I'll stitch your arm." I put on a cheerful tone, though I have to force it. "There's food and water there beside you. You need both to get your strength back."

I flip on the projector, and it whirs to life, the light brightening the center of the room as it shines on the white screen in front of it.

"Come here, starlight."

I turn to find him watching me, his bare chest lifting and lowering with each deep breath he takes. I expect to see some heat behind his eyes with the way he called me back to him, but I didn't expect to see them so somber, shining at me with gentle longing.

"Look," he says, reaching over to pick up a glass of water from the tray Luna and Stefanie had brought back. "I'll drink." He takes two long gulps. "I'll eat. Just come here and be close to me."

I bend to grab the small kit with medical supplies before making my way to Arlo. I step in close, placing one boot on the ground between his slightly spread legs, the other on the opposite side, before I lower over his knee.

I settle my feet beneath me and shift forward on my knees to straddle his thigh. I sit, landing heavier than I'd meant to. His flesh is warm, pressed firmly between my legs, and impossibly, I feel desire for him now. I have to ignore the feeling, though, so I can focus on his arm.

I glance down at the wound, and the sight is instantly sobering. I don't even know how to describe what I see, but I'm so damn thankful that the bullet merely grazed him. This particular injury will be a challenge, but I know how to stitch a flesh wound. I wouldn't know where to begin if a bullet had burrowed inside him. I tremor at the thought of it.

"It's only flesh and blood…That's nothing to be afraid of." Ellary's voice is clear inside my mind. *"It's injuries of the heart and soul that make me uneasy."* That's what she'd told me once when I asked her how she was so good at managing gruesome injuries.

Ellary is such a natural caregiver, truly gifted with medicine and healing. She would be so much better than me at stitching this wound, and I wish she were here right now to help me.

I just hope that she and Cambria are safe.

I didn't see Ellary at the gathering this morning. I know some were grabbed by men, while others were chased by the Control as they ran, and I don't know who was caught or how they'll be punished.

I hope they ran early and that they thought to seek safety at Sanctuary. It's naïve of me to think that any rules designed in the favor of women are sacred in Ember Glen, but perhaps the men will honor the one that prevents them from stepping foot inside Sanctuary without the unanimous permission of every servant within.

Perhaps if they stay in Sanctuary, they'll remain safe…at least until the next full moon.

I open the medical kit and twist to place it on the ground beside me. Arlo's hand touches my cheek, and it stills me. A wave of loving energy flows from his palm through my entire body, the warmth of his touch reminding me that it was only last night that I thought I'd never feel his touch again.

His thumb brushes my skin, and all the emotions I've been suppressing rise against the dam wall I've built, threatening to break through and flood me. I shut my eyes and inhale slowly, trying to steady myself as my head drifts naturally into his palm. When I open my eyes, I find him watching me with a small smile, and my lips curl in response.

There's a beat of peace now that we're alone, away from all the world and safe for the moment…I should be happy, and I am, but I'm also intensely aware of how broken I am from the events over the last few days.

I feel tears prick my eyes, but I don't want to cry anymore.

I'm so sick of crying.

I sniff them back and force a brighter smile through my expression. His hand falls from my cheek when I turn away from his touch to reach over and grab some rubbing alcohol from the kit. I pour a small amount on some fresh gauze, then begin to clean the area around his wound, disinfecting while scrubbing away the dried blood in preparation for stitches.

Silence surrounds us, and it begs to be filled.

The one truth I don't want to acknowledge gnaws at the inside of my cheek, grinds through my teeth, then sneaks out past my lips the moment I let them part…

"You almost died today."

It's a thought that has me twisted up in knots on the inside, though the words sound so ordinary, as if I'm engaging in small talk and this is a normal topic of conversation.

Arlo remains quiet as I work, and just when I start to think he's not going to respond at all, he quietly replies, "Almost."

I swallow against a thick lump that's risen in my throat, blinking a few extra times to bat away the tears dotting my lashes. I finish making a clean circle around the wound, then pick up a new square of gauze from the kit and pour more alcohol so I can clean the wound itself.

"This might hurt," I warn before gently working to cleanse the injury.

It's a canyon dug into his flesh, raw and open, reminding me just how fragile we are—how easily their bullets could tear us all to shreds. All I can do is close the wound by stitching the broken flaps of skin together, seal it from infection, and hope his body knows what to do to repair itself in time.

I work gently but quickly to disinfect as much of the wound as I possibly can. I try to focus on the whirring of the projector, to tune out the sound of him hissing and groaning in pain. When I finish, I discard the blood-soaked gauze. Before I reach for the needle, I drench my hands in alcohol, rubbing them together to disinfect my skin thoroughly.

"You promised you would eat," I remind him as I clean the needle, then work on threading it.

"Were you really going to burn with me, Mercy?"

My breath stutters in my lungs at the question, and for a moment, I'm frozen.

"Yes," I whisper.

My hands are suddenly trembling. I stare at them intently while struggling to thread the needle, trying to avoid his gaze. But then I realize that I need him to know clearly, without a doubt, that it was my intention to die with him when I climbed onto that platform and stood with him at the stake.

I meet his eyes. "Yes, I was going to burn with you, Arlo. I was ready to die with you."

Arlo sighs. "Starlight…I wish I could find a way to put my thoughts into words."

I grin, looking down at my hands again, finally managing to work the damn thread through the loop. "The poet is at a loss for words?"

"A complete loss. A blank page."

What does that mean?

Does he think I'm weak?

Does he think less of me for choosing to die with him rather than face the final trial without him?

I don't know what to say, and he's quiet again.

The silence festers between us.

Letting out an anxious breath, I bring my hand to his shoulder, turning my palm above his wound to get a good grip. I shift closer and bring the needle to his arm.

"This will hurt," I tell him.

From the corner of my eye, I see the motion as his head bobs in understanding. I can feel him staring at me. I know he's studying each twitch of muscle through my tense jaw, watching every subtle shift in my demeanor.

"Do you regret it?" he asks.

My head turns with a snap, and I quickly meet his eyes.

"If you had the choice to make again, not knowing that my life would be miraculously spared today, would you still choose to run to me? Would you still choose to burn and die with me?"

"Arlo, that's…it's an impossible question to answer."

He glances at my lips before returning to meet my eyes. "Then give me an impossible answer."

I don't know how to answer his question, though it's not because I don't know the answer. It's because I'm afraid of what he'll think of me once he knows the truth.

He leans forward, pressing a sweet kiss to my shoulder. "Please. Tell me the truth, starlight."

My body softens as he drops his forehead to my shoulder, turning his head to nuzzle his face into the slope of my neck. His breath is warm as it breezes across my bare skin, softly dripping heat down my body.

He melts me.

My skin prickles and my muscles release their tension as every part of my body begs me to relax into his touch, to find comfort in his nearness. Yet I know comfort can only be found with the truth, and so I have to speak mine.

I let the words drip from my lips. "The impossible answer is yes, Warden Rainn."

His head rises from my shoulder, and our eyes connect deeply. I didn't intend to call him Warden Rainn, yet the honorific came out so naturally. His blue eyes give me clarity, reminding me of who he was, who he is, and all he will become.

Arlo Rainn has always been, and will always be, my warden. Not the warden assigned to ensure my punishment in the trials; he's the warden of my heart, the jailor of my soul, the captor of my desire, and only because I *choose* him to be the keeper of every part of me.

"You can ask me this question a thousand times on a thousand different days," I whisper, "and my answer will always be the same. Forever, my answer will be yes. Forever, I would choose to die with you, to burn with you."

His chest sinks. "Forever...I would burn with you, Mercy." He leans closer to kiss my neck, trailing his lips up to my cheek. They skim along the line of my jaw until he reaches my ear and whispers, "I would die a million deaths for you."

"My lips part, letting out a breath of relief, releasing all the fear I held that he might think less of me for my answer. Of course, I should've known he wouldn't, because in my heart, I knew his answer would be the same.

My parted lips draw his gaze to my mouth, and the promise of his kiss hangs heavy in the air between us.

"I need to stitch your wound…" I remind him.

Arlo slowly nods. "Go ahead."

His fingers brush over my cheek before they comb into my hair. A tremor runs up my spine as they curl and flex, fingertips gently rubbing against my scalp as he indulges in his obsession with my hair. My eyes flutter shut at the soothing feel of it.

I swallow, my mouth suddenly dry. "Do you want me to give you a warning or just begin?"

"Starlight," he whispers. "There is no warning you could give that would sufficiently prepare me for your touch."

I open my eyes to find his gaze roaming across my face, touching every feature, slipping through my hair, tracing the curve of my neck. His eyes could easily be his hands, because I feel every sweep of them over my skin.

"Arlo."

His eyes shift to meet mine. "Go ahead."

His thumb moves back and forth, gently rubbing a spot on the side of my head, and it calms me.

I need to focus.

I need to stitch this and get it covered.

"You're not going to make this easy for me, are you?" I squeeze my hand over his shoulder, leaning in and preparing to sew.

"I just need to touch you. I don't mean to make this harder on you than it is." He continues to stroke my scalp and play with my hair.

It feels so good; I want to drop my head into his palm and let him touch me like this forever. It's so soothing, so loving, so calming, yet arousing all at once. Perhaps I can give into it once the stitching is done, but it has to be done now.

I wait until I feel his fingers draw through my hair again, and when they're halfway through the strands, I whisper, "Hold on tight."

Then I plunge the needle into his flesh.

He tenses, groans, and just as I told him to, his hand closes around a tuft of my hair, holding on tight. My head tilts back slightly as he pulls a little too hard, but he quickly relents, loosening his grip enough to allow me to lower my head.

"I'm sorry," he says. "Did I hurt you?"

"No," I tell him breathlessly.

I feel awake.

I feel alive.

My scalp tingles from the pull, prickling like tiny bursts of lightning all around my head.

"You don't have to let go," I tell him.

I sew another stitch.

His groan is feral.

His grip is tight.

He tugs my hair so hard that my chin aims skyward.

I gasp at the feeling of pleasure that ripples through me, surprised at its presence, heat touching my cheeks with the awareness of desire coursing through my veins.

I feel the tremor through his arm, though he doesn't release me. My hands are still, holding the needle at his arm, waiting for him to let go. His lips graze the hollow of my throat and I shudder, letting out a whimper.

The tease of his touch—of feeling him *alive* when only hours before we were both preparing to die—makes my eyes fall shut in ecstasy.

Gradually, his grip loosens, though he doesn't entirely let go.

"Don't stop," he breathes the words along my collarbone. "I've felt so cold. I've felt so lifeless since your trial, since I found out what it would be like to lose you. The pain of you sewing me back together is *divine*, starlight."

His hand shifts to find a stronger grip, to sift more of my hair between his fingers from the base of my skull. His hold on me is possessive, and I cherish it, crave more of it. A rush of warmth drips down the center of my body as liquid heat stirs my lust for him.

I let out a breathy moan as my body loosens to his touch. I sink heavier against his thigh, and he flexes, shifting the hard muscle beneath me. He groans as my hips drive forward, rubbing myself along his thigh.

"Please," he begs, his voice soft with desperation. "Mercy, *please*. Let me feel you. Give me pain. Make me feel alive."

He lets me loose enough to drop my head so I can see what I'm doing. I line up the needle for the next stitch, and a rush of anticipation overcomes me.

I want his hand in my hair, gripping tight, pulling hard.

I press the needle through his skin to make the next stitch.

I nearly cry out with how hard he jerks my head back.

"*Mercy…*"

The way he says my name makes my thighs clench.

My head drops forward and I tug the thread through, taking a split-second to make sure the line I'm stitching is straight. His injured arm moves slightly as I inspect my work; he reaches forward to grip the smallest part of my waist, his other hand still tangled with my hair.

I sigh, arching my back. "I missed your hands on me." My hips drift forward to drag my pussy shamelessly along his thigh.

He groans, his hand squeezing my waist before slipping down my hip. "I thought I'd never touch you again."

"Touch me now." My hips move back and forth, grinding down hard. "I need you."

He holds my head steady, then dives in to kiss me, bruising my lips with the pressure of his. I open for him, begging to taste him with a moan he eagerly swallows. His tongue sweeps heavily against mine, taking command, tasting me exactly how I need to be tasted.

I cannot control myself, though I wish I could. Wanting him this way, desiring him *here,* in the midst of this brewing rebellion, feels wrong, like something only a sinner would do…

And that makes me want it all the more.

I can't stop rocking my hips.

His sweeping tongue forces heat down my throat that sinks straight through me, melting my core and dripping wetness between my thighs.

I pant as he drops his mouth to the hollow of my throat, licking and kissing a sensitive trail that travels up the side of my neck, along my jawline, right beneath my ear.

"I want to be inside you while you mend me. I want you to make me hurt while I make you come."

I don't even know how he manages it, but in a swift motion, he sweeps me up, lowering me quickly on my back. I lose my grip on the needle, and it dangles from his arm, miraculously hanging onto the thread. I reach for it, but he pulls back, rising onto his knees between my spread legs.

"The needle…" I warn.

He ignores me, staring into my soul as he unbuckles his belt.

The dangling needle puts me on edge. I'm anxious to grab hold of it before it falls, before it accidentally punctures his skin somewhere unintended, yet he remains entirely unconcerned.

I'm almost bothered by it until he grabs my skirt with both hands, shoves it up my thighs, then slaps his hand over the wet spot soaking through my underwear. He circles his fingers, rubbing me over the fabric, and all rational thought spills with the rush of wetness between my legs.

I reach down to slip my underwear over my hips, lifting my legs so I can kick them off, tossing them away somewhere, forgotten forever.

"Lay down; let me take care of you." I try to sit up, but he quickly bends over me, placing both hands on the floor to cage me in. "You're going to hurt yourself." He slowly smiles at me as I speak. "Sit back down the way you were and I'll…"

I'll…what?

What was I going to say?

The full length of his dimples slices down his cheeks, and his divinely unholy grin shuts me right up.

His hips move forward, and I feel the tip of his cock rub against me. He shifts until he's perfectly aligned to enter me, and with a slow, steady stroke, he sinks inside me.

My eyes slam shut, my back arches off the floor, and I suck in a sharp breath. He's as deep inside me as he could possibly be, and it feels so perfect that I don't care if he moves. I don't care if he fucks me; I don't care if he makes me come.

The feeling of him inside me is all I need.

"Starlight," he says, and I open my eyes. "Stitch me up."

The needle still dangles from his arm, literally clinging to him by a thread. It takes me a few seconds to regain enough focus to reach out for it, plucking it between my fingers. Arlo remains still as I shift beneath him, reaching up, aligning the needle with his flesh, and then I pierce him.

He hisses through his teeth, his eyes clamping shut.

I watch his face as I slowly tug the thread through behind the needle. As I drag the thread, he drags his cock, pulling out of me at a speed that matches mine.

I twist the needle around to position it for the next stitch.

And at the moment I pierce his skin, he slams deep inside me again, making me gasp at the rush of it as my back arches from the ground.

I pierce and pull.

He thrusts and drags.

Arlo fucks me in time with the movement of each stitch.

It's a tease, a game, a gradual build-up of need.

By the fifteenth, and final, stitch, we're both panting, throbbing, needy to have our hands on each other.

"Wait," I tell him before he moves again, reaching over to grab a strip of clean gauze.

Quickly knotting the stitches, I wrap the clean strip of gauze around his arm as he pulses inside me, making my hands shake as I hurry to finish the task.

I tie a knot in the gauze to secure it around his arm, and the moment I tug it tight, he adjusts the angle of his hips. The tip of his cock thumps against a perfect spot inside me as I let my hands fall away, dropping to the ground on either side of my head.

His hand collars my throat, and I gasp at his touch. One of my hands comes up to circle his wrist as I watch him fuck me. He thrusts deeper, moving with a steady rhythm that lets me feel every inch of him slip along my inner walls.

"Can you feel the way I need you? How hard I am for you? Can you feel how desperate I am to come inside you?" He slams into me so hard that my body slips backward, grinding against the rock floor.

"I want you to." I reach up to grab his cheeks and he thrusts again. "Always inside me."

"Always. *Sweet sin*, the way I love you."

He kisses me and it hurts.

It hurts because he's deep inside me, filling me entirely, yet it doesn't feel like enough.

I need more of him, desperately, but more isn't possible.

I've never known such pleasure as what he gives me. I didn't know it was possible to desire so deeply. It's physical, but it feels emotional, too…it feels *spiritual*. Rushed and desperate as it is, we're connected in every way, and it's beautiful.

This is more than sex, more than using each other physically to chase an impulse for release. I won't deny that we're both chasing that release—of course, we are—but more than that, this is a reminder that we're both *alive*.

Our hearts beat.

Our lungs burn.

Our bodies beg.

I feel every part of him, and he feels every part of me.

We're alive, we're together, and we're in love.

It's an act of rebellion so blasphemous that it makes me hot, like my warden is fucking me in hell. My stomach clenches at the thought of it, and a devilish grin lifts the corners of my lips.

My hands slip along his cheeks, his unruly beard scratching my palms. I comb my fingers back through his tousled strands, tugging at the ends.

"I love you," I whisper, and with a sigh, he drops his forehead to rest against mine. "I love every version of you…dark and light, angel and demon, saint and sinner."

"Sweet sin…you're *mine*." A demonic growl rumbles through his chest, and he fucks me faster.

My stomach clenches against the flurry of pleasure building through my core, both from the way he moves inside me—as though his anatomy was crafted for the sole purpose of making me come— and for his words, his voice, and the vulgar, intoxicating sounds of his desire.

The hand around my throat slides around to the back of my neck, fingers climbing up to sink into my hair as his palm cradles the back of my head. He holds me tight so he can pound me hard, dragging his nose up my cheek, drawing in a deep breath to inhale my scent along the line of my hair.

"Wildflowers," he mutters. "Wildflowers and starlight."

Those words will never fail to kickstart my heart, and I wrap my arms around him, hugging him as tight as I can. We hold on to each other desperately as he fucks us toward oblivion. He's so heavy against me, every inch of our bodies kissing. I angle my hips just right to feel his body rubbing against my clit while he moves inside me. His cock is so hard, so beautifully thick, and it pulses with his onrushing release.

"*Sweet sin*," he groans. "Come with me. *Fuck.* Come with me, starlight. *Please.*"

It's not as though I could ever come on command; it only works because his timing is exquisite. He pays such careful attention to the way I move, the sounds I make, the way my pussy clenches around his cock. He holds off his release until he knows I'm near mine, edging himself until he's sure I'm ready to come hard on his cock.

And I'm there…ready and needy.

Three perfect thrusts bring me to release. I come so hard, it's silent. So hard that it freezes me in stillness, traps me for seconds that feel like hours in the stagnant tension that holds him tightly inside me…and then the pleasure crests, crashes like a tidal wave against the shore, breaking to release its hold on me.

He pumps into me twice more before the grip of my cunt squeezes him to his own spectacular release. He bites my shoulder to stifle the sound of his groan as he spills warmth inside me, spurring another small aftershock of pleasure that twitches through my insides.

We fight together to catch our breath. Still held close in each other's arms, he rolls us to our sides, and though the ground is painfully hard, I don't care. My head is cradled in his arm wrapped around me, his fingers splayed over the back of my head. Our hips still rock lazily as we come down from the high.

"I love you," he whispers. "I love you more than my own life."

"And I love you more than mine."

I work my hand up between us, my fingertips playing through

the overgrown hair of his untrimmed beard.

He grins at me. "That makes us dangerous, you know."

"I know. You and I will be the most dangerous threat to ever rise against Ember Glen."

"Of course. That's why they want us dead."

"Well, they already tried to kill us, and they failed, didn't they?" I press a kiss to his perfect lips.

"If only they knew what they were really up against with you, Mercy Madness." A smirk curls one corner of his lips. "A woman who evades death *and* can stitch a man's gunshot wound while he fucks her across the floor? They don't stand a chance."

"And that doesn't even speak to what I can accomplish when I'm on top."

"We'll have to explore that once my back is healed."

"Are you in pain?"

"Mercy, I just came inside you; that's all I feel. Ask me again in ten minutes."

"Okay, I will."

And I fully intended to ask him again in ten minutes, but I hadn't realized how utterly exhausted I was. My attention had been given to everyone else, and I neglected myself.

But I think Arlo knew.

Despite his injuries, he laid there beside me, gently playing with my hair until I drifted into sleep.

And through the hours, I was trapped in nightmares of blood and fire, battles fought and lost, women kneeling before violent men.

There was nothing I could do to help.

I couldn't escape my own mind.

The only way to end it was to burn it all down.

The only way to end the nightmare was with fire.

BRYNN FORD

chapter twenty-one
Mercy

IT'S DARK ASIDE from the lantern's light, and everything feels so quiet, so still…except for the low moan of pain from Arlo beside me. I find I'm still curled against his chest as I awaken, his right arm beneath my head to give me a pillow against the hard ground.

I breathe in and his scent fills me, instantly bathing me in comfort. My hip aches from the rock beneath it, but I feel well rested, calm, and more at peace than I have been in a very long time. It's because I'm with *him* and we're together freely, unburdened by the fear of being found out.

My lips curl up into a grin as I press them to his chest. He stifles a groan, leaning away from me, though I don't get the sense that he wants to. His left arm is tense, ramrod-straight, resting on top of his hip.

I untangle myself from him and push to sit up, gently laying my hand on his forearm. "Are you in pain?"

"Yes," he hisses, tilting toward me.

I shift back on my knees, giving him some space to roll onto his stomach.

"You could have moved."

"I didn't want to wake you."

I reach out to stroke the back of his head, hoping to ease him back to sleep, but my fingers slip down the back of his neck as he unexpectedly pushes to his knees, then sits back on his heels. He hangs his head, pressing his palms to his thighs as he blows out a heavy breath.

"What can I do?" I ask.

His hand floats out to the side, and without looking up, he catches my fingers and pulls my hand onto his lap. "You're already doing it."

I scoot closer, reaching up with my other hand to sweep an untamed strand of hair across his forehead. He tilts his face toward me, granting me a small, pained smile.

"I wish I had one of those little white pills to give you now."

The medication he'd given me after Killian made me push my hand into the bonfire had effectively ended my pain, and how I wish I could give Arlo one now. I wish I could do anything to end his pain.

Arlo's brow furrows. "Even if you had one, I wouldn't take it."

"Why?"

"Because I deserve the pain."

"You don't—"

"How much pain have servants suffered at the hands of men? How much suffering have I caused? We forced pain and granted no relief. We have medicine that ends pain, yet the servants who need it most don't have access to it. We hurt them in service, and then we just send them to Sanctuary…injured, alone, in pain…" His blue eyes darken.

Air rushes from his lungs, the feeling of dread slipping out with it, and I'm forced to draw it in with my next breath. "Mercy, I need to tell you something."

"Okay…"

"I don't know how to tell you this because it's going to break your heart." His eyes flick away from me.

"What is it?" I move closer, placing my hands on his cheeks, turning his face toward mine.

He's quiet for a moment as I search his eyes.

"Just say the words, Arlo. Whatever they are."

"I should have told you last night in the foyer, but I didn't think it would matter then. I thought I would be dead by now, and that you would be soon after…I just wanted that time with you; I didn't want to cause you more pain."

"Arlo…"

"Something happened at your trial," he hesitates, and his reluctance agitates me.

"A lot of things happened at the trial. Can you be more specific?"

"Cambria and Ellary were meant to be set free once you were in your grave."

"Right," I pause, "and they were. I saw Cambria at the Homestead."

"Cambria was there, yes, but Ellary…"

"But Ellary, what?"

His chest sinks as his warm breath quickly fills the space between us. "Ellary fell from the cliff."

My hands drop from his cheeks and they land on my lap. I sit back on my heels as my eyebrows knit together, my head inclining as I watch him.

"I don't understand…What do you mean?"

"Ellary fell, and she landed on a ledge. The drop was twenty or thirty feet."

I hear what he's telling me, the words he speaks, but somehow, they aren't making sense to me.

A lump rises in my throat, and I blink as I swallow against it. "W-What are you saying?"

"Mercy…" He reaches out to touch my cheek.

I slap his hand away reflexively. "What are you *saying*?" My voice sounds angry, though I don't mean for it to be.

His eyes harden, hiding his gentleness from me so he can spit out the truth. "Once you were lowered into the grave, Killian pushed Ellary over the edge. She fell as much as thirty feet and landed on a ledge. We had to bury you and Delle first, but then I went over the edge to retrieve her. She had a pulse, but she was near death. Park took her back and left her alone in Sanctuary, and that's the last I know. I don't know if she's alive or…"

Alive or…dead.

.

.

.

.

.

Arlo is in front of me, but I don't see him.
My eyes are unfocused.
Everything's blurry.
My mind is a blank void.

.

.

.

.

Arlo speaks to me.
His hands are on my cheeks.
His forehead touches mine.

.

.

.

It's dark all around me, and I'm lost in empty space.

.

.

Liquid runs hot down my cheeks.

.

His arms close around me.

I'm warm.

My body forces me to breathe.

I smell him.

Instead of drenching me in comfort like it did before, it shocks my senses and awakens me, brings me back from the dead.

I'd rather be dead.

I want to return to nothingness.

This sudden pain in my chest, this sob bursting out of me, these tears that burn like fire are too much for me to bear.

"No…" I think the word came from me, though I'm not sure.

I didn't think it.

I didn't choose to speak it.

All I know is pain.

"She's okay," I mutter against his chest. "She's okay. She's not dead. She wouldn't die. She couldn't."

"I'm sorry. I'm sorry, Mercy."

Sorry?

I jerk back, my palms on his chest, shoving. "Don't be sorry. There's nothing to be sorry about. She's fine." I feel tension through my forehead, misplaced anger touching my expression. I sniff, willing the wells of my tears to dry up as I blink rapidly to bat the remaining droplets away. "She's *fine*. I survived being buried alive, and she can survive a fall."

"Starlight—"

"*No.* Ellary's alive. The servants will care for her in Sanctuary. She'll heal and she'll be fine."

If she's alive, she's certainly in pain.

Are her bones broken?

Did she bleed?

I meet Arlo's eyes for a moment, but he looks at me with pity and despair, and I have to look away. I reach around him to grab the one lantern that's lit and start crawling toward the exit.

"Where are you going?"

"To find Luna and Stefanie. I want answers."

"Right now? After what I just told you? Take a minute, Mercy, you're—"

"Shut *up*."

His hand grazes my ankle as I reach the opening, but I jerk my leg away.

He groans in pain, and a twinge of guilt passes through me. I hesitate for a moment, but only just. I reach through the opening to place my lantern on the other side, but just as I duck my head to crawl through, Arlo's hand clamps around the back of my knee, and it makes me jolt with surprise.

"Let go!" I turn my head over my shoulder, looking at him sternly as I reach back to grab his arm.

"Stop. Come here." He tugs at my leg, and it makes me furious.

Fine. I'll be furious, then.

Anger is better than heartache.

Rage is better than sorrow.

Action is better than stillness.

I let go of his arm just so I can smack it hard. "Don't *touch* me!"

Conviction shadows his expression with darkness, and his grip tightens. My leg rises from the ground as he pulls hard, dragging me backward toward him. I try to crawl forward, but he unbalances me, and the shin of my opposite leg—still planted on the ground—grates against solid rock.

"Stop!"

I drop on my hip as I twist, then sit my ass on the ground as I bring my arm around, aiming without thought to slap his cheek. He snatches my wrist just before it lands…and I'm glad he did.

I don't know what I'm doing.

I don't want to hurt him.

Was I trying to hurt him?

Was he trying to hurt me?

"I'm not trying to hurt you," he says as though he can read my mind. "I don't want to hurt you. Just let me hold you."

He huffs as our eyes meet, and it settles me to see his own heartache ripple through the blue. I go still, blinking up at him with wide eyes.

"You can't run from the pain," Arlo whispers, his grip on my wrist gradually loosening. "Don't run from me." He moves over me, his other hand slipping around my waist to splay across my back. "If you go through hell, then I go with you." He lifts, slowly bringing me against him.

I'm trapped by his gaze as he holds me there, chest to chest, eye to eye. The longer we stare, the more the pain grows, the faster misery fills me like a rising tide of anguish that drowns the world until the black waters of despair are all that's left.

And as his forehead touches mine, I cry.

Ellary is my best friend; she means everything to me. They knew this, and they made her walk to the cliff's edge to serve as a sacrifice for my trial.

And I sacrificed for her.

I did what I was supposed to do to save her. I climbed into my own coffin, let them *bury me alive*, and it was all for nothing. Because they pushed her anyway.

Killian pushed her. Killian fucking Cole…

I'm going to learn the truth about Ember Glen, and then, I'm going to murder Killian Cole.

He owes me a debt in blood, and I'll make sure he pays.

I weep in the sanctuary of Arlo's arms until there's nothing left, until I'm an empty black void and the only thing that can fill me is rage…

The only thing that can fuel me is revenge.

chapter twenty-two

Mercy

ARLO'S ARM IS around my back, hand curled around the side of my waist to keep me close to his side. I hold the lantern as we navigate the dark passages back to the main cavern. Even with the lantern's light, we can only see a few feet in front of us as we move through the black-as-night corridors.

Arlo navigates the way for us so easily, especially considering how dark it is. I can remember it always seemed so effortless the way he took us through the paths and tunnels in the cave system beneath the Homestead. I suppose he just has a good general sense of direction, and I'm grateful for it because I think I'd be lost on my own right now. It's hard for me to think straight with the chaotic swirl of emotions muddling my thoughts, keeping me in a constant state of anxiety.

Will this sense of unease live in my soul forever?

I grip the back of his belt, holding on so he can't slip away from me. "I don't remember it being so dark when they led us through before."

"It wasn't, but night must have fallen." He squeezes the side of my waist and guides me to veer right. "This way. This is the main cavern."

The sunlight that filled the space when we first entered has faded, leaving only the soft ring of moonlight that outlines the circular opening far above the pool.

"Did we sleep the entire day?" I whisper. "It's so quiet."

"It seems that way."

We creep forward into the wide-open space, and it almost feels like an intrusion.

"Should we just go back?" I wonder. "Try to find them in the morning?"

"That would probably be the polite thing to do."

"I've never known you to be particularly polite." Despite the disquiet in my mind, he was just asking for a response like that, and I grin as it slips out so effortlessly.

He stops us, turns his head to look over at me. "I used to have very good manners, you know. It earned me quite a bit of power…" his mouth curls up on one side, "but it certainly never got me beneath your skirt."

My grin broadens, though I force my eyes to roll. I feel heat flush my cheeks. I don't know if I'll ever understand how he affects me the way he does. I suppose it doesn't matter why; it only matters that he does.

Despite thinking it may be best to head back, he leads me forward anyway, on a slow walk through the dark, and it's peaceful. I might even venture to say it's serene, despite the horrors that haunt us. Yet any serenity we find is soiled by the invisible fragments of each trauma we've faced, like speckles of stardust which constantly trail behind us, pulled along by the gravity of our dark souls.

Even so, there's something ethereal about this place in the quiet night—I half expect to see tiny flakes of starlight following behind us as I glance over my shoulder, the dark remnants of my pain lit up bright and sparkling in this safe space as I drag them behind me.

I feel open here…I feel free.

Free to feel joy.

Free to feel pain and heartache.

Free to exist as I am, even when it hurts.

In a strange way, this place reminds me of Sanctuary. The week we were required to spend in Sanctuary following a night of service was always filled with pain and suffering. Yet there was freedom found in just existing there with my sisters.

Though I couldn't speak freely with my dissenting thoughts, I was free enough to let myself *feel* them—free to cry, free to scream, free to sit quietly and drift into my own mind without interference. Those were the only weeks I felt safe, and in that safety was my freedom.

No man is allowed to enter Sanctuary—not ever. The only exception is the Control, and even so, they can only enter if every single servant within agrees to *allow* them to enter. And I don't think that happened once in my four years of service.

Although…

Arlo said Park took Ellary back and left her alone in Sanctuary.

Did he leave her outside, on the landing?

Were some of the servants inside, and they agreed to let him in?

Did they take Ellary from him and bring her inside themselves?

I shake my head, forcing it from my mind. If I think of Ellary again and what happened to her, I'll fall apart entirely. She is family to me, and the thought of her suffering, dying—perhaps already dead—will break me beyond repair. So I tell myself that she's fine, that she's alive, that she's not suffering, even if I'm only lying to myself.

I force myself to think of Arlo's fingers at my waist, the comfort I find in feeling his touch and having him near me. I feel his warmth against my side, though the warmth isn't just from him—I feel it radiating from the pool as he leads us nearer. Stefanie had told us that the water was warm, a natural hot spring or something.

We stop at the edge of the water, standing still in the silence. Without the sunlight shining through the opening far above, the water appears glossy black. Warm air from the water rises against the cool air from the night sky above, with soft, nearly translucent clouds of steam rolling in the space between. My gaze tracks the steam, following it upward until the night sky steals my attention.

A clear, black sky.

A sliver of moon glow from the waxing crescent.

Bright white lights speckling the dark canvas.

"Starlight," Arlo whispers.

I glance over at him, thinking he's calling for my attention, but I only find him looking up at the same night sky, marveling at the beauty of it.

And I marvel at the beauty of him—he's war torn and battered, but he's alive.

And he's mine.

"I thought I'd never see the stars again," he mutters. "I thought I'd never see you." He looks down at me, and even in the dark, I see the depth of his love.

True love is a divine thing—they had that much right. But Arlo and I would never have found it if we'd lived the way they wanted us to. It wouldn't have been some celestial blessing from God that we miraculously found as assigned domestic partners; it came to us as a sinner and a self-proclaimed saint.

We had to choose it.

We had to fight for it.

There's a light splash somewhere in the water and our heads turn at the same time to search for the source. Holding out the lantern, I don't see anything in the pool before me, but I'm certain I heard the ripple of waves…

And then we hear it again, followed by a muted whimper.

What if a child has fallen into the water?

I step closer to the edge, and Arlo grips my dress, bunching the fabric in his grasp to tug me back.

"Careful, Mercy…"

Leaning forward, I look out as far as I can, but it's all just dark, black water. There's a moan, and I'm fearful again that someone needs help.

"A child might have fallen in," I rush, tugging myself from his grip as I walk to the edge of the pool.

"Mercy…"

I stop about halfway to the outer edge of the main cavern, noticing there's a path that cuts across the water. Trusting my instinct, I turn and follow it.

The farther I go, the more my light reveals—there's an arched opening up ahead where the path continues through on the left side, water flowing through into a smaller pool on the right. My pace hastens when I see the flicker of firelight emerging as I move into the alcove, growing from shadows from around a bend that cuts left up ahead.

I move slower as the light grows brighter. That odd feeling I had before washes over me—like moving through these caves at night is an intrusion.

Yet, I'm still worried someone might be hurt. It would be too easy for a child to fall in if they decided to wander at night.

So I creep ahead, and turn the corner, revealing another cavern, as large as a house. The path I'm on continues in front of me, opening into a wider expanse of bedrock that reveals a baby sleeping comfortably, tucked safely into a corner, laid on piles of soft blankets.

I'm almost certain it's Soleil, and I lift my foot to rush to her.

But then I stop abruptly when my eyes scan right.

No one has fallen in.

No one needs help.

And I have most certainly intruded where I shouldn't be.

My hand comes up to cover my mouth as I'm frozen there in surprise, stuck and staring.

The water here is shallow enough for Luna and Stefanie to

stand. It only reaches the middle of their waists, revealing both of them bare-chested and tangled in each other's arms. Luna's head falls to the side and Stefanie's lips land on her collarbone.

I should go…

I know I should turn and walk away, but I'm completely stunned by what I'm seeing.

I fully comprehend the nature of Luna and Stefanie's relationship—she made it very clear in her admission earlier, though I'd already suspected it before.

Yet it still stuns me to stumble upon this intimate moment despite the debauchery I've been privy to from my four years of service. I've never seen a domestic be physically intimate in any way before, let alone like *this*—domestics are meant to be modest and humble.

Though I know that's not all they are.

After all, I was never what they wanted me to be.

I need to step away quietly, go back the way I came and walk away…But a twinge of curiosity gets the better of me, and for just a few moments, I watch.

I'm not sure how I ought to feel seeing two women together this way, but I feel a little in awe of this moment. They're entirely lost to each other, unaware of my presence, and that's something I'm familiar with. It's the same way I get so lost in Arlo when he loves me in that physical way.

A trace of desire whispers low in my belly, and that feels wrong. Shame quickly rises, threatening to take hold of me, but then that feels good, too. Ember Glen gave me that shame, and my mind somehow knows it shouldn't exist.

Why should I feel shame witnessing beauty from love when I feel none witnessing beauty from nature?

I can lie in the meadow among the wildflowers and watch the stars at night, feeling a different kind of pleasure and warmth at the beauty that surrounds me, leaving me in awe. Witnessing the love they share is no different.

I give myself permission to let go of the shame because I understand that the desire I suddenly feel isn't desire for them—it's desire to feel the way they're feeling, to have the touch of the person I love, and share pleasure with him.

I should go.

They don't want to be seen.

I take slow, careful steps backward, though my eyes are still fixed on the scene. I watch them kiss and touch, I see the way they hold each other. I watch for moments too long and witness the shift from slow exploration to urgent pleasure-seeking...

And every second of it is beautiful.

I'm intruding.

I force myself to turn and softly pad back along the path the way I came. I'm surprised Arlo isn't already right behind me, surprised still when I don't crash into him along the path across the water in the main cavern. As I near the end, I see him standing there, waiting in the dark for me to return to him.

He looks at me quizzically as I hasten my pace, reach out to snatch his right hand, and drag him with me as I move away from the pool, back toward the passage we came through.

"What did you—"

"Quiet."

I don't speak a single word until we've crossed the main cavern and entered the dark tunnel.

"Are we being polite, then?" he asks. "Waiting until morning?"

"Yes," I whisper.

I stop abruptly, turning to look behind me, as I'm suddenly so flustered that I can't remember if we turned left or right.

"To the left," he says, and I pause to meet his eyes. "Are you all right? Did you see something?"

My face heats. "It was nothing. You should be resting, anyway."

He inclines his head. "If there's something I need to know—"

"Trust me, you don't want to know about it."

"And now that you've said that, I'm certain I *must* know." He takes a step toward me. "Tell me."

"Don't press, Arlo."

As if in direct defiance, he presses forward, moving me backward until I collide with solid rock against my spine. "It's in my nature to press, especially with you." He plucks a short strand of hair that hangs in front of my cheek, dragging his finger slowly down. His body kisses mine in a manner that's achingly indecent—he takes the trace of desire and magnifies it until I feel it through my entire body.

"Tell me, starlight."

The way I always ache for him…

How does he do that?

I lift my hands to his chest as he leans in and pins me in place before kissing my cheek. He sighs as he slips his one uninjured arm around me, splaying his fingers over the small of my back. "Why is every part of you so tempting? So distracting? Sweet sin, I want you so much…but I don't think I have the strength right now."

"You don't, and you shouldn't."

I wish he did.

I wish he could.

"If you saw something sobering, Mercy Madness, now would be the time to share."

I swallow both my desire for him and my apprehension for telling him what I saw. And then I tell him, anyway. "I saw your sister…"

"Luna?"

"And Stefanie. In the water."

He pulls back slightly and looks at me, perplexed.

"They were sharing an intimate moment."

"What do you mean?" He looks genuinely confused, and for some reason, that amuses me.

"Arlo…" I grin at his continued confusion, "surely I don't need to put two and two together for you. They were seeking pleasure together."

His brow furrows, and though the confusion fades from his features, a serious consideration of what this means filters him instead.

"Are you upset?" I ask.

"I'm…not sure."

"What do you feel?"

"Conflicted."

"What is there to be conflicted about, love? They care deeply for one another. They share a passion for each other, similar to what you and I share. Shouldn't they be able to indulge as we do without judgment?"

"Everything I've been told my entire life has led me to believe that it's wrong for a domestic woman to seek pleasure, and least of all, with another woman. It's sin—"

"According to the documents of God's word written by men. Documents we've never seen, and documents that probably don't even exist."

"I understand, Mercy. I know. Give me some grace." All at once, his hold on me loosens, he steps back, and turns away. His hand scrubs over his beard when he faces me again. "My mind is… it's my greatest enemy now, and everything is changing so quickly." His voice is pained. The strain of conflict and confusion pulls at his features, so I remain quiet and let him speak.

"I was one of the Control. I was a man of God in all manner of speaking, and I learned to be faithful to the Edict. I know it's all wrong now. It *has* to be wrong, because I'm fated to be yours. I will *always* be yours. That's a simple truth I know in my soul that can't be refuted or denied, even if the Edict says we don't belong together.

"But knowing what's true doesn't help my mind escape the conditioning any easier. I cannot help that there's a voice in my mind that rushes to judgment of my sister's choice, even though I know it's hypocritical of me to pass judgment on anyone now."

He glances down with a shake of his head. "She's my *sister*. I've always cared for her; I've always wanted her to be happy. If Stefanie makes her happy, then I accept it. Deep down, I know that's all I feel about it. Acceptance. Just a fact about her life. But that *voice*…"

I step forward, laying my hands at the sides of his waist.

"That voice keeps trying to sway me, and I fear it will always be there. I'm fighting to silence it. I promise that I am." He bends to press his forehead to mine, reaching out to cradle my cheeks. "Please be patient with me, even though I know I don't deserve it."

"I have patience for you, Arlo." I hug myself against him, careful to avoid the wounds on his back. His arms close around me, and I let out a long-held breath. "I know the voice…I still hear it sometimes, too."

"Do you?"

"Yes. I think we all do, and I think we all *will*. I think it's always going to be there. Our minds don't always tell us the truth, not at first. Sometimes they tell us what we need to hear to protect ourselves. Even when that old, small voice has to tell us a lie for self-preservation's sake."

"But you learned to ignore it, didn't you? How?"

"Truthfully, I'm still learning. It's there sometimes, telling me that I'm wrong, that I'm a sinner, that I should feel ashamed for what I've done and who I've become. And sometimes I feel the shame for becoming the woman I am."

Admitting that out loud nearly brings me to tears—something I hadn't expected—and I bury my face in his chest.

"That kills me, Mercy. Knowing that is more painful than

any physical wound. The voice of your shame is…it's *mine*. It's *my* voice you hear whispering in your mind, isn't it?" He squeezes me as though his loving embrace could put me back together, as if it will mend all the pieces of my heart and soul that he played a role in breaking.

Arlo has hurt me in so many ways.

It's a fact that can't be denied.

It's a fact that demands to be acknowledged.

"I've laid so much guilt upon you," he continues. "I've called you a sinner more times than I can count. I've told you it was all your fault, that you deserved the punishment of the trials, that you deserved to *die* for your sins…"

He releases me and paces away, leaving me so abruptly that it feels as though he's sucked my soul from my body and has taken it with him. I pause for a quiet moment and watch him stop a few feet away with his back turned to me.

"The voice is my own," I tell him gently. "At least, it sounds like my own voice. I know it's not really mine, but Arlo, I know it's not yours, either. It can't be because we both know that the words you spoke to me in judgment didn't really belong to you, either."

Arlo turns to face me.

"That voice," I continue, "the one that sounds like your own, the one they try to make you believe is your conscience, or the voice of God trying to lead you down the right path, the voice that brings you shame…That voice wasn't born with you; it was created.

"They put these so-called morals in our minds, told us what was right and wrong to believe before ever giving us a chance to figure it out on our own. And it's why we feel such shame with that voice, because it isn't *ours*. It doesn't match the truth that we know in our souls.

"We feel shame for not being true to ourselves, and fear for our disobedience against the voice all at once. It's troubling. I've felt troubled all my life. And I'm willing to bet there is no person in all of Ember Glen who can say they haven't felt the same."

His chest rises as he takes in a deep breath, then lets it out heavily in a rush of relief that I can feel as it leaves him. He hurries to close the distance between us, touching his forehead to mine the way he always does as he pulls me into his arms.

"Mercy Madness," he whispers my name with a sense of honor and pride. "I'm in awe of you…perplexed by the way your curious, brilliant mind works, and completely, *madly* in love with you."

chapter twenty-three
Mercy

"BEFORE WE SHOW you the real story of Ember Glen, I think we should tell you how we found this place," Luna says.

Arlo and I waited the night to find Luna and Stefanie again, but now that the sun has risen, we've made our way back to the hidden space with all the plastic bins and the projector.

Stefanie brought more pillows back with her, which she drops on the ground, then glances up. "You might want to sit."

Her expression tells me I should take her seriously, so I do, lowering to sit on a small, square throw pillow. I'm about to order Arlo to do the same, given how weak he is from his injuries, but he has the good sense on his own to sit beside me this time, probably wanting to avoid another fainting spell.

Luna hands Soleil—who's sound asleep—to Stefanie. She brings the baby against her chest to snuggle her close with a soft smile, appearing as natural with her as Luna.

A few feet in front of me, Luna bends to snap open the lid of one of the plastic bins on the floor, setting the lid aside. She doesn't take anything out of it. She straightens and looks at me, wringing her hands together in front of her.

"I feel like we owe you an apology, Mercy." She bites her lip as her eyebrows knit together.

"For what?"

"Your father's home—*your* home—was left behind, empty, when you were first taken to the Homestead for the Trials of Dissension. When Stefanie and I found out that Hyatt had…that he'd set a servant on fire during service, we were horrified. He'd done a lot of terrible things, but setting someone on fire…?" Her face scrunches with disgust. "How evil must his soul be to have such an impulse?"

"Anyway," her eyes cast downward, "I was scared for her, and of course, she was terrified of him. We both…Well, we needed to find some comfort. We needed to be with each other. We needed time together, in a safe place, to take care of one another."

Luna glances back at Stefanie, who gently sways with Soleil in her arms. She briefly meets Luna's gaze before Luna turns back to face us with a tense grin.

"We knew that your house was empty, unwatched. We went there to be together, and Mercy," she sighs, placing a palm over her heart, "we were finally free in your home. We could finally love each other without fear. We only meant to meet there once, but then we just kept going back. I'm sorry. We used your home without your permission to *be* with each other. And with everything you were going through—"

"Stop." I gently lift my palm. "Luna, it's okay. You don't need to apologize. I'm not upset."

"You're not?"

"No. For all that you've done—finding this place, bringing the children here to safety, bringing domestics together in rebellion— how could I be upset? I understand the need for comfort, especially when you're going through hell."

I glance down as I rub my palms over the velvet soft fabric of my red gown, suddenly wondering if it would be worth the risk of going back through the secret space to my father's home to find something black instead. I want to wear black for my sisters, for Ellary…

No, no, no. Don't think of Ellary.

I draw in a cleansing breath and lift my head. "When Arlo and I stopped hating one another and started to find love, it was all I wanted—finding comfort in his arms, being alone with him every moment I could before death found me." I glance between them. "I understand the need. No apologies are owed."

Luna drops to her knees and reaches out, dragging me into a hug. "Thank you. I didn't know I needed to hear that, but I did. I felt so awful."

I already have a deep fondness for Luna. Her natural kindness and concern for others are so genuine, so endearing. She's a lot like Ellary in that way.

Stop…

My breath stutters as I fight rising tears, and I quickly grip Luna's shoulders to push her away. Heartache looms behind my appreciation of Luna's kind nature. Holding her at arm's length, I grant her a smile, hoping she doesn't see the tears glassing over my eyes.

"So," I redirect, hoping I don't sound entirely depressed, "you and Stefanie were meeting at my house. But how on earth did you find the way here? I've cleaned those floors a million times, and I never noticed anything that would ever make me think I should try prying up a floorboard."

Luna smiles, and for a moment, it brightens the shadowed space. "Of course. Who would think to do that?"

She pushes to her feet again, turning to pace away. She reaches into the bin she'd opened before and pulls out a black leather journal, bound by a black leather strap.

"What is that?"

Luna looks at it with a conflicted expression, etched with pain as she draws her fingers down the front cover. "We didn't know what it was at first…Odd scribblings, ranting and rambling passages that were difficult to read, and none of it really made any sense. There's a list of names at the front, and it's actually where I saw the name Soleil." She glances back at Stefanie and smiles at her baby.

"The rest of its contents didn't make sense to us when we first found it, and it wouldn't have made sense to your father, either. He couldn't have known what it was; you should know that. But when we found out…" She grips it in one hand and holds it out to me. "This is the Impulse Edict."

I look over at Arlo, and our eyes lock in shared confusion, apprehension, anticipation, and outrage. I tear my gaze from his to look at the journal, hesitating for a beat in knowing that everything is about to change.

Luna must be wrong.

The Elders are supposed to be the keepers of the Impulse Edict—the only ones who have access to it and know the laws of God.

Slowly, I reach out, grip the journal, and take it from Luna. I hold it and stare, running a finger over the leather cord that secures it shut.

"We were in your house one night, and there was something I wanted to write down before I forgot it." Luna chuckles a little. "Actually, I did forget it. We were trying to find some parchment and a pen when I went into your father's room. I sat on the bed and pulled open the drawer on the nightstand."

My head snaps up.

I'd found my mother's journal in the nightstand drawer beside his bed.

"It was empty," Luna says, and my forehead creases in confusion. "At least, I *thought* it was empty. I was about to close it when I saw what looked like the corner of a page sticking up through the bottom. I was only able to tug it out about halfway, and I could see it looked like a letter or a journal entry that someone had written. I actually thought that if it was something from your father, then maybe I could find a way to get it to you; though, of course, that was a foolish thought. Still, it seemed important, so I called Stefanie in to help."

"We couldn't pull the page out." Stefanie speaks in a hushed tone, mindful not to raise her voice too loud over the sleeping baby against her chest. "I didn't want to risk tearing it, so I figured I'd try prying up the bottom of the drawer so we could pull it out carefully. It was surprisingly easy because it was meant to be pulled out—the drawer had a false bottom."

"That's where we found this." Luna points at the journal in my hands. "The page that was peeking out must have been from a different journal, though—it was smaller and a slightly different color. There were two other pages with it, all laying on top of the journal."

"There were three? Three torn pages?" I frantically look at Arlo.

"Mercy found her mother's journal in that drawer after her father died," Arlo explains. "She'd never seen it before then, like perhaps her father had left it for her to find? Three pages were torn from it, though…missing."

"Oh." Luna's head tilts, giving us a quizzical look. "I'm surprised by that."

Stefanie shares the same expression. "So am I. It seemed clear that he meant for you to find those pages."

"Eventually, at least," Luna adds.

"You read them?" I ask. "What do they say?"

Luna nods at the black journal in my hands. "I tucked the pages inside the cover. Open it."

My heart races as I eagerly uncoil the leather cord, impatient to see what's written on the three pages—equally nervous that I may learn something I wish I hadn't. I lift the black leather cover to open the journal, and there they are…

Three torn pages, the same size and color as the pages of my mother's journal. I let out a breath as I stare down at the page on top, my eyes unfocused as I search for courage to move boldly forward. I search for the courage to read them and learn the truth I've been searching for my entire life.

"What do they say?" Arlo nudges.

I turn my head to stare into his blue eyes, knowing I'll find strength I can borrow from him—and I do find it. Then I look down at the journal placed on my lap.

With trembling hands, I slip my fingers beneath the three pages and lift them from the journal, easily recognizing my father's handwriting.

I steel myself and read the words of the first page aloud.

Buried beneath Ember Glen,
secrets below soil found in corridors of stone.

Tunnels weave through layers of hell,
from mountain to mountain,
forest to forest,
and into the great beyond.

Beyond…the place where fabled hostility still reigns.
Yet, it reigns no longer.
Peace was won.
Though we are lost in Ember Glen.

Hostages.
Captives.
Unwilling savages.

Everything is buried.
The truth is beneath us.
The only way out of hell is through.

Dig.
Burrow.
Bury yourself alive.

Seek hell beneath your feet,
and should the demons show you mercy,
you'll find the path to the truth.

Peace.
Harmony.
Freedom.

It's all beyond…

Copied from the "lost" journals of E.K. and T.W.

My eyes narrow, fixed on the page. "I don't think I understand…"

"Neither did we," Luna says. "At least, not at first. Flip it over."

I glance up at her briefly and she gives me a nod. I turn the page and look at the other side. There are a few lines of text at the top, still in my father's handwriting.

It's right in front of you…the way to hell.
Lift the rug.
Pry the floorboard.

A crude map is drawn beneath the lines of text my father wrote. I stare at it as Arlo moves closer to view it with me. He seems to work it out almost immediately.

"This shows the way we came," he says. "The tunnel we crawled through," he reaches out to trace the path with his finger, "the passages we followed. And here's the main cavern where the water is."

I nod, starting to see the familiarity of it as he draws along the corridors, and the strange verse of text on the front of the page begins to make sense...

Buried beneath Ember Glen,
secrets below soil found in corridors of stone.

"These are the passages we took to get here, and this," he circles a spot with the tip of his finger, "is the alcove we came through on the other side of this room."

"It took us longer than it should have to figure out that we needed to move the boulder," Luna says with a grin.

On the map, it appears that the corridor we traveled to get to this room extends past the alcove, branching off into several different paths. And those paths branch off into even more before the page comes to an end.

It appears similarly on the other side of the page, paths extending out from the opposite side of the main cavern—tunnels leading to more tunnels that end with the paper's edge. And my father scribbled a note in the blank space between lines that outline a path, at the spot where one path diverges into three.

The way out?

"The way out?" I speak his words aloud, glancing up at Arlo, then looking at Luna and Stefanie. "What does that mean? The way out...of Ember Glen?"

"We think so, maybe. But that page is the only map we've found. Those paths can lead anywhere. They can be dead ends, or they can extend for miles. It would be so easy to get lost if you didn't know exactly where you were going. I think your father was trying to figure it out, or at least, leave behind enough information for you to do it."

I blink at her, my lips parted because I want to say something, I just don't know what.

"But over here," Arlo says, and I glance down to see him point to a spot on the map that's closer to where we are on this side of the cavern. Another note is scribbled where the path diverges.

Homestead?

"I wondered…" Arlo looks over at me. "I've been thinking perhaps these caves connected with the ones under the Homestead."

"You knew about these caves?" Stefanie asks with an accusatorial air.

Arlo meets her gaze directly. "There are caves under the Homestead, and I knew about those. Theo and I took Mercy and Delle there to prepare for the trials because it gave us privacy. I've been exploring them carefully for two years since the last Shift when I became one of the Control. All the Control know they exist, but mostly, they don't seem to care. I might be the only one who's done any exploring down there." He nods, turning his attention back to the map. "It makes sense that it's all connected."

"I don't understand. Why would my father be trying to find a way out? And who are," I pause to flip the page back over, then read the last line aloud, "Copied from the lost journals of E.K. and T.W. Who are E.K. and T.W.?"

Luna shrugs. "We don't know."

"E.K.…" Arlo mutters, and then his face tenses with recollection. "Ethan Kaine?" His head snaps up with recognition. "It's Ethan Kaine and Tucker Whitler. I recognize the names from the record of the Control." He looks at me pointedly. "Do you remember what we talked about the morning after the last service, when your hand was burned and I had you take the medication before we went to deliver the news of Hyatt's death to Stefanie?"

"Vaguely…bits and pieces, I suppose. I was so high on that little white pill you gave me."

"We talked about the three pages torn from your mother's journal. One of them was torn out right after a passage that told of the strange and untimely deaths of two members of the Control when your grandmother was a child."

"Right," I nod, "I remember that. The deaths occurred only days apart, and the Control and the Elders had just labeled them as tragic mysteries."

He nods. "Yes. I never told you this, but while you were healing from your burns, I went to the Control's library on the third floor of the Homestead and did some research. I looked back through the records denoting all previous and current members of the Control and the Elders, dating back from the very beginning. Ethan Kaine and Tucker Whitley were both listed as deceased in the same year. It was…twenty-one forty, maybe forty-one?"

I quickly do the math in my head. "That would've been around the time my grandmother was a child. That could be who she was talking about."

"It makes sense," Arlo agrees. "If they were on to the secrets being kept—if they knew about the caves and that maybe there was a way out of Ember Glen—then it wouldn't surprise me at all to learn the Elders had orchestrated their deaths."

"Wasn't that…" Stefanie starts, then stops, eyes turning up toward the ceiling in thought before a realization changes her expression. "That would have been when the last Trials of Dissension were held. Forty-five years ago, right?"

"Yes, I think that's right," Arlo confirms. "So, during the last trials, two members of the Control learned things the Elders didn't want them to know, and they had them killed. This," he points at the page, "could be the only remaining record of the secrets they learned."

"It's not…" Luna's voice is soft.

Arlo and I both look at her.

"It may be the only record of what *they* documented," Luna says, "but what was copied on that page led us to this room. And this room holds a history of Ember Glen that's…"

"Disgusting," Stefanie finishes for her. "The history of Ember Glen is disgusting."

chapter twenty-four

ARLO

THE HISTORY OF *Ember Glen is disgusting?*

"Mercy, I think you should read the next two pages," Luna says gently. "It's a letter…from your father."

Mercy blinks, tearing her eyes away from me to look down at the pages in her hands. She seems to hesitate, as though the idea of knowing more is painful.

"Do you want me to read it?" I offer.

Her head turns in my direction, her face blank, lost, overwhelmed. But then she nods. She lifts the pages and hands them to me, fixing her eyes on my face as I take the first page from the pile of three and set it aside. Quickly turning them over, then back again, I see with a glance that these two pages are filled with text—a complete letter from her father.

I give Mercy a cursory glance, lifting my eyebrows to ask if she's ready. She responds with a quick bob of her head, watching me as I read the letter out loud.

My dear Mercy,

I don't know how to begin this letter. I suppose I should start by telling you that I'm a coward. I didn't have the courage to tell you what I was doing, that something had been eating away at my mind since your mother died. I didn't have the courage to confess all the ways I failed you as a father, though

I'm certain you're aware of them all the same.

I'm the reason your mother is dead.

The guilt of that has chipped away at my sanity since she died, and I think it's what has slowly been killing me.

I need you to understand something; I was in love with your mother. I loved her from the moment we were married. I thought she and I were divinely blessed in our assigned domestic partnership. I confessed my love to her when you were only three years old, and she denied that she felt the same. I thought in time she would come to see what I knew— that God had blessed us. But as you'll know by now, having read your mother's journal, she would never come around.

She eventually entangled herself with someone else.
Another woman.
They'd been sinning in secret.

I reported her indiscretions to the Control when I lost myself to a jealous rage. And Mercy, please know that I have regretted it every moment of every day since. Had I understood then what I understand now, I would have loved her better. I would have helped her find a way to be with the woman she loved, if only to make her happy.

Instead, I sentenced her to die. I took her away from you. I forced you to live a life without Mira Madness, and I can say from experience that a life without her is misery.

I am so sorry.

I thought it was the right thing to do when I made the choice, but since the day I stood and watched her go up in flames, my relationship with God has changed. It's been gradual, so slight that I didn't even notice the changes happening myself. I didn't dare speak of them with you. I didn't know your mind, and that's my own fault. I was not the father I should have been.

But now, in my final hours, none of it matters. I have been so sick lately, and I feel the end is coming. I wish I were brave enough to give you this face to face, but I'm not. I just hope you find this before the Control does.

I found the journal entries of E.K. and T.W. a few years before you started service. It was in a box of books that had been taken during a raid by the Control—books that were meant to be destroyed. I couldn't just take the journal—they'd already catalogued all the books and were taking inventory before throwing them in the flames.

I'd been carrying your mother's journal with me everywhere back then. I was always afraid it would be found if I left it behind. Even as I write that, I'm not sure I can say exactly what I was afraid of…only that I was afraid. It was all I had on me, so I flipped to the first blank page I could find, and quickly copied the text and map into her journal.

I didn't understand what it was a map of, and it took me forever to figure out the text. But once I did, I began chipping away at the stone beneath our feet, and I've been chiseling into the ground for years…burying myself alive to find my way to hell.

I became ill before I could explore much beyond the map for myself, but I can proudly say that I finished cutting the way through for you. Hopefully, the tunnels will lead to somewhere special, somewhere new…perhaps to freedom.

You were not born to be a servant of men, Mercy.
You were born for something more.

The nearer I come to death, the more vividly I see you—your compassion, your strength, your unyielding nature…You are so, so much like your wonderful mother.

And so I leave you with this, hoping your curiosity leads you beneath the surface, and you find what I couldn't…I hope you find the path to truth.

I love you, Mercy.

I watch Mercy as I lower the pages. Her silvery-blue eyes are unfocused, looking off into the distance.

"I…I don't understand," she whispers.

Luna crouches in front of her. "Your father dug beneath your home. He chiseled through stone to make the tunnel we crawled through. He cut the way through to these passageways. This is where the *tunnels weave through layers of hell, from mountain to mountain, forest to forest, and into the great beyond,*" she quotes from the secret message left by E.K. and T.W.

"I can't believe this," Mercy says slowly. "I can't believe *him*. Why didn't he bring me here before he died? Why didn't he just *tell* me?"

Luna shrugs, glancing at me for help in responding, but I have no response that will offer Mercy any comfort. I can already feel the electric current of anger flowing through her, making the hairs on the back of my arms stand up.

Mercy's voice is quiet, but the tone of resentment is clear. "He could have brought me down here. He could have protected me, kept me hidden away so I wouldn't have to serve," she huffs and her expression twists, the anger clear through her slanted eyebrows.

She tears the pages from my hand. "Why bother to write me a damn letter just to remind me that he's the reason my mother is dead? That he's a coward who can't stand face to face with me and speak his truth? I don't *want* this." She balls up the letter and tosses it aside.

I'm hesitant to speak against her anger because it's fully justified, and I understand it. But I also think I understand her father. Though I don't care to defend a man I didn't know—a man who has clearly hurt Mercy so deeply—I want to service her compassion. She's at her best, her strongest, when her empathy is triggered, and I have a feeling this is only the tip of the iceberg.

She's going to need her strength.

"I agree; he was a coward," I tell her calmly. "He even admitted as much himself. But I think he was also afraid. You understand what fear does to you, Mercy. You were so afraid that you served for four years while hiding your dissenting thoughts. You had to in order to survive."

Her head snaps in my direction, as does her voice. "Don't you *dare* speak to me about the things I had to do in service. My father was too afraid to speak to his daughter; I was afraid for my *life*. It's not the same thing, Arlo Rainn, and you know it."

"You're right," I concede. "But so am I. Fear is the same for everyone, Mercy. When fear finds you, it takes control of you. It clouds your judgment. It doesn't matter what the fear is from, whether it's from a threat that's real or a threat that's perceived. It alters your decision making.

"Your father made a terrible choice to hide this from you, only hoping you would find it. By all accounts, you, me, and Stefanie should be dead right now, and those pages should still be hidden in the false bottom of that drawer, trapped there forever, never to be found.

"I'm angry at him, too. I'm furious that he hid this from you. He *is* a coward for avoiding you, but he had at least one moment of clarity. He had just enough courage, for just long enough to write the words on paper…and that may be an even more courageous feat than speaking.

"Writing requires bravery. It requires acceptance that your thoughts are printed eternally, acceptance that whether you're right or wrong, your words might be read by anyone at any time—perceived and accepted for what they are, or twisted and used against you in judgment.

"And you must see that your judgment of your father is also a judgment you hold over *me*. I was a coward, the same as he was. I have to accept that, and I do. I was too afraid of my feelings for you when they were first forming. I couldn't say them to you, so instead, I wrote them down. I never intended for you to find the poetry you inspired, but I always knew it was possible. It took me a very long time to find the courage to give you those pages.

"Perhaps," I pause to collect myself as I process my own truth, "perhaps it's time for you to recognize that you are gifted with more courage and strength than any of the rest of us could ever hope to have."

"I don't want to be strong," Mercy whispers, and saying the words brings tears to her eyes. "I don't want to be brave. I just want to be…I don't know. I just want to be angry."

She starts to cry, and it guts me. I put my arm around her, but she shrugs me off.

"No. Please, just let me be angry." She looks at Luna. "Tell me the truth about Ember Glen and let me be angry at someone other than my father."

Luna seems to hesitate. "Maybe this is too much all at once. Maybe we should wait—"

"*No.* No more waiting, no more delays. I want to know about vicious circle. I want the real story of everything, and I want it *now*."

"Okay." Luna nods, slowly rising to her feet before she turns and goes back to the open bin. She reaches in and pulls out a video reel for the projector. "A lot of archived videos seem to be stored in these bins—hours upon hours of them—but we only need to show you five of them for you to see the truth." Luna pauses, then asks, "Are you sure you're ready?"

Mercy nods. "Yes."

Luna moves toward the projector to set up the first reel. "Then I'll let the footage speak for itself."

video record one
instigation

March 31, 2032
One Year Before the War

THE REEL BEGINS with a black screen. White text fades into the upper left corner to reveal the video has been catalogued with a title and a date, this one is revealed to be 'Instigation' on March thirty-first, twenty thirty-two.

The video begins to play with a flurry of noise—a large crowd cheering with loud music in the background. The visual is confined to the shape of a rectangle in the center of the screen, the longer edges running from the top to the bottom. There's a brief flash of text to indicate the video was recorded on the personal cellular phone device of someone named Violet Clare.

A throng of people are packed together in an outdoor space, continually moving, swaying, and dancing to loud music being played by a group of people on stage. It's nighttime, and bright overhead lights artificially illuminate the space. Many of the people raise their hands and cheer, singing along with the song that must be familiar to them.

The recording device is clearly held in the recorder's hand—Violet Clare. Violet's voice—clearly the voice of a happy young woman—is the loudest as they cheer and sing along.

Violet pans the crowd with her device as she sings out of tune. A couple of rows ahead of her is a woman with both arms raised, her right arm adorned with bangles and bracelets. But more notably are the two solid black lines encircling her forearm. The tattooed bands are about two inches apart.

"Hey, hey!" Violet shouts with excitement, her voice loud near the microphone of her device. "Vicious Circle!"

"Oh! Where?" asks another female voice nearby.

"Over there!" Violet's left arm stretches out to point, and we see a glimpse of the same two-banded black tattoo on her forearm. "Vicious Circle!"

The woman with the bangles turns her head over her shoulder, and when she spots Violet recording from rows behind her, she smiles.

She can't be heard over the crowd and the music, but her mouth moves and it appears as though she shouts, "Vicious Circle!" as emphatically as Violet had while waving her left arm.

She taps the shoulder of another woman standing beside her, and that woman looks back. They look friendly in a way that might suggest they see someone they know, though it doesn't seem Violet knows them.

The women being recorded both raise their left arms, revealing that both of them have the same tattoo. Violet and what sounds like three or four other loud female voices beside her all scream excitedly, having found a common bond with strangers.

There's a clear sense of camaraderie.

Violet pans her device to record the people next to her, scanning across the faces of six women to her left that wave and cheer, or sing dramatically along to the song being played on stage. It's clear they're all friends who are attending this concert together, and when they move their arms, we can see they also have the same tattoo.

"Hey!" a male voice from somewhere behind Violet bellows,

and she must whirl around to face him with the way the recording spins with her. A man with anger etched on his features stands closer to Violet than he needs to be. There's a close-up of his face, showing his dark eyes and light hair. "Cover that up or put your fucking arm down. No one wants that VC bullshit here."

"Excuse me?" Violet says from behind her device, an attitude of annoyance detected in her voice.

"I said, put your *fucking* arm down."

"No. Fuck off."

"Fucking bitch."

"What did you just call me?"

"I said, you're a *fucking bitch*. Is it too hard to hear me over the music, dollface?" He raises his voice. "All of you are *fucking bitches*, and your little *Vicious Circle* camaraderie is dumb as fuck."

"Do you realize I'm recording you?"

"I don't give a shit. Record me." The man moves into her space, and the recording shakes as Violet is forced backward.

"Get your—hey!" Violet shouts, as other voices rise around her. "Get your hands *off* me!"

The video is a jittery blur as Violet fumbles with her device, but it all steadies when she drops it and it lands on the ground. The perspective is now that of someone lying on their back, looking up at the sky. However, the sky is merely the backdrop for a chaotic visual where several sets of hands are pushing and grabbing while contradictory shouts of protest and encouragement are flung violently through the brawl.

"Fucking trash," the angry man mutters.

Though, truthfully, with so many people speaking and shouting all at once, it's difficult to tell if the voice belongs to him or to another of the men who seem to have joined in.

"You want rights? Then act like a goddamn lady."

"Don't touch her!"

"Fuck off!"

"Where's security?"

The voice of the woman singing stops mid-chorus, and her spoken words echo through the speakers. "Hold up. Cut it, guys. Hey, cut it off…" The music stops discordantly, with individual musicians ending at different times. The disharmony lends to amplify the sounds of the fight, and the tone is unsettling. "They need help back there. Hey! Get my girls some help back there! Where's security?"

A woman's dark brown hair whips across the screen as she falls over the camera. Her feet—adorned in black, lace-up ankle boots—fly up as she's knocked sideways, landing on the concrete.

It's difficult to make out the words over the scuffle, but it sounds like "…snap your fucking arm in half right between those lines…"

A man's foot lifts over the camera, then comes down hard on the other side of it, out of sight. At the same moment, a subtle, yet harsh, sound strikes, and it's reminiscent of a twig snapping in half.

The fallen woman screams, "My arm!" The voice is easily recognizable as belonging to Violet. Her pained sobs are distressing as they echo through the recording.

Some people wearing bright yellow coats appear, moving into the middle of the brawl, and they nudge the two conflicting groups apart. One of the yellow-coats crouches toward the ground, asking Violet if she is all right..

end of video

video record two
national news

April 17, 2032

Eleven Months Before the War

THE VIDEO FILLS the entire screen, displaying two women sitting on tall chairs that are angled toward each other. The image is bright and clear, slowly zooming in as music fades out, and a red banner appears across the bottom of the screen with text that reads, "Exclusive Interview with Violet Clare."

The same white text that appeared in the first video fades in at the top left corner of the screen. This time it reveals the title as 'National News,' dated April seventeenth, twenty thirty-two.

The woman on the left side is dressed in a cream-colored blouse that's tucked into a bright red pencil skirt—and her attire matches her serious expression. Her blonde hair is styled in a perfect sweeping wave that frames her face, and her make-up is done impeccably.

"We are live in Denver today, here with an exclusive interview with Vicious Circle activist and recent alleged assault victim, Violet Clare," the blonde woman says with an even, practiced cadence to her voice. "Better known to her social media followers as Vicious Vi, she's recently garnered the attention of news outlets across the country with her video of a brawl at an outdoor concert that resulted in a broken arm for her, and broken faith in humanity for her following." She makes a show of turning to face Violet directly. "Violet, thank you for joining us today."

Violet gives the blonde woman a tight grin. "I appreciate you having me, Lindsey."

Everything about Violet's appearance is in direct contrast to Lindsey's. Violet's dark brown hair is pin-straight, stopping just at her shoulders, and her precisely trimmed bangs draw a straight line across her eyebrows.

The neon green cast on her left forearm brings out the color of her striking green eyes, which are noticeably bright against her tan skin. Aside from that, and the deep burgundy shade painted on her lips, the rest of her clothing is dark. The black T-shirt makes the perfect canvas for the bright white letters displayed across her chest.

The words *Vicious Circle* are printed in all capital white letters, and the Latin—*circulus vitiosus in aeternum*—is printed directly beneath it in lowercase cursive. Her dark jeans are faded gray and torn in spots, and she wears the same black boots she was wearing in the first video.

"Violet, your video of the assault has stirred up quite some controversy online."

"It's not exactly controversy, Lindsey. Right and wrong are clearly defined in this situation. If you want to call the online attacks launched against me and my followers since I posted that video 'controversial,' I suppose you can, but it's not the correct term. Controversy implies there's an argument to be made for each side of a debate, but I think it's pretty clear from that video what happened. My friends and I were assaulted, and that's not really up for debate."

"Hmm. It seems there's a rather significant portion of your online following that disagrees, but your stance is that their opinions don't matter. Well, I have to say, Violet, your position on this seems rather...*controversial.*" She laughs to herself, as if she believes she said something truly humorous. "So, if controversial isn't the right word to describe what's been going on, then what word would you use?"

"What word would I use to describe the cyber bullying and stalking instigated by Ian Cole and his friends? Hostile. Aggressive. Repugnant. Any of those would be better. That significant portion of my following you mentioned—the ones who seem to disagree with the *fact* that this was a bias-related assault—aren't my followers.

"I had eighty thousand engaged and respectful followers before I posted that video, and within three hours, I'd surpassed a hundred and fifteen thousand. At least half of those new followers were in *support* of Ian Cole and his friends and their assault against me and mine. He was praised for, and I quote, 'Putting a VC girl in her place.' There were thousands of new comments on nearly all of my videos, and they were hateful, disrespectful, targeted, and outright disgusting. I won't even mention the emails, phone calls, and the attempts at doxing me."

Lindsey turns her head away from Violet, looking straight out from the screen as if she's speaking to the viewers directly. "Ian Cole, the son of presidential candidate Frederik Jay Cole, has been named as the alleged perpetrator in the assault." She shifts her attention back to Violet. "Now, Violet, some have said that you're capitalizing on the attention this video has received to increase your following."

Violet shakes her head. "No, I didn't want to increase my following of misogynistic men who feel the need to be heard in situations that don't involve them. Their comments on my videos and the videos of my loyal followers have been atrocious."

Lindsey's forehead creases as she nods with a tilt of her head. "Yes, we actually have a few of those controversial comments here." She lifts her hand to indicate a screen on the wall behind Violet.

Violet turns her head to glance at the screen, but quickly snaps back to look at Lindsey. "I'd actually prefer it if we didn't show those comments. I'm not here to give a larger platform to men who hate women. I'm actually here today to talk about Vicious Cir—"

"Let's take a look at this comment," Lindsey cuts her off as a white box containing text comes up on screen.

"So sick of these VC girls and their bullshit. So concerned about their rights, but these bitches don't give a shit about men's rights."

"What's your take on that comment?" Lindsey's voice can be heard, though all that we see is the comment on the screen.

"What's my…I'm sorry, did you just ask me what my *take* is? Can you even show those words on the news?"

"This is a privately operated news station."

After an unusually lengthy pause, Violet speaks again. "Okay, then, my *take,* Lindsey, is that men like that commenter are so privileged that they've lost their ability to empathize with the female experience in this country, especially over the last decade, where our rights have been so subtly stripped that most women don't even realize it's happening.

"It started with our right to access appropriate health care, our right to make decisions about our own bodies, and these changes have been happening ever since. Just last week, the federal government introduced a bill that makes it *legal* for employers to require female applicants to sign a disclosure as a part of their application, stating whether they plan to get pregnant in the first five years on the job. And if they get hired, and become pregnant within those first five years, the company has full rights to *terminate* her employment without cause."

"Wouldn't most of those women be planning on taking a maternity leave, anyway?"

Violet's eyes widen, gaping at Lindsey. "Is that a serious question?"

"Well, wouldn't they?"

Violet blinks. "Sure, Lindsey. Sometimes, when women get pregnant, they take maternity leave. But typically, they value the right to take that leave by choice—maybe even with pay—and *certainly* with the option to return to their jobs. Instead, they're being punished for having a uterus."

Lindsey leans in as her head inclines. "So, you view this bill to be…what? Detrimental? Wouldn't you agree that employers have a right to know that information when making hiring decisions?"

"*No.*" Violet glances around, her gaze stopping straight ahead, as though she's looking straight out through the screen. "Is this a joke? Really, is this a prank show?"

Lindsey chuckles. "I assure you it's not, Violet."

"Then let me be clear; the proposed bill is most certainly detrim—"

"Let's take a look at another comment," Lindsey cuts her off again.

"VC girls should all have their arms snapped right between the lines tattooed on their precious little arms. Nice work, Ian C."

There's a long beat of silence, then Lindsey says, "Give us your take on this one, Violet."

Violet glances down at the neon green cast on her left forearm, then with a hard expression, she simply says, "No."

Another pause.

"Okay, then let's take a look at this one."

The comment on screen fades out and a new block of text appears.

"These sluts couldn't even come up with their own name. You

know who did? A man. So fucking dumb. Next time you open your mouth, you'd better be on your knees so I can shut you up, Violet Clare."

"Are you kidding me?"

"Now, this has always been a controversial point of discussion surrounding the Vicious Circle, hasn't it? What's your take on this?"

Violet sighs, leaning her elbow on the wooden armrest of her chair. "You keep asking me about my *take* on these hateful comments, Lindsey, but I guess I'd like to hear *yours*. Given the shocking manner in which you skipped over this man's flagrant insinuation that he'd like to 'shut me up' with a non-consensual sexual act, I'd like to know…Is there a take on rude comments from hateful men that *isn't* absolute disgust?"

Lindsey leans her elbow on her armrest, then delicately places her fingers beneath her chin. "You seem angry, Violet."

Violet's face scrunches as she tilts her head with a sarcastic expression. "Do I?"

Lindsey gives Violet an inquisitive look and waits for her to respond. When she doesn't, Lindsey continues, "Is the commenter correct about the source of the name for your activist group, Vicious Circle? Did a man come up with it?"

Violet huffs, "Fine, let's talk about the name if it will steer us back in the right direction, because frankly, I'm not a big fan of the direction we're heading here, Linds. When my girlfriends and I—"

"*Girlfriends*…Can you clarify what you mean by that? It's often been speculated that all the women who support Vicious Circle are lesbians."

Violet claps her hands together, leaning even closer to Lindsey and looking at her sideways. "Do you think I'm a lesbian? Is that a question you'd like to ask me?"

"I'm certain our viewers would like to know."

Violet bobs her head with a look of disbelief, sitting forward and looking directly at the viewers. "Viewers, let me be very clear about this. *My* sexual orientation is irrelevant; the sexual orientation of the women who've chosen to associate themselves with the Vicious Circle is irrelevant. Our activist group celebrates all sexual orientations and preferences, or the lack thereof, and that's all I'm saying on the subject."

"Could you—"

Violet sits back, turning to look at Lindsey. "That's all I'm saying on the subject. Now if you'll allow me to speak…"

Violet waits for a cue from Lindsey, or to see if she'll cut her off again. When Lindsey doesn't speak, Violet goes on, "As I was saying…When my *girlfriends* and I started protesting together nearly a decade ago, we had no intention of forming an activist group for women's rights. We just wanted to bring awareness in honor of our friend Kendra, who died well before she should have at only eighteen-years-old.

"She died because the teaching assistant in her freshman biology class decided that he wanted her, and she didn't have the right to tell him no. She died because that man just couldn't control himself, because he decided to follow her home from class and insist that she say *yes*. And when his insistence was still met with her refusal, he beat her, raped her, and left her bleeding beside the dumpster behind our dorm…in broad daylight.

"My friends and I were heartbroken, but we wanted to take action because accepting what happened to her was unfathomable. So we went to a women's rights protest because that's what our safety boils down to—men's perception of whether women *should* have rights. The right to safety, the right to bodily autonomy, the right to say *no*."

Violet pauses, and miraculously, she isn't interrupted by Lindsey. "Anyway, the name came from the first protest we went to after Kendra's death. While we were preparing, we were trying to think of a way to honor her at the event. We were talking about her and who she was, and remembered the way she always had two elastic hair bands on her arm—always two, and always black. She would joke it was because she always wanted to be ready to throw her hair up and get in a fight to defend one of us."

Violet gives a small smile, lost in her story. "Really, it was just because she was always too warm to keep her hair down for long, and she had very thick hair, so the ties were always breaking. But we couldn't think of Kendra without those two black bands around her arm.

"One of my friends got the idea that we should all wear two elastic bands as our way of remembering her at the protest, and we did. At the end of the event, they had a moment of silence, and we didn't plan it, but me and the six other girls found ourselves forming a circle together, our arms wrapped around each other in comfort.

"Kendra's death was still so fresh, so raw then, and I don't even know why…I just felt compelled to reach out to her. Like I wanted to show her the bands on my arm so she'd know I'd always remember her. So I reached my arm straight up toward heaven, and before long, the rest of the circle did, too. The photo that was taken of that moment is what started it all."

A photo fades in to fill the screen. A circle of seven women together on a city street as dusk falls, a traffic light shining red nearby. A crowd of mostly women fills the background, but they're blurred. The focal point is clear—the circle of young women, all wearing matching pale pink windbreakers. Their left arms are all raised, their fingers splayed, and each arm is adorned with two black bands outside the long sleeves of their matching jackets.

"It was a really powerful moment for us. After that, we started going to every protest, every activist event for women's rights." The photo fades as Violet speaks, returning to the view of her and Lindsey sitting on the two tall chairs. "Eventually, we started organizing our own events. It was at one of the events we organized that a drunken group of white guys decided to start spreading hate.

"Our security staff were talking to them, trying to get them to leave, but one of them just kept arguing, so I came over to help. That man told me that all women were vicious and vindictive, and that our event was proof of it. Now I'm all for free speech, but he was spewing a lot of hateful comments and badgering protesters. And when he grabbed one of my friends and snapped one of the black bands on her arm, we had to call the police to intervene.

"It was after that event that we decided we'd all get tattoos of black bands around our arms so men couldn't go around snapping them. And that spread like wildfire. We were kind of shocked with how many women across the country started getting the tattoo to honor their own female friends and family who were victims of violence. It's like wearing a name badge or club pin—we can find each other easily, spot solidarity in sisterhood from a simple mark.

"So that man at the protest was arrested for drunk and disorderly conduct, and as they were putting him in the police car, he started yelling nonsense about how we were vicious, vicious women, and how we should all stand in our vicious little girl circle like we were in the photo. We had a good laugh about it and started calling ourselves a vicious circle as an inside joke…but then it sort of just stuck.

"We took what this man had intended to be an insult and made it ours. We took ownership of being a vicious circle of women who would not stand by and watch our friends die at the hands of men. We're proud to be considered vicious if it's what we have to be to make sure no other circle of friends has to go through what we went through."

"Wow, I'm…Thank you for sharing this story," Lindsey says. "I'm sure that was a difficult time for you and your friends."

"Yes, it was." Violet appears pleasantly taken aback by Lindsey's response.

"But just to go back to the comment, you are verifying that a man at one of your protests came up with the name for Vicious Circle, and your group has taken credit for it ever since?"

"That's…Is that what you took from everything I just said?"

"I'll take that as confirmation. Why don't we move on?"

Violet's jaw visibly tenses. "*Yes.* Why don't we?"

Lindsey looks out at the viewers. "As we're committed to unbiased reporting, and we've provided Violet with ample time to speak today, we also have a special guest joining us for this exclusive interview to talk more about the alleged assault—"

"Again, it's not *alleged* if it's on camera…" Violet chuckles humorlessly.

"Ian Cole is here to tell us more about the events of that night. Ian? Why don't you come on out?"

Violet's eyebrows shoot into her hairline as she leaps anxiously from her seat. "Ian is here? *No.* If he's here, I'm done. I have a personal protective order against him for cyber stalking…"

Violet freezes, staring wide-eyed with fear as a clean-cut man in his mid-twenties steps into view. Though he has a pleasant expression on his face, he's clearly the same angry man who started the fight with Violet at the concert. He wears a pressed, pale-blue button-down shirt tucked into his khaki pants. His blond hair is styled neatly, and his brown eyes appear dark as night on screen. Not dark in color, but dark in expression…dark with ill-intent.

"Violet, let's just talk about this calmly," Ian says, holding up a palm. "I know we can find common ground on our differences."

Violet nearly stumbles over her own feet, rushing to take a step backward. She raises her hand, pointing a finger at him. "You… you're in violation of the protective order and the terms of your bail."

"I just want to talk about this," Ian says. "Let's come to an

agreement on dropping the charges."
     Ian steps forward and Violet steps back.
     "Violet, be reasonable."
     He takes another step.
     Violet turns, runs, and disappears off screen…

end of video

video record three
the edict

May 14, 2032

Ten Months Before the War

IAN COLE APPEARS on screen as he lowers to sit in a chair behind a desk. The wall at his back is light-gray and bare—no picture frames, no shelves, no indication that this is a space where someone frequently spends their time. His sandy-blond hair is swept neatly across his head, styled intentionally in a clean-cut manner that suggests his outward appearance is important.

There's a brief flash of text to indicate the video was recorded on his personal cellular device, which must be propped up somehow, as the video is clear and steady. He sits centered within the rectangular frame created by his device, and the familiar white text fades in at the upper left corner of the screen, revealing the title of the video to be, 'The Edict,' and dated May fourteenth, twenty thirty-two.

He sets his arms on the table, folding his hands in front of him, his expression contrite and reflective. Turning his gaze downward, he sighs.

Slowly and softly, Ian begins to speak. "I tried to reach out to Violet Clare again today. She just doesn't seem to understand how sorry I am for what happened at that concert; that all I want to do is apologize to her and her vicious *fucking* circle of friends." When he cusses, his palms slap the table with a jarring snap that shakes his perfectly styled hair out of place.

Gradually—*eerily*—a broad smile draws across his cheeks as he presses slightly forward on his palms, and his sinister grin displays straight, white teeth. He lifts his eyes to look directly at the camera, as though he's staring at the viewers.

"Violet Clare," he begins quietly. "Violet, Violet, Violet. Vicious little Violet. If she had any idea what's waiting for her, she would keep my *name* out of her fucking *mouth*."

He leans back in his seat, then combs his fingers through his hair, drawing in a deep breath as he stares straight ahead.

"This is what I'm here to talk to you about, my brothers—my most loyal, faithful followers. This situation with Violet Clare has reached an impasse, and the time has come for action. The cushy little plea deal Violet's lawyers offered me? It's gone. They took it off the table yesterday when they realized the pretty little bundle of flowers she'd found on her doorstep were from yours truly."

He throws up his hands. "It's what I get for trying to be a gentleman with a woman who *refuses* to be a lady. Let that be a lesson to you, brothers. Treat her how she deserves to be treated, how she *demands* to be treated. I've tried to be nice, but Violet has affirmed time and again that she doesn't *deserve* nice." His dark eyes narrow. "So she's not going to *get* nice from me anymore."

He begins to unbutton the cuff of his long sleeve shirt, working to roll it up his forearm as he speaks. "Without that plea deal, I've been assured that we're going to trial. And though my father could easily find a means to sway the jurors, that alone just doesn't satisfy me. You see, my inclination toward Violet Clare is..." he pauses, glancing up at the ceiling as he searches for the exact right word, "*obsessive*. And gentleman, I don't think I will ever get these fantasies of her crying face pressed to the ground beneath my polished leather shoe out of my mind. Not until I act on them. So what exactly am I telling you?"

He moves on to the other sleeve, unbuttoning it at the cuff, working to roll it up his forearm. "Well, I'm telling you that I'm leaving. I'm going away for quite some time. My criminal record isn't exactly clean, and my father's lawyers have assured us both that there's no way I'm walking away from a trial by jury with less than five years—and that's if I'm lucky. Felony assault, bias-related hate crime, stalking… They say it's astonishing that I'm out on bail right now given my past. I think it's astonishing that they seem surprised by how easily the system can be bought."

He pauses mid-twist of his sleeve and looks straight out at the camera. "Well, not *all* of his lawyers are surprised, of course. Certainly not my father's dearest friend, Waylon Creed. He's actually the one helping my father—the one and only Frederik *fucking* Cole—to hash out this plan of ours. Spoiler alert: they're going to buy me a playground and help me…*disappear* before my trial."

Ian stops talking long enough to finish with his sleeve, then he folds his hands on the tabletop. "In case you didn't know it by now, my father is the filthiest fucking politician to ever grace these glorious states. Everyone knows that, even the people voting for him know that. But none of you know just how filthy he is because he's so *precise* in his manipulations, so practiced, so clean.

"You see, I *am* my father's son…an apple that certainly didn't fall far from his tree. But I'm not quite as polished as our dear elder Cole has been with his own little obsessions, not nearly as neat and clean. I've been learning, I've been growing." He waves his hand like this is a normal topic of conversation. "But with my criminal record, and this latest blow from vicious little Violet, I'm afraid my time for learning and growing has come to an end. So, as my father would say, it's time to purchase ourselves a solution.

"And oh, what a beautifully twisted solution it is. I don't want to give away all the details just yet…I think I'd rather show you when the time comes. But allow me, if you will, to give you a little preview of what my disappearing act is going to look like."

He reaches off camera, and when he pulls his arm back, he holds a black leather journal. He uncoils a leather strap from around it, then drops it on the tabletop in front of him before flipping open the cover. He straightens in his seat and brings the side of his fist to his lips before dramatically clearing his throat.

"*This*," he begins, turning his palm toward the ceiling and floating his hand over the open pages, "will be my gift for Violet Clare. A gift she'll receive when she's finally brought before me on her knees, where she fucking belongs. Call it my playbook, my manifesto, my Bible, my *edict*…my written documentation of the feral *impulse* I have to destroy her."

He strokes his hand down the pages. "It contains the details of every terrible thing I plan to do to her in my new playground, but I've left a lot of blank space, spots that she and I can fill in together as I ruin her."

He flips a page and slaps his hand down on it. "Here is a list of fourteen names. Mine and Violet's names are the two at the top, of course. I even drew a little heart in between just so I could scribble it out. But what are the names of the other twelve? Well, half of them are *your* names, my brothers. My father and I have chosen six of you to join me—six of you connected to very powerful men in this country who will help us keep this secret safe. You're going to help me keep our playground secure and our playthings under control. Because *we* will be in control.

"And the other six names…Can you guess who those names belong to? I'll give you a hint. The name beneath Violet Clare is Jada Johnson." He pauses and waits, as though he expects an actual reply. "Another hint, you say? Well, I'll tell you that name number three is…" he drums his hands on the table to build anticipation, "Soleil Garcia."

His head inclines with a self-satisfied smirk. "Catching on now, aren't you? Violet and her six besties—those bitches who started Vicious Circle—are coming with us when we disappear, though of course, they don't know it yet. Violet and I are going to have a surprise reunion at the new property—our new playground—where I'll have free rein to show her *precisely* what I think of her.

"Now *this*, gentleman, is the secret project that my father, Waylon Creed, and our favorite corrupt Senator Bright are working on to get me out of this mess that vicious Violet has put me in. Right as we speak, they're searching for the perfect property upon which we'll build this playground of ours—a *community* where we can *finally* be real men again.

"Somewhere hidden away, so deep that no outsider will ever stumble across it. Somewhere far enough that it's treacherous to reach, impossible to leave, yet near enough that our dear elders— Cole, Creed, and Bright—can continue to funnel in the resources we need for survival and debauchery for however long we need to exist apart from this world…this *fucking* world that wants us to sit down, shut up, and let the Violet Clare's speak their heinous thoughts of men.

"And, of course, the collective wealth of our founding fathers… did I call them 'elders' before?" He tilts his head and chuckles to himself. "Actually, I like that."

He sits back and spreads his arms wide before dramatically bellowing, "Our *glorious* elders!" He laughs again before gradually bringing his arms down.

"They have so much wealth between them that they'll be able to keep this secret for years…decades. *Fuck,* even generations of Coles if it's what we want. We'll finally be free to exist how we were born to be—as brutal, savage men who *take* their power and maintain it with violence. We won't be held to the laws and standards of the world around us. *No.* It's time for us to return to the days where men held all the power and the women existed to serve our needs.”

He leans forward, pointing his index finger out at the viewers. “Men rule, and women do whatever the fuck they’re told, and that means *you*, Violet Clare. I’m coming to get you, dollface.” He slowly grins and whispers, “You better be ready for me…”

end of video

video record four
day one

September 19, 2032
Six Months Before the War

THE SCREEN IS black.

The darkness creates a disturbing background to the sound of distressed whimpers, soft crying, and pleading. The voices of several young women are amplified in a deeply unsettling manner without a visual to provide context.

It remains this way for mere seconds, though one might feel as though they stretch into hours, like a looming threat about to fulfill a sinister promise. The only place to focus one's visual attention is the upper left corner of the screen, where white text fades in, displaying the title of this record to be 'Day One,' and the date as September nineteenth, twenty thirty-two.

Just as the darkness begins to settle as familiar, the camera abruptly switches on to reveal another cellular device recording. The camera is aimed at the gravel-covered ground, revealing the toe of a man's polished leather shoe peeking out from beneath his clean, pressed black slacks.

The fearful crying of several women continues as the man holding the device slowly pans upward, and our view gradually rises. The camera adjusts as the light changes, a bright-white flash of sunlight filling the rectangular frame and momentarily obscuring the scene. But quickly, the flash is gone—the sunlight returns to its single point in the sky, becoming mere backlighting as the camera refocuses, revealing a frightening scene.

Directly in front of the man holding the device are seven women, all on their knees upon the gravel, and each placed a few feet apart from each other. Their hands are bound behind their backs and black hoods are pulled over their heads.

One woman's head is hung low in fear.

Another's shoulders shake while she sobs.

The next rocks back and forth as she mutters, "Please…"

And another is stark still, like a kneeling statue.

The subtle clack of a man's dress shoes against concrete draws attention. The man holding the device turns slightly to the right, revealing Ian Cole as he slowly descends a set of stone steps from a grand manor that rises from behind them.

He steps down onto the small, gray stones, and he pauses, taking his time to adjust his cufflinks beneath his sharp, black suit—it fits him precisely, as though it was tailor-made. He smooths the lapels of his jacket, then slowly lifts his chin.

Ian turns his head—scanning the line of women to his right, then to his left—and satisfied with the sight before him, he lets his grin spread. He takes a step forward, and the sound of his sleek shoes crunching over the shifting stones seems to startle the women. They take turns whimpering fearfully, flinching at the sound of dread approaching as he steadily stalks toward them.

He finds the woman kneeling at the center of the line.

He stops directly in front of her.

He looks down at her, appraises her…

And then his grin broadens.

Five other men move to stand behind the line of women—all looking perfectly pleased with themselves—and there's also the man who's filming. With Ian, that brings the count of men to seven.

Seven men.

Seven women.

The fourteen names written in Ian's journal.

Ian reaches forward to grip the black fabric covering the head of the woman who kneels directly in front of him. He glances up and gives a nod to the other men. "Take them off."

Each man tears off the black hood of the woman kneeling in front of him. As their hoods are tossed aside, the women are brought into overwhelming sunlight—they blink and twist their heads, turning away from its source. As they begin to adjust, batting their eyes against the bright light, they begin to glance around at their surroundings, at each other, trying to make sense of it all.

And that's when they begin to recognize one another.

"Jada?" It's the girl kneeling in the center of the line—the one directly in front of Ian Cole—who says her friend's name…

It's Violet Clare.

"Soleil?" says another woman, recognizing a familiar face beside her.

The collective suffering crescendos as they realize this harrowing experience is shared, not just with other women, but with their closest friends.

Ian steps in close to Violet, and she lifts her head, squinting and blinking against the light, trying to make out who stands before her.

"Hello, Violet…" Ian says.

It seems to be his voice that triggers her instant recognition.

He reaches out to snatch her by the back of the neck as she lets out a gut-wrenching scream. With force, he slams her down sideways onto the gravel. He presses his palm to the side of her head to hold her down, though he rises just enough to replace his hand with his shoe.

Violet's friends scream, shouting and crying for him to stop.

Yet it doesn't seem to faze him.

Instead, a look of relief relaxes his features.

He straightens to his full height, unaffected by their pleas. His eyes fall shut as his leg pushes down, squishing Violet's cheek to hold her in place beneath his foot.

Her body thrashes.

Her bound hands are useless.

Ian's head rolls back on his shoulders as he draws in a deep breath. Then he grins as he opens his eyes, dropping his head forward again.

He looks down at Violet—his new plaything.

His expression could be described as hungry, and Violet Clare will be his favorite meal.

"There you are," he croons, "*finally*. Right where you belong."

His foot begins to twist…

THE VIDEO CUTS to black, and there's a beat of darkness before a new clip appears on screen. The device is laid on the ground, camera pointing straight up to show the clear night sky. It's a black canvas spotted with white dots of starlight. The angle is just wide enough to reveal a bright, full moon.

The sound of a woman stifling her cries—trying to choke down her whimpers while fighting to catch her breath—crescendos just before the top of her head comes into view over the camera. Inching forward, presumably crawling on her hands and knees, she continues forward until her entire face is centered within the rectangular frame of the device. Her eyes are closed as she fights through fear, and her dark hair dangles toward the camera.

"Right there, stop," Ian Cole's recognizable voice commands. "Don't move another inch, my vicious little Violet. Open your eyes and look down."

With dread painted across her face, Violet Clare obeys, and she does it easily. A conclusion about the nature and length of her suffering on this night could surely be drawn by her quick compliance alone. Yet it's the distant echoes of her friends—screaming and crying from faraway places spread across the property—that serve as true evidence that they've been drawn into a nightmare.

Blinking open her eyes, Violet looks down at the device, and her gaze burns a hole straight through the screen. She stares into the unseen faces of the viewers on the other side.

Someone's finger reaches out in front of her eyes, seeming to tap the screen of the cellular phone, and a light from the device switches on. She squints, slightly turning her head against the shine that brings unwanted clarity to the injuries marring her face.

With eyes clenched shut, she cries out as a hand lashes out, tangles in her hair, and twists her head to bring her face fully back into the frame.

"*Violet.* I told you to open your eyes. Now do it. Take a good fucking look at yourself."

Trembling against his grip, she slowly opens her eyes and looks down…and the image of her face is haunting.

Bloodied with scrapes.

Covered in dirt.

Darkening skin from fresh bruising.

Bloodshot, weary eyes.

Though no tears presently spill from her eyes, clean streaks cut like riverbeds down the layers of soil and blood on her cheeks.

And despite all that grime, her green eyes remain vibrant and striking.

"Don't you look pretty now that your face is all made up? *Fuck,* I wish I could put you on live with your followers. I wish they could see you just like this…Sadly, this recording is just for me."

Violet Clare continues to stare straight down—straight out

toward the viewers—as Ian speaks. Her breaths are heavy, drawing rapidly through her lightly flaring nostrils. One might think she's restoring her strength as she watches herself reflected in the self-view. Another might think her strength is restored in knowing that someday, someone will see this, and know what really happened to her…They'll know Ian Cole for the monster he truly is.

The slight quirk of one corner of her lips—a brief twitch that shows a smirk for no more than a second before she hides it again—is telling that it's the latter.

"It's not like I could send it, anyway," Ian goes on. "No Wi-Fi out here, so far away from the world. No cell phone service either, in case you were thinking of trying to steal my phone. Dear old Dad has his own private satellite that only three people on the outside have access to.

"Now don't worry, dollface. Even if you did manage to get a hold of my phone without me realizing it—which is next to impossible because it's always on me—you'd have to know the password to access the satellite cellular. And if your tiny little brain managed to figure that out—*and it won't*—there are only three people you'd be able to call. Can you guess who those three people are, Violet?"

Rage creeps into her expression, like a filter slowly making its way up from chin to forehead, scrubbing away at the fear. When humanity is lost, and all seems hopeless, passionate fury may lead the only path away from fear.

And Violet Clare is traveling that path.

Without hesitation, and without inflection, Violet simply replies, "Your father."

"Yes!" Ian says. "That's one. The *obvious* one. Anyone could have guessed that. Why don't we play a little game for you to guess the other two?"

Her eyes briefly shift to glance sideways as a sneer flattens her lips. "A game…"

"A *game*," he repeats. "It's very simple, VC girl. You guess the names of the other two people who know this place exists—the last of our three glorious elders, if you will—and I won't fuck you so hard in the ass that you bleed for days."

Her eyes widen slightly as fear tries to drag her back, but she lets them fall shut briefly as she takes a deep breath, bravely refusing to let it take her.

"So, are we going to play? Or should I just skip to the good part—"

"I'll play," she says, nearly interrupting him as her eyes snap open.

"Oh, this should be interesting. A little game of 'How Much Does Violet Know About Ian Cole.' Fuck, if you win, I might just force you to come for me as a fun little treat for you. Because let me tell you, Violet, that would get me *right* the fuck off, knowing you've been paying such careful attention to me."

Violet can hardly hide the look of disgust.

"Okay. So, one down, two to go. Who else do you think is involved? Ten seconds on the clock, Vi."

Her brow furrows, creasing her forehead. Her eyes dart around as she searches her mind, but then they brighten a little, perhaps as she latches onto an idea.

"Five, four, three…" Ian counts. "Two—"

"Bright!" she shouts. "Senator Bright…"

"*Violet*, you sneaky little thing. You have been paying attention to me." Then he mutters, "Fuck, that gets me hard."

She sprints the path from fear and reaches passionate fury in an instant.

"Your father is a fucking presidential candidate. I haven't been paying attention to *you*; I've been paying attention to *him*, you dumb fuck. I've been actively campaigning against that sick son of a bitch all year!"

There's silence for a moment, and it's filled with tension.

"No, go on," Ian urges with an eerily calm tone. "Keep talking, dollface. Talk yourself right into another broken bone."

A flicker of fear shows in her eyes, and she presses them shut, huffing it out with a heavy breath.

"I almost don't even want to finish the game now, Violet. You hurt my feelings, and it makes me want to hurt yours." He sighs. "Though, I suppose fair is fair. I did lay out the rules, and the rules are meant to be followed, so we must continue with this game to determine what happens to you next. So, let's see if you can get out of the most brutal ass fucking you've ever had. Tell me, baby, who's the third person? You have ten seconds."

Violet's head shakes with such a slight subtlety that it can probably only be seen by the viewers. As moments creep past, her eyes seem to shift away, less and less focused, and it becomes clear that she doesn't know the answer.

"Five more seconds. Come on. Make it fun. Take a guess."

"I-I don't remember his name," she mutters.

"Who's name?"

"The…his lawyer. Your father's friend."

"Oh. This is getting interesting. You've almost got it. Three seconds. Come on, now, throw out a name…any name…"

The urgency strains her features. "Reed?" She quickly guesses. "Is it Raymond? Raymond Reed?"

"*Raymond Reed*?" Ian laughs.

Her eyes widen a hair as something seems to click. "No! It's *Creed*. Raymond *Creed*…"

Ian is still laughing. "No, Violet. It's not Raymond Reed, and it's not Raymond Creed. It's *Waylon* Creed."

She sighs, distress taking hold of her expression, eyes darting wildly. "But I said Creed…The second time, I said Creed…"

"And sadly, time was already up, buttercup. But good effort.

I'm truly impressed that you figured it out, even though you got Mr. Creed's name wrong. Well, rules are rules. I'm gonna have to fuck you now. We can do this the easy way or the hard way. It's up to you."

"No!" Violet screams, her dark brown hair swinging as she crawls forward, her head moving away, up the screen.

But then her face rushes past in the opposite direction, entirely awash with fear as she's violently jerked backward…

THERE'S ANOTHER JARRING cut to black, though it only lasts a moment. The video jumps around the screen as Ian Cole fumbles with his recording device. He appears to be indoors—somewhere with fluorescent lighting—and there's a pervasive buzzing sound in the background.

"Just a second, doll," he says. "I want to record all your cute little whines and whimpers."

The video stills when he places his device on a flat surface beside him. He appears sideways within the rectangular frame on the screen, and the view peeks up at him from below.

"I don't want it," Violet quietly cries. "Please…" Her voice is unusually soft, weak. "Did…did you put something in the water?"

"Of course, I did. I can't have you squirming and messing up my artwork."

Ian leans over the camera, looking down at his device with dark eyes, and raises his hand above it to show that he's holding a tattoo machine—the source of the pervasive buzzing in the background.

"You'll ruin it," Violet pleads. "You can't…It was for my friend; it was for Kendra. Ian, *please*…"

He brings his free hand to his heart. "Violet, *please*. If you say my name like that and beg so sweet, I'm gonna have to stop and fuck you again."

"Y-you can. You can stop. Just…don't draw over my tattoo and I'll let you. I'll let you, Ian."

He looks down and rolls his eyes at the camera, as if he's glancing over at a friend to share a look.

"Of course, you'll let me, Vi. You're gonna let me do whatever I want to you forever, because you don't have a *choice*."

Violet cries. "Please…"

"Shh. Quiet now. I want to make sure you understand why I'm doing this before you fall asleep. It's funny actually, because you could've prevented all of this from happening. There was a plea bargain on the table for the charges you had brought against me, and I was fully prepared to accept it. I would've accepted it, and you and I would've continued on as we were, sharing our sexy little aggressions toward each other in secret—"

"I…I never shared…" Violet's voice is fading.

Ian continues as though she hasn't spoken. "I would have kept messaging you, and you would've kept blocking every new account I made to follow you. But do you know what happened to that plea deal? Of course, you do, because *you* were the one who told them I'd come by your shitty little apartment and left those flowers on your doorstep.

"Those were a *gift* for you, Vi. I was being a gentleman. But you went and cried to your lawyers and they pulled the deal, so it's kind of like *you* made a decision that would send me to prison. I wasn't going to go to prison; my father was not going to allow that to happen. So I need you to understand that this game we're all playing here now…it's all your fault."

"It's…not…" She's barely audible.

"So because you wouldn't accept my flowers, VC girl, I'm going to make you wear them forever, right here on your forearm with your stupid little black bands. Now, there's no need to worry. I know how to use this. And if you bothered to learn anything about me, you'd know that I'm actually a rather talented artist—a tortured soul, if you will—and I will make this the most beautiful bouquet of wildflowers you've ever seen. I promise, you're going to love it."

He sighs. "It's just rather poetic, isn't it? I've plucked you from your meadow, my little wildflower, just so I can watch you wither and wilt and slowly decay… Violet?"

Ian's head turns, and he looks down at the camera. "Oops, she's asleep." He reaches out to tap the screen with his finger…

end of video

video record five
new world

March 31, 2033

The Civil War Begins

AN OLDER MAN with salt and pepper hair appears, centered within the rectangular frame on the projector screen. A bit of white text fades in briefly to indicate that this is a recording from Ian Cole's personal cellular device. His face appears within the rectangular frame as well, but it's confined to a smaller rectangle in the upper right-hand corner.

"Mr. Creed," Ian says from the smaller box, his face visibly tense and his voice clearly strained. "I was expecting my father to call. Where is he?"

"I have to say, I'm rather surprised to hear you ask," Waylon Creed responds—the man who appears largest on screen. He's well put together in a sharp gray suit, but he looks tired, stress clear in the tone of his voice.

Ian's head tilts to the side. "Why? Do you think I don't care about my father? Of course, I fucking care, *Waylon.* He's my father, and he saved my life with this property. So where the fuck is he? I'd like to know he's safe."

"He's safe, Ian. He was gone before the worst of it came through. Intelligence had already predicted an attack; they just hadn't expected a group of women to be so—"

"*Vicious*," Ian finishes for him, turning his head over his shoulder to look behind him. "See what you did, Vi? You had those angry little VC girls wound so tight before you disappeared that they just couldn't play nice anymore, could they?"

"What?" Violet's voice is quiet from somewhere in the background. "What do you mean? Did something happen?"

Ian snaps, whipping sideways, "*Yes,* something happened, Violet! Your Vicious Circle followers have started a goddamn *war* over you! Went into D.C. today, guns blazing—*literally*—because they think my father had something to do with your disappearance."

There's an odd pause where everyone seems to wait for the obvious to strike.

"And yes," Ian says a touch more calmly, "I'm aware he *did* have something to do with your disappearance. But that doesn't stop me from being angry about what your girls are doing, Vi, so don't give me that goddamn look like you think I'm stupid." A pause. "I'm fucking serious. Fix your face or I'll tie you to a damn tree again and leave you for days." Another pause. "That's better." Ian turns to face forward again.

"Ian," Waylon begins calmly. "You do understand that their motivations are more complex than you're making it seem, right? The Vicious Circle has coordinated attacks across the country in all the places where your father facilitated the stripping of certain women's rights. This isn't just a VC protest for a proper investigation of Violet and the other girls' disappearance. I'm not trying to be condescending, Ian, but it's incredibly important for me to know that you have a clear understanding of the nuances and complexities of this situation before I give you the power I'm about to give you."

Ian's demeanor switches from self-righteous anger to calm and collected in an instant. The change is harsh, rehearsed, disingenuous... He puts on a charming façade that's reserved for the outside world, one that's necessary for politics and deception. It's a mask he likely destroyed six months ago when he made the property his new home.

Ian folds his hands on the desk in front of him and speaks deliberately—deceptively. "These events have been rather difficult for me to process, and my fear over what this world is coming to got the better of me. I apologize for the outburst, Waylon. I regret you saw me in a moment of weakness. Yes, I understand the complexities of this situation."

He lifts his eyes toward the ceiling, as though he was going to roll them in a sarcastic manner but fought the urge mid-roll. Then he sighs and bows his head, casting his eyes downward.

"It's tragic that these women have felt the need to resort to violence. While I certainly appreciate why they might feel afraid and confused as we work to change our laws for the greater good, I see these attacks as their attempt to…to cry out for help.

"They need guidance from men, solid leadership and great care as they come to terms with these changes. It will be difficult for them, but these women of the Vicious Circle are simply victims of Violet Clare, brainwashed by her hate and hostility, and they've become cult-like in their mentality. We must grant patience to those willing to change, but violence shall be met with violence when they leave us without a choice—"

"All right, Ian," Waylon says flatly, with an annoyed expression. "That's enough."

Ian switches back to his former—and truer—persona, dropping his palms to the table as he leans back. "Thank fuck."

"I'm glad to know you can still turn it on when it's necessary. We've all been more than a little concerned about your ability to do that. Frankly, we hadn't expected you'd be capable of attempting to take this role until you were much older and we had more resources in place—"

"You're talking around the point, Waylon. Let's get down to

brass tacks."

"Are you recording this call?"

"Of course."

"Good, because we have a lot to discuss and you may need to review this later. Just remember the protocol. Immediately convert to reel, then make a duplicate. Store them properly for longevity, place them separately for security—"

"And wipe the data clean. Yeah, I've got it down to a science."

"Good. It's important because at some point soon—far sooner than we were thinking due to the recent attacks—we're going to need you boys to go dark on all devices. For good."

Ian's brow creases as he straightens in his seat and leans forward on his elbows. "I'm listening."

"When we purchased this property we had two goals. The first was to get you out of the impossible situation you'd gotten into with Violet Clare. Actually, your father and I had already foreseen that something like this would be coming, so we'd been discussing it off and on for years. I don't need to explain to you why we've both had concerns for your…proclivities."

"I live with my *proclivities*, Waylon, so I think I have a good understanding of your concerns," Ian says with a proud grin.

"This is serious, Ian. Your father is being targeted by the Vicious Circle, and it puts all three of us at risk. And if we're at risk, then all of you at the property are at risk without the appropriate infrastructure in place."

"Okay, I hear you. So what's the plan?"

"Senator Bright is making arrangements for the three of us to go into hiding, and he's handling the press on that. And we've decided that we will be in hiding for a very long time. The VC have made it abundantly clear that they do not intend to stop fighting until their rights are restored and your father is thoroughly investigated regarding the disappearance of their founding members."

"Well, shit." Ian combs a hand through his hair, leaning back in his seat.

"The situation is dire. The VC are increasing their numbers as we speak, and they've declared their intent to engage in civil war if their demands aren't met. That was the purpose of the recent attacks…to demonstrate on a small scale what they're capable of. Intelligence has confirmed their growth, and they're recruiting men, too—their weak-minded husbands and brothers."

"Waylon, seriously, tell me. Is this a joke? We're really talking about a bunch of angry women who were followers of Violet? *My* Violet? Did anyone think to wait a week and see if it's not just collective PMS hysteria from their cycles all syncing up at the same time? Christ. Give them a week to finish bleeding and maybe they'll all go home—"

"This is serious, Ian. It's not just women associated with the Vicious Circle who are involved…it's women from *our* side, too. This was our fear. It's one thing for them to be stupid women, but an entirely different thing when they start brainwashing the good ones—our obedient wives and demure daughters. *I* have daughters, and I don't want to see them get dragged in by VC rhetoric."

"Okay." Ian nods. "Okay, I get it; you're being serious about this."

"Things are going to have to change. They were always going to have to change…we just thought we'd have more time to prepare. We thought we'd have years to plan and prep, but we have to move quickly."

"So what's your plan?"

"This is the second goal we had when we purchased this property—creating a community that serves the needs of men like us; a community committed to serving the needs of *men*. But it requires a beginning with the right people: those who are already committed to our beliefs, and those who are susceptible enough to commit under the right circumstances. And there are seven 'right circumstances' already living on the property."

"You mean, me and my friends."

"Precisely."

"Sounds like the perfect job for my father. Why doesn't he come live here himself? It's probably the safest place in the world."

"It probably is, but only because we've worked very hard to make it that way. And as soon as we've finalized the selections for the first generation, we'll have them delivered to the property. Once they've arrived, it will be your responsibility to ensure the community is built properly. Once they've arrived, we'll have to shut down all communications for a while—at least a month, maybe two."

"Stop. You're going to bring more people to the property, which means more mouths to feed and more resources used…And then you're cutting off communications? How the fuck am I supposed to keep them alive, Waylon? Where are they supposed to live? The boys and I are *not* giving up the mansion, and there are only three houses in that little village area down the path."

"We'll do a major supply drop along with the first generation— everything you'll need to get started—and then once a month thereafter. And we're selecting the population *carefully*. You'll have people who can plan and build, people who can heal, people who can teach. Women who can care for their homes and children…women you can breed."

"Go on."

"You know you can't make wives and mothers out of those heathens there with you now. And you *certainly* shouldn't be breeding with them—which reminds me of another item you'll need to resolve."

Ian's face hardens. "You're not taking away my plaything, Waylon…*our* playthings. My father promised me Violet Clare, and I will be keeping her for as long as I choose. It will be *my* choice when she fucking dies and no one else's. Do you understand me?"

"No one is trying to take away your playthings. They'll be an important part of this new community. You know as well as I do that men don't just need subservient wives and dutiful mothers for their children; we need sex and violence. It's a primal, natural need that we've all been suppressing for far too long…and we need women upon which we can unleash."

"So how the fuck am I supposed to unleash on the mother of my children?"

"You're not. Are you suggesting that Violet Clare should be the mother of your children?"

Ian glances off screen. "No."

"Good, because I just told you that she and her repugnant friends aren't fit for breeding. Are you listening carefully, Ian?"

"*Yes.*"

"There are good, faithful women we are bringing to you, and they must be treated differently than the others. They are perfect to breed a future generation of domestic daughters from. Those daughters will be the first generation born and raised on the property, the most important for ensuring that this community will continue on for decades to come."

"And what makes you so certain these women will be willing to have those daughters?"

"Because your brilliant father has already convinced them that *God* has chosen them for this task."

Ian chuckles. "He is fucking brilliant that way."

"Oh, he is. He's convinced them that—"

"*Circulus vitiosus,*" Violet whispers from somewhere off screen.

Ian's head snaps toward the sound.

"*Circulus vitiosus in aeternum.*"

"The *fuck* did you just say?" Ian's eyes widen as he looks at something we can't see, then abruptly rises to his feet. "Violet, put that down. Put it down right this goddamn second…"

"What's wrong?" Waylon asks.

"Violet, stop…*Stop*…I swear, if you try to slit your wrist one more time, I will fucking murder you. *Violet!*" Ian bursts forward, instantly darting off screen.

There are sounds of a struggle happening off camera—grunting, fighting, skin hitting skin.

Waylon pinches the bridge of his nose.

"I will *always* be with the Vicious Circle." Violet's soft, sad voice drifts through the speaker. "VC forever…*circulus vitiosus in aeternum*. No…*No!*"

"Let *go*," Ian grunts. "Give me the knife, Violet!"

Silence falls, immediately following the reverberating sound of skin slapping skin. There's a clang, like the sound of something hitting the floor. Then further struggle as Violet whimpers—

chapter twenty-five

Mercy

I DON'T REMEMBER standing.

I don't remember screaming.

I don't remember shoving the projector to the floor.

Yet I do remember glancing at Arlo, and I remember seeing him with his legs bent, his elbows on knees, his forehead against the heels of his hands, and his fingers tangled in his hair.

And I remember his silence…

He hadn't said a word as we watched, but that's not the silence I recall. It was the silence of his soul that I remember, a silence so deafening that it will haunt me forever.

It felt like moments where he ceased to exist.

It was the revelation of the truth that broke him.

It broke me.

It broke *all* of us.

And I had to make it stop.

The projector is on the floor, but the video still plays, the sound still surrounds us, and the echo of Violet Clare's broken whisper, *"Circulus vitiosus in aeternum…"* brings me to my knees as I sob.

And I whisper the words *with* her.

chapter twenty-six

ARLO

I DON'T KNOW who I am.

Everything I believed was a lie.

Everything Mercy went through was for nothing.

I let them hurt her in the name of a god who doesn't even exist.

I hurt her in the name of a god who doesn't exist.

I am nothing.

My life has been meaningless.

Meaningless until Mercy...

The haunted past of Ember Glen demands atonement, and my soul rips itself apart, offering the pieces of me as payment. I'm in pain, and I don't mean in the physical sense. I can't feel the wounds on my body while my soul is being shredded in this excruciating manner.

I exist in the shell of my body, trapped in this spiritual agony, and my only earthly awareness is of Mercy—my starlight—the strongest woman I've ever known. She had sensed all along that our world wasn't right, that something didn't fit, that we were all broken. I should have listened to her sooner, yet I resisted—and for far too long.

My resistance brought her here, to this place where she was forced to witness the *disgusting* truth she feared.

I brought this misery of humanity upon her.

My head is planted firmly on the heels of my hands, fingers

gripping my hair and pulling so tightly it aches. I don't realize Mercy has moved until I hear the projector crash to the floor, and even then I'm frozen.

The sound of her sobbing doesn't just surround me, it *fills* me.

Where my soul is shredding, hers has been lit on fire.

Where my misery is quiet, hers is loud.

Where the void of my mind's entrapment is cold, hers is blistering hot.

The truth has set Mercy on fire.

Though her flames roar with pain too unbearable to fathom in this moment, I know that soon she'll burn to ashes only so she can rise renewed.

But the sparking embers of Mercy's soul will always remain… at least, I hope they will. I'll forever need the shock of her embers setting me on fire to ensure I never forget this moment when we learned the heinous truth—this moment where I realized that without her, I am nothing.

I was a soldier before her, blindly following orders.

And now, I am *hers*—a broken man willing to kneel before the fire's glowing truth while she burns for us all.

chapter twenty-seven

Mercy

NOT A WORD has been spoken about what we saw. I don't know how long I sat and sobbed. I've been left alone here, and I don't know where they all went. I know comfort was offered, though I can't say for sure by whom.

I couldn't stand to be touched.

I couldn't bear to listen to a single word that was spoken.

I shrugged off a gentle touch on my shoulder.

I covered my ears when someone asked if I was okay, if there was anything I needed.

I wanted to scream at them…

There's nothing you can give me that will make it right!

But I couldn't even bring myself to speak—no words had meaning. None except for Violet's dying whisper…

"Circulus vitiosus in aeternum."

Did Violet die that day?

Did she survive, only to suffer more in the days to come?

I suppose it doesn't matter. It was a century-and-a-half ago, and they're all long since dead now.

It almost feels like nothing matters…

My tormented thoughts want me to believe that, and I'm trapped within that belief for the longest time.

I allow myself to believe it as I sit alone, my back to the wall of stone that encloses the projector room. It must be hours that I wallow, that I remain in silence, encased in hopelessness and despair.

Yet eventually, a moment comes where I realize that a decision has to be made.

I have a choice to stay here. I could sit still, refuse to speak, refuse to eat or drink…I could decide that nothing matters and there's nothing left worth fighting for…I could lay down and wait for death—and I hate to admit it to myself, it's a choice I'm tempted to make. My heart hurts so much that I think it might give out, stop beating, and make the choice *for* me.

But then a realization dawns on me, a sudden understanding that I was missing before—the lesson I was meant to learn from watching the video records.

"I *have* a choice." The words tumble free from my lips, the first words I've spoken since learning the truth.

"Starlight?"

I turn my head toward the sound of Arlo's voice, sneaking in through the low entrance to the projector room. He must be out there in the alcove, maybe waiting for me, and I didn't even realize he was near. I've been so lost that I hadn't even sensed his presence.

"I thought you left."

"No," he says from the other side. "It was clear you needed to be alone, but I couldn't leave you. I wouldn't."

It's a relief knowing he's there. I needed the space, and the fact he recognized that warms my heart. As I crawl out from the depths of my mind after the initial shock of it all, I can feel the vibration of his existence flow through me, and my senses feel renewed. I find enough clarity to know I can't process this alone—and since I'm not alone, my thoughts easily tumble out of me.

"I'm horrified, Arlo. I never would have guessed that was how we came to be, and it makes me feel lost. A part of me wishes I didn't know the truth, but now that we do, I realize that it gives me a choice. We have a *choice*. The way we lived, the way they meant for us to die…we never had a choice before. We were forced to live the way we have because following the word of *God* was the only option. We were told there was nothing for us beyond the mountains. That leaving was impossible, that even if you *could* leave, there's nothing good out there.

"They told us we were safe in Ember Glen because we had rules and laws and were governed by God. But this God they spoke of was nothing more than a man who scribbled his violent obsessions in a book—a book we were told the Elders had possession of, yet it was here in Ember Glen the entire time. Everything they told us was made up; it was fiction. Every rule was just a game."

I pause to take a deep breath against my building anger.

"They told us we were lucky to be born here, but we weren't. Our ancestors were lied to, and those lies trapped them here—it trapped *all* of us here. We would've died by their lies, never knowing what was real. But the truth gives us a choice. We can take what we know and run…or go back and fight like hell to end this madness for good."

I could just be imagining it, but I can almost feel him drawing in a deep breath. "So tell me your choice, Mercy."

"You know my choice."

"I do."

"But you want to hear me say it."

"I'm not…I don't want to make assumptions about anything anymore." His tone is contrite. "I thought I had all the answers, but I was wrong. I was so…I was so *wrong*, Mercy." His voice breaks, and I hear him take a stuttering breath. "And you were right…"

It's unmistakable that he's crying. His heartache quickly brings me to my hands and knees, and I crawl to him. I move into the alcove through the low opening connecting the spaces, and I find him directly beside it, sitting to my right with his back leaning against the rock wall. He's cast in shadow with the light of a lantern on his opposite side, but when he looks at me as I move through, everything stops.

I've never seen such pain in his expression.

For a moment, we're both still.

And then he reaches for me.

I launch myself into his arms, and we hold on to each other stronger than we ever have before. We shed tears together from the agony of knowing the truth.

"I doubted you for so long," he mutters against the side of my neck, his tears slicking my skin. "I'm so sorry. I'll never doubt you again."

"None of this is your fault. It's not your burden. You were told what to believe; we *all* were."

He draws his arms back and reaches up to grab my cheeks, gently tugging to bring our faces together, leaning in to touch his forehead to mine. He peers into my soul, his blue eyes faded in the dim light.

"We wouldn't be here right now if it weren't for you." Arlo's tone is resolute. "You need to know that. None of this would've happened without you. We would never know the truth, and this choice wouldn't exist. All of this is happening because you chose to run from service, and if you make the choice—if you say the words—then Ember Glen ends with you. Say the words, Mercy, and we will *all* be with you. Say the words, and we'll burn this place to the ground."

My choice was already made, but his encouragement emboldens me further. "We're going to war, Arlo. We're going to take control of Ember Glen, destroy anyone who gets in our way, and leave the ashes of this wretched place behind us for good."

chapter twenty-eight

Mercy

"I FEEL LIKE I have more questions than answers," I tell the others, and I'm met with sounds of agreement.

All the women—save for a few with the children—have gathered in the main cavern, and we sit together near the crystal blue water. It radiates a pleasant warmth that rivals the cooler air of these underground spaces. The afternoon sun fills the cavern, and I'm so grateful for a clear day where the light can reach us.

The warm water was soothing against my skin when I took a quick dip before we gathered. Luna had showed me and Arlo to the shallow point of the pool so we could finally get clean. That shallow point happened to be where I'd accidentally witnessed her and Stefanie together, though I wouldn't tell her that.

One of the women, Silvia, brought us fresh clothes. For Arlo, she had some items from my father's room, and for me, she brought black outfits from my closet. Strangely, I find comfort in wearing black again. I'm no longer in red; I'm no longer a trial participant. Dressed in black, I feel solidarity with my sisters.

Though I was grateful that Silvia brought us clean clothes to wear, I expressed concern that she compromised her safety when it wasn't necessary. She explained that she's still in good graces with her husband, that she and two other younger domestics—wives who haven't yet had any children to worry over—had volunteered to go back and forth between the caves and the village. They hadn't engaged in the fight at the Homestead, and they've been supplying everyone here with all the resources they need for survival. Secretly, they've also been able to collect information about what's going on above to help keep everyone down here safe.

The three of them are young—only sixteen and seventeen years old, and brand-new wives—and their bravery is inspiring. They remind me of Delle, who I often think has been the true unsung heroine throughout our nightmare journey. I imagine Delle's choice to participate in the Trials of Dissension would have inspired other young women her age to *think*, to challenge their thoughts and beliefs.

I'm told that Delle's still alive, being kept within the Homestead. It's a relief to know they haven't made movement on her third trial, yet I know that decision could come any day now.

I swear I will save her before they hurt her again.

I will not leave Delle behind.

"Every day I have a new question," Luna agrees. "I still wonder where the Elders are, whether they know the truth about Ember Glen's founding. But they *must* know…"

"Not necessarily," says Enid, the woman who guided us into my house when we fled the Homestead. "They might be hidden away from the rest of the world, too. And maybe Ian Cole had, at some point, created the true version of the Impulse Edict—something that wasn't nonsense like his black journal. They could be in the dark about the truth just as much as we were."

"Perhaps," says another woman named Willow. "I might be able to believe that if *all* the Control become Elders and they go to the same place at the Shift, but only *three* of them become Elders. So, maybe those three could be hidden away from the world and sealed off from the truth. But then that means the retired Control are, too. How could there possibly be three secret locations that no one from the outside knows about? How could they keep everything a secret from all the people in Ember Glen, all the Elders, *and* all the retired Control?"

"But we know the place where the retired Control are sent. They go to the Land of Kings—the place where the Impulse doesn't exist. The retired Control are assigned domestics and sent to live there, where they are finally allowed to have a wife and children, their happily-ever-after..." Enid tilts her head with a puzzled look, trailing off as if she's just realized something. "Though...how do they have children with their domestics in the Land of Kings without seed from a donation? Who would be there to perform the fertilization?"

"No one." Arlo's voice is loud and clear, every head turning to look in his direction. He enters from the arched entryway that leads to the tunnels. "The Land of Kings doesn't exist."

I stand and rush to meet him as he moves into the cavern. "Where have you been? You said you'd be gone ten minutes, and it's been nearly two hours." I throw my arms around him as we collide, and though he groans in pain, he hugs me back. "Where did you go?"

I release him and step back, though I reach out my hand for him to take. He quickly latches onto it, locking our fingers together, and lifting our hands to kiss my knuckles.

"I wanted to test a theory," he says.

"What theory?"

I lead him back to the gathering of women, and we sit together on the ground beside Luna and Stefanie.

"I had a theory about where one of the passageways would lead, so I followed it. It led me to a forked path and I'm almost certain it's the one I was looking for. If it is, then I think I know the correct path to get to the Homestead."

"You *think*?" Luna chides.

"As I said, I'm almost certain."

"Certain enough that it's worth the risk of getting lost forever in the winding tunnels?" asks Luna.

"Sure." He shrugs, giving a dismissive look.

It gives me the urge to throttle some good sense into him—and Luna shares the same look of frustration.

"What did you mean when you said the Land of Kings doesn't exist?" Willow asks.

"I have no evidence to say whether I'm right or wrong, but my gut tells me it doesn't exist," he says.

"I suppose a gut feeling is as useful a measure as anything else when you have no measuring stick," Stefanie says.

Arlo nods. "Right."

"Did you…Did the Control know anything about the Vicious Circle?" a woman named Kinsley asks Arlo.

He shakes his head. "I didn't. Though I do remember Killian saying something odd about it at the Homestead before we were freed. Do you remember the speech he gave while holding the gun? He said something about Stefanie having cited ancient texts, *unholy* texts that were forbidden, which, of course, isn't true. It's a great way to twist the narrative in their favor to ensure the people would see Stefanie as unholy before setting her on fire. I think the Elders just told him to say that without offering further explanation. He would've done what they asked without question."

"That wouldn't surprise me," Stefanie says.

"Nothing surprises me anymore. Nothing ever really did…" My eyes drift to focus on a spot far away. "A new violent encounter every single month, and no way to escape it…"

There's a beat of quiet.

Then Kinsley speaks slowly. "Arlo…Do you think Killian knows the truth?" She pauses, and when he doesn't respond right away, she continues, "Killian Cole *has* to be a descendant of Ian Cole, don't you all agree?" She's met with nods and whispers of agreement. "Maybe the Coles have known everything all along…"

Arlo's brow furrows, his head tilting slightly to the side as he considers it. "I don't know," he says slowly. "Anything is possible at this point, but…no, I truly believe that he doesn't know anything."

He looks out at the women gathered. "I can't think of a single interaction I've had with Killian that suggests he might know more. I think the history of Ember Glen was buried intentionally. They wanted this to become a community to last generations, and the only way to achieve that goal would be to maintain the secret until it naturally died out. They would have had to stop telling their children.

"And maybe…maybe it's only revealed to the Elders. They would be the only people who need to know the truth, and they *only* need to know to ensure our survival, to ensure resources from the outside world are delivered."

"And how do they deliver those resources?" Kinsley asks. "I've honestly never even thought to ask, and it seems so silly now that I haven't. I guess in my mind I'd always just assumed that we were mostly self-sustaining."

"That's what they told you to believe, and why would anyone question it?" Arlo replies. "Our community has done well in creating many of the things we need for daily sustenance, but some things come from the outside, too. I don't know exactly how they arrive, but about once a month, the essentials are left for us to collect. We never know when or where the boxes will be left until they've already arrived, and then we go and collect them."

He chuckles humorlessly, glancing down. "They told us that *God* provided our supplies, and I'm embarrassed to admit that I never thought twice about it. The supplies came from *God*, and it's all I thought I needed to know."

There's another lingering silence that surrounds us, though I'm certain no one's mind is quiet.

"Do you think it's safe out there beyond the mountains?" Luna's question cuts through the silence, and all heads turn to look at her, though she's looking at the ground. "Do you think it will be better than it is here in Ember Glen? I just don't know what to think, and I'm…afraid.

"They always made the Civil War seem like it was so devastating across the entire country, like the world beyond the mountains was cast into an apocalypse. But maybe that was a lie, too. Maybe the Vicious Circle won their fights, and there's a place out there where women have rights and freedom. Some place that maybe even Stefanie and I could just…*be*."

"I don't think we can trust anything we were told," I tell her. "I think we have to question all of it." The wrinkle of her brow suggests she's not quite satisfied by my response. "I think anything's possible now, Luna. But the only way to know is to find out for ourselves… and we will."

She turns her chin to glance at me with a smile, and I'm glad that something I said gave her some hope. She deserves to have it.

"So, what do you think we should do, Mercy? What's the plan?" Enid asks.

I shrug. "I guess I don't really have one…not yet. I just know that we need to fight for control of Ember Glen and save as many women as possible before we find a way out."

"How are we going to save *anyone*?" a woman sitting farther away asks.

"If we leave these caves," Willow says, "the men will capture us the moment they see us, and there's no telling what they'll do. They put you through the trials just for turning and running from service. What are they going to do to us for fighting against our husbands at the Homestead? For taking their children away and hiding them here?"

"That's the point of fighting," Stefanie says. "You would have to be willing to end the life of any man who tries to take you."

"But that's not really fair, is it?" Enid says. "Not all the men want to see their wives punished. Some of them are only living the way they're told to live. They might even be on our side if they knew the truth. How can we fault them for falling victim to the same lies *we* fell victim to? This has gone on for generations, and no one knew. We can't just kill anyone who tries to stop us from taking control."

"But how do we know who's with us or against us until we fight?" Kinsley asks. "We can't know that *any* of them would be with us just for knowing the truth. There will undoubtedly be some who are still unwilling to relinquish control, some who may fight harder to keep it. We don't know their hearts and minds. And because we can't know which men are safe, we have to assume *all* men are dangerous."

There's a flurry of agreement from the women.

"But how can we justify faulting every man without giving him a chance to choose? If we do that, where do we draw the line?" Enid asks. "Should we go after the domestics who chose not to join us in the caves as well? The wives who turned to help their husbands fight against us at the Homestead? They're all victims of these lies, the same as us, aren't they?"

"So, what do we do?" Luna asks. "How can we give them a chance to choose when they don't know the truth?"

"I have an idea," Arlo says, and all eyes land on him. "I don't know if it will work, but I'd like to try."

He glances over at me, and I nod, encouraging him to speak.

"Inside the Homestead, there's a door that leads to a system of caves, which I believe are all connecting with these tunnels and passageways. If I can successfully navigate my way through, and sneak in through that door, there might be a way to show everyone the truth."

"How?" I ask.

"Theo Hughes has always been good with the technologies we

have. He's set up all the broadcasts and livestreams, all the cameras and projections for the trials. He connects us for every call we have with the Elders, and I think—I *hope*—that maybe he can help us. If I can find my way into the Homestead with the reels, then perhaps he can broadcast the videos across Ember Glen."

"What makes you think he'll help?" Willow asks.

"I don't know if he'll help," Arlo replies. "But I have a feeling that he will. He's shown kindness and care toward Delle as her warden, and I believe he grapples with conflict over his role with her. I have great hope that once he knows the truth, he'll help us."

"Okay," Willow says. "Then let's say for argument's sake that your plan works, and the entire village sees the video records all at once. What do we do then? Domestics will be with their husbands; servants will be in their homes with their fathers and brothers. If the men choose to turn a blind eye to the truth, or if they simply don't believe it, then they'll keep the women from leaving and we won't be able to save them, anyway."

"That's true," Stefanie agrees, "but I think there's a way around that. And it will give us the time we need to plan this well. The full moon will be in nine days, and we all know there will be a short period of time where everyone is separate before service begins.

"The servants will gather in Sanctuary before heading into the forest. At the same time, the domestics will be left alone in their homes. And, of course, the men will have to make their monthly deposits to the Bank before heading out for the purge. If the timing is precise—if the videos broadcast at just the right time—there would be enough separation for everyone to have a moment to reflect. There would be just enough time to let them make a choice."

She's right…

I hadn't thought about that, but it would certainly allow time for everyone to make a decision. I'd nearly forgotten that the men would first have to gather at the Bank to make their monthly deposit. All the men of Ember Glen who *can* produce viable seed *must* provide it—and it can only be done on nights of service, on the only night pleasure is allowed.

I nod in agreement with Stefanie. "That would help us know the men who are with us and the ones who are against us. Those who still want to purge will have proven they don't care about us. I don't know about the rest of you, but that's enough justification for me."

"But what about the…" Kinsley begins, then lowers her voice as if the word itself is taboo, "*guns?* Killian had one at the Homestead, and we all saw the damage it did. Are there more guns? Will the Control have them?"

"There's no way for us to know. We were trained in how to use them at the last Shift, but they're only to be used in times of rebellion and war—something none of us ever really expected to see," Arlo explains.

"There's one gun for each of the seven Control, and our bands are required to gain access to them, though mine has already been deactivated." He twists the black band still affixed to his wrist absentmindedly. "No one person can access all seven guns—each of us has access to only *one.* And they can't be accessed without permission, which the Elders control electronically with a certain activation in the bands.

"It's possible that Killian may be the only one of them with a gun…" he says, "but it's equally possible that they all have. And given that the children have been taken, I wouldn't put it past the Elders to ask them all to be prepared to…take action as needed."

"And this is why I'm not…I can't just leave my children to fight," Willow says. "I refused to go the first time because it was too dangerous to try to rescue Stefanie. But this? There *will* be bloodshed over this. You know there will be."

"Yes, there will be bloodshed if we do this," I say honestly. "But there will be bloodshed all the same if we don't. Maybe I'm asking too much of you all to try to understand what the servants go through on nights of purging. Maybe it's unfair of me to ask anything of you at all.

"But the fact is that we are all *so* lucky to be here right now. We're free to speak openly about this, free to choose what we do next. But the women left behind are up there right now, and I beg of you to think of them as you would want someone else to think of you. You would want someone down here to think you deserve a chance. You would want someone to come back for you. You would want someone to fight for you. And we're the only ones who can fight for them."

I pause and take a deep breath. "We don't all have to go. We'll need some to stay behind with the children. And no one is going to force anyone to do something they don't want to do. But the more of us who are willing to fight for this, the better our chances will be. It's a game of numbers, and we won't know which side is outnumbered until the truth is revealed to everyone. I just…I can't stand by and watch my sisters endure another purge. I *won't*. And I'm asking for your help."

Tears well in my eyes, and I glance down as I shake my head. It feels like hours slip by as I wait in silence for someone else to speak.

"So, this is the plan." Luna speaks with finality. "On the next night of service, Arlo will go through the tunnels to the Homestead. He'll find Theo Hughes and convince him to broadcast the video records just before it's time for the servants to leave Sanctuary. Once the videos are broadcast, we demand that the purge be canceled. The men who still insist on seeking service after learning the truth will have made their choice."

"And we should hold no remorse for shedding the blood of those men," I add. "By choosing to purge after they know the truth, they will have proven that they'd show no remorse for you."

I hear Arlo's sharp intake of breath, but I don't have to glance at him to know the look of pride in his eyes. I can feel the way he looks at me, his gaze reflecting his desire to praise my bold declaration.

And then I wait, unsure of exactly what might be said next.

Then finally, Enid stands and glances around at the others. "Well, it sounds like we have nine days to prepare, so we may as well get started on gathering the supplies and resources we'll need. I don't know about the rest of you," she says, "but I'm done living a life that was chosen *for* me. I'm ready to fight for freedom."

chapter twenty-nine
ARLO

"IT MUST BE difficult to write by lantern light." Mercy's voice surprises me.

I'd expected she'd come looking for me soon, though I didn't know exactly when. I lift my head from where I've been staring down at a blank journal in my lap, one in which I hoped to pour my thoughts onto the pages with new poetry…something to give to Mercy in case we're not able to retrieve the ones left behind in the Homestead.

It seems odd that the words evade me, though I have to wonder if it's due to the fact that I've had ample time to whisper my words of desire directly into her ear. Instead of flowing from my mind to the pages, my poetry has spilled directly from my lips and splashed inside her mind. Perhaps that's why it's difficult to write—because I haven't needed to leave anything unsaid.

I smile at her as I close the journal, placing it and the pen on the floor beside me. I straighten my legs from bent knees, then gesture for her to come to me.

"I wanted the quiet more than I wanted to write," I tell her as she crosses the dark enclosure—a hidden alcove we found together while exploring the caves.

"That makes sense," she says, lowering to sit sideways on my lap. She settles against me with her head on my chest. "The children were particularly chaotic today…I could nearly see your headache forming when you left."

I smile at that. "They can't stay down here much longer. All that energy has to go somewhere."

"I don't think it does. I think it just bounces off the walls and then goes right back into them."

"How's Adam?" I ask, wondering how Delle's brother is doing. Witnessing his sister being buried alive has obviously done something terrible to his mind.

Mercy sighs. "I wouldn't say that he's well, but I did get a small smile out of him today. So, it's progress, at least."

"That's great progress," I tell her. "You've done a lot for him over the last few days."

"It feels like the only way I can help Delle right now."

"Speaking of…"

"I know," she mutters. "I heard."

Silvia—one of the younger domestics who is secretly moving back and forth between the caves and the village—had come forward with news earlier today.

Delle's trial date has been set.

Service from Bloodshed—the final trial—is set to take place on the next night of service, which is the day we've chosen to fight for control of Ember Glen.

"At least the timing of it works out in our favor, don't you think? It should work for our plan…" Mercy's palm slides up my chest. "If they plan to set her up to begin her trial at the start of service, then we'll be able to find her easily. We'll be able to save her once the videos have been broadcast—maybe *while* they're being broadcast. We'll make sure she's freed before anyone lays a hand on her."

I rub my hand over her back as I place a kiss on the top of her head. "She'll be fine."

"What do you think they had planned? How do you think they mean to…kill her?"

I sigh. "I'm not sure I want to speculate on that too much. But if they arranged it to take place at the start of service, then I think it's safe to assume they mean to involve all the men of Ember Glen in her trial."

"All of them…and with the intent to make her bleed. I don't want to think about it." I can feel a tremor ripple through Mercy, and it's followed by a beat of quiet. Her fingers curl, gripping the open collar of my button-down. "It's so strange to think of it now as something separate from me. I never dreamed there would be a way out of it. I was prepared to die in the trials, right along with her. And I don't know what to make of the fact that it somehow feels *worse* to think of it happening to her than it does to think of it happening to *me*."

"I don't think that's strange, Mercy. I can empathize with the feeling."

She lifts her head to look up at me, reaching up to wrap her arms around my neck. Her forehead wrinkles as her eyes narrow on mine, giving me a serious expression. "If I had to help them bury you alive—stand by and watch it all happen while pretending I was okay—then I…I wouldn't have been able to do it."

"It was a waking nightmare, but it was *nothing* in comparison to what you went through. I won't allow you to minimize it just because you have compassion for me. That compassion is your greatest strength. It's one of the reasons I fell so hard for you, but I don't want you to misplace the use of it on me. I hurt you as much as any other man in this village, and I don't ever want you to forget it."

"Do you think I could ever forget? Arlo, I've forgiven you for every pain you've caused me, but none of them will ever leave my memory. They've left scars on me—the same as every other pain I've endured—but the scars you left are the only ones I *want*."

"Why would you *want* them?"

"Because they remind me of yours."

She draws her arms back from around my neck to lift my hand away from her waist, bringing it up between us as she presses her palm flat against mine. With her other hand, she traces the lines and ridges of the old burn scars across the back of my hand.

"You were only a child when you started to burn yourself, punishing yourself for urges, which I'm now certain we all have. You were praised for seeking pain instead of satisfying your need—a need you were told could *only* be satisfied by a servant once a month when you'd reached a certain age.

"And that was all for nothing. Now that we know what Hyatt did to Stefanie, we know the purges haven't done what they were intended to do. We know that whatever rules we were made to follow were arbitrary, made up by the original founders, who were doing nothing more than playing a game with money and power.

"We've both been scarred by this place, Arlo. You hurt *me* because they hurt *you*. And that doesn't make it right; it's not an excuse for anything…it's just the truth. But you should know that when I think about the hurt you've caused me, I think of your hands, too. When you hurt me, your hands belonged to them…but now they belong to *you*."

I lean my forehead against the side of her face, letting my eyes fall shut as I breathe her in. I bring my fingers between hers to lock our hands together before she pulls our shared grip against her chest.

"I won't hurt you with them again." I brush my nose across her cheek, nudging her hair away so I can whisper near her ear, "Not unless you ask me to."

She lets out her breath, sinking into my hold. I kiss her cheek as her eyes drift shut. "I could be convinced to ask you to…"

"No, starlight. I won't try to convince you of that. I'll only give you that when you beg me for it on your own."

"Then don't give me pain, Warden Rainn. Use your hands to give me *relief* instead. Take care of me." Her head turns and with her eyes still shut, she plants a whisper-soft kiss on my lips. "And then, perhaps, I'll beg you for it."

I groan with the visceral shift in her energy, and it rumbles through our lips as she kisses me again—it's light, gentle, teasing with soft pecks that seduce me to open for her. Mercy's tongue sneaks past my lips, deeply yet delicately licking against mine with soft sweeps that drag me under her spell.

So easily, I'm lost in her.

Every fear, every ache, every worry fades away.

I could stay like this forever, with her close against me and feeding me love through her delicate kisses. I still don't feel I've earned what she gives me, and this kiss feels too sweet for a man who doesn't deserve it…yet it's because she gives it so easily that I *want* to deserve it.

I want to be the man who deserves Mercy Madness.

Her grip on my hand tightens, and I feel her entire body tighten with it, holding my hand firm to her chest. I deepen our kiss, feeding my tongue so deeply that it takes her breath away. She gasps, breaking the kiss, and I take the opportunity for my lips to draw a trail across her cheek.

"Tell me what you want from me, starlight. How should I make you come?"

"Love," she says, twisting her head to look at me. She fully captures my attention with her silver gaze. "I can't believe you would ask me *how*…" My head inclines as I watch her, trying to work out what she's saying. And then her lips curl up at the corners. "You should be asking how *many*."

I'm on her in a flash.

Ignoring the ache in my arm, I wrap both around her to ease her landing, lowering her sharply to the hard stone floor. She lets out a yelp on the way down.

"Awfully bold of you, Mercy Madness." I grin at her as I plant one elbow on the ground beside her head, tracing my fingers down her throat.

"You like it when I'm bold," she says as a matter of fact.

I bend to follow the trail of my fingertips with my lips, dotting soft kisses down the line they draw from chin to chest. "I *crave* your boldness, at least as much as I crave these curves." I lift my head to watch my fingers glide up the slope of her breast. "So boldly tell me what you want from me. Ask me for anything, and you'll have it."

Moments pass as her chest rises and falls. I get lost in the motion of her curves as her breaths quicken, but my eyes are torn away, called back to her face when she finally speaks. "I want you to undress me…"

That doesn't seem like a very bold demand, so I look at her expectantly, waiting for her to say more.

"Strip me bare…"

She looks so serious that it draws my face closer to hers, and I wait. Looking deep into her eyes, I know there's something more to this that I'm just not understanding.

"You and I have never been fully undressed together. Every time we've come together, one or both of us has been at least partially dressed."

I nod, realizing she's right. "It was always in secret or in a rush…"

Her hands find my face, thumbs brushing my cheeks. "I want to feel your skin against every inch of me. No barriers between us, no rushing." She lifts her head from the floor as she pulls me closer, brushing her lips over mine. "No secrets. Just my skin against yours."

Sweet sin…

That sounds like the most provocatively *perfect* thing I could ever give this woman.

I force her head back to the ground as I kiss her hard, and she moans into my lips. Her fingers sink into my hair and tug, triggering a shockwave of need that makes me shiver. I sit up sharply, pulling out of her grip to the sound of her whimper. I sit back on my heels between her spread legs and grab her left ankle, moving it in front of me. I drop the heel of her boot into my lap and start to untie the laces, my eyes locked on hers as I remove her boot and sock. I toss the shoe over my shoulder, and it lands somewhere behind me with a heavy thud.

Lifting her leg up with my hand at her ankle, I lean in to kiss the side of her knee. I raise it a little higher and kiss the back of her leg, where it creases behind her knee. She startles at the touch of my lips, drawing in a quick breath, so I kiss her in the same spot again, eliciting the same response, which gives me absolute satisfaction.

Grinning down at her with my lips pressed to her skin, I start to nip at the inside of her thigh, watching as her stomach visibly clenches. My cock twitches at the sight of her pink lips parting to gasp before whispering my name. I repeat it all with her other leg— removing her boot, kissing behind her knee, then gently nipping along the inside of her thigh.

I cross my arms before grabbing her hips, and with a quick twist, I roll her onto her stomach. She plants her palms on the ground as she lifts onto her knees, only just enough so she can shift her body backward through her pressing palms, ass pressing toward me, back arching like a cat.

I reach forward to unzip her layered black skirt, then slip my fingers beneath the waistband—beneath the underwear, too—and slowly drag both barriers away. I bend over Mercy to kiss her skin, covering each exposed inch with my lips.

Slowly, sensually, I bare her hips and the breathtaking curve of her gorgeous ass. I ease the fabric down to her knees, and she lifts each leg so I can remove it entirely, tossing it aside.

I take a moment to appreciate the beauty of Mercy on her hands and knees in front of me, hips squirming, back arching, already so needy for my touch.

When she whimpers, desperation punches through my gut, and I absolutely *must* taste her. I cup her cheeks in my palms, squeeze and spread as I shift my knees back. I lower my head behind her and dive in to taste her. Mercy rewards me with a gasp and a moan, pressing her ass back to bury my face as my tongue finds her pussy.

I lick until she twitches, spending minutes right there with my face submerged in the delicious rising waves of her lust. I get lost in her perfection, obsessed with her taste and scent. My hands are around her thighs, fingers digging into her flesh to hold her still as I try to satiate this never-ending thirst.

This—right here between her thighs—is my favorite place in the entire fucking world. I would move mountains for a single taste.

"I'm…" Mercy pants. "Love, I'm…*Oh*…"

Her hand swings back and smacks my forearm, and the strike is enough to bring me back. I promised her I would never hurt her with these hands, yet my fingers are sunk so deep into her fleshy thighs that I know they must *ache*.

All at once, I release, and her body launches forward, but I quickly grab her hips to drag her back and steady her. The hand she smacked me with reaches back again, her palm covering the back of my hand on her hip. Her head hangs as she fights to catch her breath.

How long was I there between her thighs?

"I'm not ready to come yet…" Her fingers curl and her nails dig into my knuckles. "You nearly made me come and I'm still half-dressed…"

I blow out a breath, knowing I have to pace myself.

I let go of her hips, slowly bringing my palms over the curve of her cheeks. I slide my hands up her back, then slip my fingers beneath the hem of her black lace top. I move in close behind her on my knees and drop my hands along her sides, slipping around to the front of her to palm her breasts beneath her shirt.

I fold over Mercy's back, molding to her body as her head rises, the back of it touching my shoulder. I nuzzle my face into her hair, brush my nose across her cheek…I kiss along her jawline, lick down her neck, paint her skin with her scent which coats my tongue.

Closing my arms around her waist, I lift her as I rise on my knees, keeping her flush against me as we kneel together on the bedrock. She raises her arms as I peel off her shirt and toss it away, then pull off her bra beneath.

She sighs the moment she's bare, relieved, letting her weight fall back against me.

"Take off your clothes," she whispers as my hands roam over her body. "Let me feel you hard against my back."

I squeeze her breast, drawing my fingers back slowly across her nipple to tease her. "Move forward, starlight. Put your hands on the wall and wait for me."

I guide her forward, moving until she can flatten her palms against the stone wall when she bends. I have to force myself to back up with the way she arches so beautifully, but I hastily remove my clothes because it's what she asked me for.

And I'll give this woman *anything* she asks me for.

As soon as I'm naked, I press in behind her, nudging her knees apart with mine between hers. I reach over her head to wrap my hands around her wrists, her palms still flat against the rock wall that rises before her. She whimpers as I dip to kiss the back of her neck, making sure she feels my hard cock just begging to force its way between her cheeks.

"Sweet sin, Mercy. I'm so hard for you right now. So fucking hard…"

"Fuck me," she commands. "I want to feel how hard you are when I come."

I lasso one arm around her waist and angle her hips. My fingers slip down over her curls as I eagerly reach for her clit, and I know I've found the right spot when her entire body jumps at my touch. I find an easy, gentle rhythm with my fingers, and I continue until her belly is clenching, twitching against my arm, her entire body trembling.

"Arlo…I can't…I want…."

"You want my cock?" I kiss her shoulder.

Her head bobs in a jerky nod.

"Are you trying not to come right now, starlight? Are you letting me edge you until you have me buried deep inside you?"

Again, a tense bob of her head.

I rub harder, faster, and then abruptly, I stop.

"No…I need…"

"What do you need?"

"Inside me…"

"Fast? Hard? Gentle? I want you to tell me."

She hangs her head, gasping, steadying her voice. "Fuck me hard. Make me come fast, even if it hurts."

I drop my head onto her shoulder. "Sweet sin."

I flatten my palm over her curls to draw her body back, encouraging her to arch deeper, to angle her hips for me to enter. I bring my arm around behind her so I can fist my cock and run the tip along her slick folds. I thrust inside her in one long, deep stroke, and we groan in unison at the shared relief of being connected. I hook my arm beneath her waist again to find that swollen nub, rubbing in a steady rhythm that quickly draws her into tension.

"Yes. Warden Rainn, *yes*…I feel you…every inch…"

Just as she wanted, every inch of my skin is touching every inch of hers, and *fuck*, it feels so perfect.

She feels so perfect.

I turn my face against her shoulder, press it into her neck and whisper, "Wildflowers and starlight."

She gasps, as if it's my words that cause the full body tremor down her spine and not my fingers on her clit or my cock deep inside her.

I start to move, giving her fast, hard strokes that have us grunting together with every slap of our bodies. We move with pure carnality, letting our bodies take control. Our movements are utterly indecent, vulgar thrusting in physical desperation. Yet each motion is driven entirely by our deeper connection—our spiritual devotion, our unconditional love. The physical need for one another couldn't exist on its own; sex would *never* feel this perfect without the guiding passion from our souls.

I plant my palm over Mercy's mouth as she cries out with her release, keeping my rhythm steady with my cock and my fingers to draw it out as long as I can.

I don't stop until she's shaking—until she reaches back to *make* me stop—and when I settle to be still inside her, she lets out a small chuckle. She turns her head slightly over her shoulder, not enough to fully look at me, just enough to get my attention.

"That's one." Through her profile, I can see her smile. "I want more."

Sweet sin, she wants more.

And because she demands it, I give until she's spent.

And I'll give her so much more once we've won this war.

"PROMISE ME YOU'LL be careful," Mercy whispers into my ear. She rises onto her toes to wrap her arms around me tighter.

It's when her fingers slip up from the back of my neck, tangling in my hair, that I feel it—the pang of saying goodbye once again. My arms circle her waist, pulling her closer as I draw in a breath filled with the wildflower scent of her hair.

"When all of this is over," I whisper, "promise me we'll never say goodbye again."

She nods, her cheek brushing mine as she gives a final squeeze. "I promise."

Reluctantly, I let her go, let her slip from my arms as she gradually releases me. I stand still and stare at her as Luna hooks her hand through the crook of Mercy's arm to drag her back—as if she knows there's no escape for me if Mercy isn't anchored.

"You really should go," Luna says. "You'll have to find Theo without getting caught, and even then, he'll need enough time to set up the broadcast without the rest of the Control finding out."

"I know. I'm going, just…"

Sweet sin, just one more.

I reach out to snatch Mercy's wrist and yank her from Luna's grip. I drag her straight into my arms, cradle the back of her head in my palm, and kiss her hard.

Hard, but not long because time is running short.

I drop my forehead to meet hers. "I know I'll never convince you to run if this all goes sideways, so I won't bother trying. I'll just tell you that I love you, Mercy Madness, and I need you to survive." I sink my fingers into her hair, hold her in place, press my cheek to hers, and whisper in her ear, "I haven't spent nearly enough time with my face between your legs, and I won't be able to rectify that if you get yourself killed."

I pull back to look at her, and find a grin on her face, her eyes fluttering open to meet mine. "I can't think of a better reason than that to survive," she jokes. Her chest rises, then her shoulders drop as she exhales. "I love you, Arlo Rainn."

I plant a heavy kiss on her forehead.

I nearly give into the urge to lift her over my shoulder, to drag her away with me through the tunnels to avoid this rapidly approaching battle for freedom.

Yet I know I can't do that.

This fight is hers, and I have to let her lead it.

I force myself to release her, then sling the messenger bag with the video reels over my shoulder. I take a step backward, and she lurches against Luna's hold. I know it was unintentional—a natural urge she has to be with me. I know it because I feel it, too.

There's a painful tension through the invisible rope that binds us, and my muscles strain to fight it. I force myself to take another step backward.

"You're the sinner we all needed, starlight." Another step. "And you're the only one who can lead us out of hell."

With all my might, I turn away from her, flinching as the imaginary rope snaps, untethering us as we separate on the brink of war.

With a quick pace, I head into the dark passageway to leave for the Homestead, charging out of sight because I'd never be the man who deserves Mercy Madness if I didn't fight for her…and fighting for her means fighting for what's right.

So tonight—beneath the light of the full moon—we fight for freedom.

chapter thirty

Mercy

THE SUN HAS nearly set, and the full moon will be rising soon. The last remaining glimmer of daylight gives way to the falling night, crushed beneath the descending darkness. The way the light fades beneath our feet feels visceral, like our steps are stomping out the final embers of the dying sun.

Most of the domestics have arranged themselves around the village in smaller groups, spread out and ready to fight. We know there will be some men—and probably some women, too—who will reject the truth when it's revealed to them. We're prepared for those who reject it to react in one of two ways.

Our hope is that they'll recognize their part in our suffering—that they'll stand down and step back. But that's not the reaction we expect; that's not the reaction we've prepared for.

Tonight is meant for the purge, and the men are primed for violence.

The men see this night as divine, a night that's *owed* to them after the month-long suppression of their depraved urges. Yet we're going to stand before them once the truth has been revealed, demanding that their one glorious night of debauchery be canceled immediately, insisting that we be granted freedom from service and forced domesticity.

We already know this will end violently.

So, we're prepared to meet them where they stand.

It looks like most of the men have already arrived at the Bank to make their deposit before the purge—a few here and there crossing the way to enter. The servants have already gone to Sanctuary and have been there for a while now. The domestics are home alone, and the Control could be anywhere.

My goal is to be at the center of the action because these women are looking for me to lead. Though it's terrifying, I'm committed to this fight, and even if I don't survive, maybe some of the others will see freedom come morning.

And the thought of that is worth risking *everything* for.

Stefanie and Luna make their way with me behind the houses, winding through the village in shadowed spaces that provide good cover in the dark. It's not a challenge to make it from my home to the backyard of the house nearest the sloped path without being seen. But it *will* be a challenge to make it across the open village square to Sanctuary.

We can make it soundlessly up the sloped path that leads from the village to the square—grass lines the edges of the gravel path, which will keep our steps muted. But once we reach the top and the ground levels out, the gravel beneath our feet will surely give us away, and there's no way around it. And of course, there's the possibility that they might simply *see* us running across the square. It's a vast open space without any spots to hide.

I turn to Luna and Stefanie behind me and speak in a quiet voice. "We just have to make a run for it. When I move, you follow. Don't stop, don't look back, just *run*."

"We'll be right behind you," Luna says.

I look out to scan the path and find it's all clear.

The opportunity is now…and I decide to run.

We take off, running single-file up the narrow patch of grass that lines the upward-sloping gravel pathway. As I approach the top of the incline, I steel myself against the fear of being seen, not knowing if the Control may be in the square or watching from the Homestead. Though truthfully, it doesn't matter if we're seen—we have to push onward all the same.

The square opens before us, and my boots land on gravel. The sound seems so much louder than I anticipated, and it's further amplified by Luna's and Stefanie's footfalls as they follow. The slipping stones beneath our feet only serve to slow us down, so we push harder, running as fast as we can across the square.

Sanctuary is in sight…

We can make it.

We're halfway across the square when bright lights switch on at the exterior of the Homestead.

"Hurry," I urge. "Faster."

"Mercy…" Luna's voice holds a tinge of warning.

"Go!" Stefanie shouts, and the volume of her voice alone suggests that we've already been seen.

And Killian Cole's booming voice only confirms it. "I see you, Mercy Madness!"

I glance right, watch as he charges down the front steps of the Homestead, and panic strikes me.

"Mercy, *stop*!" I see Owen running out the front doors of the Homestead, and he chases after us, too.

My lungs ache, my calves tighten as my feet slip over the shifting stones, but I keep going.

"Open the door!" I cry out, hoping the servants in Sanctuary will hear me, that one of them will let us in. "Please, open the *door*!"

Luna and Stefanie shout with me.

We run, we scream, we *hope*.

I reach the bottom of the stone steps that lead to Sanctuary, and the moment my boot lands, one of the two heavy wooden doors swings inward.

"Mercy?" It's Cambria at the door.

"Let us in!"

Her forehead wrinkles, but then she must spot Killian charging after us because her eyes widen.

She steps back. "Hurry!"

I reach the landing and stop, turn sideways to usher Luna and Stefanie through first. "Come on!"

Luna enters first, closely followed by Stefanie.

And Killian's halfway up the steps.

Cambria grips my arm.

I turn as she pulls me, then sprint across the threshold and slam to a stop just behind her. We turn together and see Killian crash to a halt. His hands come up, slamming against the closed door on one side and the frame on the other, bracing himself in the opening.

"You can't come in." Cambria hastily steps forward, blocking the way, holding the door open with her hip.

Killian cocks his head to the side. "Cambria—"

"You can't come in," she repeats. "You don't have permission from me, so there's no way you'll get permission from *all* of us."

I gape at her, stunned at her boldness, especially with Killian.

"I don't need to come in, Cambria. I just need *her* to come *out*."

Maybe I only see it now because I know the truth about his ancestor, but Killian and Ian Cole share the same darkness in their eyes, the same penchant for obsession, control, and violence.

I move to step in front of her, but her hand swings out to stop me, her eyes never leaving Killian.

"Ten minutes." She grips the side of the door and starts to push it shut.

Killian sticks his foot out to stop it, the toe of his polished leather shoe slamming into the wood.

Cambria's head drops to look down at his foot, then she slowly drags her gaze up to his face. "Killian Cole, remove your foot from our Sanctuary *at once*. You're a man of *God* and you need to behave as such. This night of service has not yet begun, and until it *has*, I suggest you control your Impulse."

He drops his head and chuckles darkly before looking up at her from beneath his lashes. "Cambria Miller, you're testing my *fucking* patience."

"And I'm sure you'll test mine for the remainder of the night, so let's call it even. *Ten. Minutes.*"

This time, she moves behind the heavy door and shoves, forcing his foot out before she slams it shut. She spins to face me, and for a few moments, we only stare at each other. Then, we move at the same time, and throw our arms around one another.

She exhales heavily, her body sinking just before she releases me and steps back. "That was terrifying," she says. "I thought he was going to force his way in. What are you doing here? Where have you been?"

"There's so much I have to tell you, and I will." I glance around, seeking Ellary, expecting to see her lying broken in a bed. But the beds are all empty, so she must be doing better—yet I don't see her among the servants gathering around us. "Where's Ellary? I need to see her. Where is she?"

Cambria's lips part, but she doesn't speak, and her relieved expression melts into something somber. "Mercy, she—"

"Where is she? I know she survived the fall; Arlo told me she did. And she's had all this time to heal…Is she walking? Is she moving without trouble?" The words all come out of me in a rush, filling time, delaying her from telling me what the glassy sheen over her eyes implies.

Cambria's head falls with the weight of the truth. "No, Mercy." She lifts her head again to look at me as a tear streaks down her cheek.

My eyes shift, drifting away to peer at a faraway spot, my vision becoming unclear and unfocused. My eyes feel warm and wet, but I can't be crying…

Because there's nothing to cry about.

I blink and shake my head, forcing my gaze to refocus as I look squarely at Cambria. "Where's Ellary?"

Cambria shakes her head.

"Where's *Ellary?*" I insist.

"She died! She's gone, Mercy. Ellary's *gone.*" Cambria gasps as she looks at me, and I don't know what she sees in my expression, but she hurries to close the distance between us, grabbing and pulling me into a rough hug. "Ellary died. She's dead, and they didn't even hold a remembrance. No honor or gratitude was given." She grips my shoulders as she pulls back, looking directly into my eyes, waiting until I meet her gaze. "Mercy?"

"I thought she was okay…"

Her hand touches my cheek, her thumb brushing beneath my eye as if she's brushing away a tear.

Am I crying?

"No. No, she wasn't okay. She never even woke up."

"When did she…"

"Six days ago."

"Oh…*no*…" Tears fall like rivers down my cheeks.

"I know," she mutters sadly. "I know…"

"Where…where is she?"

"You can't see her, Mercy."

"But where *is* she?"

"They burned her after she died. All that's left of her are… ashes."

"I-I can't see her?"

Cambria shakes her head.

"So, she's just…"

"She's gone."

Ellary's gone.

"Killian did this," I mutter.

Cambria nods. "He did. He pushed her; I know he did. Mercy, I'm afraid. I'm afraid to go out there tonight and face him. We're *all* afraid."

I look up to find my sisters have gathered around us, and every face is awash with fear. I turn my attention back to Cambria, giving her a questioning look.

"I don't know where you've been or what you know, but things in Ember Glen have turned for the worse," she tells me. "The Control, the husbands…they're so angry that the children are gone and that half the domestics have disappeared. Their rage has been building since the incident at the Homestead, and we don't know what will happen to us tonight in service. We have to serve—we know we do—but how can we walk out there and offer ourselves freely, knowing how angry they are tonight? And what if the Control brings their guns? What if their Impulse is to use them against us?"

Their fear surrounds me, consumes me, triggers my compassion so strongly, it's sobering…and it reminds me why I'm here. I have to take my despair over the loss of Ellary and box it up, wrap it tightly, and store it away somewhere deep inside my mind. Ellary is gone, but these women are still here and they need me.

I press my eyes shut. I allow myself to endure a single sob that twitches through my gut, let out the cry that claws up my throat and forces its way out from between my lips. And then I straighten my spine, pull back my shoulders, and lift my chin as I open my eyes.

"A plan is in motion—that's why we're here. And I'm going to tell you *everything*," I begin. "But know that if everything goes right, none of you will serve tonight. None of you will ever have to serve again."

chapter thirty-one

Mercy

"WHAT'S HAPPENING, MERCY? I don't hear anything playing yet." Cambria's ear is pressed to the door. "The men are out there. They expect us to be in the forest already for the purge. What do we do?"

I told the servants everything. I told them about the video records, and the real story of Ember Glen. I told them about the plan for Arlo to engage Theo's help in broadcasting the videos. They listened to me, and many of them seem to believe me.

The ones who don't believe me insist upon proof, and that's understandable. Yet I don't know when that proof will be unveiled because we're still waiting for the damn videos to broadcast.

They're late...

What's going on?

Is Arlo okay?

What am I supposed to do?

"Let me think," I tell Cambria as I pace the floor.

"The longer we wait to serve them, the worse this night will be," says Phoebe, one of my sisters in service.

"You said there was proof," Ruby says. "I want to believe you, but if there's no proof, then we *must* go out and serve. It's our duty."

I whirl around to face her. "It's not your duty to serve those men, Ruby. I swear to you, it isn't. Everything I told you is true. I just...I don't know what's going on with the videos. Something must have happened to delay them."

They're delayed…

What would delay them other than being caught, captured, or killed?

"We've seen the videos," Luna says in my defense, gesturing to indicate herself and Stefanie. "I promise you, it's real. What Mercy told you is true. Service is not God's will for you; it was the will of *men*."

Phoebe points at the door. "And those men out there have provided for us. We owe them our gratitude for that…We owe them our *service*."

"Those men have done *nothing* for you. They are not the providers in this village. Our providers are right here." I point to where Luna and Stefanie are standing. "The men do *nothing* in comparison to what the domestics do. Domestics are the pillar on which our community stands, and truthfully, they should be named the same as us—*servants*.

"We may serve the men's brutality once a month, but domestics serve their husbands daily in all other manners of speaking. Those men who purge with us go home when the sun rises, and their domestics take on the burden of caring for the remainder of their needs for the rest of the month." I glance over at Stefanie. "And some of them have served in violence."

Stefanie gives a brief nod, then steps forward and raises her shirt, pushing down the waistband of her skirt to reveal the letter 'H' that Hyatt had carved into her flesh.

"What is…" Phoebe steps closer, staring. "Is that a scar?"

"Yes," Stefanie says, covering it again. "My husband gave me that. You recall Hyatt Price? The man who set your sister Ivy Jane on fire. Sadly, her *service* that night was meaningless since he hurt me when he returned from service that morning because his breakfast wasn't ready. Violent men are violent, whether during a purge or in their homes with their wives. You will not spare the domestics from violence and fear by serving those men tonight. I'm sorry to tell you that you never have."

Cambria looks around at the servants. "I feel like my eyes were opened when Ellary was pushed. Killian's Impulse to shove her from the cliff proves that his violent urges were not satisfied from the previous purge. I think what Mercy's telling us must be true. I think the Impulse is a lie. And given how angry those men are that so many of us helped Mercy when we were gathered at the Homestead…I fear that some of us will die tonight in service."

I smile watching Cambria as she speaks, my heart beating wildly to hear her, of all people, speak those words. *Cambria*—the woman who always wanted to feel the pain from her service in reverence of how dutifully she served.

Her eyes are open…*finally* open.

"I have faith in Arlo…faith that he and Theo will succeed. You will have your proof tonight, Ruby." I turn to Luna and Stefanie. "I think we have to stall. The timing is all wrong. We expected everyone would still be separate when the videos were broadcast."

"You're right," Stefanie agrees. "The men won't wait forever."

"And by the sound of it," Luna says, "they're growing angrier the longer the servants make them wait."

"What if Arlo fails?" Phoebe asks.

"Arlo won't fail, not with this." I pause to take a steadying breath, then I turn to face Cambria. "We need to stall the men. We need to give them a plausible reason for why you're all making them wait, and I think I have an idea. I need you to open the doors, and I need you to speak to Killian."

"What? Me?"

"Yes. He listened to you before, and he'll listen to you now. You need to convince them that the servants *want* to come out, convince them that you're all planning to serve tonight."

"No, I can't—"

"Cambria, *listen*. Tell him that you all want to serve, but you're afraid of retaliation for what happened on the day that Arlo and Stefanie were meant to burn. Draw him into a negotiation."

"But what am I supposed to negotiate?"

"Tell him…" I pause to gather my thoughts. "Tell them that you want to negotiate certain restrictions for tonight's service; that you want to limit certain acts of violence."

She shakes her head. "They would *never* go for that. And even if they agreed, it wouldn't matter. Any acts they commit against us tonight will be forgiven by God. They could lie and say they agree, then commit those acts anyway."

"That doesn't matter. It's not the point. *No one* is serving tonight—that will happen over my dead body. The point is to stall until the broadcast comes on. You can do this, Cambria. Just keep him talking…for as long as you can."

She's hesitant. I can see the muscles in her neck working as she swallows hard. Her eyes cast around the room, but finally, they land on mine.

"You swear that it's true?" she asks me. "Can you swear to me that everything you told us is true and there are videos to prove it?"

"I swear it, Cambria. On my own life, I swear."

Slowly, she nods. "Okay. I'll try."

THE DOUBLE DOORS to Sanctuary are open wide and Cambria stands between them. She remains inside, just a few feet back from the threshold. Though I know the men believe that entering Sanctuary is a sin against God's will, it's still unnerving to see her so exposed. The crowd of men are gathered outside, and their voices rise in anger and frustration.

Killian slowly approaches, moving away from the gathered men to cross the gravel-covered square alone. He comes to a slow stop at the bottom of the stone steps, and for a beat, he watches Cambria.

Then, he raises his arm to demand silence.

As the voices of men fade toward quiet, I see something I hadn't noticed before. I'd been so focused on getting to Sanctuary when we ran that I must have missed them. Two screens are set up in front of the Homestead on either side of the staircase, and what they show makes my blood run cold.

On screen is a livestream from within the forest—from the clearing where the bonfire roars high and hot. Delle is positioned away from the fire, her wrists bound in rope. The ends are tied to trees on opposite sides of the clearing, stretching her arms out and up. She stands barefoot on the ground, wearing no clothes except for underwear and a bra on this cold November night.

Seeing her like that—alone, shivering, and frightened—sends anxiety tearing through me.

Why haven't they broadcast the truth yet?

"Cambria," Killian's voice is deceptively gentle. "Would you please enlighten me as to what the fuck is going on in there?"

"We have some demands before serving tonight."

Killian chuckles. "My apologies if I'm a bit confused. I thought there was a full moon tonight." He turns his head, lifting his chin skyward, spotting the full moon as it's revealed from behind a gray cloud that's sweeping away. "Yes, there it is." He turns back to look at Cambria. "And under the full moon, it is your *duty* as a servant to come out to the forest and *serve*. So I'm going to need you to be very explicit with your words, if you're capable of such articulation, because none of us understand why you're all in *there* when you should be out *here*, asking how you may serve our needs."

It's subtle, but I see her pull her shoulders back. "On the day Arlo Rainn and Stefanie Price were meant to burn, some of us behaved in ways that were…inconsistent with our role as servants. Naturally, we fear retaliative acts being performed against us out of spite for our actions that day. And for us to serve such retaliative acts would be beyond the scope of our duty. We are beholden to serve the needs of men by their *Impulse*, not by their acts of aggression in revenge. Now, if you would kindly receive our requests in good faith, and grant us certain reassurances for this night, then we will gladly come out to service you all." Cambria pauses. "Was I explicit enough with my words? Or should I find a way to be more *articulate*?"

Killian shows a tight grin, glancing down at his feet as he takes a single step up the stone staircase. "Quite articulate." He looks up at her. "Let me grant you the reassurance that no retaliation is sought *tonight*. The men you are beholden to simply want to purge, and it is their holy right to do so. Now, tell me what must be done so you will all come out and serve God's will."

"No guns," Cambria says.

Killian cocks his head to the side, watching her.

"You will not allow guns at service, tonight or any night hereafter."

Slowly, menacingly, Killian climbs the steps without speaking a word. He stops on the landing, looks at her for a beat, then takes a single step forward. He stands right at the edge of the threshold, though thankfully, he doesn't cross it.

He lowers his voice. "Are you asking me to deny my Impulse to make you come around the barrel of my gun? Surely, you don't wish to deny us both such *fun*, Cambria Miller."

Her neck works as she swallows, eyes widening slightly, though she manages to hold her ground. "That's precisely what I'm saying, Killian Cole. Guns are tools of war; they were never meant to be involved with service."

He nods, pursing his lips. "Perhaps you're right." He reaches behind him, lifts the bottom of his jacket, and pulls a gun from his waistband. "I'll make a deal with you. In good faith, from *both* sides, we'll relinquish one gun per servant. I'll put down this gun, and you send out a servant. *Or...*" He stretches his arm, aiming his gun at me.

"Send Mercy out to service us all, and we will relinquish every gun immediately, banning them from use in service forevermore."

I fight the panic that sharply rises, keeping my body still and steady.

"No. She's not coming out," Cambria says. Killian turns his arm along with his eyes, pointing the gun at her instead. Her eyes press shut for a moment, but she doesn't falter, quickly opening them again. "Put down your gun, and I'll come out."

His eyes scan her face, and he looks pleased with her response.

I'd been so busy watching the gun that I hadn't noticed Owen charge up the steps with Wesley right behind him, each holding two guns—one in each hand.

"Hand it over," Owen demands as he climbs onto the landing.

Killian glances over at him. "I have this situation under control."

"You most certainly do *not*," Owen says. "Their request is fair. Our guns were never meant to be involved in service. Any one of us might mistake the power we feel when holding one as an Impulse that must be satiated. Half the domestics have already disappeared. Would you like someone to accidentally plow through half the servants as well?"

Accidentally?

How would one accidentally *fire a gun at multiple servants?*

I'm outraged by that statement alone, but by sheer force of will, I bite my tongue. Cambria is stalling successfully, and any time we can buy is necessary.

Owen tucks one of the two guns he holds into the back of his waistband, then holds out his empty hand to Killian. "If you want to purge, hand it over."

Killian turns sideways, facing Owen fully. "Are you really suggesting that we leave ourselves and our men unprotected right now? Do you see who's here?" He points back at me. "Mercy Madness has crawled straight out of hell and barged back into Sanctuary like nothing's changed. And she brought *domestics* with her, no less! Clearly, she's been keeping them captive somewhere and poisoning their minds—she's probably poisoning the minds of the children, as well!"

"The only ones who have poisoned our minds are the men of this community," Stefanie says, and all heads snap in her direction.

"And that one should already be dead!" Killian bellows.

"Once the servants are out," Owen says, "we can deal with them, and we will. But our men need to purge, and that *must* come first."

With a sneer, Killian points his gun at the ground, swings his arm forward, and hands it to Owen.

Owen looks over at Cambria after he takes the gun from Killian. "There. The guns are gone. We'll take them back to the Homestead right now."

Killian huffs in frustration, turning to face Cambria again as he lifts his palms to show her his empty hands. "There. See? You got what you wanted. Now, will you *kindly* exit your Sanctuary and do your duty?"

Where is the damn broadcast?

Cambria looks over her shoulder at me, and I know she doesn't know what else to say.

But it doesn't matter because Killian crosses the line a moment later. He shamelessly charges into our Sanctuary—a space no man is allowed to enter—and snatches Cambria around the waist.

"No!" I shout as he lifts her from the floor.

He backs out of the open doorway, dragging Cambria in his arms. He swings her around in front of him, sets her on her feet, and shoves her forward. She tries to stay on her feet as she's flung toward the steps, but she trips and falls, rolling as she lands sideways on the gravel at the bottom.

"Gentleman," Killian announces. "You've been given permission to enter Sanctuary and take your selected servant by force." He gestures toward the wide-open doors at his side. "By all means… help yourselves."

Cambria climbs to her feet and backs away as a sea of men rush toward Sanctuary. Killian chases her down the steps as the wave swallows her whole, and then, she disappears…

This is not what we had planned.

This is not how this will end.

I shout at the others to shut and barricade the doors, but I don't stay to help them. Instead, I run full speed after Killian Cole.

I fight the hands of desperate men as I shove my way through the crowd, force my way past them down the steps, and rush out into the open space of the village square.

I leave the sound of pandemonium at my back, forcing myself to ignore the servants' screams, and I dash across the pebbled-ground chasing Killian as he chases Cambria.

"Cambria!" I yell after her, hoping she'll stop. If she stops, then I can catch up, and when I get my hands on Killian, I will *end* him. "Cambria, stop!"

She must hear my voice because she slows, then whirls around to face me before taking a few staggering steps backward.

I expected her to stop.

I *wanted* her to stop.

But I didn't expect Killian to do the same.

He slams to a halt.

He turns to face me.

He grins.

The unnerving look forces my feet to stop, and they skid across the stones as I slide to a halt.

He chuckles darkly. "You're so predictable, Mercy Madness. And you're late for your final trial."

Did he pull Cambria out of Sanctuary just to lure me out?

Anger rises, burning hot in my chest.

I'm going to kill him.

I charge, slamming into him so hard that it knocks the air from my lungs, but I also manage to knock him off his feet. I fall on top of him as he falls backward, but he's ready for it. He grips my waist and rolls us both, slamming me to the ground, my spine crushing against the gravel.

I try to kick up my foot, reaching for the small, sharp knife that's sheathed in my boot—a leather holster some of the domestics sewed in for each of us before this battle. But he's over me fast, straddling my waist, heavy as he pins me to the ground…and I can't reach it. His hand closes around my throat, and I swing my arms at his, wildly trying to knock him loose.

But he only squeezes tighter, presses down harder.

A sandy-blond strand of hair—one that shook loose from the knot tied at the back of his head—falls over his eyes…

And they're dark—dark, cold, and callous.

I think of Violet Clare. I think of how hard she must have fought Ian while she was in his captivity. I think of her voice and the last words she spoke before the final video record ended—before *I* ended it because I couldn't bear to hear another word.

And though it's her voice I hear in my mind, I speak the words out loud, letting them whisper from my lips as Killian tries to steal my breath for good.

"*Circulus vitiosus in aeternum.*"

His rage-filled expression twists in confusion. "What did you just say to me?" He lets go with one hand to swing his arm as he turns his head. "Get *off*, Cambria!"

His shove sends her flying, and she drops harshly to the ground. Then, he returns the hand he pushed her with back to my throat. With both hands wrapped around my delicate neck, he squeezes.

He lifts my head, then slams it back to the ground again, so hard that my vision momentarily blackens at the edges.

I kick my foot, trying uselessly to get it out from beneath him…
and the absurdity of this situation nearly makes me want to laugh.

Is this it?

After everything, is this the way I die?

I look past Killian, gazing up at the sky, noting the clouds above
me have cleared.

I see the stars.

I see the full moon.

And in my mind, I see Violet Clare.

Somehow, the vision of her weakens me. All at once, I let my
arms fall back…I stop kicking, I stop swinging, I stop fighting. My
body is still beneath the crushing force of Killian's hands.

I'm lying on the ground, looking up at Violet Clare as she crawls
over me, as though I'm the camera laid on the ground capturing her
first night of horror as Ian Cole's captive. Her face appears above
me, dirt-smudged and bloodied. She looks down at me when Ian
demands it while she fights back her tears.

"Circulus vitiosus in aeternum."

I don't know whether I said the words out loud or heard Violet's
imaginary voice say them in my mind, but it doesn't matter. Her face
above me begins to fade, but I'm not fading with her…I'm not dying.
The haunting vision of her has breathed air into my lungs.

Her voice cuts through the fog in my mind, and it brings me
clarity…it brings me back to reality. "Hey, hey! Vicious Circle!"
Violet's voice is amplified, playing from the video she recorded at
the concert.

Killian's grip loosens.

The servants' screaming ends.

The men's desperate demands fade.

And all of Ember Glen is quiet as the truth is finally revealed.

chapter thirty-two

Mercy

KILLIAN SLOWLY RISES, his gaze fixed on the screens in front of the Homestead—screens they'd intended to use to display Delle on trial.

But Delle is no longer on display as the video records play.

Everything around me has stopped…

The men and the servants all stare at the screens in silence.

Killian is on his feet, slowly taking a step away from me toward the Homestead. He seems bewildered, transfixed, as if he's drawn in by some unseen force.

This is my chance to free Delle.

His attention is focused on the screen, but I still need to move quietly. He won't give up on killing me so easily once he snaps out of it.

Drawing my knees and elbows beneath me, I sneak sideways, creeping like a crab as my eyes stay fixed on Killian, watching for any subtle indication that he's going to lunge for me. Cambria is on her hands and knees nearby, slowly rising to her feet, though she remains bent over to keep herself small and unseen.

She reaches out for me, her eyes darting up to watch Killian. I twist to grab her hand, let her help me to my feet, and we slowly, quietly back away.

Then, we turn toward the forest and run.

My lungs burn before we even reach the tree line that separates the square from the forest, but I keep pace with her all the same as we sprint into the darkness. We move as fast as we can, heading in the direction of the clearing with the bonfire, the twigs and leaves crunching beneath our boots.

Too soon, we hear footsteps behind us.

"Mercy Madness!" Killian roars.

"Go," I pant. "The clearing. Get Delle."

"Where are you—"

"Get Delle. He's after *me*. Let him chase me."

"Mercy—"

"Do it!"

I see her silhouette shift in the black forest, heading in the direction of the clearing.

I turn to circle around it, and just as I expected, I hear his footsteps behind me, keeping pace. It's not long before I see the tree line ahead of me and the meadow beyond it. The moon's spotlight glows above the wildflowers, guiding my path through the darkness among the trees.

The threshold is right in front of me, and I force myself to move faster toward it. But just as I reach it, my foot catches on a fallen branch, and I tumble into the tall grass.

Coming out of a roll, I scramble forward, fighting to get my feet beneath me. I try to run too soon and stumble over my own feet. My arms shoot out to catch my forward fall at the same moment Killian barrels into me from behind, slamming me face-down among the grass and wildflowers.

I clench my hand into a fist and swing my elbow back hard, twisting my body with the thrust to nail him in the ribs. He groans, his weight shifting sideways from the hit, and it gives me enough relief where I can push up to my hands and knees.

I manage to crawl out from under him and stumble ahead a few steps more, but then breathlessness catches up with me. My reserves are depleted after the run, my muscles are weak from the oxygen-deprivation, and my body gives out.

I fall to my hands and knees as he catches up to me, crawls over me, and climbs onto my back. The weight of him forces me down, flattening me beneath him.

I throw my arms out in front of me, claw my fingers into the ground, grasping at the stems of wildflowers that only snap in half.

"Well, this is a surprise." Killian reaches over me to grab my wrists, painfully yanking my arms behind me. He holds them in one hand, pressing them down against my lower back as I buck my hips, trying to throw him off me. He groans. "You made me hard with this little chase, sinner. I think God wants me to fuck you before I choke the life out of you."

"No!" I cry out, thrashing uselessly beneath his weight.

Still pinning my hands against my back with one hand, he lifts my skirt above my hips with the other. I fling madly, wildly, thrashing with every last ounce of energy I can muster. His rough fingers slip beneath my underwear and graze me dry as he tugs them to the side.

"Killian, don't! Don't do this!"

"Quiet, you little sinner. You deserve this for all the stress you've caused me."

"Stop!"

I hear his buckle.

"No, *please!*"

His zipper.

"Killian, st—"

He steals my voice.

He stuns me.

He forces himself inside me with a dry, grating thrust.

I can't think; I can't move. The world has gone quiet.

All I hear are his groans, the crude sounds of him moving inside me as unwanted wetness floods to protect me from the pain he inflicts.

I'm motionless.

I'm still for so long that he gradually loosens his grip, slowly releasing my hands. I let them slip from my back and drop to the ground at my sides. Arms restrained or freed, I'm still trapped beneath him, pinned to the ground in this nightmare.

A light breeze rustles the grass, and the wildflowers whisper as they dance around me…

Wildflowers and starlight.

The blooms are shades of amethyst and ruby, though they're shadowed in the night. And with each of Killian's painful movements, they grow darker. He's blackening my meadow, taking the color from this place with every vile thrust.

This place isn't for him.

This place is for love…

For wildflowers and starlight.

And he ruined it!

His palms grip my thighs so he can spread my legs, and he fucks me harder.

I bend my knee, sliding it up beside my hip.

"That's a good little sinner. Spread wider for me."

I twist my body toward my knee, reaching down with my hand. He's so consumed that he doesn't get what I'm doing. He doesn't know that I'm reaching for something. He's not aware that my fingers are grazing the handle of a knife that's sheathed inside my boot.

I grip it.

I start to pull.

Killian groans…

And then he's gone.

In a single motion, I unsheathe my knife and roll to my hands and knees. I look up to find Arlo tangled with Killian, tumbling through the grass. Arlo lands on top of him, slams his fist down into Killian's face, punching him over and over again.

I climb unsteadily to my feet, stumbling and shivering as I twist the knife in my hand while I move beside them…

Arlo continues to pummel Killian, his nose cracks and blood splatters. It splashes across my arm, dotting speckles of red across the wildflowers in my tattoo—the blood of a Cole spilled on the image meant to silence the Vicious Circle.

I want more of it…

I raise my arm.

I fall to my knees.

And finally, I drive my knife into Killian Cole's chest.

chapter thirty-three
ARLO

WHEN I SEE him on top of Mercy and realize what he's doing, violence mingles with adrenaline as it shoots through my veins. I charge after Killian, tumble with him through the meadow, and pin him to the ground.

My hand forms a fist that I pound against his face.

I keep hitting him, even when I hear a crack and blood sprays from his broken nose. I'm determined to hammer him with my fist until he stops moving, stops breathing, until he *stops fucking living.*

But I blink, startled back from the darkest part of my mind as blood erupts from Killian's chest. Then, more blood splashes up, so much that it makes me flinch as it covers my face.

Mercy…

She's on her knees beside us, pulling her knife out of his chest, driving it down again, causing another eruption of blood.

Her face is blood-soaked, twisted in rage, and the sight of her in action stuns me. I'm amazed by the look of her, confused by my reaction because all I see is beauty drenched in red…

My Mercy.

I slip off Killian as Mercy stabs, as she lifts, then lowers, and lifts her knife again. I stay there beside her as she unleashes her rage, watching her massacre this man who deserves every slice of her unbridled fury.

Gradually, her pace slows, and then she stops with her knife raised above him. She looks down at him as she fights for each breath. And then she drives her blade into his flesh—one final time—and her fingers remain settled there, gripping the handle.

I see the whites of her eyes as they slowly lift to look at me, peering through the red that soaks her face. "Arlo?" she mutters.

I reach forward, gently wrapping my fingers around her wrists, and as I rise to my feet, I pull her to stand with me. I step over Killian and drag her into my arms, reaching up into her tangled, starlight tresses, which are threaded with streaks of blood.

She hugs me around the waist, lifts her chin to look up at me, and for moments, we simply stand this way and stare. My hands move to her cheeks, unfazed by the blood that coats my palms as my thumbs brush with a comforting stroke.

In this quiet moment, it's only us.

I press my forehead to hers, tell her with my gaze that I'm so sorry I was late, that our delay caused this to happen to her. Her gentle eyes tell me that she's already forgiven me, yet we both know she'll never forget.

Just like all the pain I've caused her, she'll remember this. But this scar is not worth remembering how she got it. This pain is a burden that will haunt her. And though I did everything I could to be on time, though there was no avoiding being late from the malfunction with the technology, I will *always* blame myself for this.

I will always blame myself for *all* of this.

She should not have been alone. She should not have been Killian's target. But there's no doubt in my mind that this end was always coming. Mercy had to take back her power, and the only way was with violence—the men who built this place made sure of that.

And if violence is the only end, then I'll be violent with her. I'll fight to give her the life she deserves, because this brutal, beautiful, bloodied mess of a woman in front of me deserves peace, happiness, and freedom.

Mercy silently begs me for comfort, so I tilt my chin to kiss her lips softly. Though they're slick and red, I'm unbothered. His blood was meant to be spilled, and she earned the right to spill it.

I was just coming out of the Homestead when I saw Killian disappear into the woods, sprinting like he was chasing someone. I knew right away who he was chasing, but I scanned the crowd of servants and men, nonetheless. They were all just standing, staring, transfixed by the videos playing on the screens.

When I didn't quickly spot her in the throng, I ran into the forest after Killian. I went to the bonfire, assuming Mercy ran off to help Delle, and that's where Killian chased her.

Neither Mercy nor Killian were in the clearing. Instead, I found Cambria fighting tight knots in the ropes that held Delle, struggling to free her. I asked her where Mercy was, and she screamed at me to find her, that Killian had been chasing her, intent on killing her.

That's when I realized she'd lead him to the meadow.

Maybe she did it on purpose, or maybe she just felt the pull, but this meadow became ours the night we chose sin, when we declared our intentions to sin *together*.

That night—as we stood in the pouring rain, beneath the storming sky, with the wildflowers whipping around us in the wind—we'd declared a commitment to stop fighting the passion between us and give into it instead.

Maybe she knew I would find her here.

And when I did find her here, it took me moments too long to understand what I was seeing. I knew right away he was hurting her, but it took a few seconds trapped in shock to see *how* he was hurting her.

That monster was *fucking* my Mercy.

And when it hit me, I snapped.

I glance at Killian on the ground, Mercy turning her head to do the same. His chest doesn't rise and fall; he's as still as a statue. His blood still flows out of him in seemingly endless streams.

Killian is dead.

And my Mercy is the one who ended him.

Pride swells within me, and I feel no shame for it.

Still cradling her cheeks in my palms, I turn her head to face me. I dip to level my eyes with hers and let my wide grin tell her of my pride. Her smile shines through the crimson that coats her face, and though her eyes are filled with tears, I feel relief flow through her. I'm not sure whether the relief comes from the fact that he's dead or from my acceptance of her brutality against him. But it doesn't matter to me as long as she feels a burden lifted.

I take her hand, lock my fingers with hers, and lead her back to the bonfire.

"I'M SO SORRY," Theo's voice is frantic as he quickly works the buttons on his shirt.

The knots that held Delle have been undone, and I'm surprised to find her held in Luna's arms as she shivers. I don't spot Stefanie, but Cambria is nearby, hugging herself with her arms across her chest. Delle's arms are tucked up in front of her, pinned between her body and Luna's.

Mercy and I approach them, coming around from the opposite side of the fire. She tugs her hand from my grip, and I stop with her, both of us watching as Theo removes his button-down shirt. Then, he and Luna work together to put it on Delle, helping her slip her arms through before Luna quickly fastens the buttons in front of her.

"I knew y-you would c-come." Delle's voice tremors as she shivers through her words. Her head is turned toward us, and she's looking directly at Mercy. Delle smiles at her, then turns her gaze to look over at Theo. "I t-told you she'd come back and f-fight."

I look at Mercy, expecting to see her crying or grinning madly, maybe taking off at a run to drag Delle into a hug, so I'm shocked to find her expression impassive. Her face turns away as she casts her gaze toward the fire, then slowly, she walks toward the flames.

"Mercy?"

She crouches to her haunches beside the bonfire, watching the blaze expectantly—it looks as though the fire is speaking and she's listening intently.

Her hand moves forward, and my heart leaps.

Thinking that she's lost her mind—that she's going to thrust her hand into the flame—I cry out, "Mercy!"

She doesn't seem to hear me as she lowers her hand…but then it falls in *front* of the fire, not *through* it, and I let out a sigh of relief.

Her fingers wrap around the end of a small branch that sticks out from the burning pile of brush. She drags it out, bringing fire along with it, and she slowly rises. One end of the branch burns like a torch as she holds it out in front of her.

What is she doing?

She turns and slips away into the forest, heading back in the direction of the meadow. We all call after her, but she's either ignoring us or she's so focused on what's going on in her mind that she can't hear us. Either way, I'm frightened by her lack of response.

We all follow her.

We follow, though none of us makes a move to stop her.

Even when she's broken, even when she's hurting, even when her mind is lost to the darkness and pain, I have faith in her. I will follow her into flames and *burn* with her if that's where she leads me.

She enters the meadow, holding her makeshift torch in front of her, and though she continues forward, the rest of us stop. I can't speak for the others, but I feel *compelled* to stop. There's an internal sense of knowing that I should bear witness to whatever this is, though I'm not meant to participate.

So, we all wait, silently watching from the tree line.

She moves deeper into the meadow, to the spot where Killian lies nestled among the tall grass and wildflowers swaying ever so gently in the light breeze.

She stops beside him.

She stares down at him.

She takes in the vision of her brutality…

And I take in the vision of her reclaimed power.

Holding the flame, she's the light in the center of our meadow. Though darkness wraps around her—though shadows blacken the colors of our meadow—her glow remains bright, her internal flame still burning.

And when she speaks, we're compelled to listen.

Her voice is filled with malice, reflecting the contempt in her heart, and she directs her final words downward at Killian. "*Malo mori quam foedari.*"

Death before dishonor.

Chills ripple across my skin, a tremor running up my spine as goosebumps rise on my flesh.

She drops the burning branch over his body, then steps back.

The flames catch on his clothes.

The orange blaze spreads, then rises.

And we all watch as Killian Cole burns.

For moments, we're all transfixed, lost in a trance with Mercy as the fire dances. Sparking embers leap from his burning body, land on the blooms of wildflowers, and singe their petals.

Though her body faces the fire, Mercy's head turns to catch my stare. She draws in a breath so deep that her shoulders rise as her lungs fill. And when she lets it out again, I see the satisfaction in her subtle grin.

I will never forget her perfection in this moment.

She walks toward me, and I move to meet her halfway. I grab her cheeks and kiss her hard, stealing the last moment we'll ever see in this burning meadow.

Her hands touch my wrists as the kiss breaks, and with her sparkling silver-blue eyes on mine, she whispers, "Wildflowers and starlight."

My smile is wide and proud, and I'm immensely grateful that I get to call her *mine*. I drag her against me, embrace her close, and tangle my bare, bloodied fingers into her hair.

This burning meadow will forever hold the memory of the night we kissed in the rain, the moment when we declared our intent to sin together until the day death finds us.

But death hasn't found us yet.

And death won't find us today.

And now that he burns, Killian's violence won't sully our memory of this place. The fire is cleansing, and Mercy made it.

This meadow is ours again—hers and mine.

I whisper three words, "Wildflowers and starlight."

And they're the only three words she needs to hear to know that my love for her is eternal.

chapter thirty-four
ARLO

WE REACH THE square to find the entire village gathered in front of the Homestead—the servants and men were already there, but even the domestics have come out from their homes to join the population. A swarm of voices—loud in their confusion, fear, and outrage—all swirl together, creating hectic noise.

Wesley and Park stand halfway up the stone staircase, shouting down at the crowd, trying to give answers they don't have. Mercy and I walk hand-in-hand toward the back of the gathering with Theo, Delle, Cambria, and Luna all behind us.

Heads turn at our approach, and I'm certain the sight of us is jarring. Mercy looks like she's come straight from battle, as though she's killed a hundred men—and I suppose, in a way, she has.

Ending the life of Killian Cole—the ancestor of the man who's mad obsession resulted in the founding of Ember Glen—feels like poetic justice. She stabbed him countless times, and a part of me wonders if she stabbed once for each generation of Coles that survived and thrived in the brutality of this place.

Probably not, but the thought of it feels so *right*, that I decide it's what I'm going to believe.

One person from the throng spots us over their shoulder, and they draw the attention of others around them. More and more heads turn in our direction, looking back at us as we approach, and the crowd begins to part. A path opens for us through the gathering, and we follow it as voices gradually fade to silence.

Stefanie forces her way through the crowd ahead of us, and I follow her with my gaze. She runs for Luna and throws her arms around her in relief. I breathe a sigh of relief, too. It would hurt me if my sister's heart was broken—and it would have been broken if something had happened to Stefanie. She joins us as we approach the stone staircase.

Wesley and Park move in front of us about halfway up the steps. "What's going on?" Wesley asks. "Do you know anything about this?"

I ignore his question. "Where are Owen and Ryker?"

"They're inside, trying to get in touch with the Elders to find out if it's…Is it true? Is it all true?"

Mercy releases my hand and turns outward, facing the crowd. When she speaks, her voice is loud and clear. "What you've seen is the real story of Ember Glen from footage that was found hidden in the caves beneath our feet. And now that you know the truth, Ember Glen no longer exists.

"Men, in case you were wondering, there will be no purge tonight. The servants will no longer be happy to serve your violent and sexual needs. As you now understand, it is not God's will for them to serve you. It was the will of a madman named Ian Cole, and I'm certain no servant here would like to serve you in his honor.

"In two hours, we're leaving Ember Glen. Arlo Rainn will lead us through the caves to the world beyond the mountains. You may choose to come with us, or you can remain here in Ember Glen…" She turns her head toward the forest, looking out toward the smoke rising in the distance. "But if you choose to stay, then I suggest you hurry to put out the fire I set over Killian Cole's dead body before it spreads to the trees."

Everyone looks out toward the forest, but it's only about a dozen men who run from the crowd, shouting about hurrying to put it out.

Mercy turns on her heel. "Move," she tells Wesley and Park. They looked stunned, horrified, but they step aside to let us pass.

As we ascend, my gaze sweeps over the images of wildflowers etched into the massive wooden doors.

Did Ian Cole carve those images himself?

If he did, I'd like to watch them burn.

Stopping just in front of the doors, we move aside to let Theo reach out with his banded arm to unlock it. We enter the Homestead together, then turn left, heading directly for the courtroom.

Down the hallway, the courtroom door is open—which is unusual—and we can hear Owen's voice carry down the hall as we approach.

"And you *knew* this? You *knew* from the moment you became Elders?" Owen asks with a tone of incredulity.

"Yes." I hear Clyde's voice.

The Elders must be on screen.

Mercy and I glance at each other, then hurry to the door, rushing into the room.

"What are you—" Owen gapes at us with wide-eyes. He's leaning forward on his palms, standing behind the black, semi-circular table. I can see his face in the spotlight as he leans forward out of the shadows behind him. "I don't even care." He shakes his head, writes us off, and turns back to speak to the Elders. "How could you lie to us? How could you…Why would you…" he sputters, seemingly at a loss for words.

Ryker seems unfazed, sitting just a few seats away from Owen. "They still have to maintain control of this community. The so-called *truth* doesn't matter."

Owen swings his head to look over at Ryker. "The truth doesn't *matter?*"

"He's right," Lawrence says from the screen. "It didn't matter to you until you knew it."

"Well, now that I know, it *matters*." Owen stands, putting his hands on his head as he spins away, pacing into the dark shadows behind the table.

Edgar appears somber on the screen. "Now that everyone knows the truth, it's over. It all ends at sunrise."

I step forward, moving to stand in the spotlight that shines over the center of the space in front of the table. "What do you mean? What ends at sunrise?"

"Arlo Rainn," Edgar snarls, "I suppose you're the culprit behind this little…*unveiling*."

"Tell me what you mean." I put a hard edge to my voice. "It all ends at sunrise…?"

"You ask for truth so insistently," Edgar says. "So let me tell you the truth of the world outside of Ember Glen. Out here, you don't *exist*. You were never born, you never lived, you have no records… You are *nothing*. Because you don't exist, there is no life you can have beyond the mountains. You can't work, you can't earn, you can't purchase food or acquire housing. You would all *die*, starved and homeless if it weren't for us keeping this secret for you; if it weren't for us providing everything you need in Ember Glen—"

"We don't want you to provide for us!" Mercy shouts, stepping forward into the light. There's a chorus of gasps as they take in her rough appearance, but it doesn't give her a moment's pause. "We want to be free. We want to choose how we live our lives, and not be held to arbitrary rules made up by a madman."

"You *cannot* be free," Lawrence insists. "You don't exist beyond Ember Glen, and there is no way for you to survive. All that you have done, Mercy Madness, is provide hope to these people…hope where there is *none*."

"There *is* hope," Mercy insists. "We're leaving this place tonight. You no longer control us."

The Elders laugh.

"How exactly do you think you're leaving?" Clyde asks. He tilts his head, regarding her. "Ah. I know. You're going to try to find your way through the caves, aren't you? Well, go right on ahead and try. We wish you luck."

Mercy's brow wrinkles—the response surprised her.

It surprises me, too.

"The caves lead to escape," I tell them. "I know they do."

"Sure," Lawrence says with a shrug. "I'm sure they do. But those tunnels and passages are vast and winding. One wrong turn will get you lost for days. How much food and water can you carry with you traveling through? How many mouths do you have to feed if they all follow you?"

"We'll make it through." Determination is unwavering in Mercy's voice.

"Go on and try," Edgar says. "No one here is going to stop you. But let's say you do escape. Let's say you do find your way out to the world beyond. What then? As I told you, *you do not exist.*"

Mercy tilts her head. "You keep saying that, but it doesn't make sense. If *we* don't exist, then *you* don't exist. So, how are *you* surviving?"

The Elders seem to hesitate, each waiting for the other to speak. But they don't have to speak…because I think I know the answer.

"You've had to take on new identities on the outside, haven't you?" I ask.

"You were always bright, Arlo," Clyde says. "And if you'd only been patient, you would've known the truth when we made you an Elder at the next Shift."

"That wouldn't have been for…what? Another twenty-three years? Do you really believe that twenty-three years of our women suffering would have been worth the time it took for me to learn the truth at the Shift?" I chuckle without humor. "And I'm right, aren't I?

What are your last names on the outside? I bet I can guess. You had to change them, didn't you?"

Slowly, quietly, Mercy says each name. "Cole. Bright. Creed."

"You've been given identities as though you were their descendants, haven't you? You gained their wealth and power on the outside, and you had to keep this secret or you'd lose it all. And in that case, as you've said, you wouldn't exist."

Edgar's expression indicates he's grown weary of the conversation. "Of course. There would be no other way to live outside of Ember Glen."

"So, that's why only three of the Control are selected to become Elders. And what of the Land of Kings? That's a lie, too, isn't it?"

"You seem to be answering your own questions," Lawrence says.

"Well, here's one I don't know the answer to. What happened to the three Elders before you? When the three of you became their replacements, what happened to them?"

"They were old," Edgar says with an air of annoyance. "They died."

"How?" Mercy takes a step forward. "How did they die?"

We're met with silence, and it's telling.

The conclusion we've all come to is spoken aloud by Luna. "You killed them."

"None of you are capable of understanding," Lawrence says. "It's an *honor* for the retiring Elders to give their lives, to make way for the next generation. They were seventy-five years old by then— they'd lived their lives on the outside and were ready to die."

"It's an *honor* to have kept these secrets from you," Edgar says. "We have kept you *alive* in Ember Glen. We've kept you housed; we've kept you fed. For God's sake, all your men would be *imprisoned* on the outside. They would be called *criminals* for the things they've done on nights of service."

"Then why didn't you simply *stop* them?" Mercy raises her voice. "Why did you continue this *game*? You could've put an end to it all—you *should* have!"

"It's too late to stop anything by the time one becomes an Elder. By then, we've spent twenty-five years with the Control and participated in countless nights of purging. By the time we reach fifty and learn the truth as new Elders at the Shift, it's already too late. If we put an end to it, then *we* would be the criminals. We'd be imprisoned for the things we've done in Ember Glen, and that hardly seems fair."

Mercy throws her head back and laughs. "Fair! Don't you dare speak to me about what's fair…"

"This conversation is pointless," Edgar says. "Come morning, Ember Glen will be gone. All of you will be dead, and it's all your fault."

"Let me make sure I understand," Mercy says. "You're going to wipe out an entire community of people, and all because you don't want the outside world to find out the truth about you? All because you're scared to admit that you're heinous, disgusting old men who get off on playing God? Because that's all this is; that's all that this has ever been. Ember Glen only exists because privileged men like you wanted to play God." She shakes her head. "But no more. We *will* find our way out."

"You'll never find the way out. You'll die in those caves."

"And so what if we do?" Mercy snaps. "If you're going to destroy this place anyway, at least we will have tried." Mercy takes a step closer to the screen. "Mark my words, gentlemen…we will find our way out. And when we do, I *will* find you. I will hunt you down, and I swear, it will be *my* face you see when you take your last breath."

Mercy turns, stomps from the room, and we follow her. She stops in the foyer, standing at the center of the starburst pattern on the tiled floor.

"Luna, Stefanie, start gathering everyone who wants to leave. Get the others to help you and lead them to the caves through my house. Tell them what the Elders said; tell them whatever you need to make them hurry. We have enough food and water to last four, maybe five days for the women and children who were with us, but we'll need more for the others. Have everyone gather as much as they can carry and tell them all to *hurry.*"

She turns to look at Delle. "Go upstairs and get dressed. Then see what you and Theo can gather from the kitchen."

The front door suddenly opens, and Wesley enters.

Mercy charges toward him, boots stomping over the tile floor. "Are you with me or against me?" she asks Wesley, coming to a stop directly in front of him.

Wesley looks bewildered. "I…I don't know what I am."

"Well, make up your mind," she snaps. "We don't have time to wait for you to decide. If you're with me, then gather kindling for a fire, bring it here, and pile it in front of the staircase. We're leaving Ember Glen forever, but not before I watch it burn."

I SPENT FIFTEEN minutes in the shower with Mercy. It took that much time to help her scrub every last trace of Killian's blood from her skin and hair. She's dressed in red again—no black clothes in the Homestead for her to choose from.

We have everything we need packed and waiting for us to grab from the main cavern, so the only thing we cared to collect was her mother's journal which has the poems I'd written for Mercy tucked inside.

Some of the people have decided to stay. There's a group who don't believe the truth we revealed to them, and they most certainly don't believe the conversation we had with the Elders.

They think this is a test of faith.

They believe they'll meet God come sunrise.

The rest are ready to go, and they're all coming with us. I have to lead our people through the caves, and the idea of it is daunting. But the time to do it is now—whether I'm ready or not—and somehow, I'll find a way through for them.

Everyone who wants to leave has already been led through Mercy's home to the main cavern. They're waiting for us to meet them there…They're waiting for us to lead them.

Yet there's something that must be done before we go.

I tuck her mother's journal beneath my arm, pinning it to my side as I stand with Mercy in the foyer. The front doors of the Homestead are propped open wide, and there's a pile of brush and branches in the center of the sunburst tile.

"Ready?" I ask.

Mercy nods.

I strike the match, but this fire is hers to ignite.

I pass her the lit match and she takes it delicately between her fingertips. She steps closer to the kindling and crouches to her haunches. With one hand, she sweeps aside her crimson skirt, making the flower appliques dance with the motion. She lowers the small flame that's held between her fingers and keeps her hand in place until the brush catches fire.

She drops the match onto the pile as she rises, then returns to stand beside me. Together, we watch the flames grow, standing still as the entire pile catches fire, mesmerized for moments as the blaze reaches for the ceiling.

I tug on her hand. "Come on."

She turns with me, lets me lead her through the double doors, but then she stops. She lets go of my hand and turns around to face the flames. She stands centered within the frame of the open doors, just outside the threshold to the Homestead in an elegant red dress.

I need to see the entire picture…

I need to see her watching the fire she sparked.

I descend the stone steps, realizing this is the last time I'll ever walk them, that this is the last time I'll see the Homestead. I hesitate to turn, feeling the finality in my chest. Yet when I finally turn and look up, there is nothing in my heart but hope.

Beyond Mercy, there's nothing but fire.

It catches on the curtains, and it burns up the banister.

Flames fill the foyer entirely.

All I see is a backdrop of fire, and my Mercy standing at the center. Her starlight hair bounces as she turns her head over her shoulder. She sees me and smiles, and the world shifts into slow motion as she spins to face me.

Everything has slowed, my mind allowing me to catch every detail as she bends, as she lifts her skirt to reveal her black boots beneath, and she jogs down the steps to meet me.

She stops on the second to last step and reaches out to touch my cheek. The sound of the roaring fire crescendos—crackling, scorching heat behind us.

"Take my hand, Warden Rainn." She leans forward as her thumb brushes my cheek, pressing her lips to my ear. "Take us all away from here and lead me home."

My hands work secretly between us as she pulls back to look at me, her smile shining with a brightness that rivals all the stars in the sky.

I step back and hold out my hand for her.

She glances down at the fresh pair of black leather gloves I've put on, then looks at me quizzically.

"For old time's sake." I give her a smirk. "Come with me, sinner. I'll take you home."

Mercy lets out a cleansing breath as her grin rises.

She places her palm on mine, steps down beside me, and that's the moment all the stars in the sky align.

I have no fear of the journey ahead, no worry for life beyond

Ember Glen. I only want to lead her home.

Yet our home isn't here.

Our home is beyond the mountains, waiting for us to find it.

So, I'll find it for her.

We run, hand-in-hand, crossing the empty village square beneath the star-speckled sky. Under the glow of the bright full moon, we leave the Homestead burning in our wake.

Our lives ended the night she ran from service, but a new one begins tonight, born from the ashes of Ember Glen.

We all rise from the sparking embers of Mercy.

*circulus vitiosus
in aeternum*

epilogue

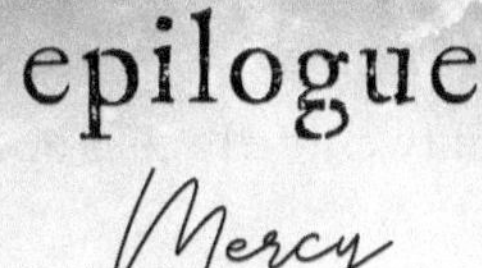

July 21, 2188
Three Years Later

"EVEN MOM SAYS it's weird," Stefanie's oldest daughter, Heidi, informs me. "People out here don't wash their dishes by hand. They use a dishwasher machine. I know you have one."

Heidi and I are speaking through a small rectangular screen that's built into the wall beside my kitchen window. It's much like the screen in Ember Glen where the Control would speak to the Elders, but the screens in the outside world are much brighter and clearer, the technology far more advanced. I can speak to so many more people during the day than I could before—just a tap on the screen, and there they are.

I rinse a plate beneath the faucet. "Well, your mom also knows that I'm not the kind of person to do something just because everyone else is doing it. So, tell her I'll continue to be *weird*, and she should mind her own business."

Heidi turns and yells off screen, "Hey, Mom! Mercy says that you should—"

"Heidi!" I snatch her attention back, but it's too late.

Stefanie moves her face into the frame. "I heard every word.

385

Happy birthday, by the way."

I grin. "Thank you."

I'm twenty-three years old today, which I've learned is considered rather young out here in the outer world. I've come to find that an Ember Glen twenty-three is about the same as an outer world forty.

Life moves slower out here…life is *kinder* out here.

When we fled Ember Glen, it took us four and a half days to navigate our way through the tunnels to escape. We came out onto a dirt path, which led us to a road. The road led us to people, and the people found us help.

We were granted government-issued housing for a while as things were sorted out. We all lived in the same apartment building in the city. It was a strange experience because it was nothing like Ember Glen, but at least we were able to be together so we could look after one another.

The Elders had been right about one thing—we didn't exist outside of Ember Glen. And because we didn't exist, we weren't able to secure jobs until about a year ago. That's when we were finally granted official documents and records.

That process was long, difficult, and exhausting.

But it wasn't impossible as we were made to believe.

We had to jump through a million hoops, tell and retell our individual stories to authorities, government officials, and social workers.

The men of the Control who fled—all but Ryker—were called to appear individually before a judge for rulings against any of their potential wrong-doings in Ember Glen. I can't speak for the others, but Arlo and Theo both had to jump hurdles to clear their names. But it was thanks to the testimonies from the other members of our community that they were cleared. Instead of imprisonment, they were appointed rehabilitative services instead.

And now we live happily, just outside the city. Our small house is within walking distance of everyone I love in our own little neighborhood that we call home.

"Is Arlo around?" Stefanie asks. "Luna and I were actually hoping we could talk to you both today…"

I freeze for a moment, my hands going still around the dish I'm holding beneath the faucet. I force myself to blink as I swallow hard. "Is it about…um…"

"Scoot," Stefanie tells Heidi, shooing her away. She moves closer to the screen. "It is about that, actually. Luna was going to drop all the kids off with Archer and Diane later today. Let them all run around at the new house."

"Oh, the new house *and* the new wife." I make a face. "How is Luna getting along with her?"

"Diane and Luna are basically the same person, so naturally, they don't get along at all." Stefanie grins.

I laugh. "Well, I'm glad Archer found Luna's double. He had the hardest time getting over her."

"Believe me, I know. It's better for all of us this way. Anyway, since we won't have the kids, we were hoping we could walk over and chat for a bit."

I try to mask my stuttering, anxious breath with a smile. "Of course, you're always welcome. You can come over anytime. You really don't have to ask first."

"Oh, yes, we do. We do have to ask."

"You're family, you don't—"

"We love you both, Mercy, very much, but not enough that I want to see you strung up naked in your living room because you and Arlo forgot we'd be coming by and you told us to 'let ourselves in' when we got there. We're not *that* close."

"And again, I am *so* sorry about that," I laugh.

"Speak of the devil…"

"Hi, Stefanie." I feel Arlo's heat at my back just before I hear his voice.

He comes in so close behind me that he pins me against the countertop. He brings his left arm around me, plants his hand on the counter, and leans forward. Except it's not just his hand that he's placed on the counter—he has a length of rope coiled in his grip.

My eyes widen a bit when I spot it, then I quickly draw my attention back to drying the dish I'm holding. I'm thankful our camera doesn't pan wide enough to show his hand on the counter.

"How's my sister?" Arlo asks casually.

His hips shift forward, and I feel him rock-hard against my ass. His right hand palms my cheek, and when he squeezes, I let out a small yelp. I quickly drop the dish as a cover, pretending that's what startled me.

"She's good. Everything okay over there?"

"Yes. I just dropped a dish. Soapy hands. Slippery."

"Maybe that's another good reason to use your dishwasher?"

"We'll see." I chuckle nervously. "I like to do it myself."

"You should at least make Arlo do it on your birthday."

His hand dips between my legs. "I couldn't agree more. That's exactly why I'm here, Stefanie. To give her a helping hand. She shouldn't have to do it herself on her birthday."

I glance at the upper corner of the screen to see whether my cheeks look flushed.

"Right. I get it." Stefanie rolls her eyes. "We'll come over at two. Do you think you can finish by then?"

"Two or three times, easy," Arlo says. He twists his head to look at me, but I don't dare look back. "Maybe four if we do it well? It *is* your birthday…"

"Oh, wow. Okay, see you at two," Stefanie says quickly, and the screen goes black.

He presses his lips to the curve of my neck. "I thought she'd never hang up…"

"We hardly spoke before you interrupted us."

"I'm sorry." He dips his hand further between my legs. "Would you like me to stop so you can call her back?"

"No need. She's coming over at two. I'll talk to her then."

"Good. Because I'm *desperate* to fuck you." He pushes harder against me, crushing my waist into the edge of the counter.

His hand slips down my throat, fingers tugging at the collar of my shirt. With a quick pull, he jerks down my top and my bra to expose my breasts. I'd sink to the floor with the way his fingers play with my nipple, except he's pushing so hard against me that I couldn't slip away if I wanted to.

And I definitely don't want to.

His lips sweep my neck. "Put your hands behind your back, starlight."

Instantly, I comply, folding onto the counter as he takes my arms behind me. He binds my wrists together with ease, and I'm already panting by the time he's done. He reaches around me to unfasten the button of my jeans, huffing a breath of frustration as he works the zipper.

"I fucking hate these." He chuckles, yanking my jeans down with a sharp motion. "I miss the accessibility…"

"I'll wear a skirt for you the next time I do the dishes if you'll quit complaining and get to work." I wiggle my hips.

One hand grips the rope as the other tangles in my long hair. He lifts me off the counter, my back arching as he curves me back against him.

"Lucky it's your birthday, Mercy Madness. Normally, that kind of snark earns you edging for hours."

My belly clenches. "No one asked you to make any exceptions for my birthday."

"Well, in that case…"

The screen on the wall interrupts us with a trill, showing that there's a call coming in from Theo.

"My phone's still connected to the screen…I think?" The technology is still a struggle sometimes. "Just grab it and turn it off. It's there by the sink."

With one hand still tangled in my hair, he reaches around me with the other to grab my phone. He fumbles with it in one hand, but then, the noise stops.

"Whatever I did worked," he says, just as confused about these things as I am.

"It didn't work the way you thought it did," Theo says, and our eyes pitch to the screen on the wall. There he is, looking directly at us, and we're frozen in awkward silence. "Call me right back. It's urgent." The screen goes black.

We're quiet for a beat.

"He didn't tell me to finish first…" Arlo says. "I think we should probably call him back."

We burst into laughter.

That's my favorite thing about the new world—I have things to smile and laugh about.

We put a pause on our activities, put ourselves back together, and return Theo's call.

As soon as he comes on screen, he says, "I found him."

And just like that, the day changes completely.

I couldn't have hoped for a better birthday present.

"THEO FOUND HIM." The words shoot from my lips the moment I open the door for Stefanie and Luna.

"He did?" Luna's eyes are wide with surprise. "When?"

"A few hours ago. Come in." I wave them inside.

Luna crosses to give Arlo a hug, and we all sit around the small table in the kitchen.

Stefanie glances over at Luna sitting beside her. "Do you think we should…"

Luna eagerly nods. "Definitely. We should definitely tell her because it's her birthday, and she's been waiting forever for an answer."

Stefanie's hesitancy makes my chest tight with anxiety. I *have* been waiting forever for an answer about this, but she doesn't owe me anything. She doesn't owe me an answer. She doesn't even owe me time spent considering it.

Arlo and I started talking about it a year ago when we found out I couldn't carry a pregnancy through to term—that was also when we found out that many of the former servants were getting similar results from their doctors.

Arlo reaches for my hand beneath the table, squeezing tight.

He wants a family. He wants it with me so much, and I want it, too. I'm just so afraid she'll say no.

"Stefanie," Luna says. "Would you just tell her?"

I close my eyes, certain from that statement alone that her answer is no.

"Luna and I have talked it over. We've been talking about it for a while now," Stefanie says. "And I'd be thrilled to carry your baby, Mercy. It's the least I could do for you."

I gape at her in shock.

I look at Arlo, and he's in tears.

He drags me into his arms and holds me.

This is the best birthday I've ever had.

"WELL, HAVE YOU told her yet?" I whisper to Theo.

We're standing beside my parked car, just across the street from the small house that Delle and her friend Juniper share. Cambria actually lives just a few houses down, so we've already stopped to pick her up, and she's waiting in the back seat of my car.

"She's not ready," Theo says.

"What do you mean?"

"You and I both know that out here, everything's different. Delle was still a kid when we left Ember Glen. The time she's spent out here has been different for her than it has been for you and me. She's only nineteen."

"And she was only sixteen in Ember Glen, but you thought having 'a connection' with her was okay then. So, what's different now?"

"The *world* is different, Mercy; that's what changed. *She* changed. And it's a good thing, I'm not saying it isn't. I'm glad she's free out here. I'm glad she can be like other people her age out here. But I'm thirty years old now, and I think differently than she does. It doesn't mean that it'll never happen, it just means…" The front door to Delle's house opens, and she appears, her head turning back over her shoulder as she laughs and waves goodbye to Juniper. "It just means not right now."

It's true that Delle has changed, and like Theo, I'm glad for it. It's been a good change for her. She's freer, happier, enjoying her life. She was so young when we left, and I think that was beneficial for her in transitioning. Where the rest of us felt a little more weathered than others our age, Delle seemed to blend in seamlessly with her peers.

She practically bounces down the sidewalk heading toward us, flipping her long, smooth hair over her shoulder. Her beautiful face is caked in experimental shades of make-up, and her clothes fit in easily with the other nineteen-year-olds in this world.

I'm happy for her.

And maybe one day Theo will tell her that he loves her…but for now, I think he might be right.

It's not time.

She's not ready for that with him yet.

All the same, she does have love for him in a certain context. It's evident in the way she leaps into his arms to give him a hug. "I haven't seen you in like, two weeks! Where have you been?"

"I've been around..." He grants her a small smile.

She comes to me next, and I drag her in for a tight squeeze.

"Ready?" Theo asks us both.

I nod. "We'll follow you."

I slip into the passenger seat of my car, though Delle goes immediately to Theo's parked behind us.

"Is everything okay there?" Arlo asks from the driver's seat.

"It will be. Some things just take time."

His brow wrinkles in confusion, because I don't think he knows what I'm talking about.

I just smile at him and shake my head. "Just drive, love."

"YOU DON'T HAVE to do this!" Edgar begs.

Theo found him.

Theo *finally* found the last of the three Elders.

He tracked down Lawrence within a year and found Clyde around the time our official citizenship documents were approved.

But Edgar has been a challenge.

I know Theo struggled with finding him, but I knew he could do it. I had faith that someday we could end this, once and for all.

Arlo and Theo have tied Edgar to a plush chair pulled from his luxury dining room. The others have all gathered around to witness, because they need to see it, too. We've all been struggling to find peace since we fled. We knew the Elders were still out there and knowing that made us angry and resentful.

Why should they get to live freely after what they put us through?

They had access to the same wealth and resources that funded Ian Cole's madness, and we couldn't risk them getting the bright idea to start it all over again somewhere else.

We had to find them, and we had to end them.

And once Edgar is dead, we'll all finally be able to rest.

Luna and Stefanie are on my right, Delle is on my left, and Cambria stands a few feet behind us. A glance over my shoulder reveals her arms tight across her chest—she struggles more than she lets on. I know ending Edgar's life alone won't help her, but maybe once this is done, she'll feel safe again.

Maybe once this is done, I can help her heal.

Theo moves to stand on the opposite side of Delle as Arlo circles behind me. His right arm swings forward with the gun in his hand, and I reach down my side to take it from him with care.

"I made you a promise." I take a step closer to Edgar. "I told you that my face would be the last one you see as you take your dying breath. And I'm here to make good on that promise."

"No, you don't have to do this. I'll give you money, more money than you can *dream* of…"

I shake my head. "I don't want money—none of us do. All we want is peace. It's all we *ever* wanted."

I raise my arm, gun in hand, and aim it at his head.

Edgar shouts.

I draw back the hammer and cock it.

Edgar begs.

I slip my finger over the trigger.

Arlo steps in close at my back. And just as he did with Lawrence and Clyde, he places his feet behind my heels to ease me from the kick-back.

"Any objections?" I ask the room.

I asked them the same when we ended Lawrence and Clyde. I may hold the gun, but they're all helping me pull the trigger. If even one of them decides they don't want this—even now—then I won't do it.

I'm only met with silence.

I squeeze, and the silence erupts.

Blood sprays.

Edgar dies.

And peace finally finds me.

I lower my arm as Arlo hugs my waist, and the energy around us changes. Ember Glen is destroyed. The final legacy of the Elders is gone. And all of us are *free*.

I finally feel safe.

I finally feel unburdened.

Cleansing tears fill my eyes and rinse down my cheeks.

And Arlo whispers a promise that sets my soul on fire…

"WILDFLOWERS AND STARLIGHT."

THE END

from the author

I have no idea how we made it here.

Writing this series has been a journey. There were times I thought it would never be finished. There were times I almost gave up on it, worried I could never give Mercy and Arlo the happily-ever-after they deserved. This world is deep, these characters are complex, and this story pushed me past my limits.

I have never cried so hard after finishing a story, and though that's partly because writing it kicked my ass, it's also because saying goodbye to Mercy and Arlo is heartbreaking for me. They've been with me for two years, existing with me daily inside my mind, telling me bits and pieces of this insane story and challenging me to actually write it. That's what this entire series has been for me—a challenge.

It's exhausted me, it's uplifted me, it's made me question my own sanity. But here, at the end of it all, I can say without a doubt that I'm in love with Mercy and Arlo and their strange, wicked, sexy, dark journey to love.

And with confidence, I'm happy to tell you...

They lived happily ever after.

With love,

Brynn

brynn's books

The Four Families Trilogy
Counts of Eight
Dance with Death
Pas de Trois

The Four Families Spin-Off
King of Masters

Ember Glen
Spark of Madness
Blaze of Misery
Embers of Mercy

Senseless
Unheard
Unseen

Lawless
(Coming Soon!)
The Darkness We Hide

Standalones
Jagged Line Paradise
Sugar Wood
The Alter

connect with brynn

Author Newsletter
brynnford.com/connect

Goodreads
goodreads.com/brynnfordauthor

BookBub
bookbub.com/profile/brynn-ford

Instagram
@brynnfordauthor
instagram.com/brynnfordauthor

TikTok
@brynnfordauthor
tiktok.com/@brynnfordauthor

Facebook Page
facebook.com/brynnfordauthor

Facebook Reader's Group
Brynn's Daring Darlings
bit.ly/brynnsdarlings

acknowledgments

This book would not exist without the support of my family, my friends, and my amazing team. There are many people who were involved in this process, but three in particular who deserve the most *major* of shoutouts.

Chris, love, there's no way I could have finished this book without you. Not only did you pick up my slack with the kids and the house while I spent hours upon hours sequestered behind my laptop, you encouraged me, you pushed me, you told me I could do it when I was ready to give up and tell the world I failed. You really are amazing, the best husband ever! *Wildflowers and starlight.*

Danielle. Real talk. This book would not exist if it weren't for you, and that's a hard fact. You have been my number one supporter from the very beginning of my writing journey. You encourage me, you uplift me, but more than anything else you *believe* in me—even on the days when I don't believe in myself. I need you to understand how amazing you are, and that I'm so lucky to have you in my corner. You've become one of my closest friends over the past few years, and I appreciate you more than you know. Love you!

Silvia, my AMAZING editor...you have gone above and beyond for me with this book! I could never say thank you enough! You know firsthand how much I struggled with this book, and I am beyond grateful for your flexibility, your time, and your endless support. Your feedback is always spot on, and I can always count on you to polish up my words so spectacularly. I don't know what I'd do without you, so I hope you plan on editing my books forever!

To my dearest beta readers, Danielle, Echo, Brandy, Mary, and Amanda. How do you continue to put up with me? With all of my last minute chapters and the cliffhangers, I would've abandoned me long ago if I were you! But seriously, I have to give you the biggest THANK YOU for your countless hours spent reading and giving me feedback. You are the most amazing people, and I appreciate you so much! (Also, I'm sorry I made you domestics who got left behind in the scuffle at the Homestead…that's my bad…I'm sure everything turned out okay for you in the end…)

To my Street and ARC team and everyone who has taken the time to read, review, or post about this series…THANK YOU! Your support means the world to me, and I'm so incredibly grateful for you.

Najla, Nada, and the team at Qamber Designs, thank you so much for making my book look beautiful! I adore your team and the work you do is always spectacular. I can always count on you to create gorgeous covers and stunning interior design for my stories. You all are amazing!

My final thank you goes directly to you, reader. You picked up this book, you read the words I wrote, and for that alone, I am grateful. If you connected with the characters or the story and enjoyed this read, just know that you and I have met through these words, and I'm forever thankful you took the journey with me.

about the author

Brynn Ford is a USA Today Bestselling Author of dark romance for daring readers. She writes emotionally heavy love stories that will twist your soul and shatter your heart before pulling you back together with a hopeful happily-ever-after.

Brynn's books are dark, sometimes disturbing, and often overwhelming. But they're always brightened by an insistent, spicy romance that will live rent-free in your head long after you've turned the final page.

When Brynn isn't obsessively writing, you may find her binge-watching favorite shows while eating far too much junk food or fanatically reading, always seeking to lose herself in the emotional roller coaster of a damn good story. She's a firm believer that her characters continue to live outside the pages in the minds of her readers. Stories don't end just because there aren't any more pages to turn.

www.ingramcontent.com/pod-product-compliance
Lightning Source LLC
Chambersburg PA
CBHW051430190726
48289CB00001B/133